LADY MIDNIGHT

The moon bathed the sea ___ ilver. A warm wind wafted g___ Gwen and Roc's hea___ sand crunched ___ He stopped ___ his hands o___

She waited ___ for his kiss, but he stood m___ss, his face cast in light and darkness, his eyes wells of thought.

"Kiss me," she urged recklessly. "You said you would."

Silence grew full and heavy between them.

"If I do, I might not be able to stop," he said, his voice harsh with emotion.

LADY MIDNIGHT

MARIA GREENE

AVON BOOKS ◢ NEW YORK

LADY MIDNIGHT is an original publication of Avon Books. This work has never before appeared in book form. This work is a novel. Any similarity to actual persons or events is purely coincidental.

AVON BOOKS
A division of
The Hearst Corporation
105 Madison Avenue
New York, New York 10016

Copyright © 1989 by Maria Greene
Published by arrangement with the author
Library of Congress Catalog Card Number: 88-91352
ISBN: 0-380-75563-7

First Avon Books Printing: April 1989

AVON TRADEMARK REG. U.S. PAT. OFF. AND IN OTHER COUNTRIES, MARCA REGISTRADA, HECHO EN U.S.A.

Printed in the U.S.A.

K-R 10 9 8 7 6 5 4 3 2 1

For my friends,
Carina Wahlund and Susan Camacho

Chapter 1

"That scoundrel Dandelion deserves to hang!" Roc Tyrrell, the earl of Landregan, muttered to himself. "He obviously has more gall than all the other smugglers put together."

Yet that grim thought could not destroy Roc's happy state of mind. Sighing with pleasure, he stood at the tall windows in the Green Salon at Landregan Hall. Last night he had come home after ten years abroad, to breathe once more the sweet, humid air of his boyhood in Cornwall where he'd grown up steeped in the land's ancient lore. Hands clasped behind his broad back, he absorbed the lovely scenery. From the Hall sprawled atop an emerald hill, the land spread for miles in every direction. To his left he glimpsed a corner of the stables and the spinney; to his right, softly undulating fields and clumps of trees. The Hall was surrounded by the most fertile soil in Cornwall. Straight ahead lay the Channel. Joy surged through him as he looked out over the jutting black cliffs that edged the secluded Landregan harbor and its steeply rising lookout point.

Did the smugglers use the harbor for their illegal business? Roc had returned home not only to take charge of his family's estate, but also to catch the infamous smuggler Dandelion, whose reputation had traveled as far as London.

A slow smile curled Roc's lips. He didn't begrudge the poor village people the extra income the free trading brought in, but they need not make such bold maneuvers that tales of their infamy reached the ears of the authorities in the capital. The smugglers deserved a reprimand, and he had agreed to act as temporary magistrate since no one in Landregan filled

1

the post at present. The identity of Dandelion would not remain a mystery much longer, not if he had any say in the
matter.

Oh, but was he happy to be back home! Sunlight played
over the ever-moving sea, its greens and blues blending.
Studying the gnarled oaks guarding the estate, he knew they
had stood during the reign of Queen Elizabeth when the
E-shaped hall had been built by one of his Landregan fore-
fathers out of Pentewan stone mined from the cliffs near Mev-
agissey. Now, centuries later, the stone had weathered to a
silvery gray. Untidy ivy covered the front façade and clematis
vine smothered the entrance, the blue flowers nodding in the
brisk breeze from the sea.

That Roc's unworldly brother, Morgan, had neglected the
estate came as no surprise to Roc. Nor did he particularly
mind. He felt a need to channel his enormous energy into a
difficult project—to make the estate yield its full measure
once again.

Long ago, Roc's mother had decorated the Green Salon,
which was now somewhat shabby. The walls were covered
with soft green brocade, the parquet spread with a huge Ax-
minster carpet in soft jewel tones, its pattern duplicating that
of the molded plaster ceiling.

Roc turned to Morgan sitting behind a Boulle desk stacked
with old tomes and papers, and said, "Buried constantly in
your books, you miss the glorious season outside, old shoe.
Let's take a ride—that is, if there's any worthy horseflesh in
the stables. Tristan will arrive tomorrow, and I wonder what
old Tim Strutt will make of him. Now, that's a horse!"

"Huh? Strutt a horse?" Morgan scratched his disheveled
head and stared bleary-eyed at his older brother. Roc's deep,
tawny eyes bored into him, and he flinched. Morgan considered Roc's presence daunting to say the least; it disturbed the
old routines. Morgan buried his nose in his book once again.

"Morgan, you sapskull, wake up! How about a ride in this
lovely weather?" Roc sat down on the edge of the desk,
dangling one leg. "You can tell me all about the smugglers."

"What smugglers?" Morgan mumbled.

Roc rapped his fingers impatiently on the gleaming desk
surface, waiting for Morgan to snap out of his absentmind-

edness. "A lot must have happened in the years since I've been gone."

"No, nothing much." Morgan reluctantly closed the thick tome and placed his spectacles on top.

"I gather *you* haven't seen much," Roc commented drily. Under heavy lids he watched Morgan rise, noticing how rounded his shoulders had become and how pale his dear face appeared. He still had the air of a lost puppy, although he had reached twenty-five years of age. The only sign of their close kinship was their identical aquiline noses. Morgan was taller, thinner, and had never shared Roc's interest in sports—riding, fencing, and sparring. Morgan's hair was of a muddy reddish-brown hue, and his feet were huge. Roc smiled, realizing how much he had missed his bumbling brother. He recalled how old Nanny Simpkins used to say the gods had been unfair when dividing their gifts between the two brothers, but Roc did not agree. He had never met a more sweet-natured man than Morgan.

Roc strode purposefully to the door. Greeting Enedoc, the butler, a firm good-morning, he took a cocked hat trimmed with gold braid, his gloves, and a crop from the old retainer's hands. He pressed the hat on his head while waiting for Morgan to get his coat. Beating the crop softly against a highly polished boot, he whistled a tune.

"If I may say so, milord, 'tis a great pleasure to have your lordship back where you belong," Enedoc ventured, earning an assessing glance from the topaz eyes.

"Really?" A swift smile transformed Roc's craggy countenance. "Let me tell you a secret." He leaned toward the ancient butler. "I enjoy being back—more than you know."

Enedoc beamed and wrung his hands with joy. "I suppose those foreign countries are backward."

Roc chuckled softly and twirled his crop. "Decidedly. I say, Enedoc, what do you know about a fellow called Dandelion?"

The smile faded immediately from the old man's face. He nervously patted his pigtail wig, releasing a cloud of white powder. "I wouldn't know, milord."

"I take it you don't know Landregan is notorious for its free traders," Roc baited, his gaze piercing.

"Er? Of course one hears about it, milord, but *I* wouldn't

know who's involved." Enedoc turned away from Roc's disconcerting eyes.

Roc's tone was its driest when he said, "Naturally. Will I receive the same answer everywhere?"

Enedoc had paled considerably. "Ahem, I believe you will, milord. The villagers are very closemouthed."

"Even to a native like myself?"

"Your lordship has been gone for a long time." Enedoc's trembling fingers straightened a lace doily on a small bow-legged table and fiddled with an arrangement of roses in a silver vase.

A shadow crossed Roc's hard features. "Yes, too long, much too long."

"And if you excuse me, milord, you are the new magistrate. That'll make people more reserved."

"Do you all have something to hide?" Roc teased, glaring with mock severity at the discomfited butler.

Enedoc pretended to be absorbed in the painted landscape on the opposite wall. "I understand the poor people are in fair need of a little extra."

"Of course. Well, I will act as magistrate only until that impudent scoundrel Dandelion is captured and hanged."

"Hanged?" Enedoc echoed in a trembling voice.

Morgan returned wearing a creased and stained coat and dusty boots. Cakes of mud littered his path across the black and white marble floor. "Hanged? Who?" he asked, and righted his hat, which was at least one size too large.

"I'm going to hang you if you don't whip up some speed in those large feet of yours." Roc chuckled at Morgan's startled expression. "Come, old shoe, let's go out and inspect our beautiful land." Gripping his brother's arm, Roc propelled him into the bright sunlight outside.

A brimstone butterfly fluttered past them on the hot front steps, and a bumblebee buzzed sleepily among the flowers growing along the walls. Roc's heart constricted with pleasure. The unkempt bed of flowers made the gloomy house look more welcoming, and Roc decided to proceed slowly in making improvements around the house.

The stables had the same disorderly look as the rest of the estate, but the horses were well-fed and shining with care. The stablehands knuckled their forelocks and whipped their caps from their heads. Roc stared hard at the quiet men. Was one of them Dandelion? One of these tall, dark Cornish men with flinty eyes and a taciturn frame of mind?

The head groom, Tim Strutt, stepped forward. "Milord, I recommend White Star. 'E's th' best in th' stables—next to Blacky, o' course," he added, throwing an apologetic glance at Morgan.

"Blacky, that old nag! Is he still alive?" Roc asked.

"Aye, milord, 'e's Master Morgan's steed."

"I remember that. He's *always* been Master Morgan's steed."

On stiff legs a swaybacked stallion ambled into the sunshine, his black coat liberally sprinkled with gray. Roc turned to Morgan, his face lightened by a grin. "You don't like change much, do you?"

Morgan stared at the animal as if he was seeing it for the first time. "Blacky is a sweet-goer. He takes me where I need to go, without sudden starts and quirks. He doesn't interrupt my train of thought. I enjoy pondering the philosophical questions as I ride."

Roc had difficulty suppressing a laugh. With much effort he steeled his face into its habitual implacable mask and swung into the saddle atop White Star. In a puff of dust, White Star trotted down the drive. Blacky, as if invigorated by the pace set by the other mount, trotted off after him.

The air smelled of wild roses and sea breezes, and Roc inhaled deeply in delight. How could he have forgotten all this? Those long years abroad, under a searing sun on foreign seas, breathing foreign scents, had dimmed his memories of this lovely place. From the top of the hill he could see the deep, winding valley where slate-roofed farmhouses huddled together on meager soil. Surrounded by a brick wall stood Tremayne House, once a handsome two-story Palladian mansion with a clutter of dormer windows and chimneys, stone balusters under the windows and beside the front steps, and a carved frieze under the eaves. Even at this distance Roc could see signs of decay. Yet smoke curled from one tall chimney, and the multipaned windows glistened in the clear light.

Looking more disheveled than at the outset, Morgan reined in next to Roc. Blacky's ears twitched, and he snorted with

excitement. "Do we have to ride at such a bone-jarring clip?"
Morgan complained.

"Devil take it, old shoe! If we went any slower, White
Star would fall asleep." Roc rubbed his chin thoughtfully.
"How is Squire Tremayne? Is he still alive?"

Morgan's face lightened. "Ah! There you have a sensible
fellow."

Roc shot him a dubious glance. "I don't see any evidence
of that."

"He has invented an amazing theory about the original
inspiration of Homer's—"

"I see—hasn't changed a bit." Beginning to turn his horse,
Roc was struck by a thought. "Wait! He had a daughter, a
dirty little baggage who turned up everywhere I went. What
was her name?"

"Gwennie? Well, she is grown up, only a few years my
junior. She runs the farm now—capably, I might add."

"Married?"

"No, she's on the shelf. No one hereabouts wants such a
commanding female for a wife; sharp as a needle she is, with
a tongue to match."

A fleeting smile touched Roc's mouth. "Overpowers you,
eh? Is she beautiful?" They had turned their mounts toward
the winding cliff path leading to the sea.

Morgan frowned in confusion. "Pretty, I believe—with
brown hair, like White Star's. I haven't seen her since last
week."

"And you don't remember her face?" Roc commented
incredulously. "Don't you ever look at her?"

"She's just part of the village," Morgan said in a dismissing tone.

"And not worth your attention?" Derision had crept into
Roc's smooth voice.

"The ladies are all the same. Watch out for Gwen's aunt.
A more ill-tempered shrew you'll not find in all of Cornwall.
I always make sure the women are out of the house before I
visit the squire. Tremayne's library is comfortable, but a few
times I have had the misfortune to run into Gwen, since she
sometimes does the estate books in the study."

"Bites your head off, eh?"

"Quite. Damned unpleasant, to tell you the truth."

"Gwendolyn is perhaps a more practical person than you'll ever be?"

"Now, I don't know if I would say that. She's not womanly, you know. What lady do you know does books and talks about crops as if they were drawing room subjects? She even knows how to shear sheep. Come to think of it, last time I saw her she even drank brandy like a man.

In an undertone Roc addressed the ears of his horse. "He does remember something, sometimes . . ." Out loud he said, "Brandy? Where did she get brandy? I thought they were ruined financially."

Morgan scratched his nose. "Yes, they are, but the squire always has good brandy on his table. We do, too. Enedoc takes care of those details. Excellent stuff. You should taste a nip when we get back."

Roc scanned Morgan's face with new interest. "I will."

They spent a satisfying afternoon looking over the erratically growing crops at Landregan, Roc noticing again how much improvement the acres needed. He felt a moment of compassion for Gwendolyn Tremayne in her battle to save what had belonged to the Tremaynes for generations.

As Roc rode past the long row of fisherman's cottages down by the harbor, the villagers eyed him with suspicion. They were a tight-lipped lot, harsh and craggy like the cliffs. Roc presumed that most of these sturdy men were involved in the free trading and, studying their stubborn faces, he also realized it would be next to impossible to wring any information out of them.

The old people remembered him, and smiles of welcome creased their wrinkled faces. "Good ye're home, milord, the 'All needs a firm 'and. Th' old earl would 'ave been proud o' ye."

Not true, Roc thought grimly. Father always had a low opinion of me.

He recognized Clem Toboggan leaning against the wall of the smithy, chewing on a piece of straw. That snot-nosed urchin had grown up to be a man the size of an ox, Roc noted, with a piercing blue gaze and a bristly mop of black hair. He had a reckless air about him. Could he be Dandelion? Clem lifted a hand to his forelock with an insolent air.

"Ah, Toboggan, how is the fishing around here nowadays?"

"Th' same as always, milord."

"Still angling in the creek?"

"No, milord." Clem shifted the straw to the other side of his mouth.

"Perhaps you angle after bigger fish, eh? French fish the size of wooden barrels?"

No answer was forthcoming.

"I suppose you don't know that Dandelion chap?"

"If I did, I wouldn't tell ye, milord."

Old Mrs. Toboggan, Clem's grandmother, came out of the smithy and heard the last words. She cuffed the huge young man over the ear and shoved him through the door. "Mind yer manners, ye great looby!" She shot Roc a toothless grin before disappearing into the smithy.

"Shall we return home?" Morgan asked. "I have had more than enough air for one day, and my books are calling."

Roc shrugged. "I suppose I can continue tomorrow. Perhaps I'll visit Squire Tremayne and inspect his sharp-tongued daughter."

After he left, the villagers discussed among themselves how like the old earl Roc was. What a sad thing, they said, that the handsome young earl was a blooming magistrate and a threat to the smugglers.

Gwendolyn Tremayne crouched on the wet sand in Brandy Cove, one of hundreds of such coves on the Cornish coast. The tangy scent of seaweed floated to her, and a sickle moon played hide and seek among silver-edged clouds, pushed across the sky by a strong, humid wind from the south. She strained to see the small dinghy detaching from the sleek black outline of the French cutter in the bay. She waited, tense with anticipation, for the rowboat to land.

A nightjar's harsh cry rose over the restless water, and Gwen made a funnel of her hands and responded with an identical call. Ghostlike, the small vessel bounced over the choppy waves toward shore.

"Here they come, Clem."

"Aye, Miss Gwen. Th' carts are ready, and no excise men betwixt 'ere and Looe."

"Are you sure?"

Clem rumbled with laughter. "Aye, miss. We set up a bit o' diversion that will last 'til we've stowed this batch away."

"Officer Biggles will be angry as a hornet when he finds out we've bamboozled him."

Clem snorted. "Th' man is a numbskull and a busybody, and 'e deserves no concern, miss."

Gwen knew that after this run they would have to use another landing spot, since Landregan was infested by a small force of foot soldiers. They'd been sent by the Board of Trade to help the local revenue man, Officer Horatius Biggles, break up the smuggling ring and catch the leader.

Gwen had enjoyed outwitting Officer Biggles this past year. He was no match for her devious mind, and she couldn't have more loyal cohorts than the villagers. The reputation of the "gentlemen" of Landregan had become widely acclaimed, rivaling that of John Carter of Prussia Cove, the greatest free trader of them all. But few knew that Dandelion, the leader of the impudent gang at Landregan, was a woman, and a gently bred one at that.

The splash of oars reached Gwen's ears above the soughing wind. The boat was almost upon them. Wavelets slapped her ankles as she waded into the shallow water, sand oozing between her toes. The soft crunch of wood against grit heralded the boat's arrival on shore, and Gwen, her skirts hitched to her thighs, caught the coiled line and secured it around a rock.

Moments later the dark beach swarmed with darker shadows as sturdy men rolled kegs of brandy over the soft sand. Quietly and efficiently they stacked the contraband.

The last load bore tightly wrapped bolts of silk and Hyson tea encased in black tarpaulin. When all of the contraband had been placed on shore, the dinghy returned to the French cutter.

Gwen lighted a shielded lantern and started up the steep path, closely followed by the first man, who was carrying a keg under each arm. It was Clem, dressed in a black leather vest and old breeches, a black stocking cap pulled low over his eyes. He panted from the heavy load and swore under his breath. On the crest of the cliff the wind grabbed Gwen's skirts and lashed the loose mane of her hair. Pushing it back, she lifted the lantern high and stared into the blackness toward Wrecker's Ruin.

There came the answer—one, two, three bright flares of a lantern. The road was clear; Officer Biggles and his men had fallen for the ruse and would not disturb them tonight. He had been led to believe the cargo would be unloaded in the harbor, a mile away. With a wide, satisfied smile, Gwen led the silent line of men toward the latest storing place, the cellar of a dilapidated cottage above Yellow Rock. Tomorrow night they would transfer the goods to the cellar of the local inn, The Pilchard, and then transport them east to London.

Gwen watched the line of plodding men, urged on by a soft call from Clem as they struggled with their handcarts up the last steep incline of Yellow Rock.

The unloading went without mishap. Clem bolted the door with a heavy lock and handed Gwen the key. "There, a good round that was." He wiped the sweat from his forehead with a large square cloth. "Go 'ome and get a wink o' sleep. There won't be much o' that since we 'ave to move th' casks tomorrow night."

"I'd do anything to see the consternation on Biggles's face when he snoops down at the harbor," Gwen said with a laugh.

Clem rubbed his large nose in consideration. "Aye, that should be a sight. Per'aps—"

"No, Clem, we won't risk being seen loitering around the harbor."

She sensed his grin, although she could not see it. "Aye, miss, nobody needs to know th' squire's daughter is Dandelion, king of the smugglers."

Gwen nudged him playfully in the ribs as they walked along the ridge back toward the village. "Queen, in this case."

Rain was pelting Gwen by the time she reached the kitchen entrance of Tremayne House. The wind whistled eerily down the chimney pipes, the darkness total as she fumbled for the latch. She sniffed the salty air blowing warm and heavy from the sea and was relieved that the cutter, the *Alouette*, had attained the Channel on the turning tide before the storm had taken complete hold.

Gwen sneaked into the kitchen. The house still slept, but

it was only a matter of minutes before Marva would descend from her attic room and start the kitchen fire.

Slippers in hand, Gwen hurried to her room on the second floor. The gray glow of dawn revealed the tattered furnishings and tapestries, the paint peeling in large flakes from the ceiling, and the threadbare rugs. Lighter patches on the walls showed where paintings had been removed and sold to pay for the seed needed for new crops and equipment with which to harvest the yield.

Gwen crawled into bed. Before her head touched the pillow she was asleep, only to be awakened four short hours later. She struggled to clear her eyes and brain, both of which seemed to be filled with all the sand at Brandy Cove. Aunt Clorinda stood at the foot of the bed, her small, sharp eyes focused on Gwen.

"It is beyond me how you can sleep twelve hours in one stretch. Laziness, that's what's wrong with you," she complained with a sniff. "Only city fribbles sleep until this ungodly hour. God knows I've tried to instill some sense into your thick head, Gwennie, but to no avail."

"Aunt Clo, not now. 'Tisn't fair attacking me before I've had at least one strong cup of tea." Gwen yawned widely and rubbed her eyes. With a weary movement, she tossed aside the covers and groaned her way out of bed.

"Gwennie! You look frightful—such dirty feet! How many times—"

"I was too tired to wash last night." Gwen stepped up to her aunt's rigid form and placed her hands on the woman's bony shoulders. Her lips curved into a sleepy smile.

"How dare you tease me!" Aunt Clorinda protested. "I have tried and tried to teach you the proper decorum, but you ignore every bit of it. I swear, you'll be the death of me yet."

Gwen chuckled silently. If Aunt Clo knew the real reason for her dirty feet, she would, indeed, die from shock.

"Auntie, I'm a grown woman, and there is no cause for you to scold me like this. I'll sleep all day if I want to," Gwen retorted with mock vexation.

With an angry swish of her skirts, her back bristling, Aunt Clorinda stalked to the door. "I see that my consideration is wasted here." The door closed with a decided snap, and

Gwen sat down at her dressing table and rested her pounding head on her palms.

The nights of free trading were taking their toll. Dark rings circled her eyes, and she applied white rice powder to conceal the offending shadows.

Gwen did not resemble the Cornish people with their solid bodies and dark hair. From her English grandmother she had inherited chestnut hair, hazel eyes, and full lips. Her only pride was her peaches and cream complexion, but every trace of color in her cheeks was absent this morning. Her body bordered on being willowy, and she hated her swan's neck and tried to hide it by wearing her hair in long, loose curls, though the current fashion called for soft chignons and co-quettish wisps around the face. Her body did not give the impression of strength, but more than once she had hoisted a cumbersome five-gallon brandy keg on her back and with sheer pigheadedness hauled it up the daunting cliff.

Haphazardly coiffured, a beribboned cap perched atop her head, and dressed in a well-worn muslin gown over moderate hoops, she finally descended the stairs just in time for the midday meal served by Marva in the dining room. Marva and Arthur, the footman, were the only house servants, as the slim Tremayne purse could not support a larger staff.

Gwen saw her father's bespectacled eyes over the edge of a book propped against the soup tureen, and Aunt Clorinda's compressed lips above the rim of a teacup.

"There you are, Gwennie, looking rested this morning . . ." the squire greeted her, his voice trailing off.

Gwen met his watery blue gaze and said, "Good morning, Papa," which earned her a snort from Aunt Clo.

"Morning?" said Lionel Tremayne. "Is it still morning?"

"Of course, Papa." Gwen piled her plate high with scrambled eggs, toast, and a rasher of bacon from the sideboard and sat down, ready to devour the lot.

"Most unladylike to fill yourself with quantities that would put the stable lad to shame," Aunt Clo commented.

Gwen eyed the dry toast and weak tea in front of her aunt. "I'll be happy to share some of this with you. Terminating your self-imposed starvation might put you in a better mood."

"I'm only thinking of our narrowed circumstances." With an air of long-suffering, Aunt Clo picked daintily at her toast.

"We're not yet to the point where we don't have enough to eat." Gwen heartily proceeded with her meal. She heard her aunt mumble something like "unfeeling spendthrifts" as she rose from the table and went to sit at the window, where her embroidery frame was erected to catch the morning light. Only Gwen knew the passion her aunt had for good food at any table except their own.

With an innocent mien, Gwen turned to her father just in time to prevent the yellowed lace of his shirt cuffs from being drenched in his teacup. "Papa, do you know how long the soldiers are going to remain here on *maneuvers?*" Her derisive emphasis on the word echoed the common belief that the soldiers had been sent to Landregan solely to catch Dandelion. For a unit to be on innocent maneuvers in a small seaside village, armed not only with muskets but also with telescopes, was too much to swallow. Officer Biggles deeply resented that the authorities had seen fit to doubt his ability to catch the villain by himself.

"Eh, soldiers?" said the squire. "Oh, well, I daresay they will be gone within the week. That Dandelion fellow is too wily to get trapped by some redcoats. Besides, the villagers need the extra income . . ." Once more his voice fell away, and Gwen thought, as she took a deep draught of tea, that her father could be very sensible at times. Unfortunately those moments were all too few and far between.

Lionel Tremayne had a one-track mind, a mind that dwelled in ancient Greece and Rome, a mind that had no interest in mundane country life on the decaying Tremayne estate.

Gwen considered it a nuisance that Grandfather had let his son study at Oxford instead of instilling in him the fundamentals of running a farm. The poor soil of the Landregan valley needed sound management if it was to yield the riches it had produced under Grandfather Tremayne's strict care. Her grandfather's only fault had been to dream he could rise from squire to knight through the efforts of an educated son who would, through glorious achievement, improve the family's status. The plan had not borne fruit.

"I wonder who that Dandelion chap can be," Gwen mused aloud, filled with devilment.

Aunt Clo glared at her. "Since you're always speaking to

all and sundry in the village, you ought to know,'' she argued, stabbing the embroidery canvas with her needle.

"What . . . ?'' began Squire Tremayne, but he had already forgotten his train of thought, and Gwen released a sigh of relief. She knew that her father, when irked, could be stubborn. Aunt Clorinda had been installed in the house to teach Gwen ladylike manners, and she highly disapproved of Gwen's familiarity with the simple villagers. The squire supported the rules the spinster had established, but Gwen had long ago found ways to sidestep them.

"I've heard a new magistrate has been appointed to this area.'' Aunt Clorinda dropped the explosive piece of news with an air of superior indifference.

Gwen stopped chewing, her fork poised in midair. "A magistrate?'' Then it was true what the men had grumbled about, and she had refused to believe, last night. Faithful to their reticent ways, they hadn't mentioned any names.

"Yes, seems the authorities are bent on cleaning up Landregan,'' said Aunt Clo, "and none too soon, if I may say so. The free traders have become a shade too impudent from what I've heard. Imagine, only last night one of the soldiers was knocked down and had his uniform stolen.'' Aunt Clo bristled with indignation.

Gwen feigned a coughing attack to veil her hilarity. "Wh-who told you?'' she croaked at last, choosing not to mention that the nightly commotion had all been part of a plan to fool Officer Biggles.

"Dr. Penfield,'' said Aunt Clo. "He also told me the name of the new magistrate—and I believe *he* will be more than a match for the disrespectful villagers. We sorely lack for authority here.'' She sniffed and sent the squire a pointed glance. "More impertinent people than the villagers of Landregan I have yet to meet!'' She straightened her plain mobcap.

"Well, who is it?'' Gwen demanded impatiently.

"You know him, I believe. Not that he noticed you when he lived here.''

"Stop teasing me, Aunt Clo. *Who* is the new magistrate?'' Gwen's fingers itched to grasp the older woman and shake her.

"The present earl of Landregan Hall, Roc Tyrrell."

This time Gwen could not conceal her true feelings. Her mouth fell open in surprise. "Roc?" she breathed.

Her aunt studied her with sour interest. "You look as if you've just seen a ghost."

"Er? . . . Oh, not at all. I thought, ahem, Morgan said his brother would not return in the near future."

Aunt Clorinda tittered mirthlessly. "Morgan Tyrrell is about as reliable as the weather. He wouldn't know his own birthday."

Gwen's heart raced in her chest, and her fingers trembled as she reached for her teacup. Roc back at the Hall? It was unbelievable news! "When did he arrive?"

"He came yesterday, his traveling chaise laden with boxes and portmanteaux painted with the most outlandish patterns, Dr. Penfield told me. Rumor has it he made an immense fortune with the East India Company."

"Oh." Gwen swallowed convulsively.

"You do look pale, Gwennie. I should have had the doctor examine you. Something must be wrong since you slept away most of the day." She paused. "Anyway, the old earl always maintained that Roc was an irresponsible adventurer, and it appears his observation was true. Roc spent his time amassing a fortune while honorable men went to war against Charles Edward Stuart. The Tyrrells always had a wild streak in them."

"The English massacred the poor Scotsmen cruelly," Gwen said. "I have nothing good to say about my fellow Englishmen in this regard. It makes me blush to think that I'm related to such a heartless people."

"Nonsense! The Scots had to learn who is the master. They are a savage, unruly people, always have been." Aunt Clo's voice began to grate on Gwen's nerves so she hastened out of the room on the pretext of seeing Marva about the menu.

In a daze of delight mixed with apprehension, Gwen ran the length of the drab corridor. The man she had loved as long as she could remember had returned home! Goosebumps of excitement rose on her skin, and her chest constricted with expectation. She had never dared hope that

Roc would come back after his falling out with the old earl.

Roc a magistrate? Had he really returned to put an end to the free trading in Landregan? As long as she had breath left in her body he wouldn't succeed, she vowed fiercely.

Chapter 2

The responsibility of keeping Tremayne House from ruin weighed heavily on Gwen's slender shoulders as the deterioration of the estate worsened every year. The profits from the contraband kept the estate afloat, but how long could that continue? Gwen had no brothers or sisters, her mother having died the moment Gwen drew her first gasping breath. Under the dazed eye of her father, and the disapproving gaze of Aunt Clorinda Pettigrew, she had grown up with the children of the farmers and the sailors, learning everything about life in a remote fishing village.

Gwen was never afraid to make her views public, a trait that didn't endear her to eligible bachelors in the neighborhood. No man of her station wanted a wife with more wit than beauty, who would inherit nothing more than a disintegrating manor. Gwen's last birthday had been her twenty-third, but she would admit to no one that she longed for a man in her life, a man to love and cherish.

About a year ago, she had suppressed the longings of her heart and, with the zest of youth, had joined the smuggling gang with her childhood friend, Clem Toboggan, a jack of all trades who often assisted his father, the blacksmith on the estate.

The system Clem had devised to send messages to Gwen about the smuggling involved the use of three colored rags which he attached to a rusty nail on the stable wall at Tremayne House: white for completed mission, yellow when another load was expected, and red for danger.

It was late morning the next day when Gwen glanced out her bedroom window, one image churning incessantly in her

mind. Even the wind seemed to whisper the name Roc . . .
Roc . . . Roc Tyrrell.

Excited gossip was rife among the villagers. While taking
a ride through the village, she had heard all about Roc's im-
peccable attire and proud bearing. Even such a small piece
of gossip as that Clem had acted insolently toward Roc had
reached her ears.

Did Roc still remember her? She blushed to recall the
things she had done as a child to catch his attention. He had
been her hero, a young god who could do no wrong. She
could not wait to see if her feelings were still affected by
him, or if it was all in her imagination.

Her thoughts were interrupted by a sharp rap on the door.
Marva, panting hard from climbing the stairs, waddled in.

"Where that Arthur 'as gone 'idin' I don't know, but I do
resent 'avin' to do 'is chores." She wiped her furrowed forehead. "Mistress Pettigrew sent me to fetch ye. In a real blus-
ter she is, if ye arsk me. A guest is in th' salon with 'er."
Marva rolled her round, dark eyes. "And we know who that
is, don't we, Miss Gwennie?"

A smile appeared on Gwen's lips. "Yes, I can guess why
Aunt Clo is in a state. 'Tis not every day she entertains an
earl." Gwen patted her gleaming ringlets and smoothed the
low bodice of her rose muslin gown. Roc would surely notice
how her heart hammered under the thin material.

"Ye look beautiful, Miss Gwennie. Enough to wrap that
fella around yer li'l finger." Marva tweaked the lace-edged
neckline and straightened the folds of the cream underdress
revealed between the tied-back robings of the skirt.

"Don't be silly, Marva. As usual your tongue is running
away with you."

The cook's apple-red cheeks grew rounder as she smiled
impishly. "I 'aven't seen ye this nervous since th' old times
when Roc used to come down from Oxford. Ye can't fool old
Marva."

"Why, y-you—old *tabby!*" Gwen blurted out with an ir-
repressible smile.

She hurried the length of the corridor, her legs shaky. As
she reached the landing, a deep voice floated up to her and
she halted, spellbound by the disembodied sound. Her fingers
gripped convulsively around the mahogany banister, and she

had to take several deep breaths before she could trust herself to descend the interminable stairs. The voice beckoned her from years past, and without being aware of her feet touching the floor, she walked toward that voice. Gone was the drab hall of Tremayne House, gone was the sound of a cockerel crowing on the dung heap behind the stables, gone was the scent of mold from the mildewed spots in the ceiling.

As she reached out to open the door, his words were clearly audible. ". . . what I've heard—still as sharp-tongued as ever."

Gwen fell from her magical cloud with a thud, her anger flaring. How dared he speak of her in those terms! She stepped into the salon.

"And you're as condescending as ever." She eyed him narrowly.

Roc rose from the worn armchair whose springs creaked alarmingly, and Gwen almost gasped. He was more attractive than she had remembered, his intense topaz eyes intimidating as he gazed idly at her, from the top of her head to the tips of her slippers. Of medium height, his body a beautiful symmetry of hard muscles, he exuded authority and formidable strength. His wavy hair was tied in a queue and gleamed with blue lights like a raven's wing. There was an expression in his eyes, in his very being, that told her he wanted to touch her. He smiled and her pulse leaped uncontrollably.

In one sweep Gwen noticed his well-cut coat of deep blue velvet, the wide cuffs adorned by gold buttons and thin gold braid. His knee breeches molded thighs hard with muscles, and his high boots of supple leather hugged well-rounded calves. If not marred by that forbidding air, Roc's face would be handsome with its deep-set eyes, aquiline nose, and impressive jaw. The deep tan, no doubt acquired in foreign lands, accentuated his virility. There was an animal quality about him. To Gwen, he represented danger.

Roc bowed with easy grace and grasped her fingertips. Her stomach filled with a sweet, liquid warmth as his mouth brushed her skin. She managed to respond with a small curtsy and walked weak-kneed to sit next to her aunt on the sofa.

"The baggage I remember has certainly turned into a lovely lady," Roc murmured and, to Gwen's chagrin, she felt color rising on her face.

"And the country bumpkin I recalled has gained some town bronze," she retorted with a falsely sweet smile.

Her eyes widened in surprise as a grin softened his features. She had expected to provoke his anger.

"Gwennie!" Aunt Clo stared at her in horror, her hands fluttering nervously above the tea tray. "Watch your language. May I offer you another cucumber sandwich, Lord Landregan?"

"Thank you, no, I'm quite content sitting here eating my fill of Miss Tremayne." A devil danced in his tawny gaze, which never left Gwen's face. Perhaps he was hoping to make her blush once more.

Gwen pinched her lips together. After her first vulnerable moments in his presence, she had regained control of her rioting emotions. "You will find little nourishment in such endeavors," she murmured, trying once again to stir his ire.

A short pause filled with silent innuendo ensued. "More than you know perhaps," he said.

His smooth response set her heart pounding wildly again, and she had difficulty holding her teacup without rattling the spoon on the edge of the fragile porcelain.

"Milord," she said, "what brings you back to Cornwall? I thought you were comfortable with the East India Company." With all the calm Gwen could muster, she met his penetrating gaze.

"You must know that Morgan has neglected the Hall. It desperately needs to be overhauled from top to bottom." His eyes shifted meaningfully to a damp spot on the wall. Gwen resented his unspoken comparison.

Her swift anger burning under the smooth surface of her smile, she said, "Yes, your estate has quite gone to seed in your absence, milord."

He made no indication that her needling irked him; a taunting smile still hovered on his lips.

"Gwendolyn!" Aunt Clo exclaimed. "Lord Landregan, you must not listen to Gwennie. She's overlooking her duty as hostess." Bridling, she turned to Gwen. "Serve the earl some more tea, dear." A sharp elbow nudged Gwen in the ribs.

"I'm sure he doesn't need it. He has drunk—and *eaten*—his fill." Let the overbearing earl taste some more of his own medicine! Where had her hero of old gone, the patient young man who had sometimes allowed her to ride his horse, who had kindly sneaked her a wedge of warm apple pie from the kitchen at the Hall?

The smile fled from his face, leaving the stern mask of a man with no patience for nonsense. "Since you are hinting so blatantly that I leave, I'd first like to broach an urgent subject in hopes of gaining your assistance. I'm sure you know of the free traders—the 'gentlemen'—in this area. If you have any inkling as to who the leader of the gang is, please inform me of his name."

Gwen gasped in mock horror. "How bluntly put! I'm sure you don't expect us ladies to know anything about such rough dealings." She made a theatrical gesture of placing her hand to her heart. "Where is Papa, Aunt Clo? He should be the one to talk with the earl about such matters."

Aunt Clo pursed her lips with disapproval and flapped her fan vigorously. "Lionel doesn't remember his own name at times, much less anybody else's."

"Where *is* Papa?" Gwen had only just realized that the squire was absent.

"He partook of some tea and suddenly remembered some pressing business and went—"

"—into his study," Roc filled in, a wry smile twisting his lips, showing he knew exactly what business the squire thought more important than entertaining his guest.

Gwen instantly pictured her father snoring with his florid face in the open book on his desk top.

Roc swung one leg over the other, making no sign of leaving. "I'm sure you know of all the goings-on in the village."

"We don't make it our affair to snoop into the villagers' lives," Gwen said. "If you're angling for certain information, you ought to ask the villagers themselves."

"Surely you realize that the people of Landregan are singularly closemouthed. You must have heard that I now hold the post of magistrate in the district. If you know anything specific, you can help shorten the time needed to capture the fellow."

"If we knew, we would of course inform you," Aunt Clo piped up in her most conscientious tone. "But the villagers never tell me anything."

No wonder, thought Gwen with amusement. To the locals you are a foreigner from Devon and a meddler. Roc's disconcerting gaze raked over her. She lifted mischievous hazel eyes to his dangerous topaz glitter. She could sense him trying to probe her hidden thoughts, to sniff out any attempt at lying. In place of the amiable guest, the ruthless, predatory lawman had stepped in. In that moment Gwen felt she had met a worthy opponent. How she would love to lead him on a merry chase, with herself the victor, of course.

"Milord," she said, "you have forgotten that I'm one of that tight-lipped lot. I hope you will never catch Dandelion, because if you do, the people in this area will starve."

He snorted, anger flickering in his eyes. "You're exaggerating, Miss Tremayne. Their poverty is the result of pure and simple laziness. There is enough fishing to feed and clothe a village of much larger size than this." In his inexplicable desire to goad her, he failed to mention that he sympathized with the villagers.

"You, milord, who have been gone for ten years, might think that, but the truth is, the fishermen of the villages along the coast are squabbling constantly. They blame each other for encroaching on each other's fishing territories and, besides, people cannot live on fish alone. As for growing vegetables, you know that the soil in the village is not as rich as on the land surrounding the Hall. The stores never last through the winter. Not many can afford to buy a fishing vessel for themselves. Most of them work for a small income on the larger fishing boats, and where does that leave them? With a pittance in their pockets. On that they often have to raise a family of six or more."

A stormy look crept into Roc's features, his eyelids lowering threateningly. Soft-voiced, he said, "Smuggling is illegal."

"I don't consider it a crime to fend for one's family," Gwen retorted heatedly. "*You* don't know what poverty means, so what right do you have to judge the less fortunate? Why, the price you paid for that coat"—she pointed an accusing finger at him—"could feed a family of six for a month, but you never think of that."

When he finally responded his voice was as cold as the northern wind. "None of my tenants is starving."

"They are lucky to live on the grounds of the Hall, but not everyone does, and if you want to keep the respect of your people, you should forget that you ever expressed a wish to punish the smugglers."

"Considering your vehemence, I could almost believe you're involved yourself," he interjected.

Gwen slammed her cup onto the tray. "You arrive here, high and mighty, thinking you can ruin the free trading in Landregan and still be respected? Little do you know, milord! You ought to stop snooping while you're still well-liked around here."

Aunt Clo, her face beet-red, leaned toward Roc and placed a soothing hand on his arm. "Don't listen to her, she doesn't mean it. She has no manners."

His reaction was unexpected. He chuckled. "The smugglers are fortunate to have such a staunch defender," he said, pulling down the cuffs of his coat. "I believe the people have to accept whatever the law decides."

"That statement shows just how long you've been gone, milord," Gwen said.

Tawny eyes clashed with hazel ones for an eternal moment before Roc rose, stretching his powerful frame. "If you find any clue as to the identity of Dandelion, I expect you to inform me."

Never! Gwen vowed silently and stood, relieved to see him go. She would lead him the chase of his life. How dared he come home and pressure the decent people of Landregan. As long as she had an ounce of life in her body, she'd defend their right to food and clothing—even if it meant getting them from the other side of the Channel.

Roc bowed low and left the salon, the heels of his boots clicking briskly on the flagstones in the hall. Gwen heard him chat with Arthur as he pulled on his gloves. She knew he would glean no information from the footman, whose brain often seemed the size of a pea. Bereft of Roc's domineering presence, Gwen felt deflated, all the energy drained from her body. The impact of the tempestuous meeting had been such that she thought nothing would ever be the same in her life again.

"How dared he say that I'm sharp-tongued," Gwen declared hotly to her aunt's disapproving face.

Aunt Clo stared at her as if seeing a snake under a stone. "I've never heard anything like it! How could you behave in such—"

"—An unladylike manner. I know, you have told me many times. You don't say anything about *his* gall."

"You started it, and well you know it. However, he was not speaking of you when you entered the room. He was speaking of Clem Toboggan's grandmother."

"Oh." Angry with herself for jumping to hasty conclusions, Gwen hurried out of the room.

In her bedchamber, she sat on the edge of the four-poster bed and stared unseeing at the chaos of discarded shoes, stockings, gloves, and shifts strewn across the only comfortable chair, placed in front of the carved wooden mantelpiece. Her fingers toying restlessly with the edging on the front of her gown, she carefully recalled all the words that had flown between her and Roc. However much she hated to admit it, she was as drawn to Roc Tyrrell as ever. Her attraction to him had not been a fleeting adolescent fancy, after all. The mere memory of his face heated her blood. She longed to feel those strong fingers caressing her skin, those bold lips whispering words of love in her ears. A new restlessness filled her, an urgency tied to the yearnings of her body. She paced the floor, pressing her fingers to her blushing cheeks.

Roc rode home, oblivious to the lovely afternoon. His thoughts kept returning to the moment when Gwendolyn Tremayne had stepped through the door of the salon. Not knowing what to expect, he had found she was nothing like the urchin of old. Out of the chrysalis of adolescence had emerged a full-blown woman, not molded to perfection perhaps, but with a strength, an inner and captivating beauty and vivacity, that had enthralled him from the first moment.

He had a sudden urge to see her dressed in an elegant gown, not in the threadbare dress of indefinite color she had worn. He pondered the thought for a moment, baffled by his strong reaction to her. Despite her pride, he could not deny that her spirit had dazzled him. Excitement—and desire—filled him.

Chapter 3

Gwen went to the window to stare at the sea, longing for its usual calming effect on her sensibilities. Ever since Roc's visit, her emotions had been in hot turmoil.

The yellow rag waving on the stable wall in the gathering dusk did nothing to soothe her agitated state. A shudder of unease rushed through her. Another cargo? One had just arrived. Something must be wrong. Holding up her skirts, she fled down the stairs. Clem would be waiting for her in the spinney behind the Tremayne stables.

Clem's familiar form emerged from the shadows in the clearing of their secret meeting place. Night had already fallen among the trees.

"Clem, what's wrong?"

"Th' *Alouette* is comin' in with a cargo o' cognac on Friday." Clem sounded tense, biting back an underlying excitement.

"No! 'Tis too dangerous. Can't we stop her?"

"And lose th' cognac, th' best of th' lot so far this spring?"

Gwen groaned. "We could lose much more than that—our necks, you know."

"That night we'll set Biggles up with somethin' else to think 'bout."

"Biggles is not the problem, although he'll be more cautious after his last failure. There are also the soldiers, although they spend their time swaggering around the village flirting with every female under fifty." She took a deep breath. "And as if that isn't enough, the earl is anxious to capture Dandelion at the first possible moment, and let me tell you, he's no fool."

25

"Gorblimey, 'twill be more fun then, to lead 'im by th' nose." Clem waxed enthusiastic, and Gwen knew he was smiling in the darkness. "We'll teach 'im a lesson 'til 'e loses interest—and face."

"You seem mighty eager to show him his place." She eyed him dubiously.

" 'E needs takin' down a notch or two, and who's better at that than Dandelion and 'er friends, eh? Th' man means to take away our livelihood. I'll 'ave no regrets for pullin' 'is leg." Clem clenched his stalwart fists, his joints cracking.

Gwen also felt a keen desire to teach Roc a lesson. Her own danger did not deter her in the least. Her only worry was the safety of her men.

Clem continued heatedly. "Fancy, comin' 'ere showin' off 'is fine city clothes and manners."

Gwen smiled broadly. "What fervor! What has he done to earn your scorn?"

Clem fidgeted. "Well, 'e 'as done nuffin', 'tis just that 'is lofty airs touch me on th' raw."

Gwen's smile turned to soft laughter. "Quite a forceful personality, I agree. Anyhow, if you're game to give him a reprimand, so am I. But I warn you, it won't be easy."

"I'm game."

"I will return to the house and invent a plan," she said. "Are you sure the other men are willing to take the risk of provoking the earl's anger?" Squinting, Gwen tried to see his expression in the darkness.

"They all agreed. Th' cognac is too good to leave to th' 'gentlemen' of Fowey or Looe without tryin' to fork it in ourselves first. We need th' profit, and well ye know it. Ye need repairs on yer roof, don't ye?"

"You know I do," she said with a grimace. "There's never an end to the repairs on the house. I don't need reminding."

Early the following morning, Gwen sat atop her chestnut mare, Buttercup, trotting down the narrow, winding cobbled streets of Landregan. She alighted at Mrs. Padstow's shop to buy a skein of embroidery yarn for her aunt and ink for her father. But her real reason for riding into the village was her wish to speak with Officer Biggles. Once she knew his plans, she could set into motion her own scheme for the next load to be smuggled ashore.

It was always important to know where the revenue man would be on the night of a delivery. She almost regretted her decision to take on the load. Not only were they all being closely watched, but the moon wasn't on the dark. They would have to pray for an overcast sky, even rain. A frown etching a line between her eyebrows, she left the shop.

As she turned a corner on the narrow street, she spied Officer Biggles's scrawny back. She stepped up her pace until she was right behind him. "Officer Biggles," she called sweetly. The revenue officer turned around, sweeping his hat from his head, an ingratiating smile creasing his face.

"Miss Tremayne! What a delightful surprise." Gwen could not help but stare in fascination at the large wart that quivered on his chin. She heartily disliked having to speak with him at all, but it was important to the "business."

"How are you, Officer Biggles? I heard such shocking news." She lowered her voice. "You were attacked at The Pilchard. 'Tis awful to think of an upstanding citizen and hero like yourself becoming the victim of such bullies, only because you are doing your job." She fluttered her eyelashes beguilingly.

"Aye, 'twas a fierce evening. The smugglers' fault, all of it."

" 'Tis fortunate the soldiers are here to give you their assistance."

He snorted. "Ha! Much help they are. Think they can go around my orders. No wonder we haven't caught the scoundrels. But you mark my words, Miss Tremayne. Before the month is out, I will have captured the free traders red-handed."

"You're so brave, Officer Biggles. We need more men of your caliber in Landregan." She leaned a trifle closer. "One has to admit it is exciting to have smuggling going on in our midst." She whispered the next words conspiratorially. "Have you heard any rumors about their next load?"

"Miss Tremayne!" Plainly shaken, he added, "You should not concern your lovely head with such foul goings-on. 'Tis a matter for the soldiers to rid the area of the blackguards."

Gwen feigned a guilty expression, her lowered lashes shielding the merry glint in her eyes. "I know it is singularly forward of me, but you know how little entertainment there is in Landregan, so I thought—''

''Now, Miss Tremayne, don't take on so. If it interests you so much, and you have shown me great kindness since I came here, I will tell you something.'' He lifted a warning finger. ''As long as you keep it strictly to yourself.''

Breathless she replied, ''Why, Officer Biggles, I wouldn't dream of spreading any confidence you might deign to bestow upon me.''

He pursed his lips as if deep in thought, then maneuvered closer to her. ''Dandelion thinks he has me fooled this time, but he's more the fool. Thinking I don't know they're going to land the next cargo at Lucky Hole. Since I scouted the area last time—and the harbor—they believe I won't look there again. The only reason they got away with the contraband was that I arrived a trifle too late to catch them in the act.''

''Of course,'' Gwen hastened to reassure him, nearly bursting with a desire to laugh.

''The rumor has reached me that the 'gentlemen' are expecting another load on Friday.'' He puffed out his chest with importance.

Eyes wide, Gwen held her breath, still waiting.

''Mark my words, miss, when they say Friday, they mean Thursday or Saturday. As I told you, this time I will have Dandelion by the throat.''

Gwen released a sigh of relief. He had, as usual, fallen for her tricks. ''Officer Biggles, how clever of you! Tell me, who informs you of these things?'' she asked innocently.

Officer Biggles stared at her suspiciously, with an expression that rapidly turned to one of uneasiness. He scratched his head of lank, sandy hair. ''You know, that's the strangest thing. No one tells me directly. It sort of flows by me on the wind. You hear people talking in the streets, and so forth. Perchance this cargo is another trick of Dandelion's. They just hauled in a load.''

''Oh, I wouldn't put anything past him,'' said Gwen. ''The smugglers are probably trying to get their hands on as much as they can before the new magistrate becomes too active. They must be counting their last days, what with a capable man like you and the soldiers chasing them. And the earl.''

Officer Biggles swelled with pride, his piggish eyes, framed by pale, spiky lashes, becoming even smaller when he smiled. "You are right, of course. And a sight for sore eyes, miss. So very helpful and loyal to the law."

Gwen managed to blush. " 'Tis a citizen's duty to help the law in every way. I'm just doing what I must. And now, although I enjoyed our little chat, I must go. Pressing matters to take care of—some new ribbons for my gowns, you know." Gwen giggled with mock affectation and curtsied to the entranced officer, who swept his dusty cocked hat to the ground and presented a spindly leg.

Gwen's smile vanished as she hurried down the lane to fetch Buttercup outside Mrs. Padstow's shop.

The steady clip-clop of horseshoes against cobblestones heralded a rider she had no wish to see just now—Roc. He was mounted on White Star, and when Gwen became aware of his presence beside her, she slowed her steps. A jolt of stark physical pleasure shot through her when she met his charged gaze, but his smile goaded her.

When she had almost reached the shop, he dismounted and stepped toward her. He stretched out his hand, and Gwen felt obliged to allow him to grasp her slender fingers. His warm touch sent a shock of fire through her veins and spread a pounding heat inside her chest. His gaze rested on the tight brown jacket of her worn riding habit, and she fancied he could see her racing heartbeat.

"Miss Tremayne, what a pleasant surprise," he drawled, bending a head of glossy hair over her hand. Firm lips caressed her fingertips with tantalizing slowness. Transfixed, she lost herself in the subtle homage, her knees turning to jelly.

"M-milord." Regaining her equilibrium, she pulled her hand from his grip. "Have you lost your way? What has brought you to these humble dwellings?"

He clasped his crop under his arm, and a sardonic smile played at the corners of his lips. "I might ask the same of you. I had no idea you were on such friendly terms with Officer Biggles."

She eyed him with poisonous sweetness. "Landregan is a small place. One cannot but know all the inhabitants and speak with them frequently."

His topaz eyes narrowed. "You won't mind telling me what secrets you were sharing with him, then."

"Milord! How shocking. Don't you know 'tis bad manners to pry." Her smile was edged with frost, although she had never felt hotter inside. He looked so handsome this morning, a plain green coat stretching tightly over his broad shoulders, a snowy white jabot contrasting with his deep tan. She felt positively dowdy next to him.

"I have a strong feeling you know more about the smuggling business than you've led me to believe," he went on. "If you can tell Biggles, you can tell me." Roc's stern face held no softening promise.

"But, Lord Landregan, 'tis the other way around; Officer Biggles is the man to ask in these matters. And I assure you, about the free trading he's as tight-lipped as any. You must see that anything he utters in the village would instantly be repeated to the smugglers."

He glared at her with decided suspicion. "What then, pray tell, were you two whispering about?"

"Milord, you're overstepping your boundaries again, and you're sorely trying my temper with your shocking conduct." Breathless under his unyielding scrutiny, she gathered her wits about her and readied herself for a hasty retreat. "If you would be so obliging as to stand aside, milord, I wish to return home with my purchases."

But Roc was not in the least deterred by her vehemence. He switched tactics. " 'Tis amazing how beautiful you have grown, Gwen. A far cry from the dirty hoyden who used to follow me around."

Startled, she clutched her skirts and eyed him warily. Her voice full of vinegar, she said, "I don't remember dropping titles with you, milord." With a swish of skirts she squeezed past him in the narrow lane, ever aware that he followed closely behind her, to the small area outside the shop which the villagers called the square.

Arriving at her horse, she whirled and faced him. " 'Tis no use trying to wangle information from me. I have nothing to say to you. At best we'll only quibble, and I have better ways to spend my time. And if you desire to flirt, the village is full of willing ladies." With a toss of her head, she untied the reins.

"But I'm certain none has a perfectly acid retort to everything I say, as you do. Morgan was right, you know, when he informed me how vitriolic your tongue has grown over the years."

"What does *he* know!" She led Buttercup to the mounting block, but before she could step onto it, a pair of strong hands encircled her slim waist and lifted her easily into the saddle. Color rose over the collar of her habit, and she twisted away from his grip, yet he did not release her. His thumbs made slow circles over her stomach and a provocative grin spread across his features.

"How dare you!" she declared. "Is this what you learned on foreign soil, to take liberties with helpless ladies?" Yet, even as she spoke, she was aware of the delicious sensations created by his intimate touch. Unwillingly, as his touch scalded her through the fabric of her habit, she dragged her gaze from his face to his fingers.

"Pardon me. Do you resent being helped into the saddle?" he parried with a lazy grin.

Their eyes fought in blazing silence, and she witnessed the teasing smile slowly fade from his face. As if dazed, he glanced at his hands, then at her breasts straining against the fabric. Finally he awkwardly released her waist and handed her the reins.

"I don't mind assistance if the helper is a gentleman in the word's true meaning, not some—" Chest heaving, she sought a scathing word to describe his insolence. "Some arrogant newcomer who lords it over the entire village. If you wanted power, why didn't you stay in some heathen country where they keep slaves to do your bidding?"

"How cleverly you manage to change the subject."

"Not at all. I'm not a slave or a servant available to be manhandled by you." With her chin in the air, Gwen turned Buttercup around and kicked her heels into the lazy animal's sides. Anger flared hotly within her when she heard Roc's chuckle flying upon the wind. The utter gall of the man! She breathed deeply to restore her calm. What was he—a beloved dream of old or a nightmare come to life?

She urged Buttercup away from the village, choosing a westward path that skirted the huddle of slate-roofed granite and sandstone cottages hugging the sides of the secluded harbor. Brightly painted boats rested snugly on the shale-covered beach. Gwen saw men mending nets and chatting on the benches lining the harbor. Someone pointed at her, and they all turned and waved, their furrowed, deeply tanned faces breaking into warm grins.

Sunlight glittered on the calm sea, and a light breeze flowed over the sun-drenched landscape. The month of May was pure light and loveliness.

Buttercup unwillingly climbed the rounded hills and, at the top, Gwen turned in the saddle to look at the village in the valley below. From this distance Tremayne House looked beautiful and well-kept, with its dense spinney, stables, walled-in kitchen garden, and proud carriage sweep. She sighed with bittersweet pain. The house must always be hers; it was the only thing that held any meaning for her. Somehow, she would bring it back to its former state. She could not stand by and watch it go relentlessly to ruin.

Her mind following the familiar track of planning the gradual restoration of her ancestral home, she rode to her favorite lookout point above the sea. Here waves slapped angrily against the jagged rocks below, seething and bubbling over the treacherous reefs of Dead Man's Cove. Only a few places were safe for landing the cargo. In fear of detection, the French vessel could never land in the main harbor itself, and between Landregan and Looe only Lucky Hole and Brandy Cove were safe to enter. In dire need a shipment could be dumped outside the reef and the brandy kegs bound to a long rope with floaters. But it was risky. If not salvaged within twenty-four hours, the barrels would become soaked with sea water, which ruined the brandy. The ''gentlemen'' would go out in quay punts and haul in a few kegs at a time and hide them in hayricks, fish cellars, stables, and rainwater butts. There was no end to hiding places for a keg or two, but it took tedious time to gather them all together and send them in hiding by pony train or with the peddlers' wagons.

The peddlers pretended to lead a prospering trade of pins, buttons, bolts of cloth, gardening tools, and kitchen utensils, but when they came to Landregan, Gwen provided them with much more profitable wares. A layer of brandy kegs could easily be concealed by the usual stock in the wagons, with no one the wiser.

To take the contraband by pony train to London was risky, what with the revenue men and soldiers always on the alert along the way. Men missing from the village for several days would be instantly suspected of being smugglers. To Gwen, smuggling was a challenge to be mastered, a way to keep her mind nimble.

After sliding from the horse, she fastened the reins around the branch of a gnarled, wind-beaten oak. A seagull's harsh cry pierced the air as the bird swooped over the water.

Gwen threw herself into the soft grass with a sigh of relief. Here she could let her thoughts flow freely. Flat on her stomach, her chin propped in her hands, she gazed at the ever-changing water.

Dreamily she chewed on a piece of straw. The wind sighed in the grass and the trees. The drone of the waves upon the rocks lulled her weary body into much needed sleep, but not until the plan for the incoming cargo was perfectly clear in her mind.

Chapter 4

Something tickled her nose. Without opening her eyes, Gwen brushed a hand across her face, but the sensation continued. Only half awake, she felt a sense of sweet well-being spread through her body and heaved a deep sigh of contentment. Reluctant to destroy the pleasure, she peeked through her lashes.

She started to sit up, but something across her chest halted her. An arm.

Roc was smiling down at her. Propped up on one elbow, he was lying stretched out beside her, his thigh pressing into hers. A quiver ran through her.

"I'm sorry if I startled you, Miss Tremayne," came his slow, ingratiating voice, sending thrills of pleasure along her spine.

"Of all the detestable—" Gwen blurted out and tried to ease away. Roc's grin widened, and he chewed idly on the blade of grass with which he'd awakened her. His strong, tanned hand was coiled around her arm to detain her. She stared down at this daring intrusion on her flesh, unwilling to admit she liked it.

"You ran away so quickly I didn't have a chance to reacquaint myself with my shadow of old," said Roc. "Although you have grown into an exciting woman, I can still see that lovable urchin from my youth beneath the dignified façade."

Gwen was speechless. Her emotions ranged from indignation to anger to delight. But most of all she was confused. "You're only teasing me," she said, and pulled her thigh away. She made a motion as if to rise, but he held her fast—gently but relentlessly.

34

"Don't run away again, Gwennie. Wait awhile."

The sincerity of his voice deflated her anger. She glanced uneasily at him. "What do you want with me?"

Again he drew the blade of grass across her cheek. "You intrigue me," he said simply.

She wanted to say that she returned his sentiment, but for once her glib tongue refused to form the words. His presence, so unexpected, brought out emotions she didn't know how to explain. She couldn't remember the last time she had felt so shy. And this hot, quivery sensation in her body, what should she call it?

His gaze raked over the short jacket of her riding habit, and all at once she was aware of the wild pounding of her heart, a tickling expectation in the pit of her stomach, the promise of secret delights in his eyes.

His hand traveled along her arm, bunching the material of her jacket. The movement stole her breath away, and a spiral of desire curled along her spine. Her lips opened slightly, and she didn't resist as he pulled her down, resting her head on his arm. His thigh slid across hers. As if in a dream, she watched his lips coming closer.

Tense with expectation, she waited. The event she had always dreamed of in her lonely nights was about to happen. Roc would kiss her for the first time.

"No," she cried softly. "This cannot be true. You're merely playing a game with me." She placed a hand against his chest and shoved.

"Don't," he whispered. "Just relax and enjoy it."

She struggled out of his grip. "Yes, that's all it is for you, a nice way to pass a few minutes, but at my expense." She turned away from him. "I'd rather take a nap."

He chuckled and rolled onto his back. "You sound as if you were about to lose something."

She tightened her trembling bottom lip. "Perhaps I am. Dreams are kind, while reality is often a big disappointment."

He snorted and tickled her ear with the straw. "Little hedgehog. Reality is what it is. You can never change that. It shouldn't stop you from taking what pleasure comes your way."

She shrugged. "I don't want to *take* pleasure, and especially not lightly. I'm not your little adoring shadow anymore. You cannot play with me.''

''No, you have become a prickly hedgehog, all prim and proper with a mind for a cause. Champion of the villagers, as if they need one.''

''And you,'' she said heatedly, ''you care nothing for the children without shoes, or the widows whose husbands were swallowed by the sea. Some of them are raising six children or more all alone. Gwen's voluminous skirts hampered her movements, but she managed to stand up without his assistance. In a fit of pique, she vowed she would never let him touch her again.

He flung out his arms in disbelief. ''All this to-do over one little kiss I wanted to give you?''

She stood with her arms crossed over her chest, glaring down at him. ''That's all it is to you. One puny, disgusting kiss.''

Softness crept into his expression. ''Kisses are never disgusting. Who knows what could develop from one kiss? There is no end to the possibilities.''

''This is my spot. You have encroached on my privacy, and I beg you to leave,'' she said stiffly.

''And you're trespassing on *my* land.'' He glanced out over the sea. '' 'Tis a lovely spot, and I don't want to hinder you from coming here, but you can't forbid me to ride on my own grounds.''

Deflated, she fumed in silence. Her restless gaze traveled down to the churning water. Waves broke into furious foam over the black rocks, and two seagulls swooped toward the water. She followed their movements as one caught a fish and the other pursued the lucky fisherman, squawking with envy. Her eyes were drawn back to a dark spot beside the rocks below. Something was floating among the reeds. She frowned, and dread jolted in her stomach.

Forgetting everything, she raised a hand over her eyes to shade them from the sun's glare. The piercing reflections of the sun on the water made her doubt her sight, but then she was sure. ''A shipwreck!'' she blurted out.

Roc rushed to his feet and followed the direction of her pointing finger.

" 'Tis a small sailboat, and a man in a white shirt is tossing in the waves," she said.

Closely followed by Gwen, Roc scrambled down the narrow path to the shore below. Rocks skidded under their feet, making the descent treacherous. Gwen had only one thought in her head—to save the man. Roc must have had the same idea, since he rushed into the water as soon as he'd torn off his coat and boots.

"No!" she screamed. "You'll drown. The currents have immense suction here." But she cried in vain, and she knew she would have done the same if she'd been alone.

Roc's head bobbed on the waves. He was a good swimmer, but his considerable strength seemed helpless against the fury of the waves. He dove under and came up between two serrated rocks, close to the lifeless man.

Gwen dared not breathe. "Oh, God, please bring them back alive," she whispered over and over. She paced the narrow beach, oblivious to the waves soaking her boots.

The small boat slammed against a jutting rock, then ground between two others shaped like saw teeth. The timber groaned and splintered; waves tossed loose planks into the air, only to suck them into the blue-green water moments later. Gwen grabbed an oar as it floated ashore. Helpless, she watched Roc struggle against the elements. He had a hold on the unconscious man now and was swimming with furious energy toward the shore, only to be carried back out again.

A giant wave bore him to its crest and drove him forward with a whoosh, the limp victim dragging behind.

He's going to be crushed against the rocks if I don't do something, Gwen realized, and waded thigh-high into the water, until the current threatened to rob her of her balance. Reaching out as far as she could with the oar, she yelled at Roc to grab it. He managed to do so before the backwash of the preceding wave sucked him out again.

Gwen hauled with all her might and got a precious grip on Roc's shirt. Digging her heels into the loose shale, she pulled him in. Another wave bore them to shore.

Crawling out of reach of the water, they rested momentarily on the cold, wet shale. Roc's breath was labored, and his hair clung to his head like a smooth cap. He dragged himself to the victim a few paces away and listened to his heart. Then he looked at Gwen, his eyes pools of hopelessness. "He is dead," he said, gulping for air. "Damn!" He flung out his arms in a gesture of defeat.

The dead man was about thirty years old, dark-haired and very pale. His face was at peace but stamped with sadness. Drained, Gwen gazed out at the glittering emerald sea she loved so well. It had taken another life.

She started as Roc swore and shot a knotted fist into the air. Sorrow flooding her, she went to his side and put her wet arms around him. "You did your best. You could have drowned out there."

"You don't understand," he said. "This is James Murray, an old school friend of mine."

"An old friend?" She stared at the refined features of the drowned man, but knew she had never seen him before. She pushed wet strands of hair from Roc's face, but he dashed away her hand.

"Enough!" he demanded.

Her heart constricted as she watched his grief-stricken expression. "Murray?" she probed. "A Scot?"

Hanging his head, he nodded.

Gwen paused. "But what was he doing here in Cornwall?"

Roc sneered. "Probably escaping Butcher Cumberland's bloodhounds. There is a chase going on in the country; every Jacobite is to be hunted down and punished for treason." He stared at Gwen's incredulous face.

"You think you live far away from the winds of war here in Landregan," he continued, "but the bloodbath is being carried to every corner of the country, and it isn't over yet. The war won't be over until the killing is over."

A cold gust blew in over the shore. "And when will that be?" Gwen asked, ill at ease.

"When the English stop pretending they're involved in an innocent foxhunt, and acknowledge that the foxes are Scots," he said bitterly.

Gwen sent him a long, piercing glance. It was clear where his sympathies lay.

Chapter 5

Gwen stared worriedly at the dead man on the beach. "What are you going to do with the body, Roc? There will be questions."

"Yes, I know." He rose, balancing on the shale. His wet clothes clung to his body, and Gwen saw goosebumps forming on his strong forearms. "I'll inform his family by letter, but we'll have to bury him here. There is no way we can transport him to Scotland in the summer heat."

Gwen was relieved that he had already thought of a practical solution. "We don't have to tell anyone that he was, er, a Jacobite," she said lamely.

He glanced at her expressionlessly. "The villagers will wonder what he was doing here. Usually only fishermen drown in the sea."

"Let them wonder. They'll never find out unless we tell them."

"Very well, our secret it is then." Roc bent and hoisted the dead man over his shoulder. Struggling under the weight, he climbed up the steep cliff. She followed, her feet slipping on the treacherous tussocks.

Roc placed the body over the rump of his horse and turned to Gwen. "Thank you for helping me, Gwennie. I could never have done it alone."

She smiled in embarrassment. "Don't mention it. I'm glad I could be of help." She stared at the dead man, noticing dark smudges on his neck where the long hair had fallen away. "Look. What happened to his neck?"

Roc gingerly touched the marks, then lifted the head by the hair and studied the throat. His breath hissed between his teeth. "My God! It looks like he was strangled. You can see the bruises caused by a belt or some other device, a thin scarf perhaps."

Stunned silence hung between them. "But how—?" Gwen whispered, feeling a sudden chill in the air.

"It's odd. This means he was probably already dead when he set out in the boat. Someone placed him there, perhaps hoping the tide would carry him out to sea."

"How will we find out what really happened?"

He sighed. "I have no idea. We don't know where the actual murder took place—maybe miles down the coast." He dragged a hand across his face. "How will I tell his parents?"

Gwen placed her hand on his arm. "Don't. Not until you know the whole truth—if you ever do."

He patted her hand. "You're right. Let's get away from here."

She nodded. "Yes, this certainly has cast a pall over the day."

He assisted her onto Buttercup and released the reins from the tree, then hoisted himself into White Star's saddle and urged the horse into a trot down the hill toward the harbor. He turned once and waved at her. Gwen raised her hand and stared broodingly at her favorite spot, realizing that she would never return without remembering the tragedy.

Two days later, after having written the sad letter to the Murrays at Inverness explaining that their son had drowned, and after having attended the vicar's burial service at Landregan chapel, Roc rode down to the harbor.

His yacht, the *Blackbird*, was anchored in the bay outside the harbor. He needed to get out to the boat and think, go over in detail his last meeting with his old friend Alistair Borrodale in Calais. Borrodale was dead now, as was James Murray. Two of his old friends—both Scots—were dead. Could there be a connection between them? Perhaps they had both been involved in the Stuart Cause. Borrodale had certainly been a Jacobite.

A shiver of unease traveled down Roc's spine. Against his better judgment and because of his friendship with Borrodale, he himself was now involved in the Stuart Cause. He had to find a solution to this problem.

He tied White Star to a post and waved at the first mate, Mr. Dobson, who was waiting with the dinghy at the dock. Roc breathed deeply of the strong air, wanting suddenly to steer his ship out to sea to clear away his depression. But it was too late; darkness would soon fall.

"Goin' on a trip, milord?" asked Mr. Dobson as he rowed energetically across the bay.

Roc smiled. "No, just going out to check on the *Blackbird.*"

Roc climbed up the rope ladder to the polished deck and then down to his private stateroom below. Everything was as he had left it upon arriving from France. The oak desk was covered with charts and correspondence. The gleaming desk top was scarred where he had rested his boots. He liked to lean back in his chair, put his feet up, and look out the porthole. The water was always changing, even here in the quiet harbor. The boat swayed gently on the choppy surface of the bay.

Unlocking the bottom right drawer of his desk, Roc pulled out an octagonal brown leather box. The corners were brass, as was the stout lock. He took a key from a gold chain around his neck, inserted it in the lock, and turned it.

Slowly lifting the lid on its hinges, he sighed deeply at the glittering array of gems on the velvet interior. They sparkled multicolored fire in the orange light of the setting sun. Lovely. Charles Edward Stuart had many wealthy friends across the Channel, Roc thought as he wound a diamond and ruby necklace around his fingers. There was a tiara of pearls and sapphires, ruby and opal bracelets, black pearl necklaces, diamond brooches and pendants. Rings set with all manner of precious stones. A fortune.

And it had been entrusted to his care.

Roc recalled Alistair's last words: "Roc, you're the only one I can trust." Alistair had clutched his arms, his fingers skeleton thin. "I know very well that you don't hold with the Jacobite Cause, old friend, but I implore you . . ."

Alistair's fingers slid away, his face gray against the stark white pillows. "For old times' sake, Roc. Take the box to

England, and someone will contact you at Landregan. No one will ever know you were involved.''

Alistair's voice became thin, the specter of death already hovering in the small room under the rafters of the inn at Calais. The sounds of the streets were muted, as if they existed in another world. "Please . . . for old times' sake, don't fail me, old . . . friend.''

Roc sighed. He had never had a chance to say no. He glanced at the jewels. What should he do? The shattered Jacobite army was waiting for the aid these jewels would bring—arms, food, clothing. Roc had never wanted to play any part of the rebellion, and he still didn't, but how could he break a promise to his old friend?

Roc's father, the former earl, had had a hunting lodge in Scotland adjacent to the Borrodale estate. Roc's father and Alistair's sire had been friends for ages, and Roc himself had known Alistair all his life.

Now he was about to betray that friendship. He could not deliver the jewels. It went against everything he believed in. The Jacobites were for a Catholic king, while George II was a Protestant. The masters of Landregan had always been against the Popish religion, and he was no exception.

Charles Edward Stuart might be the rightful king by lineage, but the Stuart rule in England was over, had been since the first rebellion in 1715 when Charles's father, James, lost his only chance at the British and Scottish thrones. Bypassing her brother, James Stuart, Queen Anne had chosen her German cousin, the Elector of Hanover, as her successor to the British throne. The Stuarts had tried to change her decision by force, but the efforts had been fruitless.

"Oh, God, why did this have to happen?" Roc stared out the porthole as if expecting an answer from the water or the sky, but no sudden lightning cleaved the air in revelation.

So far there had been no message from London about the gems. It was early days yet, but could James Murray have been sent to get the jewels from him? And if he wasn't, what would the real contact say once he discovered that Roc had returned the jewels to their owners in France, which was what he intended to do at the first possible opportunity.

It shouldn't be too difficult to find Alistair's Jacobite contacts in France. While everyone in England whispered about the rebellion in the north, the French spoke of it aloud. It wouldn't be hard to return the jewels to their rightful owners.

Roc sighed heavily, closed the lid of the box. He lifted the chain from his neck and placed it in the bottom desk drawer, which he closed with an angry twist of his wrist. The simplest thing would be to toss the jewels overboard and forget they ever existed, but he could never do that.

It was too late to change the course of fate now. Alistair had placed his burden on Roc's shoulders, and there it would rest until he had delivered the box back to France, where it belonged.

On Thursday night everyone in the village knew that Officer Biggles and the soldiers were lying in ambush above Lucky Hole, taking for granted that this would be their night to capture Dandelion. As Gwen had surmised, the excise man had fallen for the rumors she had spread.

Burning with curiosity, Gwen and Clem crept down to the cove to spy at midnight.

Muffled laughter erupted from behind trees and rocks as bored soldiers lay in wait, whispering among themselves. Gwen's brow furrowed with concern. They were an arrogant lot, and if they tired of Officer Biggles's incompetence, she feared they might take matters into their own hands. She had no desire to be the target of a hastily discharged musket.

Like an excited bloodhound, Officer Biggles ran back and forth among the rocks.

Gwen and Clem sneaked to the edge of the cliff and tossed handfuls of pebbles down to the beach to create a diversion. First came Officer Biggles, his pot belly clearly recognizable in a flash of bright moonlight. He scuttled in such a hurry toward the beach that he lost his foothold on the slithery mud and tumbled down the slope, his curses shattering the stillness of the night. The soldiers rushed over to help him, pulling the deflated revenue officer to his feet. Lying low among the furze, Gwen gleefully watched the goings-on, then, with her henchman, quickly crept away from the scene, a few words drifting to them from the irate Officer Biggles.

"Cursed nuisance! They will be at it on Saturday night now. A whole night's sleep lost over nothing, and my leg aching like the devil."

The next day, Friday, Gwen saw Officer Biggles limping through the village, a dark scowl on his face. He earned no sympathy from the villagers. Satisfied with last night's work, she murmured her commiseration and hurried home, knowing that nothing would stand in the smugglers' way that night when they brought in the contraband.

The next morning Gwen moaned with fatigue as she forced herself to her bedroom window to see if a white rag hung on the stable wall. It was there. Thank God! No hue and cry had arisen; the cognac had been delivered safely to the dilapidated cottage above Yellow Rock.

She sat down at her dressing table and stared into the mottled mirror. Since Roc had returned she had been more careful with her appearance. For the first time in her life, it bothered her that her gowns in the heavy clothespress were worn and out of date.

Not that she had seen much of Roc since their sad discovery at Dead Man's Cove. James Murray had been buried quietly in the estate's chapel, the only mourners Roc and Morgan, but the incident hung like a pall in her mind, a foreboding of tragedy to come. She tried hard to push away the premonition.

"Late again," Aunt Clo greeted Gwen sourly as she hurried into the breakfast parlor.

"Nonsense, Aunt," Gwen parried brightly. "A lady needs her beauty sleep, and well you know it. Where is Papa?"

"He's in the study with Master Morgan, who arrived on our doorstep at an unreasonably early hour." Aunt Clo sniffed audibly and wiped her pointed nose with a dainty scrap of cambric and lace. "Perhaps he's escaping the hubbub at the Hall. I meant to tell you, the dowager countess is coming home now that the earl's back."

"That old tartar! Times will be lively at the Hall." Gwen chuckled. "She'll have her sons dancing to her pipe in no time."

"We'll see. The earl doesn't seem like a man who takes kindly to a commanding female." Aunt Clo sipped her tea gingerly.

"He'll have to obey his mama to keep peace in the house."

Aunt Clo snorted. "You are wrong there, Gwennie. I declare, the dowager will have to obey *him.*"

"Have you ever seen her taking orders from anyone?"

Aunt Clo grudgingly admitted that she never had, not even from the former earl.

"Are you going to call on her?" Gwen piled her plate high with toast and eggs.

"Yes, I might drive around and leave my card some time next week. You can rest assured she'll hold strictly to conventions." She hesitated. "If an invitation from her should come, I will of course accept."

Gwen patted a stray curl. "She'll bite your head off with her condescending ways."

The object of their discussion was at that very moment alighting from her traveling chaise in front of Landregan Hall. Her booming voice bounced off the imposing walls as she issued sharp orders to the footmen swarming around her. She lifted protruding eyes to survey Enedoc as that gnarled retainer welcomed her on the stone steps, his wig askew and his sky-blue satin livery sadly rumpled.

"Welcome home, your ladyship," he rasped, and bowed with difficulty, his back stiff.

"Hrmph. You look a fright as always, Enedoc. It's beyond me how Roc lets you stay on here," she stated with a disapproving tilt of her triple chins. She sailed into the cool hallway, her dress swaying precariously around huge hoops, almost sending a vase toppling to the floor. Released from her quelling glance, Enedoc rolled his eyes.

Her ladyship waved a huge painted fan in front of her face while her critical gaze flew around the room. She turned her head so quickly that Enedoc began to guess when her curled and powdered wig, adorned with a cluster of ostrich feathers, would fall off.

"Lady Landregan, how long are you planning to visit?" he asked boldly.

She cackled and whacked him over the head with her fan, sending his tie-wig to the floor in a cloud of powder. Blushing, he bent to retrieve it. "Already anxious to get rid of me, are you, you old windbag?"

"M-milady!"

Fortunately for Enedoc, Roc came swiftly down the stairs. "Mama, there you are."

"Wretch! You couldn't wait for your mama on the front steps; no, I must be welcomed and *insulted* by servants." The dowager countess offered a wrinkled cheek for him to kiss.

A smile tugged at his lips as he leaned over the powdered and rouged countenance. "That bad, eh?" He glanced at a velvet heart-shaped spot that had been applied crookedly to her cheek. With a careful flick of his finger, he righted it, earning from her a snort of outrage.

"Worse! I declare I regret the moment my chaise passed the Tamar. And what a sorry sight this house is for my tired eyes. The neglect, the decay—and you're doing nothing about it. Your papa surely must be turning in his grave . . ." She gave Roc a penetrating stare. "You look dreadful—as if you've slept too much. Lazy, I'm sure. Just like your papa always maintained."

"Of course," Roc said in the driest of tones.

With a push, the dowager righted her ostrich feathers and tottered toward the Amber Salon. "Are you going to let me starve all day in this hallway, m'boy, or am I entitled to a nip of tea on this most trying of days? How I ever let you persuade me to travel down here, when I was snug in Tunbridge Wells taking the waters, is inconceivable." She sighed heavily. "And the beds at the inn at Liskeard positively crawled with fleas."

She righted a set of figurines on a table beside the fireplace and pulled a fat forefinger along the back of an ornate chair. The amber damask walls received close scrutiny, the amber curtains a shake, and the green and amber striped chaise longue a headshake. Cradling a needlepoint pillow to her ample bosom, she sat down, glancing critically at the Oriental carpet underfoot.

"Mama, I assure you I didn't want to tear you from your friends, but I thought you might want to see me once, now that I'm home. And yes, I spent a cursed bad night."

She eyed him speculatively. "You know how much I hate the humid summer air of Cornwall. 'Twill be the end of me." She fanned herself vigorously, and Roc hid his smile behind his hand. He was saved from responding when Enedoc wheeled in the tea trolly.

"Where is that bookworm son of mine?" the dowager countess demanded peevishly.

"I believe the fact of your imminent arrival must have flown from his mind. Enedoc, please remind Morgan."

The old butler hurried from the room. The dowager slowly shifted her cumbersome frame. "Now, Roc dear, will you inform me why you have dragged me down to this godforsaken place when you know how much I detest it?" She suspiciously regarded her handsome son, his back so straight, his stubborn Tyrrell chin more pronounced than ever. He was a chip off the old block, and she heaved a sigh of regret for the days when the old geezer, her husband, had been alive.

"Bursting with curiosity about my motives, eh?" Roc tapped the carved wooden mantelpiece and eyed her with amusement. "I need someone to hostess a few parties, that's all. 'Tis about time I was married, don't you agree?"

"Married?" she shrieked, her fan falling to the floor. Roc watched her chins drop even farther down the ample chest. "Took you by surprise, eh?" he said with a laugh.

"And whom do you have in mind?" she demanded.

Enedoc interrupted the charged scene by announcing that Sergeant Adams had arrived on urgent business and requested a private word with the earl.

The dowager bellowed. "Don't you dare leave the room before giving me the name of this *person* you're going to marry!"

"Sergeant Adams, milady," Enedoc repeated.

"Not *you*, you addlepated toad," she burst out, pushing a fleshy finger into the earl's middle.

"All in good time, Mama." Firmly he lifted her finger from his body. "You'll have to excuse me. Enedoc, where is Sergeant Adams? In the library?"

The butler nodded since his voice could not be heard over the dowager's piercing protests.

"Mama, control yourself!" Roc snapped, and left the room. "Phew." He wiped his forehead and took a deep breath. His former composure returning, he stepped into the library.

The first thing that met his gaze was Morgan's stooped

form bowed over a book. Then his eyes traveled to the young officer attempting to converse with his absentminded brother.

"Morgan, the dowager countess is awaiting your company in the Amber Salon," said Roc.

"Eh? . . . Oh, yes, that was it. I had quite forgotten what Enedoc told me to do." Without another glance at Sergeant Adams, he disappeared, the cherished book clamped under the arm.

"I'm awfully sorry to disturb you at this ungodly hour of the morning," Sergeant Adams said in hushed tones, "but I find it of utmost importance to inform you that the smugglers hauled in a load last night."

Roc stared at him in disbelief. "Another cargo? But you told me they just made a delivery, right after the dark of the moon."

The sergeant squirmed, pressing his hat more firmly under his arm. "Yes, that's true, but the French cutter evidently made another trip."

"Damned impudence!" And he had slept like a dead man all night. He motioned Sergeant Adams to an upholstered leather chair in front of his desk. "Please, sit down and tell me all about it." His tawny gaze bored into the uncomfortable officer.

"We should have caught them, of course, but Officer Biggles was sure the delivery would not happen until Saturday—since it didn't occur on Thursday." He gulped for air and bravely met the earl's narrowed gaze. "I regret complaining about Biggles's incompetence."

"Then don't. You already know of his, er, difficulties and should assist him in any way possible, as I'm sure you have more, er, upstairs than he does."

"Yes, milord, I swear this will not happen again. The next time we'll be sure to catch Dandelion on whatever day he chooses to do his dirty deed."

"Tell me, *how* did Officer Biggles know about the load in the first place?"

"Oh, he claims he has reliable ways. I suppose the villagers tell him." Too late Sergeant Adams realized the folly of that reply and hastily tried to undo the damage. "I mean, he must have spies, you know."

The contempt in the topaz eyes told him what Roc thought of that explanation. "I expect results soon," said Roc, "or I shall be forced to seek more competent help."

"Aye, milord. This was an unforgivable mistake." Adams stood abruptly and walked to the door, the heels of his boots clicking against the polished floor. "I promise 'twill not happen again." He bowed deeply, saluted, and left the room.

Roc rubbed his aching forehead. The dull throbbing reminded him of one night when he had been very ill and had taken laudanum to make him sleep. I can smell the fox, and he's much too clever for comfort, he thought.

Chapter 6

"They *are* weeds, you know." Gwen held up a gloved hand covered with soil to shield her eyes from the glare of the sun. Today of all days Roc had chosen to visit her. Speckled with mud to the elbows, she looked a fright. Her dress bore a multitude of small holes and tears, and a battered straw hat with faded ribbons barely concealed her limp curls.

Despite her efforts, she fought a losing battle with the weeds on the lawn in front of Tremayne House. On this occasion she was digging up dandelions. How fitting! She held a crushed dandelion in her hand and said to Roc, standing on the other side of the drive, "The lawn is overgrown with this nuisance, and if you leave the smallest part of the root in the ground, 'twill grow back." She refrained from informing him that the yellow flower had inspired the name for her secret identity.

"I daresay the whole village is overgrown with them," Roc responded drily and alighted from his chestnut stallion, Tristan, who had just been delivered to Landregan Hall. He patted the noble head. "I have recently received the disturbing information that Dandelion has struck again."

"So you hotfooted it over here to find out if we know anything about it. I assure you, we know no more than you do. At that time of night we're sound asleep in our beds." Her eyes twinkled impishly at him. "And so you should be." She laughed as his lips set into a grim line. "But you weren't in your bed, if your visage is any indication. You look harried and exhausted. Did you have a sleepless night? Chasing free traders, perchance?"

Her mocking voice made him coolly disdainful. "On the

contrary. I can't remember a time when I slept more deeply. Well, I should not keep you from your simple chores. Is your father at home?''

"How ill-tempered you are this morning. The smugglers must have slipped through your fingers." Her eyes lost their teasing glint and became points of steel. "You're out of luck, milord. The squire has gone to Plymouth on business. And I should not keep you hanging about here, as I have nothing to tell you. I'm sure it must wound your sensibilities to speak to such a lowly working creature as myself. Good day, milord." She turned her back on him.

"Ah, Gwen, you must always get in a last lash of that tongue of yours." He laughed, the sound jarring her. "Indeed, you look fetching in that, ahem, costume, and your nose is burned by the sun. I almost didn't recognize you." Instead of leaving, he sauntered across the lawn toward her, his attractive form clad in tight-fitting breeches and a brown riding coat with wide cuffs and pocket flaps adorned with gold braid. His top boots shone mirrorlike in the sunlight, as did his sleek raven hair.

Gwen's breath caught in her throat, and she swallowed hard. She smoothed down her patched dress and threadbare apron in a futile effort to make them appear less timeworn. "Roc, if you're seeking to spar with me, I warn you I have no time to listen to you. I have too much lowly work to do." She averted her head to hide the bitterness in her eyes. His next words startled her.

"I did not come here to clash swords with you, Gwen. I deeply admire your struggle to save the estate."

She peered suspiciously at him from under thick lashes. His gaze caressed her briefly before moving to the façade of the old brick manor. "You have been working very hard, I can tell—all new window sashes."

"Yes." She lovingly scanned the plain two-story house. The windows were newly painted, and the shutters had a fresh coat of green paint. Ivy climbed the old walls all the way to the wooden gutters. "The window sashes are all new." And paid for with proceeds from the smuggling. She had spoken a shade too quickly and prayed he would not notice the breathless quality of her voice. "The house needs a lot more work, a new roof, ceilings, and the floorboards are—well, I don't want to bore you with the details. We are getting along quite adequately.''

Thoughtfully he slapped the crop against the cuff of his boot. Gwen held her breath, sweat breaking out on her palms. *Next he will ask where I got the funds. He might even suspect . . .*

His disconcerting gaze crossed her face, locked, held, taunted, tamed. Excitement surged between them, mingled with a spice of something forbidden, something dark and sweet and wildly exhilarating.

Gwen dropped the small garden spade from her nerveless fingers and stood motionless, enchanted. When his long fingers reached out to touch her cheek, she did not pull away. For one endless moment, as if his face closed the distance between them, she thought he would kiss her, but only his breath rasped against her heated skin. His virile scent enveloped her, and she realized how much she had always liked it. But this was the first time she was aware of its subtle seduction. Heady desire wound slowly through her, gathering hotly at the joining of her thighs.

A swift movement bore his finger like a butterfly across her lips, teasing, branding, and she gasped, a delicious shiver coiling in her abdomen. She laughed, a low, throaty sound. ''Taking liberties again, Roc?''

He expelled his breath slowly, deliberately. ''I'm lost in an exquisite dream,'' he murmured. ''Simply exquisite.''

Gwen hesitated. *Did he really mean that she was a dream?* Her breath shuddered with longing. She wanted the moment to go on forever.

To hide any telltale sign of her churning emotions, she bent awkwardly to retrieve the shovel. ''There are no exquisite dreams for people like me—only plenty of hard work every day. I suppose a person like you can idle away your time without worrying about the roof caving in over your head.''

''Well, I'm sadly neglecting my work at the moment.''

She glanced sharply at him. ''Work? And what could that be?'' she chided gently.

''To establish Dandelion's ways more firmly in my mind. Not that I've had any luck, but sooner or later someone will let slip a snippet of information, and I will catch him.''

All magic evaporated from the moment. ''I can't say I

wish you luck, Roc. In fact, to put it bluntly, I hope you never find him. I hope he leads you a merry chase until you tire.''

"By Jove, that rather spurs me on, you know. I won't rest now, if only to make you take back those words.'' He returned to Tristan, who was methodically tearing grass from the lawn, and heaved himself into the saddle in one fluid movement. Gwen squinted up at him. He was, indeed, a formidable enemy, and a remarkably attractive one, too. Did he know the effect he had on her?

"We will see who has the last word,'' he called as he wheeled the horse onto the graveled drive.

She turned on her heel, ready to fling another sally at him, but his unyielding back forestalled any more taunts, and she held her tongue. Listlessly she pulled out another sagging dandelion from the unkempt lawn.

During breakfast the next day, Arthur delivered an envelope on a tarnished silver platter. With an owlish look on her face, Aunt Clorinda opened the stiff missive and read it, her eyes growing rounder. She began to flutter around the breakfast parlor like a nervous moth.

"Are you going to keep me in suspense forever, Aunt Clo?'' Gwen asked.

"This note is from the dowager countess of Landregan. She has invited us to take tea with her tomorrow at four.'' The monotony of Aunt Clo's voice told Gwen of her great emotional tumult. The missive sailed to the patched tablecloth. "Good grief, we don't have anything to wear,'' Aunt Clo wailed suddenly, as if she were seeing her dream fading into nothing.

"I'm sure we'll find something sufficiently elegant to wear,'' Gwen assured her. "Landregan isn't London, you know. This is the country, and she can't expect us to be dressed in the latest style. After all, 'tis only an invitation to tea.''

"Ha! 'Tis not every day you get invited to take tea with a countess. She will not deign to speak with us again after she sees our dreadful gowns. We'll look like paupers.'' Aunt Clo sniffed, a look of long-suffering sagging her face.

Gwen shrugged. "That's what we are, Auntie, paupers with no decent clothes on our backs."

"How can you be so cruel, Gwennie, reminding me of our straitened circumstances?" Aunt Clorinda sucked in her lower lip with disapproval, evidently forgetting her own complaints.

"I assure you, we'll make do."

The next day, twenty minutes before the appointed hour, Aunt Clo waited impatiently in the hallway, her eyes redrimmed from worrying all night. A respectable if old blue silk dress over moderate hoops adorned her scrawny body. Her best lace shawl, starched and pressed to perfection, crossed her chest, concealing her lack of bosom. Pulling on her gloves, she looked up the stairway, her growing anger appeased as Gwendolyn emerged from her bedchamber only five minutes late.

But as Aunt Clo viewed her niece, she began to wring her hands in despair. "This won't do. You should have had a new gown made for this visit. You look like a servant," she wailed. "Beside my gown, yours looks worse than ever." Dazed, Aunt Clo sank onto a chair, refusing to budge.

"Very well, we won't heed the invitation," said Gwen. "I'll send Arthur over with a note saying you've suddenly taken ill."

That cool announcement brought a fresh wail to Aunt Clo's lips. "How can you be so heartless! This is our only chance to be included in the right circles."

Gwen shrugged. "Why that is so important is beyond me." A third wail rent the air, and Gwen received a ferocious glare.

" 'Tis your *last* chance to find a husband, silly girl! If we play our cards right—"

A peal of laughter erupted from Gwen's lips. "And *whom* do you have in mind, dear Aunt?"

Aunt Clo blew her nose loudly. "You never know who you might meet in the Landregan circle."

"Lud, no doubt some painted, mincing fop from the capital, like our cousin Vincent. Spare me such a fate," Gwen added with mock horror as she pulled on her yellowed kid gloves. "Well? Are we going?" Her hands placed on her hips in an unladylike manner, she loomed over her seated aunt, who sent her niece a calculating sideways glance and rose to her feet.

"Perhaps you should walk behind me as we enter Landregan Hall," Aunt Clo suggested, "so that the countess won't immediately notice the state of that hideous gown." She looked askance at Gwen's outfit, an overdress of red muslin so faded that it was hard to decide whether to call the color rose or beige. The cream underdress patterned with flower sprigs had a clearly visible patch at knee height.

Gwen smiled sweetly. "I'm sure we'll contrive something."

The graveled sweep leading to the Hall had been raked and the holes filled in. The borders were free of weeds and the hedges trimmed, indicating that someone other than Morgan now held the reins of the estate. On the lawn in front of the imposing entrance, the blossoms of a cluster of rose bushes sent out a delicate fragrance.

Enedoc bowed on the front steps and helped Aunt Clo to alight from the Tremayne gig.

"Good afternoon, Miss Pettigrew, Miss Tremayne," he greeted them. "The dowager countess is awaiting you in the Rose Sitting Room." As he showed them in, Gwen could not help but notice that the old mansion held a newly scrubbed and polished look. Roc obviously did not waste time.

The Rose Sitting Room was located on the second floor, part of the countess's private suite of rooms. As the name indicated, the predominant color was rose. The walls were covered with watered rose silk. The taffeta draperies and carpet sported the same color. I will quite blend in with the walls here, Gwen thought, ruefully glancing down at her gown. Her giggle threatened to grow to a volcano of laughter when she laid eyes on the dowager countess.

The woman holding that title occupied a whole sofa, or at least her dress did. What made her appearance so ludicrous were the enormous paniers protruding on either side of her hips, making her look like a packhorse. The startling puce color of her taffeta gown clashed wildly with the walls. Gwen noticed how Aunt Clo slowed her steps in surprise at the vision, and Gwen gave her a sharp nudge in the back.

"Ah, *there* you are!" the dowager boomed. "Such a long

time since we last met." Her bulbous eyes sought Gwen. "Come here, gel. Don't hide behind your relative." As Gwen stepped forward, she heard Aunt Clo gasp at being called a relative.

"Squire Tremayne's daughter, eh? Lud, but have you grown tall, gel! Positively *lanky.*" A growl of laughter surged from the dowager's ample bosom. "Hard to believe the squat Squire Tremayne is your father." She eyed Aunt Clo disdainfully. "And I can tell you haven't gained your looks from your mother's side, either, although your mother was quite lovely in her day." With a pudgy, beringed hand she motioned for Gwen to turn around. "With a decent gown, you *might* pass for a handsome woman, Miss Tremayne."

Gwen, seeing the absurdity of the situation, smiled as she faced the old woman's hard scrutiny. "You make me feel quite like a prize cow, your ladyship."

"Gwendolyn!" Aunt Clo moaned.

The dowager's eyes threatened to pop, and Gwen waited with wry amusement for her reaction. The dowager surprised her by bursting into a laugh so boisterous that the sound seemed to bounce off the walls. "Dear me." She hiccupped between bouts, her face turning a mottled red. As the mirth slowly subsided, the dowager wiped her perspiring forehead with a handkerchief. "I declare I've never been more entertained in all my life. Prize cow, indeed!"

She peered at Gwen through watering eyes. "I say, an eccentric hidden out here in this godforsaken hole." Dabbing repeatedly at her eyes, she continued, "My stay might not be as boring as I feared. Sit down, gel!" She patted the chair next to the sofa, then leveled a haughty stare at Aunt Clo. "Ah, yes, Miss Pettigrew, sit over there." She waved vaguely at a chair at the other side of the tea table, indicating that she had no interest in continuing a conversation with the aging spinster.

Gwen noticed the hurt look on her aunt's face. "I will join my aunt, if you don't mind. She will feel quite abandoned over there."

The dowager countess snorted. "If that's what you want, miss." She rang a silver bell and Thomas Strutt, the footman, wheeled in the tea trolley. A silver tray groaned under the weight of tiny cucumber sandwiches, hot crumpets, and sugared rolls. A gleaming bowl held clotted cream, another contained strawberry preserves, and a plate overflowed with chocolate bonbons.

The dowager poured tea into thin porcelain cups, and the bewigged Thomas handed out the steaming cups with a cautious glance in the dowager's direction. The haughty peeress once more raised her bulbous eyes to gaze coldly at the pair across the table.

"Beautiful salon, this," Aunt Clo blurted out. "The earl has exerted himself to restore the place since he returned."

"That's more than one can say about Tremayne House," the dowager replied, filling her mouth with an entire cucumber sandwich.

Aunt Clo bristled. "We do our best, milady. Gwen works very hard to keep the estate together."

Lady Landregan snorted contemptuously. "That old pile of rocks!"

Gwen stood, her temper flaring. "I hope we were not summoned here to be insulted! I will not accept further harsh words."

Baffled, the countess fixed her with a terrible eye. "Don't get into fidgets over nothing." Her lips curled in a reluctant grin. "You're not only eccentric, you have pluck as well. My son was right when he insisted you had a sharp tongue. Naturally, I had to hear for myself."

Damn Roc! Boiling with anger, Gwen did not trust herself to speak. She felt Aunt Clo tugging at her gown in warning. Gwen paid no heed. "Well," she said, "if we're here solely for your ridicule, I think we have entertained you long enough, or do you expect me to stand on my head as well? It is poor amusement to get one's laughs from unsuspecting guests. Come, Auntie, shall we depart before the dowager countess suggests we should earn our keep by joining a traveling theater company as clowns?"

At that moment Roc sauntered into the room. "Raking them over the coals already, Mother?" he asked grimly. He bent to kiss his parent's proffered cheek while eyeing Gwen's fuming countenance, his smile sympathetic.

Casually addressing Aunt Clo, he said, "The dowager could make cream curdle with her acid words, and she's quite the horror of any gathering, so don't pay any heed to her. I apologize. Please enjoy your tea."

The "horror" huffed and muttered. "Mind—manners," were the only words Gwen could discern. She sat uneasily on the edge of her chair and nibbled a sandwich, staying only in deference to her aunt. Aunt Clo seemed to forget the insults they'd suffered as her eyes glowed at the many delicacies. While Gwen looked on, a frown of irritation between her eyebrows, Aunt Clo nimbly filled her plate.

Gwen knew Roc had instigated this charade of a tea party, but why? What reason did he have for introducing her to his mother? She glanced at his inscrutable face but read nothing there except good humor. She would see that he paid for this disastrous afternoon!

Roc leisurely chewed a cucumber sandwich. His gaze wandered over Gwen, from her flaming cheeks to the tips of her shabby slippers, which once must have matched the awful gown she was wearing. He could feel resentment surging from her in waves, and he wondered what the dowager had said to earn such wrath from the proud young woman. She ate almost nothing, her chin high, her flashing eyes seeking the patch of blue sky visible between the curtains. He felt a potent urge to seize her chin and claim her mouth with his own, to kiss her until she softened in his arms. His gaze flickered to his mother. Would she understand why he had wanted her to meet Gwen? Would they accept each other? He was toying with the idea of making Gwen his countess, but as yet he'd not fully considered the possibility.

"One reason I requested your presence," began the dowager, "is that my son has begged me to hostess a few gatherings, and you will, of course, be invited. Some of my personal friends will have to be asked here to liven things up a bit. Landregan is so shockingly dull."

Gwen could not hold back a scathing comment. "It was perfect until you—" Halting her words in the nick of time, she took a shuddering breath. "Perhaps someone ought to warn your friends to stay away from *dull* Landregan."

The dowager roared with laughter, and Gwen stared at her, aghast. Her confused gaze sought out the earl, who smiled mischievously at her. Gwen's eyes narrowed to a deadly gleam, and she clutched Aunt Clo's arm, none too gently.

" 'Tis time we left," she said. As Aunt Clo hastened to stuff another bonbon into her mouth, Gwen added, "Thank you for inviting us to tea, Lady Landregan, but we can't idle away all day."

Once again wiping her eyes, the dowager waved at her. "Most amusing—you *must* come again."

Roc followed them to the door. Gwen burned to whack him over the head with her fist. "How could you do this! I won't be treated like a fool. You should check to see if that enormous wig has boiled your mother's brain."

"I knew you two would get along famously," he said, a flicker of a smile on his lips.

As Gwen clenched her fists at her sides, her face pale with anger, Roc was flooded by another powerful urge to take her into his arms, to make love to her, to see the storm die from her eyes and contentment grow in its place.

Chapter 7

In June, at the time of the next dark of the moon, two intriguing events occurred. First, the load from France arrived, as punctual as the clock in the village church tower. Second, the marchioness of Camelford appeared at the Hall, her nubile daughter, Louise, in tow.

Like the other villagers, Gwen followed the goings-on with great interest, especially since strangers were such a rare sight in Landregan. But jealousy speared her at the thought of a young, unmarried woman living at the Hall; her own attraction for Roc had grown rather than abated. Still, she had no time to brood since Dandelion had a singularly busy schedule ahead of her.

The yellow rag—the signal of an approaching load—had fluttered on the stable wall all day. As soon as the house quieted for the night, Gwen sneaked down the stairs and out of the house. This night she took special caution in her dress. If they were captured, by no account did she want to be instantly recognized as a woman. She wore a pair of knee breeches and one of Arthur's old dark shirts. Around her hair she wound a black kerchief, and her face was dark with soot from the fireplace in the kitchen.

Wraithlike, she melted into the night. Clem was waiting at his usual spot in the spinney. She immediately sensed his exhilaration, but anxiety plagued her. The free trading was becoming exceedingly difficult, yet she had no desire to abandon her smuggler friends. Roc needed to learn a lesson—especially now, after the disastrous tea party at the Hall. She still seethed from the memory.

Meanwhile, Roc had not been idle. When not working on

his estate, he had drilled the soldiers on the village square. Officer Biggles had watched and fumed in silence, pacing the square from one side to the other.

Clem jokingly maintained that Biggles would soon be ripe for corruption, since the revenue officer evidently resented Roc's authority. A bribe in the right pockets would work wonders, Clem said.

"What is the shipment this time, Clem?" Gwen whispered as they moved soundlessly along the familiar path, skirting the village.

"Cognac, miss."

Gwen wistfully thought of shimmering silks and satins, but the image faded rapidly at the prospect of the dangerous venture ahead.

"When will it land?"

"At two o'clock, miss. We'll 'ave plenty o' time to get there. The men ain't likin' it, miss. Those Looe smugglers are a rough lot, and what d'ye think they'll do when they see *two* cutters in th' bay? They'll try takin' our stuff, mark me words."

"We'll have to work faster than ever, that's all," Gwen said with more confidence than she actually felt.

Spies had informed her that soldiers had been posted at every cove around Landregan, training their telescopes over the black sea. They were evidently waiting for the French cutter to run straight into one of their ambushes. What they did not know was that Gwen and her men had decided to take a great risk this night by encroaching on the Looe smugglers' territory. From there, they would transport the cargo back to Landregan at the darkest part of the night. They could only pray they escaped detection by the rival gang, or a fight over the cargo would be sure to ensue. And later, when they led their laden ponies back through the village to the hiding places, they could only hope the law enforcement officers had ceased their vigil for the night.

A light breeze carried the potent scent of seaweed to Gwen's nose as she trotted along the ridge bordering the sea. A gull's sharp cry and the crashing of waves against the rocks below drowned out all other sounds. The heavy air echoed the mounting tension inside her.

Eventually the fang-shaped cliffs at Looe rose black out of

the night. The waves churned and slammed against the rocky
outcrop below. Gwen cautiously lit the lantern in the lee of
a huge rock and pulled up one of the darkened panels, di-
recting the feeble light toward the beach below. She heaved
a sigh of relief when the answering flash promptly appeared.
The men were all gathered in the tiny cove among the rocks,
the ponies tethered in the shelter of a belt of stumpy willows.
Now they must wait for the signal from the *Alouette,* hovering in the Channel.

Gwen followed Clem down the winding and treacherous
path. The men were huddled among the reeds under a protruding arch-shaped cliff, their eyes turned to the dark, restless water.

"Alfie, have you seen the *Alouette?"* Gwen inquired of
the man closest to her.

"Aye, she's out there, but this is a tricky landin' place,
and I'm sure th' captain will be none too pleased with us.
Those reefs to the east can cut up a boat badly. But th' *Alouette* can easily get through 'ere, if th' captain ain't three
sheets to the wind." Alfie chuckled. " 'E often is, y'know—
with all that good cognac in the 'ull."

Gwen strained to see the outline of the French vessel.
"Have you seen any sign of our competition?"

"Naw, I believe th' Looe boat's landin' farther down, at
an easy spot o' beach since no revenue men are breathin'
down their necks. They don't 'ave to be careful. Now, if they
knew 'bout all th' good cognac—"

"We'll make sure they don't."

Gwen felt the touch of an eager hand on her arm. "Look,
there she is! She's cleared th' reefs."

Squinting, Gwen saw the blurry outline of slack sails flapping in the wind. The waves tossed two dinghies like nut-
shells toward land. Reaching the beach with difficulty, each
boat bore two kegs. Strong hands lifted the contraband
ashore, and the murmured conversation between the men carried on the air. Two of the smugglers accompanied the sailors
back to the *Alouette* for the second haul. Gwen realized the
exchange would take more time than she had calculated.

Since her help was not needed for the unloading, she
walked back up the ridge to stand guard. The view was clearer
from this higher vantage point, and she noticed the shadow

of another swift cutter making its way east. The Looe smuggling vessel! Bruising and scraping her ankles, she traversed the mishmash of jagged rocks and lay down in the scraggly patch of furze to look for the signal that would reveal the position of the other gang.

When the flares finally pierced the darkness she drew in a sharp breath. Much too close! They were literally on the other side of the massive rocks, less than four furlongs away.

Wasting no time, Gwen crawled away from her post, lucky to have escaped detection. Who knew how far spread out the Looe sentinels were?

She returned the way she had come, cursing as she acquired a new collection of bruises on her ankles. She must warn the men. An owl swept past her head, almost making her lose her balance on the shale as she rapidly descended to the cove below.

Down on the beach twenty barrels were neatly stacked on the sand. Gwen recognized Clem's sturdy form and urgently gripped his sleeve.

"Tell the men to be extremely careful and not to smoke. The Looe gang is just around the corner taking in their load."

"Gorblimey! Of all th' rotten luck—"

"We haven't lost yet, but some of the men ought to leave with their kegs right away. The ponies aren't exactly soundless. Split the men into two parties. If a few get caught, we'll at least have saved some of the cognac." She more sensed than saw Clem nod. A light mist had formed over the water, making it harder for the small boats to find their way ashore.

Clem efficiently divided the gang, and the men began trudging up the path, groaning under the weight of the kegs. Gwen went to fetch Farmer Polpenny's ponies, one at a time, from the copse. She whispered soothing words to the animals and prayed fiercely that they would not whinny. As if they understood the hushed tension in the air, they stopped chomping and turned alert eyes on Gwen.

She released the first and, skirting the copse, brought it to the top of the path. The pony stomped impatiently on the hard ground, and Gwen nervously stroked the silky neck to soothe the animal. Clem's head appeared over the edge. He was panting hard after laboring with two six-gallon kegs, one under each arm. Without speaking, he slung them across the strong back of the pony, and Alfie arrived promptly to lead it onto the dark path toward Landregan. Gwen returned for another animal, and so it continued until all the kegs had been loaded, and all the ponies but two, the ones Gwen and Clem would lead, had set off.

Clem had just finished loading the last kegs when heavy footsteps pounded on the rocks to the east. As if on cue, Gwen and Clem grabbed the reins and pulled the ponies into the shadow of the willows.

"Who goes there?" boomed a deep voice.

Three dark forms appeared out of the mist, and Gwen clenched her hands. Clem secured the reins to a branch with a swift movement, and as he did so, one of the ponies whickered. The penetrating sound cut through the thunder of the waves below. The men turned suspicious eyes toward the trees, and Gwen pressed her lips together in a thin, determined line.

Crouching, she searched frantically for a rock to shove into an old stocking she kept in her pocket for just such emergencies. Clem waited, tense and menacing, next to her, ready to spring.

"They're th' Looe men," he whispered. "Must 'ave 'eard somethin' an' come to investigate."

"Ho there! Come forth, or we'll 'ave to fetch ye," came a hoarse command.

"Wait 'ere, Miss Gwen. I'll 'andle 'em meself." Clem walked out of the shelter. Stretched to his full height, he was an imposing figure. "What're ye barkin' at?" he growled at the ominous shadows. "Bain't forbidden to cross th' ridge at night."

" 'Tis now. What're ye doin' 'ere?" Gwen held her breath as the men advanced toward Clem.

"Nuffin', just passin' with me ponies. Was up Liskeard way on business. Who're ye and what's yer business in th' middle o' th' night?"

Silence strained between the men. Gwen firmed her hold on the improvised cudgel in her fist, wrapping the stocking around her hand several times.

"If I bain't mistaken, there's th' smell o' brandy in th' air, and it bain't ours," said one Looe smuggler.

"Ye must be all about in yer 'ead! Brandy? In th' middle o' th' night? Ye must be foxed."

A fist whooshed through the air, connecting with Clem's chin and hurling him to the ground. "I've 'eard that rough voice afore! One o' th' Landregan smugglers if I bain't mistaken." The three men fell on Clem.

Before they had a chance to pin him, he swung his hamlike fists and drew up his knobby knees. Gwen winced at the sound of bone smashing against bone. Grunts and curses flew through the air, but all she could see was a welter of dark limbs. She knew Clem could not hold off three heavy fellows alone, so she crept up to the unsuspecting man closest to the trees.

Her arm trembled as she swung it over her head and let the cudgel fall. *Clonk.* She flinched at the impact. He fell into a heap on the ground with a loud grunt. She bent over him. He smelled strongly of brandy, and a raspy breath confirmed she had not put him out for good. But just as relief flooded through her, a stinging blow to the ear felled her to the ground, and the world swirled crazily, pain roaring through her. The man who had hit her fell over her, lifting his arm for another swing.

She gritted her teeth, expecting her skull to shatter. Then his weight miraculously lifted and she could breathe again. Clem delivered a well-aimed blow, sending the man groaning amid the bristly furze. Gwen regained her feet, and as a blow from the third man grazed the back of Clem's head, she swung her cudgel and landed it on the man's head with a thud. He squealed with pain as he tumbled to her feet.

Clem stood with his arms limp at his sides, his breathing labored.

"Phew, a close call," Gwen said, her head still ringing from the blow. She reached up and wiped Clem's sweaty face with a handkerchief, feeling a rising lump on his temple. "Good God! You'll be purple and yellow tomorrow."

"Don't matter," he said. "We 'ave to leave afore th' other blokes start searchin' for their mates. I don't think I could take on another 'un tonight."

He stumbled toward the ponies, and Gwen followed meekly. Though her legs were still trembling, she led her animal briskly along the ridge, anxious to put as much distance between herself and the Looe free traders as possible.

"Outright dogmeat, they are," Gwen heard Clem mumble to himself. "A rough, inhuman lot." When they were out of possible earshot, he turned to her, and she saw his teeth flash white. "Ye were a right 'un, miss. Felled one o' them mongrels with one well-aimed blow. Without ye, I would have been th' one sprawled on th' rocks, with me skull caved in."

Her head still ringing, she admitted, "It was foolhardy of us to venture into these parts. Mark my words, we've not seen the last of them. They'll be thirsting for revenge."

"Naw, a bit o' fisticuffs 'as never 'urt anybody, an' they—"

"They knew we were from Landregan. We cannot repeat this venture; on the next dark of the moon they'll be lying in wait for us."

Clem scratched his head and winced. "You might be right, miss. We'll 'ave to search for another spot to land."

Gwen sighed. "That will take a miracle. I can't think of any new place the cutter can put ashore. We've searched every inch of the coastline."

"Hmm . . . a smaller boat could do it." Clem slowed to a walk alongside Gwen.

"Perhaps, but we don't have a smaller boat except the rowboats, and they're too small to go outside the reefs. They'd be smashed to pieces."

"Aye, but I know o' one. Th' earl, or rightly Master Morgan, owns the sailboat *Seahawk* in th' 'arbor. Th' size would be perfect. And 'e wouldn't know if we used it durin' th' night. We'd clean it ever so carefully to keep away the brandy smell."

"Of all the brazen ideas!"

"That vessel could land right at Dead Man's Cove if we set our minds to it, and we could get Captain Polson to sail 'er. Th' goggle-eyed dragoons at Lucky Hole and Brandy Cove wouldn't be able to see us at Dead Man's Cove."

Gwen pondered the possibility. Clem was right, the plan *could* work—the most daring she'd heard of yet. Dead Man's Cove lay deep among the treacherous reefs, protected from view by the ring of sharp rocks that formed the natural harbor of Landregan. Only a sturdy boat like the *Seahawk* could maneuver the narrow opening in the reefs without being instantly tossed onto the treacherous rocks and ripped apart.

"You're too reckless, Clem. One of these days you'll be swinging from the gallows."

"Naw, one 'as to take a risk or two sometimes."

Gwen glanced at him from the corner of her eye. "Perhaps you should be Dandelion from now on."

His chin fell toward his chest. "Miss Gwen, ye know I bain't good at makin' fast decisions. Tonight ye knew exactly what to do, and it worked. If only them roughs from Looe 'adn't—"

"That's the risk we took and we were lucky to get away with the cognac," she said, shivering at the memory. Glancing at the softening sky, she added, "Dawn is almost upon us, and who knows how many soldiers are lying in wait for us at home."

Clem grunted and lengthened his strides. Gwen had to struggle to stay apace with him, but she didn't complain, as it was of the utmost importance to stow away the loot before dawn. Since all the hiding places along the shore were known to Officer Biggles, Gwen had decided to stow the kegs wherever there was a cavity big enough to hold them.

They arrived at the outskirts of Landregan just as dawn's first red glow was tinting the horizon. They paused in a copse, listening. A frightened starling dashed through the foliage, making the ponies twitch their ears and fidget. Gwen placed a clammy hand over their muzzles. No movement came from the path along the ridge, but Gwen had an uneasy sensation of a human presence. Her gaze flew from one boulder to another, to the trees, to the ground. Nothing.

"I think we should unload, now," she said. "Find any burrow or crevice and hide the kegs. You can retrieve them tomorrow, when the exitement has died down in the village."

Clem did not argue. Soundlessly he lifted the kegs from the ponies while Gwen crept through the undergrowth looking for a good place. The empty burrow of a fox proved large enough to house one keg. The second they stowed in a hollow oak, and the last two in an opening between two rocks.

Gwen wiped her forehead. This night was taking its toll on her nerves, and a throbbing lump had risen above her ear. She pulled her kerchief deeply over her eyes. From the shadow of a boulder she scanned the area. Would it be safe to take the ponies through the copse?

Tension crackled, and she wondered why she had such an acute feeling of danger. The countryside remained peaceful, only the warble of an occasional bird breaking the stillness. Clem stood motionless next to her, having sensed her tension. The ponies grazed calmly at a patch of grass, their solid bodies concealed by the abundant leaves. The sound of their grinding jaws grated on Gwen's nerves, but she could do nothing to stop it. She grabbed the reins. "If someone comes, leave the ponies and hide," she whispered. "The horses can't talk, y'know," she added with a wry grin.

Walking along the narrow path, they watched the first rays of the sun bathe the landscape in gold, painting brilliance in every dewy leaf and blade of grass. Had Gwen not been so tense, she would have enjoyed the delicate freshness of the morning. A curlew flapped up from the tussocks. Her gaze darted to the shadows still lingering under the trees. Then her eyes were drawn to the flash of a red uniform touched by sunlight on the shore path, only a hundred yards away.

"The soldiers are still around," she whispered to Clem, placing a warning hand on his sleeve. "We should part here, and—remember, leave the pony behind if things get out of hand."

Clem drew his stocking cap deeper over his eyes, determination gleaming there. Pulling his pony by the bridle, he soundlessly slipped into the green dusk under the trees. Gwen continued along the path, trepidation dogging her every step. Seeing the soldiers once more from between the trees, she halted and breathed deeply to calm her trembling limbs. She decided to leave the pony behind. In a sunny clearing, she fastened the reins to a bush and hurried from the animal as fast as she could, soon reaching the edge of the trees. Now she had only to pass through the village to the safety of her home. She kept to the hedges, praying that none of the soldiers would spot her. If she were recognized in men's clothes . . . The thought was too harrowing to—

The sound of voices broke the silence, and Gwen threw herself to the ground, burrowing deeply into the grass. She hardly dared to breathe, her face pressed to the damp earth.

Two soldiers on foot were arguing as they walked down the lane leading into the village, their voices soon accompanied by the clomp of horses' hooves. The soldiers greeted the rider. Gwen tensed further as she recognized the low timbre of Roc's voice. "Any signs yet?"

A negative murmur answered his query.

"Damnation! The chaps have slipped through our fingers again. We *all* knew the drop was to happen tonight."

"Dandelion has outwitted us again, milord."

"I was so sure that this time we would capture him. Dashed annoying! Where could they have hauled in the load?"

His voice trailed off as they disappeared down the path. Roc up at dawn! Gwen thought. He *was* very serious about his new status as magistrate. Magistrate Roc, bah! Gwen breathed hard, glancing at an orange butterfly perched on a straw. How lucky that they had not brought in the cargo near Landregan!

The sun's gilded rays flowed warmly over her as she slipped homeward. Unseen, she reached the spinney behind Tremayne House and was finally able to breathe freely. She had escaped detection by a hair's breadth.

"We fooled them all," she whispered with a contented smile and closed the kitchen door behind her.

Chapter 8

Half an hour after Gwen had consumed her breakfast on a tray, she gazed out over the bay and village as she absent-mindedly brushed her hair. The houses slumbered in the midday heat, and there was not so much as a cat out of doors, though every window stood open to invite in the sea breezes.

A knock sounded on her door. In sepulchral tones Arthur informed her that her presence was requested in the parlor.

"Very well, I'll be down in a minute." She applied a drop of cold tea to her eyes to remove the tired film. The liquid stung, but she paid no heed as she hurriedly applied rice powder to the dark smudges beneath her eyes. Critically she studied her face. Did she look as if she had enjoyed a peaceful night's sleep? Hardly. She shrugged her slender shoulders and hurried downstairs.

Voices wafted through the open door of the parlor. To her surprise she recognized her father's words. What could have brought him out of his study?

Through a crack in the door she spied the squire's old pigtail wig hanging over the back of an armchair. Her gaze slid to the opposite chair and her heart skipped a beat at the sight of raven-black hair. What was Roc doing here?

When she entered the parlor, she noticed that Aunt Clo was part of the small party. Squire Tremayne looked up, his gaze decidedly bored.

"Ah, there you are, my gel. I thought you might take over entertaining Lord Landregan, as I have some urgent business to take care of, concerning, uh, the farm." He flapped his hand in a vague gesture.

Gwen planted a kiss on his florid cheek. "Of course,

Papa." She waved as he left the room. From the corner of her eye, she noticed that Roc had risen, his face a bland mask.

"Lord Landregan, what brings you here at such an early hour of the morning?" she asked gaily and fluttered forward, her hand outstretched for his dutiful kiss.

As always, his presence overwhelmed her and she was powerless to stop the wild gallop of her heart.

"Miss Gwen, you look glorious this morning. You're a sight for sore eyes."

"Why, thank you, milord." She studied the dark rings under his eyes. "I'm sorry I can't say the same about you." She smiled brightly and sat down next to her dour-faced aunt, though what she really wanted to do was to trail a finger across Roc's face, to wipe away the tired lines that ran from his nostrils to his chin. His lips formed the parody of a smile.

"You look most disturbed, milord. Is there something bothering you?" Gwen prodded.

Roc's tawny glare penetrated her heart, which threatened to bolt out of her chest. Such force! She dared not think of what would happen if he ever discovered her dark secret.

"No, only I'm a trifle short-tempered this morning, and I beg you to bear with me," he answered.

Gwen contemplated his commanding appearance, his blue coat adorned by black frogging, worn over his vest of blue and cream stripes. His hair looked slightly mussed, as if he'd pushed his hand through it repeatedly. He looked at ease, even seated in the threadbare wing chair set against a faded and flaking wall fresco of a family of deer in a sunny glade.

"In fact," he continued, "Mother sent me here with an invitation." His gaze raked over her simple cream muslin gown, the modest decolletage, and her hair hastily coiled under a small cambric and lace cap. Suddenly Gwen yearned for a new gown—gossamer cloth shimmering like a rainbow, silk petticoats, laces, ribbons, jewels . . . "An invitation to a small affair."

"Oh, how *very* kind of her," Aunt Clo exclaimed. "The dowager countess serves a most delicious tea."

"Hmm, I'm afraid this is another kind of gathering. A ball. My mother has invited—well, *forced*—a few friends from Tunbridge Wells to attend, including the Camelfords. As it turns out, they're already here."

Aunt Clo gasped, as if she hadn't known the exact moment when the marchioness had arrived. "The *marchioness* of Camelford?"

"Well, yes. Naturally Mother is inviting all the local nobility as well."

"How very thoughtful of her." Aunt Clo fluttered her hands in excitement. She nudged Gwen in the ribs.

Dazed, Gwen came out of her contemplation of Roc's glossy hair and noble nose. "Huh? Yes—splendid, indeed. Most kind of you to deliver the invitation personally, but we won't be able to attend."

Silence fell.

"Why?" Roc asked, surprise raising his eyebrows.

Gwen felt color surge to her cheeks under his probing gaze. "I, er, we have other things to attend to," she invented lamely.

"Gwennie! How *rude* of you!"

"I beg your pardon, but I must be adamant." Gwen glared at her aunt and saw understanding finally dawn on the woman's face—their lack of suitable garb for a ball must prevent their attendance.

"Yes, of course. How silly of me." Aunt Clo turned to the earl. "Gwen is right, you know. I had quite forgotten—a previous engagement."

"But I haven't yet told you the date." A shadow of amusement lurked in Roc's eyes.

"Oh." Aunt Clo's face looked like a deflated soufflé.

"Thank you all the same, milord." Gwen hastened to change the subject. "Tell me, are you feeling well? There is, if you'll excuse me, a positively haggard look about your face this morning. Don't tell me you're working too hard at restoring the Hall."

"No. Surely you must know that the smugglers indulged in their illegal trade last night. I had planned an outing with my yacht, but 'twill have to be postponed now."

Roc silently cursed the smugglers who had ruined his plans for returning the jewels to France. Ever since his mother had arrived, there had been no time to attend to the pressing business. It appeared James Murray might have been the contact who had planned to take the jewels to London, but since he was dead, the mission was over. I have to return the jewels, Roc thought. The longer he postponed the trip, the more guilty he felt, as if he'd betrayed his old friend, Alistair Borrodale. He sighed. "Yes, the smugglers are a constant thorn in my flesh."

"I see," Gwen said. "Yes, 'twas the dark of the moon last night, but what does it have to do with you?" she asked, mischief bubbling in her eyes.

"Well, Officer Biggles needs all the support he can get from the locals to catch the Dandelion fellow. 'Tis my duty to help him, especially since my assignment is to uphold law and order. But I've been away from Landregan for a long time, and I don't know all of Dandelion's tricks. I'm appalled at the deviousness of the villagers. It seems they've gotten worse with time—or do I recall wrongly?"

"In those days you saw them through the innocent eyes of youth, milord," Gwen said with a smile.

He sighed. "Unfortunately, the impudent fellow has outwitted us again. It'll take some time to put myself into his way of thinking. Intelligent rascal, I believe."

Gwen clenched her hands in the folds of her dress and turned innocent eyes on him. "Poor man."

A swift smile crossed his drawn features. "Who? Me or Dandelion?"

She smiled sweetly and batted her eyelashes. "Why—you, of course."

He chuckled, then a glint of steel appeared in his eyes and he raised one eyebrow disdainfully. "How flattering, unless you mean to mock me."

She slowly expelled her breath when he shifted his probing gaze. "How unkind of you, milord, to suspect such inconsideration of me."

"I don't take kindly to false flattery."

Gwen felt her aunt's uneasy glance. The older woman was tittering nervously at the earl and fanning her troubled countenance until he suddenly relaxed, folding one leg over the other.

"What an absolute bore I am this morning. I'm forgetting my manners. Quite unforgivable," he said. He adjusted one of his shirt cuffs. "You really ought to attend this ball. The opportunities for entertainment in a village such as this one must be few and far between.'' He leaned forward, amusement dancing in his eyes. ''And you know what Mother will do to me if I don't bring back an affirmative response. Her punishment is too cruel to even consider. You can't let me suffer her wrath.'' As if in afterthought, he delved into the deep pocket of his coat and handed the gilt-edged invitation to Aunt Clo.

She reverently held it between her fingertips, as if it were a treasure of inestimable value. With her eyes she implored Gwen to accept the invitation. Gwen shot her aunt a warning glance and smiled blandly at Roc.

''We're extremely flattered that the dowager countess thought to ask us. I don't want to arouse your mother's formidable wrath.'' Her eyes twinkled wickedly and his gaze narrowed. He leaned back with an exaggerated sigh, as if waiting for more teasing to come.

''We'll see what we can do about getting out of the other invitation,'' she continued with exaggerated sweetness, ''but as you must understand, I can't promise anything. I'm sure you'll find a way to handle your mother's wrath.''

He threw back his head and laughed, and Gwen was dazzled by the sudden transformation of his features. She had never been more attracted to a man, but the thought of letting him discover the dizzying depths of her feelings frightened her like nothing else. If he ever found out, he would have total power over her. To save herself from the disturbing prospect, she plunged into the burning issue of the previous night's events.

''What really happened last night? We don't hear much about the goings-on except through the servants' gossip.''

Roc's face took on its customary fierceness. ''I will tell you nothing. Do you want to turn me into the laughingstock of the village, Gwen?''

''Of course not,'' she scoffed. ''Have you so little faith in my ability to hold my tongue? Furthermore, whatever there is to know, I assure you 'tis already all over the village, so I'll hear it all sooner or later.''

He chuckled and tapped his fingers lightly on the armrest. ''Then I'll spare my breath. You already know the miscreant eluded me, and there is no trace of brandy in the usual hiding places."

"A night's hard work, I take it?" Gwen's lips curved sweetly.

"I *knew* you would only laugh at me. You're on the side of that villain, and here I sit like a fool, baring myself to ridicule." He rose lithely. "However much I'd like to idle away my time in your lovely company, I must see to my estate." He bent and brushed the air above Aunt Clo's fingers with his lips, then turned to Gwen, smiling with exasperation.

Her face devoid of any expression except innocence, she gave him her hand to kiss.

"Minx!" he murmured.

"Rogue!" she countered.

His lips teased her skin warmly, his fingertips caressing the inside of her wrist. A current of pleasure surged through her. Her heart careened, and she felt a flame of color in her cheeks, belying her pretense of detachment. Furtively she followed him to the door with her eyes, admiring his broad back and proud shoulders.

The decisive sound of his step reverberated in her tired head as he walked out, but an excitement beyond her exhausted state flowed through her, growing stronger every moment. His presence awakened spring in her heart, and quickened love in her veins, her limbs. A tremulous sigh quivered through her.

"I say, we *must* attend the ball, Gwennie!" Aunt Clo's voice sliced through Gwen's sudden happiness as soon as the earl closed the door. "You lied to him about another engagement. Bah!"

Gwen bit her bottom lip. "I have no desire to meet the dowager countess again. She won't have anything good to say about us." Perturbed, Gwen viewed her aunt's downturned lips. "So you're really set on going. Well, then you'll simply have to find a way." She did not bother to point out that they had nothing to wear for the occasion. Her aunt was well aware of the fact. She waited to see what solution to that problem her stubborn relative would invent.

Early one morning a few days later, Aunt Clo entered Gwen's bedroom and triumphantly placed two bolts of satin on the bed. One shone with a delicate apricot hue and the other was a dark forest-green.

"What's this, Aunt Clo?" Gwen hastily donned a frayed wrapper over her simple nightshift and fingered the luxurious cloth. "Where did you get this?" Worriedly she imagined her aunt dealing with free traders working out of another village.

"When I accompanied your father into Plymouth."

Gwen gasped. "You had no funds for all this finery."

With a smile of mystery Aunt Clo stated, "Yes, I did. How else could I buy it?" She fondly patted the fabric. "This will be perfect for you, m'dear." She held up the apricot satin against her niece's pale cheeks. "I say, you look positively haunted. What is it?"

"Tell me this instant where you got the funds!" Gwen's voice trembled with worry.

"What vehemence. Well, if you insist. I sold my last piece of jewelry and spent a pleasant half hour at the cloth merchants in Plymouth, selecting these bolts." She held up the green cloth and stared at her image in the mirror.

Relieved, Gwen exclaimed, "But, Auntie, how could you sell your last piece of jewelry?"

"I don't want to hear another word from you, and that's the end of it. You'll be the belle of the ball, Gwennie."

Gwen rolled her eyes heavenward.

Chapter 9

Roc was exhausted, but he could not consider sleep, not yet. After visiting Tremayne House, he swung himself into Tristan's saddle and cantered down the lane toward the harbor. As he rode through the village, the children ran after him in a long row, giggling. The fishermen down at the harbor waved at him, as did some of the older women carrying baskets of fish against their hips. The gray stone walls of the cottages huddled close to each other as if trying to protect themselves from the turbulent sea.

Roc handed the reins to one of the urchins who had been following him from the other end of the village. "If you watch him well, there'll be sixpence for you," he said over his shoulder. The urchin nodded.

The rowboat was tied to a rusty metal ring in the docks. A peaceful hour on his yacht was what he needed, Roc thought with a sigh. Ever since he had returned home, everything had been going wrong.

In the stateroom aboard the *Blackbird* he unlocked the bottom drawer and pulled out the leather box. His brow furrowed with worry, he unlocked and opened it. The note from France was where he had put it last night. After taking an inordinate time to reach Landregan, the letter had arrived yesterday from one of Alistair's French Jacobite friends. To be sure he had not misunderstood the contents, Rock read it over.

Your contact will be James Murray. He will arrive in Landregan shortly after you, from London. Give him the box.

It was signed with the drawing of a rose.

Roc recognized the design. Everywhere in England, Stuart sympathizers were secretly drinking from glasses etched with roses. Roc sighed. The Stuart followers would surely prefer to raise their glasses in a public cheer, but that day would not arrive soon. Charles Stuart had lost heavily at Culloden Moor in April, his Scottish army torn apart. Stuart was a hunted man now, and it was unlikely he would escape with his life, let alone raise another army.

Roc followed the note with shaking hands. So he had been right in suspecting that Murray had been involved. Now he was dead. When they found out what had happened, would they send another messenger? Roc wished he knew the answer.

He touched the gems absentmindedly. They seemed to burn him, and all he wanted was to return them to their rightful owners. The Jacobites would have to find another go-between. He hit his knotted fist on the desk and set the box down with unnecessary force. The smugglers stood in his way. He couldn't get away until the smuggling business was cleared up. If he left, who knew what might happen in his absence? Biggles and the soldiers weren't much help. He would have to get personally involved if there were to be any results. He felt a sudden urge to kick something.

Roc could almost sense Dandelion's tricky mind, the pleasure the ruffian derived from fooling the authorities. The man was too impudent by far! In a fit of frustration, Roc tossed his gloves across the cabin. They landed in front of the threshold. The door opened slowly.

Gwen stood in the entranceway, her face hidden in the shadows.

Roc slapped down the lid of the open jewel box, hoping she had not seen the glittering contents. He rose abruptly. "Gwen? Is something amiss?"

As she walked into the cabin, he was sharply aware of the gentle sway of her hips. "No. I was down in the harbor admiring Morgan's sailboat, the *Seahawk*, when a desire to see your yacht came over me. Your first mate informed me that you were on board."

Roc shrugged. "Not much to see, I'm afraid. 'Tisn't luxuriously appointed, just plain and practical.'' He watched as she glanced at the varnished oak plank walls, the built-in bookcases and shelves, the brass-framed portholes. She lowered her gaze demurely as it swept past the bunk bed with its striped hangings. "Very plain, as you can see," he added.

"Yes, but cozy all the same. You know, I've never been on a boat bigger than the fishing boats in the harbor." She crossed her fingers behind her back, thinking of the late-night hours when she sometimes visited the French smuggling vessels to inspect the brandy casks.

"May I offer you a glass of brandy?" he asked as if he'd read her thoughts. She nodded, and he sauntered to a glass-fronted bookcase and took out a crystal decanter and two glasses. " 'Tis very daring of you to visit me unchaperoned in broad daylight. The village will be abuzz with rumors."

Gwen laughed. "Not at all! I've long been considered on the shelf, which gives me all manner of liberty. Besides, I'm certain you'll behave as befits a true gentleman." Her lips quirked sarcastically, and he promised himself he would kiss those lips thoroughly before she left. He handed her a full glass and watched as she sipped the strong liquid, then tipped back the glass. "Ah! Very good," she said with a sigh.

Roc smiled, ruefully viewing his own full glass. "How unusual you are, Gwen. I've never met another lady who likes brandy."

"An acquired taste," she said noncommittally and patted her lips with a handkerchief.

"Would you like another glass?"

"No, thank you." She smiled. "I didn't come to drink your brandy but to see the yacht. By the way, we'll be able to attend your mother's ball, after all."

"Splendid! I look forward to dancing with you." He held out his arm to her. "Perhaps I should give you an official tour of the yacht since you show such an interest."

"Yes, but first I'd like to see the view." Gwen wandered over to the porthole by the desk and looked outside. " 'Tis a lovely day, isn't it." Her gaze flickered to his, then to the octagonal leather box.

"Yes, and it got brighter as soon as you stepped over the threshold, m'dear."

Gwen gave him a long glance from under lowered eyelashes, and his heart began thumping hard. Desire burned in his loins, and an overwhelming urge to crush her pliant body to his came over him. It had been a long time since he had felt such physical attraction for a woman. He could not recall when. The brandy was rising to his brain, coloring everything more vividly. The slanting sunlight painted golden streaks in Gwen's hazel tresses. He wanted to see what she looked like with her hair down and her face flushed with desire.

"What is this strange box?" she asked, interrupting his reverie.

"Box?" He stared at her, seeing only the slight flush on her cheeks and her moist lips. As she touched the leather top, he was jerked back to reality. The gems!

"Oh, nothing," he said and hastened across the floor. "Just some personal effects." He shoved the leather box into the bottom drawer of the desk and locked it.

"From China or India?" she probed.

"From India, as a matter of fact," he lied. "I bought it on one of my trips there."

She was standing so close to him that he could smell her light flowery perfume, and under that, the delicate scent of her skin. It distracted and taunted him. Desire pounded more recklessly in his veins. She was fresh, like a flower at dawn with dew covering its petals. She was wildly exotic when she tilted back her head and sighed, evidently admiring the sunlight playing over the water. He wanted to laugh and lick the traces of liquor from her lips, but he could only empty his own glass first lest it fall from his nerveless fingers.

"Truly, Gwen, why did you come here?"

Her eyes twinkled wickedly. "What? Are you suspicious of my motives? Are you afraid I have come to ravish you in your own chamber?"

His cheeks grew hot, and his crotch felt too tight. "Did it never occur to you that *I* might do something to you? There is no one here to save you from me. Besides, I'm the master of this boat, and do as I please."

"Yes, of course. It appears none of your thoughts are gentlemanly." She moved slowly toward the door. "I'd better save myself, then, before 'tis too late."

He stepped quickly past her and leaned his back against the door. "Please don't leave just yet. I so enjoy your presence. Have another glass of brandy," he cajoled her. "I promise I won't tell your aunt about your shameless drinking habits."

"If you insist." Without ado, she plopped herself down on a bench built into the wall. "Where did you get the brandy?"

He shrugged. *"I* didn't get it anywhere. Enedoc supervises the delivery of strong spirits to the Hall, and I don't dare ask him where he gets this, er, superior supply. From Dandelion, most likely."

Gwen's laugh rippled. "This is the finest French brandy. You are, in fact, threatening to destroy your source of the tasty stuff if you insist on persecuting Dandelion."

His eyes narrowed. "You know a lot, it seems."

" 'Tisn't the first time I've had French brandy. Even the poorest fisherman in these parts has had his fill of it at one time or another," she said, her dusky gaze boring into him.

He raised his glass mockingly. "Cheers, then."

She raised hers. "To what?"

"To your impudent weedy friend. 'Twill be the last time, because by the next dark of the moon Dandelion will be behind a stout oaken door in the dungeons of the Hall."

She shrugged. "Don't underestimate the fellow. For a twelvemonth Officer Biggles has tried to capture him, and the soldiers have been here for two months."

Roc drank his brandy testily. "Dandelion must be running out of tricks, don't you think?"

The brandy had painted pink roses in Gwen's cheeks, and brought a sparkle to her eyes. "I would put my bet on him any day," she said.

Her husky voice did something to Roc's blood, which once more pounded crazily in his veins. For now he forgave her her scornful words. All he wanted was to touch her smiling lips, perhaps crush the smile away, and see something else grow in its place: desire.

He took two long steps toward her. She rose and hurried toward the door, but he grasped her arms. Though she struggled, he pulled her into his embrace, pinning her against himself.

He reveled in the feel of her slender but rounded curves. Here, at least, he had the upper hand. His exercise in the boxing ring in London served him well today as this armful of femininity tried to wriggle out of his grasp. She stopped, and he could see her eyes dilating slightly. In such close proximity her lips looked vulnerable, inviting, and infinitely sweet. A flicker of fear darted through her expression as he bent closer. She pushed helplessly against his chest, but he could not let her go until he had tasted her lips. Her perfume surrounded him, seeped into his brain, and he wanted to drown in her, close his eyes and smell and taste every inch of her. She was so soft and supple, like a wave of warmth in his arms.

Gwen melted against him, unable to resist any longer. Her breath was coming in small gasps, and she wanted the kiss as much as he did. He gripped the back of her neck and held it firm, and she threw her arms around his neck.

"Oh, no . . ." she whispered as he captured her mouth with his. His passion burned her sweetly as his tongue explored her mouth. Desire ran hot and thick in her blood as the sheer force of his kiss robbed her of all strength. She seemed to flow into him—or did he lose himself in her? All she knew was that the touch of his lips brought something within her full circle. His touch fulfilled a deep longing in her heart.

Roc felt as if they had dissolved into each other, two energies becoming one. But when he relinquished her mouth, he saw how wide her eyes were and how flushed her face had grown.

"Did I hurt you?" he murmured.

She shook her head, and contentment spilled through him. He cradled her head close to his shoulder, immediately aware of the softness of her breasts pressing against his chest. As if by their own volition, his hands strayed down her back to test the roundness of her hips. They fit perfectly in his palms, just as he had known they would. Thank God she wasn't wearing hoops, only a simple brown riding habit.

"You're beautiful, Gwennie. I desire you. Do you desire me?" He needed to hear her say it.

Her lashes hid the truth in her eyes. "You're very sure of yourself," she whispered. "And sure of my feelings."

"I know what feels right, m'dear. You certainly feel good leaning against me like this."

Her deep breath shuddered as he slowly released his grip on her. "I like . . ." She hesitated, pressing her fingertips to her flaming cheeks. She wanted to get closer to him, to peel away the barrier of their clothes.

"Say it, Gwennie. You're not as independent as you pretend to be. Say you liked our kiss. Say 'twas all that you ever dreamed of."

"Oh, stop it!" She pressed her hands against her ears and turned toward the door. "I don't want to talk about it."

He braced his arm against the jamb. "Please don't run away."

She gave him an accusing glare. "All you want is to seduce me. I'm only a conquest for you. All you want is to make me grovel at your feet. You'll throw me away when you've tired of me."

He laughed. "Silly Gwen, you're painting my character too darkly. I never was a womanizer. I don't know where you got that idea."

"If you aren't a womanizer, why aren't you married? Most decent gentlemen are married by thirty. Only those who want their pleasure without obligation don't marry." She stared at him suspiciously and was afraid of his answer, afraid he would rip her heart apart.

She looked as if she was about to cry. He had no desire to break her proud spirit by replying with a careless remark. He could not promise her eternal happiness until he was sure he wanted to marry her as he had planned when he had persuaded the dowager to return to Landregan. The dowager saw Gwen as an eccentric freak, not as a possible daughter-in-law. With such strong opposition, he must be very sure of his love.

Holding the door open for her, he reached into a pocket for a clean handkerchief and gave it to her. "There. I'm not married because I haven't found the right woman. Wedlock is a state I don't enter lightly, not without being sure of my feelings. Let me show you around the yacht."

Gwen sniffed. "I've lost all interest in your old boat," she said. "I'll ask the first mate to row me back to the harbor."

Roc chuckled. "Lost your scathing repartee already? Well, if nothing else, 'tis an indication that our kiss didn't leave you completely untouched."

Her eyes blazed. "Touched by loathing, perhaps!" She swept out of the room and stomped up the stairs. "You take every opportunity to taunt me," she flung over her shoulder.

He laughed. " 'Tis sweet, very sweet," he shouted after her. "Do come back for more any time."

Gwen almost fell into the water as she climbed carelessly down the rope ladder in her haste to get away from Roc. She stumbled into the rowboat, averting her face so that the burly sailor could not see her embarrassment. But could she ever hide the evidence of the turmoil Roc's kiss had stirred within her?

He was right. She had longed for his kiss all these years while he was gone. And now she had been awakened to the desires she had pushed to the back of her being, knowing full well that they might never be satisfied. He had wrecked her defenses with a single kiss, and now she was helpless against the tide of passion sweeping through her. She wanted more, so much more, but she could not bear the thought that he might use her and then discard her. He was nothing like the Roc of old. He was a grown man with a man's desires.

And her own thoughts were far from angelic.

She had come down to the harbor to inspect the *Seahawk* for a possible future haul to Dead Man's Cove. When she had seen Tristan tied by the dock, she had known that Roc was on his own yacht. She could no more have stopped herself from visiting him than she could have stopped the sun's progress across the sky.

She was playing with fire and, if she didn't take care, the blaze of her passion might well burn her to cinders. But how could she stop what she had already started?

Chapter 10

By the time Gwen had reached Tremayne House, she had gained some semblance of control over her emotions. No matter what sweet things Roc whispered in her ear, he was still her enemy—Dandelion's enemy. Without the proceeds from the smuggling, the Tremaynes would lose their estate. She refused to see her family ruined.

Gwen reined in Buttercup and stared in wonder at the carriage parked outside the front steps. The roof was piled with trunks and portmanteaux. The carriage looked shabby, and the horses were dusty and thin. Who in the world—?

"And take the trunks up to the guest room immediately," a male voice lisped behind the carriage. "I need to refresh my appearance."

Gwen would have recognized that shrill voice anywhere—her cousin, Vincent Tremayne. Frowning, she brought Buttercup to the other side of the carriage. Vincent was standing on the bottom step, and Arthur was lifting down the luggage.

"What are you doing here?" she demanded.

Vincent's pale face turned to her, and his rouged lips twisted into a smile. "What sort of welcome is that, dear coz?" he greeted her.

"If you have come to ask Father for funds, you've come in vain." She slid off her horse and gave her cousin a thorough scrutiny. His narrow shoulders were padded under a tailcoat of a particularly hideous shade of green. The wide pocket flaps and sleeve cuffs were heavily embroidered with gold thread. Every time he moved his languid hand, the gold glittered in the sunlight. His head was covered with a powdered tie-wig, his cheeks were rouged, and his eyebrows were blackened. ''You haven't answered my question,'' Gwen persisted. ''Why are you here?''

He doffed his cocked hat and gave her a mocking bow. ''Always suspicious, coz. If you must know, I was wounded badly in the thigh at Flanders. I'm on leave until further notice.''

Gwen stared at him suspiciously. He was walking with a limp, but there was no trace of pain in his self-satisfied smile.

''I thought a bit of sea air would be good for me. Aren't you going to welcome your long-lost cousin, Gwen?''

Gwen snorted. ''Why? You haven't changed, I wager. Always thinking of yourself first. I'll never forget the injustices of our childhood when you let me take the blame for your crimes.''

He laughed and climbed up the rest of the steps. ''Well, well, the same coarseness, the same bitter tongue! You certainly haven't changed. You'll always be a country bumpkin.''

''I like being a country bumpkin,'' she declared. ''If you give Father any grief, you'll have to answer to me. I'm not a defenseless little girl anymore.''

Ignoring her words, he shaded his face with his hand and scanned the façade of the brick house. ''This will be mine one day, and then I'll have the power to kick you out for good.'' He whistled between his teeth. ''At least you haven't been idle the last few years. I see you've tried to keep abreast with repairs. I'm grateful.''

''Tremayne House will never be yours,'' Gwen whispered to herself, though she knew the estate was entailed to the male heirs of each generation. Vincent was next in that line. At this moment she wished she had a brother, or that she had been born a male. ''I hope your stay won't be prolonged,'' she said. ''Your leg seems to be on the mend. Besides, our provincial ways will soon bore you to death.''

He laughed, a high squeaking sound that made her shudder in disgust. ''I've heard that the earl is back and that he's entertaining at the Hall. I'm sure I'll receive an invitation to the upcoming ball.''

Gwen eyed her cousin darkly. ''If the dowager countess has any sense, she'll endeavor to forget to send you one.''

''My, my, I think Cousin Gwen has become even more

acid-tongued since I last spoke to her. You're growing into a sour old puss.'' He sauntered into the dingy hallway, leaving Gwen behind to gnash her teeth.

She remembered a time when, as a child, Vincent had stolen a prize hen from Farmer Polpenny and killed it. When the crime was discovered, he had blamed her. She could still remember the sting of the whip on her backside and the humiliation that went with the punishment, especially since she had been innocent. Father had believed Vincent, had failed to see his nephew's shifty character.

Vincent was the only son of Squire Tremayne's younger brother, who had died a few years back from a stroke brought on by the threat of bankruptcy. His creditors had taken the entire inventory of his wine shop in Plymouth, leaving Vincent destitute.

Squire Tremayne had bought a commission for Vincent, but the young man's career in the army had been less than glorious. He had always spent his leaves in London, so Gwen was surprised that he would even consider a sojourn in the country, especially since he didn't like her.

Vincent was two years her junior, but had a knack for always getting his own way—no matter who had authority over him. He had certainly never listened to her. Since she was basically a fair, straightforward person, she had difficulty understanding his crafty, evil ways. With him in the house, it would be doubly difficult to keep her role as Dandelion a secret. He would take depraved pleasure in revealing Dandelion's identity to the world.

Leading Buttercup by the reins, she stomped off to the stables. Perhaps she could make Vincent's stay so uncomfortable that he would elect to return to London. But how?

''Well, what's going on in this godforsaken village?'' Vincent asked that evening at the dinner table. He was wearing another heavily embroidered coat—this one scarlet with padded shoulders. He wore his own hair, which was so blond it was almost white, long and stringy.

Gwen shuddered as his pale blue gaze traveled from one face to the other. ''Nothing that would interest you,'' she said.

''You look as if you have lost weight, my dear boy,'' said

the squire between bites of haddock. Melted butter dribbled from his chin. "A hard life in the army?"

"The wound in my leg took much of my strength, I'm afraid," said Vincent, and squeezed lemon on his fish.

"Why aren't you wearing your uniform?" Gwen asked shrewdly.

He glanced at her calculatingly. "Got a spot of mud on it as we crossed the Tamar. Had an accident with the carriage."

"An accident?" The squire glanced over the rim of his spectacles, his eyes round with surprise.

"Yes, I'm afraid it could only be mended temporarily. The repairs require a good deal of blunt."

"Ah!" The squire looked across the table at Gwen. "We'll see to it. Gwennie, you'll forward funds for the repairs first thing tomorrow morning."

Gwen seethed inside. *The snake.* Vincent had already found a way to extract money from Father. And such an innocent face! She wanted to grab his long flat nose and twist it around until—until it came *off!* "I'm sure the ostlers down at The Pilchard will mend whatever is wrong, for free," she said. "Mr. Trelawny owes us several favors."

Venom gleamed in her cousin's eyes, but he hid the expression behind his heavy eyelids.

"You must tell us all the news from London, Vincent," said Aunt Clorinda. "Are you wearing the latest fashions for gentlemen?" She indicated his gaudy coat.

"I'm certainly not wearing the ladies' latest fashions," Vincent said with a snicker, and drank deeply from his wineglass.

Aunt Clo bristled and snorted, and the squire laughed.

Gwen quelled a desire to upend the nearest sauceboat over Vincent's head—and Father's for being so blind.

"I heard a rumor this afternoon about the local smugglers," Vincent said, neatly turning the conversation away from himself. "A daring lot, it seems."

"Yes, and a world of good it does the local people," the squire said. "Keeps poverty at bay." As he lifted a napkin to his chin, the lace of his cuffs swept over his wineglass, overturning it.

"Papa!" Gwen exclaimed, reaching out to catch the glass, but it was too late. She was grateful for the interruption. The last thing she wanted was to discuss the smuggling business with Vincent.

But he was persistent. "I've heard that the Dandelion chap's identity is a well-kept secret." He rubbed his narrow chin thoughtfully. "I've a feeling I could easily discover the truth about the fellow. Perhaps I should offer my services to the new magistrate—however much I loathe to interfere."

"I'm sure the earl will catch him any day now," said Aunt Clo with a sniff. "He'll not accept meddling from anyone, especially since you're not a lawman, Vincent."

Thank you, Aunt Clo, Gwen thought and sipped her wine. She could sense her cousin's mind considering every possible name in the village. He would be difficult. From now on, she would have to take double precautions.

As he brought in the pudding, Arthur carried a message to the table. It was for Vincent.

He unfolded the stiff missive and scanned the paper. "Well, well. Seems that news travels as fast as it used to in the village. The dowager countess has invited me to the ball." He gave Gwen a triumphant smile. "You won't get rid of me so easily after all."

The next few days Aunt Clo spent every waking hour sewing hers and Gwen's ballgowns. She was almost driving Gwen out of her mind with the many fittings, but in the end, her satin creations were beautiful.

Gwen's apricot gown had a tight, pointed stomacher with a row of echelles—bows—made of brown velvet. The wide skirt flared at the hips over paniers. The robings parted at the front, revealing the embroidered petticoat underneath. Gwen felt lovely in it. She could not recall the last time she had worn a new gown, and a ballgown at that.

Her aunt, too, looked almost pretty in her forest-green satin gown, cut in the sack style with a row of bows down the front and a lace shawl covering the low-cut neckline.

Gwen had not encountered Roc since their meeting on the yacht, and she could not wait to see him again. She was a bee drawn to his nectar and she would not be satisfied until she had tasted more of him, more of her own newly awakened passion.

On the night of the ball, Gwen walked up the front steps

of the Hall on her father's arm, her nose filled with the scent of camphor billowing from the squire's old velvet costume. She cast an uneasy glance at him. The blue velvet of his full-skirted coat was sadly motheaten, and no matter how Aunt Clo had tried to mend the holes, they were still visible. Gwen had brushed his best wig until the sausage curls held some semblance of order, and she had dusted them liberally with powder. With his spectacles pinched across the bridge of his nose, he looked like a sleepwalker. But as soon as he laid eyes on Morgan in the hallway, he beamed with pleasure.

He nipped across the room with alacrity to pump the young man's hand, leaving his ladies to fend for themselves at the top of the front steps, since Vincent was dawdling behind.

Aunt Clo fluttered her fan and glared at Squire Tremayne and Morgan. "There they go. They will closet themselves in the study and not emerge until the ball is over."

"I don't think the dowager will allow it." Gwen stepped up to Roc's formidable mother, who was regally receiving guests by the door. The dowager countess surveyed them disdainfully as they approached, Vincent at the rear. Her gaze lingered momentarily on him, and Gwen heard her sharply indrawn breath. "Popinjay," the old woman muttered. Vincent was looking particularly frightful in a bright orange coat and yellow knee breeches. His painted and powdered face looked almost sinister beside the innocent provincial faces of the other guests.

"Ah, our neighbors." The dowager's voice boomed through the cavernous hall, and the guests glanced at the newcomers. Gwen wanted to sink through the floor, but she held her chin high and her back straight.

She caught Roc's amused glance as he stood next to his mother, his hands clasped behind his back. Her heart careened madly. As usual he was the epitome of elegance in his midnight-blue brocade coat with matching vest. His exquisite jabot of spidery French lace must have cost a small fortune.

"Pretty as a picture, isn't she, Mother?" came his deep voice. Gwen clenched her fists in the folds of her gown. How dared he tease her!

"I daresay you will do quite nicely, Gwen. That gown is a shade better than the one you wore last time," the dowager said. The ears of the nearby guests seemed to grow larger and point toward the trio to catch Gwen's reply.

"I wish I could say the same about yours, Lady Landregan," she said sweetly, and a murmur of outrage swept through the guests like wildfire. But the dowager doubled over with laughter that echoed off the painted plaster ceilings and set the paintings to trembling in their gilded frames. The old woman clutched Roc's arm for support. "What a minx she is. Such a sharp tongue!" she exclaimed.

"Equaling your own, Mother," Roc murmured. He bowed over Gwen's long fingers. "One point to you," he whispered in conspiracy, and Gwen felt a wave of warmth at the touch of his breath on her skin.

Aunt Clo pursed her lips with disapproval and hid her flaming cheeks behind her fan. Roc greeted her and gave Vincent a curt nod. "Tremayne. It has been a long time. You haven't changed." Then he led Gwen into the ballroom. "You look lovely tonight. I could not wait to see you again." His eyes held a roguish suggestion, and Gwen blushed delicately.

"From now on, I'll feel safe only in a large group of people," she said. "Then you cannot press your advances upon me."

"Oh, Gwennie, fear doesn't suit you," he chided. "Besides, I would never do anything to hurt you, you know that." He patted her fingertips, lying cautiously on his sleeve.

She shot him a dark glance. "Perhaps not, but aside from that, you would not hesitate—"

"Shall we sit here?" came Aunt Clo's voice behind her. All of a sudden Gwen realized she had almost let Roc lead her out onto the dark terrace beyond the open ballroom doors.

Aghast, she disengaged her fingers from his grasp and hurried to her aunt's side. Aunt Clo was busily arranging herself on one of the gilt chairs along the wall. Roc passed Gwen on his way back to the hallway. "I will return," he murmured in her ear.

Confused and filled with longing for his company, Gwen sank down on a chair from which she had an unobstructed view of the dance floor, and fanned herself vigorously.

"He's a handsome young man, the earl," said Aunt Clo.

Gwen sensed the older woman's gaze on her and tried to hide her excitement. "Yes . . . he is." She watched the ele-

gant couples in the room. She knew her own gown of simple
cut couldn't be compared to the lustrous gowns of the other
ladies, but at least hers was new. What she lacked in style
and jewels, she would try to make up for in bearing. And
she had taken special care with her hair, brushing it until it
shone and sweeping it high over her forehead. Clusters of
curls cascaded over her shoulders. Abhorring hair powder,
she had woven a strand of pearls in the curls. For once she
felt really beautiful, and Roc's eyes had told her that he found
her very attractive.

Gwen's breath faltered as Roc returned to the ballroom, a
wisp of a girl clinging to his sleeve. Gwen's eyes widened in
awe. The girl was the loveliest creature she'd ever laid eyes
on, delicate-featured, lily-skinned, petite, her oval face dom-
inated by huge, golden-fringed green eyes.

"Louise requested an introduction," Roc explained.

Gwen shifted her gaze to him with difficulty.

"Miss Gwendolyn Tremayne, Lady Louise Camelford—
our houseguest."

"An honor to meet you, Lady Louise," Gwen greeted her
pleasantly. She was completely taken aback when the vision
opened her mouth and spoke in an extremely high-pitched
squeak.

"Miss Tremayne, I've heard *so* much about you—how you
take such good care of your *farm,* and how very brave you
are."

Shaken, Gwen met the girl's green, wide-eyed gaze. How
could such an angelic face house such an awful voice? An
urge to giggle assaulted her, and she lowered her gaze lest
Lady Louise should notice her amusement.

"I daresay it takes a lot of *work* to care for a farm," the
young lady continued.

"Quite. Tell me, Lady Louise, how do you find these parts?
I'm sure they must appear wild and rustic to you."

"Oh, yes . . . very rugged, but also intriguing." She dimpled prettily at the earl. "Roc has invited us to stay as long
as we like."

A slightly harassed look momentarily veiled his face, and
Gwen knew that the dowager was behind the generous invitation.

"I'm afraid we don't have as many balls and routs as you

must be used to in the metropolis," Gwen said with a smile. "I'd say we're rather behind fashion here. I hope you won't become bored."

"Oh, no! I'm grateful to chat with a lady nearer my own age." Lady Louise spoke so kindly, Gwen could not help but warm toward her, though the girl looked a perfect goddess.

Louise turned to Roc. "Thank you for introducing me. I'm sure you have to take care of your other guests now." To Gwen she said, "I beg of you, will you tell me all about the smuggler Dandelion whom Roc is trying to capture?" She clapped her hands together. "I've never heard *anything* more exciting in my life, but Roc is sadly closemouthed on the subject." She settled her frothy white gown around her on the chair next to Gwen. "I've never been more intrigued. In fact, I'm *bursting* with curiosity. Can I meet him?"

"I don't think that would be a wise idea," said Gwen. Realizing the absurdity of Lady Louise's request, she began to embroider a long tale about a heroic smuggler with a scarred face, a black patch over one eye, and a wooden leg.

Lady Louise's eyes grew rounder. "I would like to meet *him*," she breathed. "Why can't I?"

Gwen laughed. "I assure you, you don't want to meet a hairy lout who would only offend your sensibilities with the smell of rotting fish—or brandy, for that matter. Besides, his words would not be fit for your delicate ears."

Lady Louise gasped. "I dare suppose you've met him?"

Gwen hid a smile behind her fan. "Of course not! How could you ever entertain such a thought? His identity is shrouded in mystery. Or perhaps he's only a silly fiction put about by the villagers."

A tall lady with a horsey face and powdered hair floated across the room to join them. Her hoops were enormous, and the gold brocade of her gown was sumptuous if overpowering. "*There* you are, m'dear," she told Louise. "I've been looking *everywhere* for you. I'm sure the earl is waiting to lead you onto the floor for the first cotillion."

She glanced down her long nose at Gwen, and Lady Louise hastened to introduce them. "This is my mother, Lady Camelford."

"Ah, *the* Miss Tremayne," Lady Camelford said. "They say there is nobody like you in these parts. A virtual paragon of hard work and dedication." The words held a disapproving note. "Come along, Louise."

The girl shot Gwen a despairing glance from under thick golden lashes and followed her demanding parent.

A few minutes later Aunt Clo dug Gwen in the ribs with her fan. "Look at the young men. How they hang in droves around that miss. 'Tis close on indecent! You mark my words, we'll have that ninny as the new countess at the Hall."

"She's a nice sort, although I can't say I like that voice of hers." Gwen smiled at the memory.

"Lud! Dreadful. Look, there is Morgan. Roc must have forced him out of the library at last. But your father, where is he? I'd wager my last penny he's in the study with his nose in a book—snoring." She eyed Morgan speculatively. "If you had a bit more gumption, Gwennie, you could nip young Morgan for a husband. 'Twould be exactly the same as living with Lionel. You barely notice that type of man in the house, except when he has no more books to read."

Gwen considered the idea of marrying Morgan. Yes, he had a nice face and kindly eyes, but one bookworm in the family was quite enough. Still, a twinge of regret pinched her at the thought of spending the rest of her life as a spinster. It had taken this ball to open up her eyes to just how isolated her family was, and how easy it was to let life flow by, year after year, inexorably moving her toward a lonely old age.

The music's first frail tones wafted through the ballroom. A cotillion formed, and Roc led Lady Louise onto the floor. Gwen was so absorbed in watching him that she almost fell off the chair when a male voice barked into her ear, "Miss Tremayne! Would you stand up with me for this dance?"

Shocked, she looked into the bulbous eyes of Officer Biggles. He stood resplendent in a purple velvet coat with red trimmings, and Gwen had to squint to protect her eyes from the onslaught of clashing colors.

"Officer Biggles," she said in a faint voice. "I would be flattered." With a sidelong glance at her startled aunt, she placed her hand on the revenue officer's arm and followed him onto the floor.

How long was it since she had last danced? She could not remember. Stiffly she reacquainted herself with the steps, afraid of injuring someone's toes. Once she met Roc's hot gaze, and it had such an impact on her that she forgot to move, which resulted in having her foot ground down by Biggles's high heel.

"I'm terribly sorry," he said, wheezing, his face red with heat and exertion. "How clumsy of me."

" 'Tis quite all right; I missed a step." She could not forget the warm suggestion in Roc's eyes, nor could she stop from glancing at him over her shoulder. He was doing the same, and their eyes met again. A glow of anticipation spread from her stomach. It was as if liquid pleasure flowed through her veins, gathering in a molten longing between her thighs. His attraction was such that she could barely contain herself. She yearned to run across the room and throw herself into his arms. Instead, she lowered her gaze demurely and concentrated on the dance steps.

After the dance Gwen sat by the open terrace doors fanning herself. A balmy breeze from the south wafted through the curtains, and the air had a faint taste of salt.

Mysterious fragrances, carried over the sea from foreign countries, enticed her nostrils. Gwen breathed deeply. She loved the sea. She thought she could hear the piercing cry of a seagull in the darkness. The old people used to say the seagulls were the souls of drowned sailors, she recalled.

The touch of a hand on her shoulder abruptly dissolved her dream. Looking up, she met Roc's smiling face. His eyes seemed to sear her soul. "Listening to the night?"

She nodded. The feel of his hand on her arm sent flurries of pleasure along her skin.

"I believe this is our dance, if you can tear yourself away from the lovely night." His husky voice did strange things to her insides, sending delicious thrills along her spine and a tingling sensation to her breasts. She placed her fingers on his sleeve. Why did he reduce her to such a state?

She let him lead her onto the floor, and they took their places for the quadrille. Roc bowed deeply, his hair gleaming with blue lights under the hot glow of the many candles in the chandeliers. Pinching her long skirts on both sides, Gwen curtsied, then prayed she could rise from her bent position despite the violent trembling of her legs.

Roc's touch continued to scorch her as he led her in the steps of the dance. Every time he caught her hand, she held

her breath. Everything else ceased to exist as only a charged
delight flamed between them. She ached to know what had
been denied her for so long, the touch of a man's hands on
her body. Blushing at the wanton thought, she dared not look
at him again, fearing he would read her blazing desire. He
wouldn't hesitate to take advantage of her in her weakened
state.

But when she could suppress her longing no more, Gwen
darted a sideways glance at him. The glitter in his topaz eyes
reflected her own naked desire. Her hand missed that of her
partner. When, at the very end of the dance, the earl's hand
took hers once more, she flinched.

"You look as if you could use some air. Are you ill?" he
inquired smoothly. Without waiting for an answer, he whisked
her past the billowing white curtains and out onto the long
terrace spanning the length of the central section of the Hall.
"You're so very lovely tonight, Gwennie, so desirable." He
sighed. "I only wish you felt the same about me."

She sensed that he meant every word, but she could not
admit openly that she wanted him. "Are you angling for a
compliment?" she asked, forcing her voice to sound normal.

"Do you have one to give?"

Gwen could not answer. She was already frightened by her
body's treacherous response to his touch. It would be so easy
to succumb to his demands.

Roc strolled with her to the end of the paved terrace.
Laughter and giggles echoed from the grounds, proving that
they were not the only couple "taking air." Roc leaned
against the curved balustrade, wind ruffling his raven curls.

Clinging to a pillar, an enormous rose bush sweetened the
air. Gwen felt intoxicated by the potent fragrance and Roc's
closeness. She could not see his eyes in the darkness, but she
was acutely aware of his presence. His strength—his power
over her senses—seemed to grow stronger in the night. Her
body grew heavy with yearning as he looked at her without
touching.

Magic spun its invisible net around the night, a perfect
moment in time, so full that Gwen wanted to float into his
arms, her whole being crying out to him, every nerve responding to his presence.

With a growl deep in his chest, Roc placed his warm hands

on her bare shoulders and pulled her to him. Pressed hard against his muscled body, she breathed with shallow gasps and yielded her soft, half-open lips to him. He bent his head, his mouth crushing down on hers. Gwen was transformed into a flame of passion, responding shamelessly to the fire his roving hands evoked in her.

With his fingers deeply buried in her curls, he slid his mouth greedily down her throat, forming a moist trail to her full cleavage. When he freed one breast from the confines of her low-cut bodice, she moaned softly. His tongue glided wetly over one aching, hard crest, which had never been touched by a man before. Shocks of pleasure pounded through her. He was breathing rapidly, hot gusts on her bare skin.

His fingers dug into her spine, and she arched her back, yielding her other breast to his sensual homage. Swooning as his tongue laved the full mounds exquisitely and the valley between them, Gwen clung to him. Her hands clutched his massive shoulders as if she were a drowning person.

"I can't . . . bear," he muttered, nipping at one throbbing peak, "to have such . . . heady . . . treasures hidden from my . . . sight." His hand massaged one swollen globe as his tongue returned to the moist cave of her mouth and plundered the sweet recesses. She clung to him as if to life, all her senses acutely aware of him. His spicy male aroma sent her mind reeling, and the sensuous attack of his tongue forced her to surrender completely.

"To feel you . . . naked . . . under me would be . . . pure heaven," he murmured, and Gwen wanted nothing else. It did not occur to her for a second that his manners had flown away on the magic wind. "I'm dying to explore your every secret," he said.

"As I want to explore yours," she whispered, longing desperately to unveil her secrets to him—and to herself.

What brought her back to sanity was trivial enough, the sound of voices and sharp heels on the stone terrace. Like an avenging angel her practical mind swooped back into her, and she gasped, frantically fitting her breasts back into the bodice and smoothing down her skirts.

Her face burned with shame, and she would have escaped into the darkness of the garden below the terrace if Roc had not held a restraining arm around her waist. Soundlessly he pulled her into the shadow of the pillar, its thickness and the climbing rose bush concealing most of them. She leaned against his motionless body, his arm like a searing band around her middle.

The steps had stopped some distance away. "I wonder where the earl disappeared to," came the marchioness of Camelford's peevish voice. "I swear I saw him exit with that . . . farming female."

"Mama! How awful you are. 'Tis ridiculous to follow Roc like this, and Miss Tremayne is very nice. I'm glad I made her acquaintance. Let us return inside before we meet them. Roc will immediately know that you're spying on him." Lady Louise's high-pitched voice pierced the night.

Gwen felt Roc's chest heaving with soundless laughter against her back, and she touched her flaming cheeks in mortification. What had she almost let him do to her? And how could he violate her with such abandon? And almost in public!

The heels began their impatient tapping back to the ballroom. "Very uncouth of the earl to escape like that," said the marchioness. "I'll give him a piece of my mind when he returns."

Roc's hand brushed lightly over Gwen's still throbbing breasts. "Are you going to upbraid me before you send me off to get lashed by Lady Camelford's chastising tongue?"

Gwen opened her mouth to rail at him, but her anger evaporated at his obvious delight in her presence.

"Perhaps we should blame this madness on the seductive summer night—and your enticing body, Gwen. I meant everything I said," he whispered roughly.

Gwen placed a hand to her forehead to still her careening thoughts. "I suppose it was partly my fault, letting you . . ."

He sighed deeply. "Sweet, lovely Gwen. Please don't be ashamed of your feelings. They are quite normal." He placed a long finger under her chin and lifted her face to his. His warm breath floated over her face. "Should I apologize?"

Gwen held her breath, absorbing his words. "No . . . just forget it ever happened. And don't ever again take advantage of my weakness."

He sighed. "That will be very difficult." But she could tell he was relieved that she wasn't going to rail at him. He laughed, a low, throaty sound. "Had you a brother—or a father of a different frame of mind—I would be called out for this evening's work."

Gwen smiled at the picture of her father, sword in hand, charging at the earl. "I'm sure the squire doesn't know by which end to hold a sword."

Roc laughed. "You do paint a harmless picture. But who is going to defend you?" He held out his arm.

"I'm perfectly capable of defending myself." Gwen twined her arm through his, and they walked slowly toward the open doors where the sound of violins blended with the wind from the sea. Roc leaned over her. "Have you noticed that we haven't bickered for at least twenty minutes? Unusual, eh?"

Gwen let out a long sigh. "Yes, very unusual."

"Does that mean we're going to be friends, after all?"

Gwen fixed him with a bright eye. "I doubt it."

As they approached the doors, a shadow appeared out of the darkness beside the opening. It was Vincent, smoking a long, thin cheroot. His eyes gleamed speculatively in the candlelight.

"Ah! There you are, coz. Every day I learn more about your character. You never cease to amaze me, m'dear."

Gwen wondered how much he had seen. The smirk on his lips suggested that he had seen enough. She raised her chin. "You shouldn't be talking about character," she said icily. "You don't know what the word means."

She swept through the door, pulling Roc with her before he could get angry with Vincent. However much she'd enjoy watching Roc pound some sense into her odious cousin, she could not afford to become the talk of the gossipmongers.

"I'd be careful if I were you," Vincent said as a parting shot. "There might be consequences."

"Yes. If you don't watch your language, Vincent, you may find yourself with your tongue cut out."

Vincent had completely ruined her pleasure, and Gwen vowed he would pay for it. Somehow.

Chapter 11

He had kissed and caressed her. What she had dreamed of for years had actually happened.

As Gwen lay exhausted in her bed after the ball, her euphoric thoughts revolved irresistibly around Roc. He had kissed *her,* not Lady Louise, or anyone else. Reliving that sweet moment on the terrace over and over, she finally drifted off to sleep, a smile lingering on her lips.

"Psst, psst, Miss Gwen!" Marva stood bent over her.

Gwen peered at the cook through gritty eyes. "What is it? Do you have to make such a noise at . . . dawn?"

"Dawn! Ye're about in yer 'ead, miss. 'Tis noon, and th' sun stands 'igh in th' sky. There's a rag on th' stable wall, miss, a red one."

"Red?" Gwen sat up hastily. Clad only in her thin nightgown, she ran to the window and looked out. A red rag spelled danger. She drew a deep, frightened breath. "How long has it been there?"

"Since some time after dawn." Marva fidgeted and glanced repeatedly toward the door, as if she expected a horde of soldiers to burst in and arrest her mistress.

"And you didn't wake me?" Gwen rushed to the clothespress and pulled out her riding habit.

Marva mopped her brow with a corner of her apron. "I figured ye needed yer rest, miss. That Clem'll be back."

"I'm sure he's already at our meeting spot, waiting all day if necessary." Gwen brushed out her tangled curls and bound them carelessly at the nape of her neck with a velvet ribbon. As soon as she was dressed, she fetched Buttercup from the stables, pretending she was taking a morning ride.

As she had suspected, Clem was waiting in the spinney, lying idly among the trees in a patch of sunlight, a piece of grass clamped between his teeth.

"Have you been here long?" she whispered.

"Long enough, but I knew ye were sleepin' yer beauty sleep, like th' ladies at th' 'All." He braced himself up on one elbow. "Miss, we've 'eard th' Looe men are plannin' on takin' our cargo at th' next dark o' th' moon."

Gwen stared at him aghast. "Oh, no! That angry are they, eh? But we were only minding our own business. We didn't take anything that wasn't ours."

"Aye, but they want to show us a lesson so we niver 'aul our cargo in their waters again."

"I see. Well, I know how we can turn the tables on them." Furrowing her brow in thought, she studied the trees suspiciously, as if even the trunks had ears. "We might have to lose the next cargo to them, but mark my words, 'twill be worth it. If Officer Biggles and the earl catch a few men, *any* men, and brandy to boot, they'll be pleased with themselves—even if the smugglers are from Looe. The confusion should give them something to ponder, and then when they least expect it, we'll bring in our own load right under their long noses."

Clem chortled. "Ye're a sharp 'un, miss. I've niver 'eard anythin' like it."

Gwen turned around, her senses alert. "Shhh, someone is coming this way." She pulled Buttercup back onto the path, and Clem hoisted her into the saddle, then melted soundlessly with the dappled shadows under the greenery. Buttercup cantered along the path, and Gwen set her face in a suitable innocent mask.

Roc rode into view on Tristan.

When he saw her, he pulled in the reins. "Good morning, my sweet. Already up and about? The ladies at the Hall are still asleep. Mother never gets up before one o'clock." His gaze darted among the trees.

"I have more important things to do than to sleep all day. What are you doing here?"

His glance caressed her briefly, and she felt a by-now familiar breathlessness.

"I thought I heard voices."

She flinched at his penetrating glance. "You must have heard me talking to Buttercup." She made her voice light and dismissing. A twig broke in the thicket some distance away, and Roc whipped his head around to stare into the shady undergrowth.

Clem! Be careful, Gwen thought, holding her breath.

A wave of guilt swept over her. She hated to deceive Roc. Since their relationship had grown more intimate, she could not take the same delight in fooling him. Her deceit had a bitter taste. But the smuggling business was too important and lucrative to abandon because she felt attracted to the local magistrate.

"The smugglers might be on the prowl," he said angrily. "I can't wait to catch the ruffians."

Gwen laughed hollowly. "Smugglers? Nonsense. I believe a badger lives in a burrow somewhere close by. I've heard suspicious noises many times, and Buttercup always snorts when some wild animal crosses her path."

His narrowed gaze bored into her. "Badgers are night animals."

Gwen shrugged. "Well, in here among the trees there's almost perpetual dusk." She clenched her hands around the reins. Only when Roc's shoulders relaxed could she breathe freely. He had accepted her explanation.

He brought his horse around. "May I accompany you on your ride, Gwen?" His eyes twinkled.

She smiled, dizzy with relief. "Of course. Were you planning to visit us this morning, since you're on Tremayne land, Roc?" Her tone teased him, but he was not easily goaded.

"No, I was only taking a shortcut through your spinney. And about last night—"

Dread filled her. "Yes, Roc?"

He looked guilty. "Hrmph, I don't know what madness came over me. Too much wine, I suppose. I just wanted to say that I'll try to keep myself within the boundaries of decent behavior in the future. I'm so sorry for violating you in such a crude manner. I had no right."

Disappointment washed through her. He already regretted their intimacy. She wasn't good enough for him—past her first blush of youth, and penniless to boot. "Oh, well, don't mention it." She pushed her heels into the mare's flanks, and

Buttercup reluctantly fell into a gallop. Tristan easily matched her stride, although he seemed to dislike the restraint. He skittered and danced around her.

Ashamed, Gwen wanted to turn around, go back to bed, and pull the covers over her face. Roc didn't really care for her. The disillusionment burned within her. How could he shatter her dream so cruelly, and why had she behaved with such abandon last night? Perhaps he had lost his respect for her since she had given herself so shamelessly.

Yet he had led her to believe he cared, and now he wanted to drop her. Why? She struggled to keep her seething emotions under control. She was ugly, that was it. She berated herself for wearing such an old riding habit, and her hair had no style whatsoever. No wonder he regretted making advances. She must look a terrible fright. Touching her hair furtively, she glanced at him from the corner of her eye. He looked very serious this morning, not in the least flirtatious.

"I don't see how Dandelion could bring in another load here in Landregan," he mused aloud, pushing a hand through his curls. They hung loosely over his collar this morning, accentuating his broad, powerful shoulders. "There are only so many accessible coves."

"He'll find a way, don't you worry," she said glumly.

"Worry? I'll be right there to catch him," Roc promised with a frown. "He would be foolish beyond belief to bring in more French goods."

"Dandelion isn't foolish, you know that." Gwen dug her heels into Buttercup's flanks and shot up the ridge bordering the sea.

They rode in silence, west along the cliff path, away from the village. At some distance the hills made room for a narrow, secluded valley where cottages had been built on a stone wall at the very edge of the glittering green water. Waves crashed continually against the wall, scattering white froth in every direction.

The steep path took them past the valley and up another ridge above Fisherman's Creek. Gwen rode along the rock-strewn summit, looking down at the weeping willows lining the still water of the creek. A pair of herons stood motionless in the shallows, their heads poised over the shiny surface as if admiring their own image. The silvery belly of a fish flashed in the bright light.

"When I was a lad we used to fish here every day," Roc said. "Morgan used to hide from the tutor in those days, long before he became a prisoner of books." A wide grin creased Roc's face, and the next moment he had slid from his horse. "Let me see if the rods are still here." He disappeared down the path and behind a tree trunk, where he rummaged through the undergrowth. "Ah, I found the rotten remains, and the hooks are still intact, if a trifle rusty," he called triumphantly. "Let's try our fishing luck. I'm sure I have a string of some sort in the saddlebag."

Gwen watched wide-eyed as he went through the contents of his bag, childlike eagerness on his face. "Ah, here we are. A passable string and some stale bread."

His smile was contagious, and Gwen caught some of his enthusiasm. After stuffing the string into a pocket, he strode up to Buttercup and placed his hands around Gwen's waist. "Come, Gwennie, we're going fishing."

Before she could open her mouth to protest, he had lifted her high in the air. Slowly he set her on the ground. Her heart thundered in anticipation. He stood so close she could smell his clean male scent. She dared not look into his eyes lest he notice the desire blossoming within her. For a long moment he stood very still, his hands clasping her narrow waist.

"Let's . . . get the string into the water," he murmured, his face so close his breath fanned her hair like a gentle summer breeze. He released his hold.

Gwen followed him down the steep path and out onto a low tree branch that hung over the water just a foot above the surface. She watched him clean off the hook and fasten it to the string. "This will not be easy, but 'tis my lucky hook, so who knows what could happen. I've caught many fish with this hook, Gwennie."

"You can't catch any without bait," she said. Her heart was still galloping in her chest from his touch, and she was angry with herself for her weakness. "I'll wager you can't catch a pilchard on that hook."

"Really?" He gave her a mischievous glance. "How much do you consider 'tis worth, then?"

She pursed her lips. "My mother's locket. 'Tis pure gold."

His baffled laugh echoed as he gently lowered the line into the water. He had shoved a ball of bread on the hook, then spit three times on it, for luck. "You must be extremely confident that my chances are nil," he said. "I recall that you greatly treasure that locket with your mother's miniature."

"Yes."

A fish jumped, forming rings on the greenish water. "There it is, my catch, or his brother. You just watch."

Not deigning to respond, Gwen peeled off her boots and stockings and dangled her toes in the cool water. At that point, she didn't care what the earl thought of her lack of decorum. The morning had been marred for her when he had excused his ardent behavior of the previous night. She had quite hoped he would continue where they had left off . . .

Taken by surprise, Gwen watched him—the powerful earl of Landregan—tear off his footwear. His toes soon joined hers under water. "Ah, how good it feels to discard these tight boots. High fashion is dashed uncomfortable."

"I'm surprised. You seem—well, so at ease with yourself."

His smile flashed. "And you aren't?"

She shrugged. "Not in drawing rooms."

"You should be glad of it. Drawing rooms are a dead bore: recitals, tea parties, nosy dowagers, rampant gossip, and lackluster conversation."

She had to laugh, and she touched his arm impulsively. "Sounds like an apt description."

The willow trailed its long branches on the water, the dappled shadows it formed protecting them from the hot afternoon sun. A light wind played a song in the reeds along the shore, and wavelets lapped gently against the bank.

"This is paradise," Roc mused. "In my pursuit of worldly riches, I forgot the peace of Landregan."

Gwen listened, alert to his words. "You surely did not lack for riches before."

"Ha! My father was one for keeping up the appearance of wealth, but at one time we were almost in as much difficulties as you are today. The old earl was an incurable gambler, and he hated me for trying to stop him."

"Oh, yes, I remember now. I was young in his heyday. That's why you joined the East India Company, isn't it?"

A curlew flew up from the reeds with a startling cry.

"Yes, I couldn't live with him under the same roof much longer, so I decided to set out to make my own fortune. India holds enormous riches, but it takes hard work to extract them. Illness, stifling heat, all manner of poisonous snakes, tigers, murderers, and thieves—you meet them all out there. Great poverty and astounding wealth. The maharajas live like gods."

"Maharajas?"

"Why, the kings or princes of the different provinces. You could never find larger jewels or richer cloths than within their palaces."

Gwen's eyes grew wide. "Oh, tell me." He had her full attention now. A pleasant half hour passed while he described what he had done and seen in foreign lands, and his trip to China and the island of Borneo. They forgot all about the line floating peacefully in the creek.

"I thought I wanted to live adventurously, to be the richest man in the world, but this"—he swept out his hand—"this is to be rich. What more can a man ask for? To live in the middle of this paradise, to feel this tranquillity every day, and to have the company of a lovely woman is more than enough for me." He turned to her, his eyes shining. "You might be poor in material things, Gwennie, but you wouldn't give this up for anything, would you?"

"Of course not; there is no place I'd rather live."

"You're wise, Gwen."

"I would have thought you'd find us provincial and boring after your foreign travels."

"Provincial maybe, but never boring. As we both know, Landregan is a veritable beehive of activity," he added drily.

She laughed at his rueful expression. "I'm glad you find Landregan adequate entertainment."

He glared at her with mock ferocity. "Landregan is Landregan. 'Twill never change, I wager." He hesitated for a moment. "Has it ever occurred to you that you might marry someone outside Landregan and leave for good?"

She laughed derisively to hide how much his words touched

her on the raw. "Me, married? You ought to know that at twenty-three, I'm definitely on the shelf."

"How cruel you are to yourself. There must be a full score of gentlemen who would desire to marry you."

"Not without a dowry."

"Ah! You don't believe in love then, that a man would marry you for love." He seemed suddenly to remember the line and pulled it in, only to throw it back out again.

Gwen colored. "*I* believe in love, but I have yet to meet a gentleman who doesn't look askance at my empty coffers." She took a deep breath. "And when are the banns to be read for you and Lady Louise? I take it the marchioness wants you for her daughter."

He snorted, his nails digging into the warm bark of the tree. "Never!" He changed the subject. "I daresay the fish are lazy today. Perchance a trifle too late in the day for fishing. They strike best at dawn or twilight."

"I told you you wouldn't have any luck."

The wind ruffled his wavy hair, blowing it across his high forehead. Gwen wanted to smooth it back—just to have a reason to touch him.

Abruptly he peeled off his coat and waistcoat and threw them on the shore. His white shirt billowed gently around him, the wet lace cuffs clinging to his wrists.

Gwen trailed her fingers back and forth in the water.

"Shhh, you're frightening the fish," he warned, a twinkle in his eyes. "Trying desperately to hold on to that locket, eh?" He looked so attractive, her breath stuck in her throat.

"I'm not going to sit here and meekly lose my locket without employing some sort of strategy," she said gruffly. Her heart ached painfully with love for him.

A flurry of movement in the water startled them both. Rings spread on the water as the fish dove, almost pulling the line from Roc's slack grip.

"See? What did I tell you?" He jerked the line up, setting the hook. The fish fought valiantly, but it was a doomed struggle.

Gwen stared at the silvery, green-spotted body of a tiny salmon as Roc pulled it out of the water. "I've never!" she exclaimed, frowning. "What infernal luck."

"Your locket, ma'am," Roc crowed and tried to grip the slick, wiggling fish.

Gwen made a moue and moved a few inches closer to shore. "Put it back in the water. 'Tis too small to keep."

"Why? Smoked salmon's a delicacy, don't you know?"

" 'Tis but a baby. Put it back," she ordered.

He regarded her in disbelief and shrugged. "I must bow to your higher authority," he concluded softly, and unhooked the small mouth. The salmon wriggled readily from his grip and hit the water with a plop. With a flash of silver, it was gone.

Gwen drew a sigh of relief. "Thank you. You behaved like a true gentleman, Roc. I was nervous for a while, wondering what you intended to do with it."

"Your locket, my sweet." He rose unsteadily on the swaying branch and loomed over her. With a squeal, she began bouncing up and down on the trunk, hoping he would fall into the water, but he had excellent balance. He lifted her easily under her arms until she was standing on the swaying tree limb. Leaning over her, his lips once more formed the word "locket."

She giggled nervously, wanting to wipe the teasing smile from his face. She struggled to loosen his hard grip on her wrists, but he brooked no resistance. He bore her resolutely ashore and deftly unbuttoned the topmost buttons of her tight riding jacket. Then he pulled out the black velvet ribbon from which was suspended the gleaming gold pendant. He stared at it for a moment, then with an audible sigh, he let it fall back into the valley between her breasts. "How can I take a lady's last treasure?" he asked.

Sensing his defeat, she undid the clasp and held the golden oval in the palm of her hand. "Take it." Her gaze bored into his, daring him to accept it. " 'Tis not my *last* treasure, milord." Forcing it into his unwilling hand, she rose and strode up the path.

"Wait for me," he called after her. "I don't need or want your locket. 'Twas but a lighthearted wager." But she paid him no heed. The whole day had gone wrong from the moment Marva had awakened her. She should have known Roc would get that fish!

"Gwen! What has gotten into you?" He caught up with

her at the top of the ridge next to the horses. He thrust the locket back into her hand, only to find it pushed instantly into his pocket.

"I'm serious," Gwen explained. "A bet is a bet. I don't go back on my promises."

He grabbed her shoulders and looked deeply into her eyes. "Very well. But I'll give you a chance to win it back soon."

She glared at him suspiciously. "What do you have in mind?"

His brow creased in thought. "How about a wager concerning Dandelion? I say I'll catch him before the end of the summer."

She laughed, the shrill sound jarring her own ears. "How foolish of you. You won't catch him. 'Tis July now. The next dark of the moon will be in three days, then 'twill be August, and then autumn will be hard upon us."

He shrugged. "Is it a bet? I'll capture Dandelion before the end of August."

She grasped one of his hands and shook it. "A bet it is. August, bah!"

He smiled and gazed silently at her for a long time. "You know, Gwennie, I like you very much," he said quietly.

She could not trust her voice to speak.

"I've met many women, but never anyone whom I've actually *liked*—as a friend. They all wanted different things from me." He grew silent, and Gwen could very well imagine what those things were. No woman could remain untouched by Roc's overpowering virility and charm.

"I like you, too," she whispered, and slapped him exaggeratedly on the back, treating him as she would any one of her fishermen friends.

He would never know how much those words cost her when she wanted to say so much more.

Chapter 12

Light at heart, Roc returned to the Hall. As he entered his study, cupping the smooth gold oval in his hand, he thought of Gwen. He had to admit that more than physical attraction drew him to her. Her frankness was invigorating, and there was humor and sincerity in her eyes. Sincerity was a trait he valued highly. The ladies who had accompanied him in London had invariably harbored a streak of cold scheming, always trying to figure out how they best might use him. They had all wanted gifts—jewels, carriages, horses.

Gwen was different. She seemed to want nothing from him. All her concern centered around Tremayne House. He found that admirable, knowing the struggle she bore without a word of complaint.

He sighed and sank down in the well-worn leather chair behind the desk. A salver held a stack of mail. Yawning, he sifted through the letters. He was tired after the late night and would have liked to lean his head back and snooze for an hour, but one letter marked "personal and confidential" caught his attention.

Slipping the gold pendant back in his pocket, he broke the seal and unfolded the paper.

Roc Tyrrell, the earl of Landregan, it began with a flourish, but the script deteriorated rapidly after that.

> *Your failure to deliver the jewel box to your contact will be looked upon as treason toward Charles Stuart, and treated accordingly. But we'll give you one more chance. Another messenger will be sent from London. All you have to do is place the box in the firewood bin at the back door*

*at The Pilchard, and the messenger will collect it post-
haste. You have one day to decide, then deliver the box.
Remember, we will not hesitate to seek retribution in the
name of Charles Stuart, rightful king of Scotland and England.*

Y'r obedient servant, etcetera, etcetera.

The signature was an illegible scrawl. Roc studied the letter with a frown. The firewood bin at The Pilchard? It was
an idiotic order. If the planning of the Jacobite Rebellion had
been handled in likewise fashion, it was no wonder Charles
Stuart had lost.

Who had dared to threaten him? And who knew about The
Pilchard and its wood bin? The questions swirled endlessly
in his tired brain.

"Oh, God, I should have returned the jewels to France
immediately. 'Tis already too late." He sighed, his earlier
pleasure gone. But there hadn't been time to deal with the
box. He'd been concerned with strategies for capturing Dandelion, and the soldiers had had too many questions and
doubts about his plans. Then the arrival of the dowager had
hampered his movements. He couldn't exactly tell her that he
intended to sail to France in the middle of a war.

He rubbed his chin thoughtfully and read the letter again.
Something didn't ring true. The script had an almost childish
tilt. But who knew about the jewels? He hadn't told anyone
in Landregan about them, not even Morgan, whom he trusted
implicitly. He wished he had found out more about the Jacobite contacts in London before Alistair had died in Calais.

He didn't like this business at all. It was as if a sinister
presence was following him, yet he had no idea where the
threat was coming from. A threat it was—there was no doubt
of that. And he didn't believe the Jacobite sympathizers used
threats to get what they wanted. Alistair had insisted that the
messenger would be completely trustworthy. James Murray
had been trustworthy, but he was dead. Perhaps the person
who had written the letter had also killed James . . .

Anger shot through Roc's veins, and frustration. He
slapped the letter onto the blotter. Oh, why did this have to
happen now? Guilt nagged at him for failing to fulfill Alistair's dying wish. Time! He didn't have time to deal with it,

but he might have to find time or risk being arrested for treason, even murdered by the person who coveted the jewels!

When Gwen arrived back at Tremayne House, a handsome carriage she did not recognize was parked outside. Female voices floated from the parlor, and she immediately recognized Lady Louise's piercing tones. Gwen sneaked up the back stairs to change into a morning gown and brush her hair before meeting the guests.

As she approached her bedroom door, she heard a thump inside and a grating noise. She stopped abruptly and leaned her ear against the door. Someone was in her room.

Icy tendrils of fear slid along her spine. Taking a deep breath, she opened the door cautiously. It glided a few inches forward on silent hinges. She peeped inside and was surprised to see Vincent's bony backside sticking up in the air as he crouched to look under the bed.

She slammed the door against the wall, and he jumped guiltily. As she stormed inside, he rose awkwardly to his feet and brushed the dust off his knees.

"What are you doing here?" she demanded, grabbing the fireplace poker for protection. "Answer me!"

He shrugged and had the temerity to laugh. "Thought I'd reacquaint myself with the playgrounds of my childhood," he said smoothly.

"Playgrounds? This room was never your territory, and you know that." She raised the poker threateningly. "You were looking for money, weren't you? Well, I don't have any, so don't ever come back in here."

"Money? Me?" He spread his hands in a gesture of injured innocence. "Have some mercy," he said, his rouged lips parting in an ingratiating smile. He seemed to be thinking of something in particular. "I wanted to see if there were any clues to the Dandelion fellow. I thought I'd help Roc find the miscreant. Gives me something to do in this godforsaken hole."

Gwen narrowed her gaze. Was he telling the truth for once? That could be even more dangerous than his lies. "What makes you think you'd find clues in my bedroom?" Her legs started to tremble, and she realized that Vincent could very well suspect her.

"I've looked in every room on this floor," he said with studied innocence. "But I've found nothing."

She advanced, swinging her poker. "You've lost your common sense, Vinnie. How could you even suspect Father of being involved with a group of uncouth smugglers?"

He stepped away from the poker hovering above his head. Swaggering nonchalantly, he aimed his steps toward the door. "I never said the squire was involved. Good day, Gwen. If I were you, I would have this room redecorated. It's shabby beyond belief." With that parting shot, he closed the door.

Seething, Gwen studied the faded blue bed hangings, the spotted beige wall paper, and the peeling paint in the ceiling. He was right, of course, but this was *her* room. He had no right to tell her what to do.

She rushed against the closed door and kicked it. "Snake!" she called after him. Pain shot up her leg, and she jumped on one leg over to the bed and rubbed her sore toes. "Dash it all!" Vincent was unbearable. She would have to find a way to get rid of him. Perhaps she could get his commanding officer to call him back to the army. Mulling over the thought for a few minutes, she decided it was as good an idea as any. She would write him a letter.

Hobbling over to her escritoire, whose veneer top had bubbled and cracked because of the dampness in the air, she sat down to compose the letter. While sharpening the nib of the quill, she considered the possible reasons for Vincent's presence in her room. Something about him wasn't right.

Unease seeped through her as she tried to figure it out. Suddenly she dropped the quill to the floor. Yes! That was it. Even though he had been carrying his cane, Vincent had not limped at all as he walked out of her room. He had conveniently invented a wound in his thigh . . . but why? She wished she knew. She would have to find out before he discovered her double identity.

After writing the letter, she donned her rose muslin gown, the least faded and worn among her everyday garments, and hurried downstairs, keeping an eye open for Vincent's skulking shadow.

Lady Louise was a vision of loveliness, and her huge green

eyes glittered with pleasure. "Oh, good morning! I could not wait to call on my new friend," the artless girl exclaimed as Gwen entered. Aunt Clo presided over a tray bearing tiny almond cakes, a bowl of bonbons, and a decanter of cordial.

Gwen drew a sigh of relief when she realized that neither Vincent nor the marchioness was present. The young girl was so lovely that envy pinched Gwen momentarily. "How nice of you to come. I'm sorry I wasn't here to meet you." She sighed. How could she be envious of someone who was giving her such a lovely smile? Gwen chided herself. "I took a morning ride."

Lady Louise giggled. "I don't know how you could rise so early after dancing all night. I could never do it. Did you have a pleasant ride?" She nibbled on a bonbon.

"Yes, quite. I encountered the earl. We rode to Fisherman's Creek."

Baffled, she watched as Lady Louise paled and leaned forward. "Did he say he was going to offer for me? 'Tis a horrid thought as I have no desire to marry Roc Tyrrell. Mama has been trying to force his hand, y'know."

"You mean . . . you don't want—?"

"That's exactly what I mean. He's so *old* and so *stuffy* and stern. Entirely without humor, y'know. If Mother forces me to marry him, I will run away. I cannot abide the thought of spending my life with that man. He's positively *frightening.*"

A smile tugged at Gwen's lips. "A veritable ogre, eh?"

"To say the least! He's more your type and age." Lady Louise slapped a hand to her lips. "Oh, I beg your forgiveness for such a rude observation."

"No matter, I know I'm no schoolroom miss," Gwen said with a laugh, ignoring Aunt Clo's disapproving glare. "I daresay times will be lively around Landregan with you at the Hall, Lady Louise."

"I don't know about that, and please call me Louise." She took a deep breath. "Mama disapproves of everything. She's so difficult to please."

"She holds you under tight supervision because you're so lovely. She's afraid some rogue will whisk you away and violate you," Aunt Clo admonished, her nose quivering righteously.

Louise pouted. "I suppose. She treats me like a five-year-old.'' She changed the subject. "How do you entertain your-selves here in Landregan? With all due respect, the village people are somewhat coarse, don't you think?''

"Naturally, but we find excitement at times,'' Gwen said. "There's the pilchard shoals in July, the fair in September, and other activities.''

"Oh, you'll be meaning the smugglers. Yes, that is *so* romantic. I wish I could meet one of them, perhaps go out one night and watch them work.''

Gwen's eyes twinkled mischievously. "And get muddy, wet feet and be manhandled by ruffians? And perhaps get bitten by a rat, not to mention frightened by the hundreds of bats that dart about in the air at night?''

Louise squealed with terror, and Aunt Clo glowered at Gwen.

Gwen smiled at their horrified expressions. "I beg your pardon. How thoughtless of me to paint such revolting im-ages. I'm as countrified as the villagers.''

Louise patted her lips daintily with a lacy scrap of fabric. "Oh, no! You have great style, and you're so *sensible*. I do admire your determination to save your farm; I know I could never do it myself.''

"You would be amazed at how much you can do when forced by narrowed circumstances.''

Louise fidgeted. "How very rude of me to point out your difficulties. I didn't mean—''

The parlor echoed with Gwen's merry laughter. "I'm not going to swoon with outrage, you know. You're very enter-taining company.''

Louise smiled tremulously. "Do you really think so? How very kind you are. I know we'll be great friends. I came here in hope of soliciting your company for a little jaunt around the area. I had hoped you could show me some place where the smugglers hide their brandy, and perhaps give me a gen-eral tour of the village.''

"I would love to do that, but I'm afraid I have no idea where the smugglers hide their goods.''

"But there must be rumors,'' Louise insisted.

"You don't want to get acquainted with that lot,'' Aunt Clo said, aghast.

"There are rumors, of course, but I won't risk meeting

some ruffian with a musket. I quite like to stay alive," Gwen said.

"Muskets? Oooh!" Louise's eyes were saucerlike. "How *utterly romantic!*"

For the second time that day Gwen set out across the hills, this time in the marchioness of Camelford's well-sprung carriage with soft velvet upholstery. As they traveled down the main street of the village, Gwen saw Marva outside Mrs. Padstow's shop at the square. The fat cook waved at her urgently, and Gwen invented an excuse to stop. "Louise, in this shop I believe you could find some really exquisite hair ribbons." She leaned forward and whispered behind her fan, "I declare, they are directly imported from *France.*"

"France?" Louise whispered. "*Smuggled* ribbons?" As Gwen had anticipated, Louise took the bait. As she tripped daintily up to the door with a smile of anticipation on her lips, Gwen called after her, "I'll have a word with our cook in the meantime."

Flustered, Marva handed Gwen a basket of fish for inspection. Puzzled, Gwen lifted the cloth on top of the fish. Under it lay a folded piece of paper. Concealing the note in her hand, she returned the basket. "Superb fish, Marva."

As Gwen stepped into Mrs. Padstow's shop, she burned to read the note, but it would have to wait until she returned home.

Chapter 13

The note bore Clem's illegible scrawl. He explained he was being watched and that they would have to invent another way to communicate. A village urchin, Gus Lane, would come early that evening under the pretext of selling strawberries. She should give her instructions to him.

Gwen paced her bedroom like a caged lioness, feeling an invisible net tightening around her. Clem being watched? It was Roc's doing, of course. How could she avert his ever growing threat? Sooner or later someone would lead him straight to her, and then where would she be? He would hate her for deceiving her, and she found that his opinion mattered terribly to her.

Pain twisted her heart, and tears burned in her eyes. There were no easy answers to her problems. Her desire to cease her lawless activities fought with her need for the income they brought in. She *must* save the family estate.

By the time Gus stood on the kitchen doorstep early that evening, she had a plan.

"Be sure to tell Clem everything I tell you." Thoughtfully she bit into a juicy strawberry as she studied the red-haired boy, the pest of the village. His eyes fearlessly met her own hazel gaze. "This is the plan: signal the *Alouette* to bring in half the cargo to the usual spot at Brandy Cove as soon as they get the sign. Tell Clem I will pay double if the *Alouette* anchors off the coast until the following night and delivers the other half of the casks to the same place. That way we won't be left completely empty-handed when the earl confiscates the first lot."

"Empty-'anded? Gawd no, miss, niver while ye're Dandelion. Ye're awake on all things.'' The child's eyes gleamed with admiration.

Such a full-fledged little scoundrel, Gwen thought with a touch of sadness. In the village the children grew up rapidly.

Gus scratched his head. ''But what if th' 'gentlemen' are caught with th' casks, miss? What then?''

''They will be caught. But not the Landregan 'gentlemen.' And the earl will believe he's confiscated all the brandy.'' She tweaked Gus's nose. ''But he'll be wrong since the rest of the casks will arrive the next night. And remember this: ask Clem to send a message to the Looe smugglers that the kegs are theirs at the dark of the moon, if they come and fetch them.'' She thought for a minute. ''From now on, you'll hang the rags on the stable wall, Gus. No one will suspect you of smuggling, only of stealing food—as always.'' She eyed his bulging pockets with a stern frown.

''Me mum's sick.'' That was one of his more common excuses. The only things keeping Gus and his mother alive were his poaching and her sewing and the proceeds from their strawberry patch in the summer. He was intelligent, quick, and knew everyone in the village.

''Run along and tell Clem what I said,'' added Gwen. ''If he has any questions, come back here and I'll buy some more berries from you.''

She ruffled his hair and earned a brilliant smile. ''Sharp as a needle ye are, miss.'' Whistling, he left, pushing his cart.

The night of the dark of the moon arrived. Even if the moon had been full, it would have been hidden by the bank of clouds hanging humid and heavy over the Channel.

The tension in the village was oppressive. Burning with curiosity, Gwen could not sit at home quietly waiting while her plan was put into motion. As soon as her father and Aunt Clo went to bed, she donned her dark breeches and Arthur's old shirt, and jammed a cocked hat on her head. She simply had to find out what was happening in the village.

Running swiftly through the spinney and along the hedge bordering the lane, she came close enough to hear the curses and catcalls of coarse male voices on the square. Creeping up between two cottages, she saw the reason for their shouts.

Standing in a ring, the men cheered on two scrawny cockerels in the middle. Vulgar epithets abounded as the birds spit and hacked at each other, feathers flying.

Gwen shivered with disgust. How could they stand around watching the poor birds kill each other? Her eyes widened with surprise when she recognized Roc's dark head and powerful shoulders among the men. He was cheering quite as loudly as the others, the wretched man! Even Vincent was there, a gold coin gleaming between his fingers. Gold? Where had he gotten it? She would find out later.

Gwen realized that Roc's purpose for mingling among the villagers was perhaps part of his strategy to catch the smugglers. She had made sure that rumors had been whispered rather loudly around Landregan that a load was expected at Brandy Cove tonight. Was her plan too simple to work?

Most of her smuggling associates were present at the cockfight, the idiots! Well, she shouldn't judge them too harshly since they, too, must be itching to see the result of her plans on this most exciting of nights.

She saw Officer Biggles at the edge of the crowd as well, scratching his head in confusion. He seemed to be wondering how the Landregan men could waste their time on the square betting their hard-earned money when they should be at Brandy Cove bringing in a shipment. There was no sign of red uniforms. Obviously the soldiers were all standing sentinel at strategic spots along the shore.

At midnight Gwen crept to Wrecker's Ruin, which had once been used as a lighthouse to lure ships onto the reefs. There she would have a good view of Brandy Cove. From behind the shadow of a tree she peered into the darkness. The sky was pitch-black, with not even the glimmer of stars to show her some sign of either the smugglers or the soldiers.

The sound of a cough reached her ears. Someone was waiting next to the ruin itself.

A light flashed three times in the bay. The *Alouette* was following instructions. A signal must have been returned from the beach below because the French captain responded with one bright flare.

All was in order. Gwen strained to see the cutter. Since nothing moved on the cliff path, she concluded the Looe men must be in place down at the cove. Holding her breath, she sensed the presence of the other men, the soldiers.

Worried, Gwen waited a whole hour before anything happened. The air quivered with tension, not even the leaves on the trees seeming to move. As she considered leaving her vigil to get a closer look, a snarled curse rent the air.

Suddenly lanterns glimmered, casting the area in eerie, flickering light. The place swarmed with uniforms, and two of the soldiers held a burly, dark-clad man, a sword pointed at his throat.

The Looe smugglers were captured like mice in a trap. Gwen clapped her hands to her ears to shut out some of their foulest epithets. Clem had done his part well. The Looe men had taken the bait without a single question. They were greedy beyond belief. Gwen felt no compassion for the ruffians; a more surly and uncharitable group would be hard to find.

Mounted on Tristan, Roc arrived on the scene to take command.

Confident that both Roc and her adversaries had learned a lesson, Gwen left her lookout point. Tomorrow she would hear all about the arrests.

And she did. After a restful night, she descended bright-eyed to the dining room to partake of a hearty breakfast. Her nightly vigil had improved her appetite immensely.

Marva stood at the table, hands on hips, a distraught look on her face as she related the night's events. In her excitement Aunt Clo even failed to remind Marva that her place was in the kitchen, an unheard-of lapse.

". . . and there they were, these big louts from Looe, bound together with chains. It gave me th' shivers to see their scowlin' faces. Did th' sign against th' evil eye, I did, and 'urried on past. They were swearin' somethin' awful. It rightly scared me out o' me wits. Th' Landregan men bain't such a rough lot—"

Aunt Clo drank in the information avidly. "And what were the men from Looe doing here?" She licked her lips in obvious anticipation of Marva's next words.

"Aye, ye should arsk that question, Miss Pettigrew. Seems our lads 'ad some fun last night. Them louts from Looe swore our lads 'ad sneaked a load onto th' Looe territory last month, and then attacked a pair o' men with cudgels. This was their way o' gettin' even. The Landregan men were all on th' square this mornin', cool as cucumbers, swearin' they'd niver been involved in any smugglin'—especially not in Looe.''

Noticing Gwen, Marva said, ''Ah, good mornin' to ye, Miss Gwen. Just tellin' yer aunt 'ow them Looe smugglers got their comeuppance.'' She turned once more to Aunt Clo. ''*Somebody* must've sprung a trap on th' rogues, and I'm glad they did.'' She winked mischievously at the baffled spinster. ''Ye mark my words, Miss Pettigrew, 'twas the work o' that Dandelion. A sharp 'un if ye ever saw one.''

Gwen sent the gleeful cook a warning glance and turned to Aunt Clo. ''Have you ever heard such a preposterous story? I collect Marva has made it up to entertain us this morning.'' She seated herself with a plate of smoked ham, toast, and eggs before her.

The cook fixed her with a grim glare, as did her aunt. ''Made up th' story? Niver! 'Tis God's truth.''

''*You'd* naturally consider it an exciting adventure, Gwen,'' Aunt Clo commented with a sigh. ''I'm eternally grateful that you were not involved.'' With a wave of her hand, she tried to shoo Marva out of the room, but Gwen saved the cook from such a horrid fate.

''And what are they going to do with the smugglers?'' she asked guilelessly.

With an air of importance, Marva puffed out her considerable chest. ''I was just comin' to that afore ye interrupted me.'' She glanced furtively at Aunt Clo, who clearly wanted to hear the rest of the story. The spinster pursed her lips with disapproval, but finally allowed the cook to stay and finish her tale.

''Th' earl was there th' whole time, barkin' questions at th' prisoners. 'E was in a state, I tell ye, wanted to 'ang th' fellas right then and there. 'E's sendin' 'em back to Looe, to be punished by th' magistrate there.''

Gwen released a sigh of relief. The magistrate in Looe was as loose as any of the smugglers in his district. The Looe men were bound to go free with only a warning. Her intention had never been to ruin their business, since the Looe villagers were just as poor as the people of Landregan. But Marva's next words echoed ominously in the room. ''Th' earl's put signs in Mrs. Padstow's shop and at Th' Pilchard. 'E's goin' to pay a right large sum to get information on Dandelion.''

Gwen chuckled. ''The earl is making more enemies every day.''

''Right testy 'e was, if yer arsk me. Awake all night, most likely, lyin' in ambush down at th' water.''

Good, then he'll sleep like an infant tonight. Gwen gloated over her audacious plan. ''Well, you have not yet told us what the earl plans to do with all that brandy he confiscated.''

''Gwennie!'' Aunt Clo admonished, but her protest was lame. She turned expectantly to Marva.

''Aye, now to th' worst part.'' Marva slammed her meaty fist down on the table, making plates and glasses rattle. '' 'E's goin' to 'ave all that good brandy flowin' in th' gutter. I 'ave a mind to go there with an empty bottle and get me somethin' to warm me nights.''

''Marva! Have you no decency in your big body?'' Aunt Clo burst out.

''Aye, I do, but th' earl doesn't—a loose fish if I ever saw 'un. Bah!'' The cook bristled. ''All them stray cats and dogs'll be a-swillin' up that good brandy, and they'll be a-'owlin' and a-caterwaulin' all night, mark me words.'' She turned a ferocious eye on the sniffing aunt.

Gwen, stifling a laugh, said, ''The kegs are still in the square then?''

''Aye, that they are, and much talked about. I'd go and get me a keg if I thought I could get away with it. Bring me a cart, and—''

''That is quite enough, Marva!'' exclaimed Aunt Clo. ''I'm sure you've things to do in the kitchen.''

Marva clearly had more to say, but after a quelling glance from Aunt Clo, she changed her mind and waddled out of the room, muttering to herself. Still, she had sowed a seed in Gwen's fertile mind. How could she steal all that brandy back from the square? It rightfully belonged to the Landregan smugglers, after all.

Marva called her to the kitchen. ''Gus be 'ere, miss. Ye want any o' 'is berries?''

Still chewing a piece of toast, Gwen nipped into the kitchen.

Gus pulled his forelock. "Mornin', miss. I've some extra fine berries today."

Gwen followed him outside and pretended to take her time choosing the largest and most succulent in his cart. "I've heard of last night's business, Gus. Tell Clem he did a fine job, and that I have something more for him to do today. Listen carefully."

Gus's eyes widened in surprise. "Somethin' else, miss?"

"Tell Clem he should collect twenty empty kegs, fill them with water, and bring them to the square—out of sight, of course." She paused for a moment, pensive. "How many guards are stationed there?"

"Two, miss, and burly 'uns they are."

"Tell Clem to wear some sort of disguise to escape recognition. He should bring sacks to throw over the guards' heads and then bind them. 'Twill be easy to make away with the brandy and replace the kegs with others filled with water." She held his bony shoulders in a firm grip. "Tell him to be extremely cautious. He should act only if he considers it safe. If the earl is about, then under no circumstances should Clem do it. Do you understand?"

"Aye, miss." His face filled with admiration. "Ye 'ave things in yer 'ead, miss."

Gwen laughed. "The 'thing' is called a devious mind, Gus. I suppose one must keep up the game—to keep the earl busy."

" 'E'll be ravin' mad," Gus commented with glee.

"Inform Clem I will be at the square at exactly three o'clock. The guards should be sleepy and bored by then, and not very attentive. And remember, no unnecessary risks."

She knew her cautioning words would fall on deaf ears. When Clem found out about this latest plan, he would be ready to act instantly. But then, he thrived on the threat of danger. Still she worried she had placed him in peril with her mad scheme.

The afternoon crept forward on leaden feet. Gwen paced her room, too tense to do anything but think about the rendezvous in the square at three. At half past two she dressed in her riding habit and went out to fetch Buttercup from the stables.

The square was quiet. A couple of matrons milled about outside Mrs. Padstow's shop, two very large women whom

Gwen did not recognize. The two dragoons patrolled lazily back and forth around the stack of dripping kegs.

"Good afternoon," Gwen greeted them loudly.

The soldiers' faces brightened when they recognized her cheerful countenance. "Miss Tremayne," they said in unison and dashed off their hats.

"So these are the famous brandy kegs. Imagine the impudence of those blackguards. How they succeed in their business is beyond me."

"Blackguards they are, Miss Tremayne," one of them replied.

"Frightening scoundrels, to be sure." She prattled on for a few minutes, making much of the kegs. "Well, I must be about my errands. I do hope you will be relieved soon. You are so very brave to do this dangerous work. I vow we will have no peace until those smugglers are caught."

" 'Twill not be long now, miss," the other soldier responded confidently. "They're thoroughly shaken up by what we've done to them—taking their booty. They were too scared to even show up last night and claim it. The Landregan smugglers are a cowardly lot."

Gwen inwardly seethed at the insult. "Well, I'm certain you'll apprehend the villains any day now. Oh, by the way, where are your fellow dragoons? They ought not leave you alone here."

The men in uniform laughed heartily. "I'm sure we can guard a few kegs, miss. On the orders of the earl, the others are escorting the smugglers back to Looe, with that dimwit Officer Biggles to make the report. With him at the helm, they're not likely to return until late this evening."

From the corner of her eye Gwen saw the women at the shop avidly following her progress, and her heart rose into her throat. It couldn't be! Abruptly, she turned back to the soldiers. "Oh, how very tedious to watch these kegs for hours. But I'm certain you will contrive very well. Ta-ta." Gwen bestowed on them her sweetest smile and rode off, seemingly at ease. But inside she was quivering with dread.

She had recognized Clem as one of the "women" outside the shop and could barely restrain herself from turning back and staring at him. Garbed as he was in a voluminous black dress, apron, and a huge mobcap pulled low over his face, he presented a fairly convincing matron. But his biceps strained the fabric to its limits, and Gwen suspected that his pockets contained a heavy stone to use as a weapon if necessary. She halted Buttercup at the end of the lane at the bottom of the hill, a hand pressed over her pounding heart. Why had she urged Clem to try this mad scheme? How careless she had been, asking him to risk capture for a few casks of brandy. If he got caught, it would be her fault entirely.

She had to force herself up the hill even though she wanted to ride back and tell Clem to forget the plan. But now it was too late. When she had reached the top, she heard a cry coming from the square. She glanced at the watch pinned to the jacket of her habit. Three o'clock. Straining her ears, she listened for more shouts, but nothing untoward happened. The crashing of the breakers and the chatter of birds were the only sounds.

The only thing she could do now was to return home and wait for news. What torture!

She had never spent a longer day, and supper became an uncomfortable affair with her aunt's incessant prattle, Vincent's stony silence, and her father's monosyllabic replies. During the dessert of strawberries and cream he startled Gwen by uttering a few whole sentences.

"They will surely be captured soon, the smugglers of Landregan." He dribbled some cream down the front of his shirt. "Deuced odd spoon," he muttered, and dabbed ineffectually at his chest.

"What are you hinting at, Papa?" Gwen's fingers clenched around her spoon until her knuckles whitened. "Have you perhaps heard or seen something? You must not keep us in suspense like this."

"I took a walk down to the Padstow shop to buy more ink, and I saw an extremely disturbing sight." He peered at her over the top of his spectacles. "You will not think I've lost my wits, eh?"

Gwen patted his hand. "Of course not. We know you have all your wits about you."

" 'Twas very quiet on the square, everyone indoors and no uniforms as far as my eye could see." The squire blew out his cheeks, his eyes bulging. "Only three large women were about, rolling brandy casks down the street." He snorted. "Very ramshackle of the earl to leave that brandy unguarded in the middle of the square, if you ask me. And since when have helpless women taken to stealing?"

Aunt Clo sat as still as a statue, her eyes wide with outrage. "I truly believe you've been looking too deeply into your own brandy bottle, Lionel. Women? Nonsense!"

The squire scowled at her. "I swear they were women, one wearing a wide hat with plumes, another wearing a mob-cap." His face lightened. "Could have been that dragon dowager countess—a most disconcerting female, and built quite like a barn door, too."

"Father, under no circumstances could any of the women have been the dowager." Gwen almost burst with suppressed laughter at the thought. "You know how opposed the earl is to the smuggling business. None of his family—"

"Naught but a young pup, that earl," the squire maintained. "Dammit, I'm glad they got away with the brandy. You know, they must have had it all planned. When one keg was rolled off the square, another was rolled on, and so it continued until all of them were replaced. I watched the whole procedure."

"Papa! That could have been dangerous. Those smugglers are a wild lot."

"Pshaw! What would they do to a peaceful man like me? And it all happened so rapidly, before you could spit. What bothers me is that those women must have come from some other village; we have no females in Landregan built like that. I mean to inform the earl of that fact, to keep him from pestering our village women with questions. There is no end to his dipping his nose into our affairs."

"He's the magistrate, Papa. He's doing all he can to uphold law and order." Gwen could have danced around the room with relief. Clem and the men had gotten away with their most impertinent act so far. Roc would be furious when he found out. More than furious—*livid*.

Gwen felt a twinge of guilt, but it passed quickly.

"In broad daylight . . . who could have believed such a feat of a few women," the squire mused, rapidly losing interest in the subject. "I don't know what this world is coming to."

Aunt Clo eyed Gwen with a dazed look. "I tell you, Lionel has gone over—"

Gwen shook her head in warning.

The squire had already forgotten their presence, his face buried once more in a book.

"Father knew what he saw. How very intriguing for it to happen in the middle of our village. I wish I could have seen it," Gwen said.

Aunt Clo regarded her with frigid hauteur. " 'Tis very unladylike to harbor sympathy for the smugglers, and well you know it. Such unlawful behavior should be quelled at all costs."

Gwen snorted with glee. "On your high horses again, Aunt?" Her eyes twinkling, she teased, "But how could a foreigner from Devon feel any of the wildness flowing in our Cornish veins?"

Aunt Clo sniffed, her mouth pursed into a disapproving button. "Your unladylike behavior will be the death of me yet, you mark my words," she said.

Chapter 14

Gwen took great care not to make any noise as she slunk out the kitchen door late that night to execute the second part of her plan. She was determined to be present when the Frenchmen delivered the rest of the kegs. Darkness enfolded her like a warm, cozy blanket, and in her black clothes she looked like one of the shadows cast by the thin sickle moon.

While the village still buzzed with the news of the brandy stolen from the square, the Landregan smugglers would go to work. Tonight they did not have to worry about being caught. The soldiers were enjoying a well-earned rest, drinking ale at The Pilchard, and Officer Biggles lay sleeping in his bed. Gwen had no knowledge of Roc's whereabouts, and as a precaution she had asked Clem to find out. He would report to her at Wrecker's Ruin.

Laughter and song flowed from The Pilchard as she passed the inn at a safe distance. The soldiers were drowning their sorrows in ale this evening. Having been robbed of the kegs in broad daylight by some rawboned females, they must feel they had completely lost face. After today's failure it would be next to impossible for them to regain the villagers' respect.

A strong wind blowing in from the sea moaned eerily through the broken windows of Wrecker's Ruin. Gwen looked down at the water, a black moving mass glittering like jet in the weak moonlight.

"Psst, Miss Gwen," came Clem's harsh whisper over the soughing wind. He was hidden in the deep shadows along the ruin wall.

She joined him, chuckling. "The squire gave me full ac-

128

count of what happened this afternoon. I must tell you I have never been more nervous in my life! It was a foolhardy plan. I don't know what got into me."

Clem chortled. "A right good plan 'twas, miss. I would niver 'ave thought o' it, and th' Looe men got their come-uppance."

Gwen frowned, deep in thought. "As long as they did not mention any names to the magistrate in Looe."

"Naw, they bain't that stupid, miss. Anyway, they don't know Dandelion's true identity."

"Well, the earl will know by now that we pulled in the last load at Looe. We can't do it again, and we can never repeat today's tricks." She tried to see his face in the darkness. "Perhaps someone recognized you at the square to-day. 'Twould be better if you stayed away from smuggling for a time, Clem, until Roc's suspicions are lulled. Tonight the best thing for you to do is to be seen at The Pilchard. I'll use some of the other men to help me take in the rest of the load."

Clem sighed in exasperation. "Naw, miss, 'twill be fine, ye'll see. I want to help ye."

She gripped his sturdy biceps and shook him. "You'll do what I tell you, without a sour face, is that clear?"

"Aye, miss, ye're the master. I'll do it if ye think 'tis for th' best," he said bitterly.

"Come now, Clem, no grimaces. You've done enough for one day. As soon as the earl discovers that no bear-sized females live in the area, his suspicions will turn back to you. By the way, where is he this evening? Did Alfie tell you?"

" 'E's at Th' Pilchard swillin' ale with th' soldiers. Foxed, too. Seems he was lurkin' behind th' inn, stumblin' into the wood bin, after spendin' all afternoon broodin' in 'is study."

"Hmm. Why should he be at The Pilchard, of all places?"

"Alfie said 'e yelled somethin' 'bout 'avin' enough 'ell for one day. Bought a round of ale for everyone."

"Oh." Gwen laughed and relaxed. The fact that Roc could feel compassion for the soldiers so brutally teased by the smugglers warmed her heart. Obviously he didn't suspect that anything was about to happen tonight.

"Be off, Clem, and make sure to keep the earl's tankard full until this load is safely stowed in Mrs. Padstow's cellar."

They dared not hide the casks in one of the usual spots since their pursuers were sure to snoop around for the kegs stolen from the square. She pressed a purse into his hand. "This should buy plenty of ale."

Clem laid his meaty hands lightly on her shoulders. "Ye be careful now, d'ye 'ear, Miss Gwennie."

Three lantern signals from the sea pierced the darkness.

" 'Tis time, Miss Gwen; I'll flash th' lantern afore I go. Ye can go to th' men down at th' cove. Th' carts are waitin' at th' top o' th' path."

Gwen crept along the rocky outcrop above Brandy Cove, alert for sudden movements. Only the wind stirred in the furze, carrying an invigorating sea breeze.

Although their numbers were drastically diminished this night, the haul went smoothly, and they stowed the brandy in Mrs. Padstow's cellar. They did not have to worry about any interference from the soldiers since The Pilchard was located closer to the harbor, at the other end of the village. As the smugglers dispersed into the night, pushing their carts and barrows before them, Gwen heaved a trembling sigh of relief. She could relax at last.

Exhausted, she crept through a hedge and started for Tremayne House. A wild idea crossed her mind. She yearned to see for herself that Roc was really spending these late hours at The Pilchard.

As she neared the inn, she repeatedly saw men reeling through the door, evidently needing to relieve themselves of all the ale they had imbibed during the long evening.

How could she spy through the window without being detected? She sneaked along the wall, berating herself for indulging in another of her idiotic schemes. She recognized Clem as he staggered through the door, drunk and singing loudly.

Grease and dust covered the window, but she could make out the men at the tables, most of them soldiers. Disjointed singing and shouting echoed within the walls, and the proprietor, Mr. Trelawny, was doing a splendid business, although no French brandy saw the outer side of the counter.

Gwen's breath caught in her throat as her gaze landed on Roc's commanding figure. She studied him carefully, noting that his face bore no mark of drunken stupor. In a flash she knew what he was doing—listening for information in the rough talk going on around him. Her glance crept from one face to another. Half of her men were there, all very drunk. Biting her lip in worry, she wished they had been more prudent in their consumption of spirits.

Leaving her vigil in front of the window, she waited anxiously until Clem returned, his steps unsteady. Under the wide canopy of an oak, she gripped his arm and hauled him into the concealing blackness.

"Whatsit? Naw—wait a minit . . ." he started.

"Shhh, 'tis me." Gwen placed a hand over his mouth, and he stiffened, obviously pulling himself together. She let her hand fall.

"Miss Gwen! Somethin' amiss?"

"No, the business went well. Has someone said anything about the load tonight, or about the events on the square? The earl looks like a hawk hunting for prey."

"Eh . . . naw, 'e's as silly as th' rest o' us," Clem insisted.

Exasperated, Gwen shook his sleeve. "Don't you see? He's only pretending. You have to be careful what you say. He's out for blood, y'know. Our blood."

"Ye're worryin' too much, Miss Gwen. 'E a nice bloke—sometimes."

Gwen took him by the lapels of his coarse leather vest, and her voice rang cold with authority. "Now listen to me. You tell the men to go home, quietly, one after the other. Do you understand? Everything we have worked for might be lost if one word slips from their slack mouths."

"Very well, I'll tell 'em." Clem had sobered enough to see the importance of her statement. "I'll see to it, miss."

" 'Tis in everyone's best interests. Besides, it must be close on three o'clock, almost morning. We should all be in bed by now." With a final tug on his lapels, Gwen fled into the night, worry still plaguing her. Deep in thought, she almost ran into a man rounding the corner of the inn. But he didn't seem to hear her, and she slunk into the cover of the hedge. There was something familiar about the man, the mincing steps, the exaggerated swinging of his arms. Cousin Vincent! She had been right before about the wound in his leg. It was mere fabrication. Her heart thundered in fear. Had he seen her? She had not noticed him at the inn, but he was whistling softly and his steps weren't straight.

She followed him all the way home and saw him glance furtively around the yard before slinking in the back door, and closing it soundlessly behind him.

Gwen burned to know what errand had brought him out in the middle of the night. She listened at his door before continuing to her own room, but all was quiet.

As she tossed and turned in bed, Gwen searched for an answer to Vincent's odd behavior. A net of threats was closing in around her. It would be so easy to make a false step. Not only that, but by deceiving Roc she had further destroyed any possibility of future happiness with him. He would never forgive her if he found out the truth. Roc was a formidable enemy. One wrong step, and poof! Like a dandelion seed puff in a ripple of wind, she would be no more.

The next morning Gwen invented an excuse to go into the village and visit Mrs. Padstow's shop. She wanted to buy embroidery yarn for the canvas she had been working on the last two years.

Entering the perpetual dusk of the old shop, she stopped to let her eyes adjust to the dimness.

"Mornin', Miss Tremayne," greeted Mrs. Padstow cheerfully.

Gwen nodded to the rotund woman behind the counter. "Good morning, Mrs. Padstow."

"A perishin' mornin' if ye arsk me. Looks like rain."

"And well we need it if the apples are going to be full of juice this fall," came a man's deep voice from the opposite end of the shop.

Startled, Gwen realized Mrs. Padstow had another customer—Roc. He bowed deeply, sweeping his cocked hat off his head. "Enchanted," he greeted Gwen smoothly. To her surprise, no evidence of his lack of sleep lingered on his face. Her heart constricted with love as his gaze raked over her. She felt positively dowdy in her faded paisley gown, apron, and plain cap atop her curls.

"You look a trifle drawn, m'dear. Are you working too hard?" Roc inquired smoothly.

Gwen opened her fan and fluttered it nervously in front of her face. "Not at all; 'tis just the oppressive heat. You look quite ragged yourself.'' Would he admit to having spent most of the night at The Pilchard?

"Really? Well, I had a hectic day yesterday. You must have heard about Dandelion's latest trick." He tapped his fingertips on the wooden countertop and surveyed her through narrowed eyes.

Gwen raised her eyebrows in feigned surprise. "No, what has he done now?" With bated breath she waited for his next words. Had her men slipped him information, or was he still blundering in the dark about last night's illicit haul?

"Those barrels outside"—he motioned toward the square—"contain nothing but water. The scoundrels came away with the kegs of brandy while the soldiers spent a frustrating afternoon in Looe, trying to convince the indifferent magistrate there that his villagers had committed a crime. Bribery goes on there, if I'm not mistaken."

"Oh, dear." Gwen deliberately colored her voice with distress. So he had not found out about the haul in the night. Not yet, anyway.

"Having this problem with Dandelion constantly on my brain must be addling my senses," he continued. "I could swear there is a smell of brandy in here."

Gwen held her breath. He was right! The faint but unmistakable scent of brandy permeated the air. "It must be from those kegs out there, baking in the heat. The wood's impregnated with the smell." She wanted him to get out of the shop immediately before he found the brandy in the cellar, and before Mrs. Padstow, who only let the smugglers use her cellar in dire emergencies, could be incriminated.

Gwen turned to the shopkeeper. "Could you match this silk, please?" She placed a thread of indigo hue on the counter. While Mrs. Padstow rummaged through her boxes, Gwen faced Roc and smiled sweetly. "Would you care for a cup of tea at Tremayne House, to soothe your nerves?"

He laughed derisively. "Very kind of you to offer, but only a solution to the Dandelion problem will soothe my nerves," he retorted. "Why is everyone so damned evasive in this village? If you'll excuse my rude language." He pushed his fingers through his hair, mussing it. "What lunatic village is this, anyway?"

Gwen glowered at him. "This is Landregan, whose praises

you once sung so loudly. But I suppose you've already forgotten." She shifted her hand from her waist to mimic his tapping on the counter. "And I've explained before why people do not want to give you any information. Things were peaceful around here until you arrived."

He muttered something unintelligible, probably a curse. She noticed the stubborn set of his chin and knew for certain he would not rest until he had captured the smugglers. Her profitable profession had turned into a tricky game that was becoming more and more dangerous.

" 'Ere we go.'Tis the closest I've got." Mrs. Padstow held up a skein of silk to the light coming from the window. The shade looked close enough. At that point Gwen didn't care if it was indigo or black. She counted out a few coins from her frayed purse and slipped the silk into her pocket, her fingers trembling. With Roc staring at her so intensely, she imagined he could see to the bottom of her black heart. He stood very still, waiting.

Brightly she said, "Are you still interested in that cup of tea, Roc?" Even to her own ears her voice sounded brittle, tense. "Come, don't be such a curmudgeon. We'll leave that to the squire." She laid her hand on his arm, and to avoid being rude, he was forced to escort her outside.

From the corner of her eye, Gwen saw Mrs. Padstow heave a sigh of relief as they left the shop.

"I hope you'll excuse me, Gwen," said Roc, "but I have a great many questions to ask in the dwellings around the square. I'll have to get to the bottom of this infamous theft." Roc bowed, and Gwen felt a spurt of disappointment.

"Of course. Give my greetings to Lady Louise," she called after him as he rapidly strode away, pretending not to hear her words.

She watched as he knocked on the door of the first cottage. She imagined him sticking his nose inside the door and sniffing for the missing brandy kegs. She prayed he would not snoop around Mrs. Padstow's cellar, since those last kegs could not be moved until later in the week, once the commotion had died down. On the next dark of the moon the "gentlemen" of Landregan would have a difficult time, indeed, she thought grimly.

Chapter 15

"I think I will explode!" Roc exclaimed to himself as he finished searching the last cottage on the square. Dandelion had really made a fool of him this time, and it was too much to bear. He stalked across the square to fetch Tristan hitched to a post outside Mrs. Padstow's shop. "I'll find that devil if 'tis the last thing I do," he muttered as he swung into the saddle.

He had heard the villagers snicker behind his back as he searched their dwellings. They knew full well who Dandelion was, or they could have directed him to a smuggler who knew Dandelion's identity. But they all continued to play dumb.

"Blast and confound!" He rode up the lane toward Landregan Hall. To his right was the sea and The Pilchard. The inn bustled with activity. A maid was scrubbing the steps, and the ostlers were strapping a team of horses to a carriage. He could see the corner of the outhouse and the wood bin behind the hostelry.

Not only had Dandelion eluded him, but the scalawag who had sent him the threatening letter had never shown up at The Pilchard last night. Not that he had placed the leather box of jewelry in the bin. After looking twice in the wood bin, he had decided he could not stand around waiting for whoever wanted the jewels without raising questions. There had been no strangers present at the inn, only the local men, readily drinking anything he would pay for. And not a single clue to Dandelion's identity had slipped past their lips.

Roc ground his teeth in frustration and spurred Tristan on. It was more than he could take. If only he could penetrate the wall of mystery surrounding Dandelion. There had to be a way! And when would he find an opportunity to travel back to France with the Jacobite jewels? The problems facing him on all fronts were growing more formidable.

As he rode along the road leading up to Tremayne House, he remembered Gwen's invitation to take tea. He needed something to cheer him up after this disastrous morning. Resting his gaze on her lively face would certainly help.

He rode to the stables and slid out of the saddle. A large white rag was hanging by a nail on the stable wall. He lifted it off the nail and wiped down Tristan's sweaty neck and flanks. The stallion was suffering in the heat, and flies swarmed around him. Two brown hens pecked on the hard-packed stable yard, and a black cat slunk around the corner of the old stone building.

Roc looked toward the house and saw Vincent Tremayne standing in one of the windows. What was that ne'er-do-well doing in these parts for weeks on end? Roc frowned, realizing he was worried about Gwen's relationship to Vincent. Would there be wedding bells ere long? A hot surge of jealousy coursed through him at the thought. Fuming, he strode toward the door. The sound of a woman's singing wafted from the back garden. Roc recognized Gwen's clear voice and changed his direction, following the sweet sound.

The garden was surrounded by a stone wall. He stopped in the arched opening, watching her. Digging with a shovel, she obviously hadn't heard him. She was weeding among the raspberry canes, at the moment bending over to extract a stubborn thistle. He had an excellent view of her bosom in the low decolletage, and a hot, prickly sensation traveled down his spine. He remembered the feel of those round globes, the silky texture of her skin. Something tugged at the depths of his heart, an unfamiliar sensation of protectiveness and urgency. He wanted to rush forward, crush her to him, and never let go. He chided himself for his fierce attraction. Since returning home to Landregan, he had lost control over his life. It was as if outside forces—Dandelion, the Jacobite jewels, his family, and last but not the least, Gwendolyn—had taken over, guiding his every step. He felt trapped, agitated, as if hounded by a strange, invisible beast.

Gwen took the lace scarf hanging loosely over her upper arms and draped it over a branch. Her skin glowed with perspiration in the summer heat, and Roc could barely contain himself. His overwhelming need infuriated him. More in her presence than in that of any other, he felt vulnerable, out of control, and he didn't particularly like the novel feeling. He hoped she couldn't sense his weakness, because he couldn't bear to have her laugh at him—like the villagers.

Gwen was trying to think of a way to bring in the cargo in August. As Clem had said, the *Seahawk* might be the only solution. She wanted to win her bet with Roc to get her locket back, but so much more was at stake. Under no circumstances could she endanger her loyal men because of her own recklessness.

She pulled a folded handkerchief from her pocket and dabbed at her bosom, then at her neck. It was one of the warmest days of the year, and she had to be out in the heat digging weeds. However much she tried to control them, she could never keep the borders neat.

She raised her gaze and gasped as she saw Roc lounging against the stone wall.

"What are you doing here?" she asked brusquely to cover her confusion. He looked tired and defeated.

"You invited me to tea, remember?" He sauntered forward, his gaze riveted on her bosom.

"You turned me down quite churlishly, so I had no hope you would accept." She snatched the lace scarf from the branch and draped it around her shoulders, then crossed it over her chest.

"A pity," he mused, a smile hovering on his lips.

"Pity? What pity?" But she knew very well what he meant. She folded her arms self-consciously over her shawl. "I'll ask Marva to serve us tea in the rose arbor."

"How romantic," he murmured and stepped closer. "I hope the rose arbor smells as arousing as you do." He sighed, coloring slightly. "When I'm around you, I seem to forget to be courteous. I apologize, but 'tis all your fault."

"My fault?" Gwen blushed. "What have I done now?"

"Just being yourself is enough of a crime." He reached out and touched a stray curl at her brow. She hastily clamped it down with a pin.

"Crime?" she whispered. All the blood seemed to be

draining from her head. Had he discovered that she was Dandelion?

" 'Tis a crime what you do to a man's senses. If we weren't in full view of the windows, I would sweep you into my arms and forget that I ever was a gentleman."

Gwen took a step back. "Then I'm glad we're in full view of the windows." She gave him a teasing smile. "And if it will make you feel any better, I assure you I don't let anyone touch me without my consent." Yet, despite her words, she yearned for his touch, glad that the barrier he had erected between them after the arduous kiss at the ball appeared to be crumbling.

"I swear I've tried to behave properly in your company," he said, "but somehow you always change me into a bee. You're the nectar, of course."

"How very gallant you are this morning." She fled from his dangerous proximity and asked Marva through the open kitchen window to bring tea.

When she turned back, he was right behind her. "Is the rose arbor also in full view?" he asked.

"Well, 'tis surrounded by climbing roses, but not wholly secluded—thank God." She was suddenly afraid of the hot light in his eyes. He stirred up such a need within her, a churning emotion she had never thought possible when she had dreamed of him over the years. His presence was so much more than the remembered image of old. Before his arrival she had fantasized about him at night, wondering what his touch would be like. Now she tossed and turned—knowing but not knowing enough. His touch brought chaos to her senses. She jerked her arm away as his fingers closed around her elbow.

"Oh, I'm sorry, I didn't mean to frighten you."

"I wasn't expecting your touch," she said, having difficulty breathing. She hurried along the brick path toward the rose arbor at the very end of the garden. A richness of blossoms bent the branches over the wooden benches and sent out an intoxicating scent in the warm sunlight.

"An enchanted place, isn't it?" he said, and nipped off a full red rose. He tucked it gingerly into the V where the scarf crossed on her bosom. "There. The perfume will put you in a romantic mood."

I am already romantically inclined, her mind yelled at him, but she only smiled demurely and sat down on the edge of the white wooden seat. "Tell me, did you find the brandy on the square?"

His bemused smile disappeared. He sighed heavily and sat down beside her. Instead of really listening to his complaints about the smugglers, she concentrated on the feel of his thigh against hers. How would it feel to slide her hand along the ridge of his hard muscles underneath the gray material of his breeches?

"—but I'll catch him, I assure you. Dandelion has met his nemesis."

She was startled out of her wanton reverie. "Nemesis?"

A vein at his temple throbbed, and his eyes blazed. He stabbed his thumb into his chest. "*I* am his nemesis. I can be quite as stubborn as that 'weed' who calls himself a friend of the poor."

She placed a soothing hand on his arm. "Don't take on so, Roc. I'm sure you'll be the one to capture Dandelion—when no one else has managed."

"Was there a suggestion of derision in your voice, m'dear?" he asked suspiciously.

Gwen arranged her face into a particularly bland expression. "You're too sensitive about the subject."

He snatched off another rose. "And so would you be in my situation."

"I haven't forgotten our wager, Roc. I take it as a game, and so should you, although I sincerely hope you never catch Dandelion."

"A game!" He stood up, looming over her. "You would not see it as a game if you had to suffer the villagers' smirks and leers."

She smiled, unperturbed although her heart thumped uncomfortably in her chest. "They know how to enjoy good entertainment." She gently sniffed the rose in her cleavage and peeked at him through her eyelashes. He was flushed with outrage, and his fingers flexed as if he was longing for a convenient neck to strangle.

He restrained himself admirably and threw himself on the seat, disgust evident in his expression. "I think we should close the subject for today. I'm too angry to talk about it."

Gwen decided that suggestion was prudent, especially when she remembered the brandy in Mrs. Padstow's cellar.

Marva ambled along the brick path carrying a heavy tray. A mustache of perspiration gleamed on her upper lip as she bent to place the tray on the table. "Ye shouldn't be sittin' 'ere alone with th' likes o' 'im, Miss Gwen," she said, grunting as she dragged a fat forearm across her forehead.

"Why?" Gwen asked.

Marva pinioned Roc with a baleful stare. " 'E means to turn yer 'ead with sweet words." She motioned toward the roses. "That's what this place was built for. Yer father proposed to yer mother in 'ere. Very sweet-like—although I would niver marry someone like th' sqi— ahem, I mean like— Here's yer tea." She slopped tea in the cups to cover up her *faux pas*. "Fresh scones."

"Proposed? Father? No one ever told me about that," Gwen said in baffled tones.

"Yes, that 'e did. The Misses Pettigrew were going a-visitin' one o' th' estates close to Fowey when their carriage broke down 'ere in Landregan. They stayed at Th' Pilchard whilst it was repaired. Yer father fell like a stone for yer beautiful mother and proposed within a fortnight."

"He never does anything if he can help it, so he truly must have fallen in love." Bittersweet nostalgia swept through Gwen, and she wished her mother was here to comfort and guide her. There was so much she wanted to ask her, especially how to deal with the wild feelings in her heart and body. Had her mother ever known such breath-stopping attraction as she felt in Roc's presence?

"Well, th' squire wasn't always like 'e is today, devoted to 'is studies." Marva took a long look at Roc. "Miss Gwen, ye should not be 'ere alone with 'im.'Tis not proper."

"When did I ever care about propriety?" Gwen asked lightly and handed Roc a cup and a scone on a plate. She hoped her mortification didn't show on her face.

Marva placed her hands on her hips, maintaining the role of formidable guardian. " 'Tis about time ye did, missy." She moved not an inch, keeping her gaze riveted on Roc's face as he hastily devoured his tea. At last he stood.

"I suppose I should bow to authority and be off, then. Thank you for the tea," he said, and smiled at Gwen.

She nodded ruefully. "I warned you this arbor was in view of the house."

He chuckled, and Marva snorted as he bent to kiss Gwen's fingertips. *"Au revoir,* my sweet," he whispered. "Meet me here at midnight."

"Never!" she said. "That would be foolhardy."

"I have a feeling there is quite an adventurous streak in you," he murmured as he straightened. "One day soon I'll find out for sure." To Marva's outrage he bent and planted a kiss on the cook's round cheek. "I would not have accepted those insulting words from anyone but yourself, Marva. I still shiver in my boots when I remember how hard you spanked my bottom with your broom twenty-five years ago."

Marva bristled. "And ye deserved it all—and more, for stealin' me freshly baked blueberry pie."

He laughed, and Gwen watched his broad back disappear around a swaying rose bush. When he was out of sight, she turned to Marva. "What has gotten into you?" she asked with an angry glare.

"Why, I saw 'ow 'e looked at ye—as if 'e wanted to devour ye whole." She straightened her fat back. "I'd do anything to protect ye, Miss Gwen."

Gwen chewed on a still-warm scone dripping with butter. "Thank you, but I can look after myself."

Marva sniffed. "Naw, ye can't. Ye always loved that gent too much. 'E'll lead ye into a 'eap o' trouble, mark me words, and—"

"And not marry me?"

Marva's head bobbed up and down. "I'll be frank with ye, Miss Gwen. Ye're not exactly 'is sort, are ye?"

A cloud of doubt descended over Gwen. Every word Marva said stabbed her with truth. "Who says I love him?" she said gruffly.

" 'Tis written all over ye, missy. Ye can't fool me, since I've known ye all yer life."

Gwen wanted to cry. Why should she not take what happiness was offered her? That's what Roc was offering. Not so much in words perhaps, but she sensed the smoldering attraction between them, and she was sure he felt it, too. Before he had arrived at Landregan, nothing exciting had happened except the smuggling. Yet the happiness he was offering perhaps wasn't of the lasting kind. Doubt nagged at her.

"And what are ye goin' to do when 'e finds out ye're Dandelion, miss?"

"He never will," Gwen vowed. "The smugglers would rather die than give him any information."

Marva shook her head. "Ye're underestimatin' th' earl. 'E's a sharp 'un. Besides, 'e's a man o' action and authority. 'E won't give up until 'e finds th' truth."

A shiver of unease traveled up Gwen's spine. Marva's words rang with truth, but she wasn't sure she was ready to hear them.

"An' 'e'd niver forgive ye for pullin' 'is leg. 'E's as proud as was th' old earl, though a lot more sensible. Beware, Miss Gwennie . . . beware." The last word lingered on the wind as Marva ambled back to the kitchen.

Gwen looked unseeing at one of the red roses. The sunlight seemed to have dimmed, and her exhilaration had deflated. She had returned to reality. The latest smuggling trick had been a sort of lesson to Roc, but the pleasure she had found in it was turning sour. She was in deeper difficulties than ever, and at the same time she felt as if she were hurtling toward a precipice, below which lay a river of passion she had no power to control. It was beckoning her to taste its dulcet depths.

To get a grip on herself, she hurried inside the house and up to her bedchamber. She would contact Clem, and together they would plan the perfect strategy for hauling in the next cargo. With the intention of counting her savings, she inserted her hand under the mattress for one of her money pouches. She could not find it, and, frowning, she knelt to look under the mattress. It was gone.

Holding her breath in shock, she examined the other side of the bed just in case she had put it in the wrong place. But she already knew her effort was futile. Then she remembered seeing the gold coin in Vincent's hand at the cockfight in the square. He must have stolen her money the day she had found him in her room! Thank God she didn't keep it all in one place.

White-hot anger welled up in her, and she wanted to stalk

to his room and demand the money back. But something held her back. A doubt, a trace of fear perhaps. Stealth was the only way to defeat Vincent. A cold wind seemed to penetrate the walls. How much did he really know?

Chapter 16

Gwen stayed closeted in her room until she heard Vincent leave the guest room, located opposite her bedchamber. He was singing off-key as he walked down the stairs. For everyone's benefit he limped heavily, but Gwen wasn't fooled.

She crept into his room and closed the door behind her. From his window she had a good view of the drive and the village in the distance. The stableboy had led the squire's horse to the steps, and Arthur, the footman, assisted Vincent into the saddle. Gwen drew back behind the curtain when he happened to look up. She was sure he hadn't seen her, but he seemed to sense her presence.

Nonsense, she told herself. Nevertheless, a frisson of fear shot through her veins. She could not recall ever being frightened by Vincent, only disgusted. There was a *slithery* quality about him that reminded her of the eels the fishermen caught. Sighing, Gwen shook off her strange mood and concentrated on her errand.

Vincent's room looked neat and impersonal, unlike her own chaotic chamber across the hallway. The guest room had the same flaking paint as the rest of the house. The wall panels which had once been painted a clear bluish-green were now faded and spotted with age. The bed hangings were frayed and threadbare, as was the woven rug on the floor. Gwen ran her hand under the mattress, though she knew Vincent wouldn't choose so obvious a hiding place as she had. But then, she had never anticipated theft. The people in the village were basically honest, except where the free trading was concerned.

Renewed anger boiled in her. Vincent had taken her money,

and who knew what else? On her hands and knees, she looked under the bed, but there was nothing there except cobwebs and a pair of red satin slippers. She wrinkled her nose at them. Vincent had strange tastes, to say the least.

She upended one of his portmanteaux on the bed and sifted through the contents. Cravats, a box of hair powder, stockings, handkerchiefs, cosmetics, a dirty hairbrush, and a letter. She snatched up the letter as if it were a lifeline. Scanning the words, she realized it was sort of a love letter. A love letter to her disgusting cousin? Her jaw fell in surprise. Who would care about him? The missive was badly spelled and full of blotches and ink spots.

Dearest Vinnie,

I've desided to join you in the kountry, even though yer tole me not to. I've found out yer wher aboots, and i don't see why i can't stay at the inn. We kould meet as usual. I know yer don't want me to, but how kould yer be so mean as to leave me wiwout even saying goodby? Yer broke me hart, but I still luv you. 'Til i see yer agin, soon, hugs and kisses. Yer Mabel.

P.S. I deserve part of yer success. I invented the idea and gived you the infermation. Only to remind yer, lest yer forgit, sweeting.

Gwen glanced at the date on top of the paper. The letter had been written over four weeks ago, shortly after Vincent's arrival. Intrigued, she pushed the letter into her pocket and shoved the rest of his belongings back into the portmanteau. She opened his trunk. Judging from the number of clothes he had brought, one costume more outrageous than the next, it looked as if he was going to stay for months, perhaps *years*. She shuddered at the thought. "Never!" she said between her teeth. One year of supporting a spendthrift like Vincent would see the end of the next-to-nonexistent Tremayne fortune. She would not stand by and see him squander what she had worked so hard for.

Slamming the door behind her, she returned to her bedchamber. She had found nothing that would give her an excuse to send him packing, but she still had the letter in her pocket. Let him stew over that! He might as well realize she could be as bold as he was, searching his room.

Yet she would never stoop so low as to steal money. She had not retrieved a single guinea he had stolen. Most likely he was carrying the pouch on his person. The thought of the coins jingling infuriated her.

Her hand touched another paper in the pocket of her wrap. Curious, she pulled it out. The letter she had written to Vincent's commanding officer! She had forgotten to mail it. Cursing under her breath, she put it on her dressing table so that she wouldn't forget it when she went downstairs. She would get her father to frank it.

It was dark when her cousin returned. Aunt Clo called from the dining room, "Do you want supper, Vincent?"

He limped into the room. "No, thank you, I had supper at the inn, if you can call their meatpies human fare."

Gwen glared at his painted and powdered countenance. " 'Tis certainly good enough for you—you ate it, didn't you?"

"Gwennie, dear, don't be rude to Vincent." Aunt Clo pressed her hand to her forehead. "I don't think a minute passes before you're at each other's throats. It gives me such a headache."

Vincent's lips parted in mockery. "Cousin Gwen has a deuced hot temper."

Gwen clenched her hands in her lap and schooled her face into a mask of indifference.

"I'll go upstairs to change clothes. Then I'm going out again," he explained, wrinkling his nose at a dish of jellied plums.

"Where?" Aunt Clo asked, and Gwen narrowed her gaze as she waited for the lies to pour from his lips.

"Merely a card game at another inn along the Fowey Road. I'm going to meet a gentleman whose acquaintance I made at The Pilchard. He's on his way to Land's End. All the rooms were occupied here, so he decided to go on. I'll ride with him." Obviously believing he had given them a satisfactory explanation, he limped upstairs.

Except that there wasn't any inn on the Fowey Road. Eagerly Gwen put aside her empty plate and patted her lips with the frayed napkin. "I'll turn in early tonight, Aunt. Your raspberry tart was delicious."

Aunt Clo blushed with pleasure. "Very kind of you to say so, Gwennie. Sleep well." She gave Gwen a keen glance as she rose from the table. "I hope you're not becoming ill. You've looked pale and peaked these last few days."

Gwen hurried toward the door. "I have a lot on my mind, that's all." She rushed up the stairs two at a time and darted into her bedchamber. Behind her wooden screen painted with a motif of cabbage roses, she pulled off her gown and dressed in her black breeches and shirt. She tied her hair with a dark kerchief and sooted her face, her heart hammering in anticipation. Tonight she might find out the answer to Vincent's secrets. He was full of them, of that she was sure.

An hour later he left his room, dressed in a dark coat and breeches. Whistling a shrill tune, he shuffled outside. Gwen heard the clatter of hooves on the drive. She hesitated at the top of the stairs, worrying that her aunt would see her as she sneaked outside. Usually Aunt Clo sewed in the parlor for an hour before going up to her bedroom. Gwen hoped this evening would be no exception.

She had learned to walk soundlessly, and luck was with her tonight. She reached the back door minutes after Vincent had left. Running fast along the path through the spinney, a shortcut to the village, she soon reached the first cottages. Vincent wasn't far ahead of her. His movements took her by surprise. Instead of choosing the road to Fowey, he rode down to the harbor.

"What's he doing?" Gwen whispered to herself. She was losing her breath trying to keep pace with him, but she had not dared to ride Buttercup, since Vincent would instantly recognize the mare.

He rode up the steep incline to the outlook above the harbor, right out onto the cliffs that jutted dangerously over the churning breakers below. The serrated reefs buried under the water line could chew up a boat faster than an ax could split a log. Vincent was obviously well aware of the danger because he pulled back from the edge. The horse pawed the ground nervously. A silvery moon washed the night with an eerie light. Hidden behind a tree, Gwen studied Vincent's silhouette clearly outlined against the lighter sky. What was he doing?

He seemed to be staring at something in the water. She slunk closer to the edge, remembering that the *Blackbird* was anchored in the bay. Vincent was staring at Roc's yacht. But why? She wished she could read his thoughts. The yacht was dark, which meant that Roc was not on it.

Fifteen minutes passed before Vincent made his way back down the cliff. The horse stumbled once and let out an anguished snort. Gwen had regained her breath and was waiting tensely for her cousin's next move. He turned onto the Fowey Road, but instead of going west toward Fowey, he headed in the opposite direction. As the road wended its way up into the hills, it passed Landregan Hall.

Vincent rode slowly past the gates leading to Roc's estate. They were wide open, as always. To Gwen's surprise, he alighted some way down the road and led the horse into a thicket of trees. Gwen watched him from the cover of a tree trunk as he sneaked past the imposing gateposts and up the winding drive. He kept to the shadows of the trees, and Gwen had to concentrate sharply not to make any sound as she followed him.

Lights from the mansion illuminated the front lawns. The fragrance of roses in the borders lining the gravel drive sweetened the air, and the wind was warm and soft. But the stealthy figure in front of her filled the air with tension. She followed Vincent around the corner of the house to the back gardens. Gwen gasped as he swung himself over the marble balustrade of the terrace and tiptoed along the wall. Holding her breath, she waited for his next move.

He stopped at the tall windows leading to the study. Light streamed through the windows. Roc must be in there, and had forgotten to pull the drapes. Or it could be Morgan. Whoever was there, Vincent showed him an inordinate amount of interest.

Stubbing her toe on a fist-sized rock, Gwen bent rapidly and picked it up. She weighed it thoughtfully in her hand, then pulled out the old knitted stocking from her pocket and stuffed the rock into it, just in case she would need to defend herself. The rock would make a handy weapon.

Gwen hoisted her legs over the balustrade. Pressed to the

wall, she sidled up to a cone-shaped juniper bush in a tall urn, then to a window. She looked inside. No one was in the study, but candles glowed on the desk, as if someone had just left and would be back soon. From behind the bush, she kept watch on Vincent.

Cold sweat coursed down her spine as she saw him pull something out of his pocket. The steel of a sharp blade glittered in the light. She had to clamp a hand across her mouth to stop from shouting a warning.

As Vincent reached out to slip the blade between the sashes, Gwen acted. Raising her weapon over her head, she rushed forward and swung it against Vincent's head before he knew what had happened. With a muffled oath he toppled over, and the rock continued through the glass pane with savage force. The sound of shattering glass broke the silence of the night. As she had flung her weapon the rock had rebounded in the stocking wrapped around Gwen's fist and smashed into her arm.

She whimpered with pain and stared in horror at the broken window. Roc came rushing through the interior door, his mouth agape. Vincent was rolling in agony on the stone terrace. In a flash Gwen saw Roc heading for the window, and Vincent's fingers clawing for a grip on her leg.

She had to get away! If she was detected, everything would be lost. Roc would put two and two together and know she was Dandelion. No woman in her right mind would be roaming the night dressed up in black breeches, her face covered with soot, unless she was already familiar with such unorthodox behavior. Just as Roc opened the door, she swung over the balustrade and melted into the darkness.

"Blast and thunder! What's going on—" From the shadow of a hedge, Gwen saw Roc bend over Vincent's prostrate form. "Tremayne, is that you? What the deuce are you doing here?"

Gwen could not hear Vincent's garbled response, but she was happy that he'd been caught. He would have difficulty explaining what he was doing lurking about the estate in the dark, carrying a knife. She moved closer to hear their exchange.

"Did you break the window?" Roc demanded, brushing off Vincent's shoulders. There was no sign of the knife.

"Of course not," Vincent denied. "I was walking around the back to fetch my gloves, which I forgot last time I was here, and I saw a dark figure standing by your window."

"When were you here?" Roc asked suspiciously. "I haven't seen you since the ball."

"The marchioness invited me to tea. I had a chat in the garden with her and Lady Louise yesterday."

The two men silently took each other's measure, and Gwen held her breath in suspense.

"If you don't believe me, I can prove that my gloves are here," Vincent said in whining tones.

"Very well," Roc said tiredly. As Vincent was righting his wig and waistcoat, Roc stepped over to the edge of the terrace and scanned the darkness. "Did you see who it was or where he went?"

"No, he was dressed entirely in black."

"I'll have a word with the stableboys to see if they saw a stranger lurking about." Roc sighed and walked along the terrace to the fan-shaped steps in the middle that led to the garden.

No! Gwen cried silently. Don't go with Vincent. If the gloves are there, he put them there on purpose.

But Roc did not sense her warning. She followed behind them, the sock still wrapped around her hand. If necessary, she would risk everything to save Roc from Vincent. Instinctively she sensed that her cousin was capable of violence—even of stabbing Roc in the back, though why he would want to do it, she had no idea. Her throat was dry with fear, and she worried she would give away her presence by stumbling on the dark garden paths.

"You could have sent Arthur for your gloves," Roc said.

"Arthur?" Vincent tittered. "That buffoon. His memory span is no longer than five minutes, at most."

Roc did not join in the laughter. "You're exaggerating. Arthur is intelligent enough to hold the post of footman." His voice turned pensive as they skirted a tinkling fountain. "Tell me, Vincent, have you noticed anything out of the ordinary at Tremayne House?"

"What do you mean?" Vincent sounded cautious.

"Anything that could be connected to the smuggling business?"

Gwen shivered, but Vincent laughed out loud. "Smuggling? You mean you think someone at Tremayne House might be Dandelion?" He sounded incredulous.

Gwen sent up a silent prayer of thanks.

"Well, I have no idea if anyone there is involved, but I need to investigate everyone. As long as Dandelion is free, everyone is suspect."

"I see," Vincent said coldly. "I'm sure *all* of us have at some time in our lives done things we want to keep secret."

"What are you talking about?" Roc's voice was wary.

"There they are! My gloves, just as I told you." Vincent bent and retrieved something from one of the benches in the Landregan rose arbor. "Well, I'd better be off now." He made as if to move away, but Roc gripped his arm.

"What secrets were you talking about? Business? Politics?"

"You wouldn't expect me to tell you my secrets; you're practically a stranger," Vincent said scornfully.

"We've known each other all our lives," Roc protested. His silhouette looked tense, brooding, and Gwen waited breathlessly.

"More than ten years have passed since I last saw you, and we didn't exactly part on friendly terms. You called me a fop, if I recall."

"Well, times have changed. We could let bygones be bygones. I need you to keep your eyes open. You'll let me know about any suspicious acts, won't you, Vincent?"

He grumbled something, his limp more pronounced as he hurried toward the light streaming from the windows. "Very well. If I hear or see anything at all—"

Roc remained behind as Vincent made his escape.

Gwen sighed. She had come no closer to finding an explanation for her cousin's strange behavior. What was Vincent's real business at Landregan Hall? She would not rest until she found out.

Two days later, yet another of the dowager countess's heavily gold-embossed invitations arrived at Tremayne House, sending Aunt Clo into transports of delight. At Lady Louise's request, Gwen, Aunt Clo, the squire, and Vincent were invited to take tea at the Hall two days hence.

Vincent cried off. Probably because he was still nursing a headache after the blow Gwen had dealt him, she surmised. He had made up a story about being attacked by highwaymen on his way back from Fowey. Gwen was disappointed that Roc had seen fit to believe Vincent's story about the gloves. Somehow she had to get Vincent out of the house. She had to protect her father and Aunt Clo. If angered, Vincent might use any weapon in his defense.

"Just imagine all those heavenly crumpets . . . cucumber sandwiches . . . cakes . . . tarts," Aunt Clo exclaimed.

When the hour of departure arrived, Aunt Clo, rigid with anticipation, sat in the trap next to the indifferent squire. Gwen sighed, at the end of her patience, as she tooled the equipage through the gates of Landregan Hall. Why had she been saddled with such an exasperating family? Perhaps all families were alike. It certainly looked as if Roc's kith and kin had their share of lunacy.

Filled with misgivings, Gwen thought about the tea party. Surely it would only be a repetition of the previous disastrous affair, unless she could keep from clashing swords with the dowager countess.

Enedoc announced their arrival in quaking tones and winked at Gwen as he held open the door to the salon. She curtsied to their hostess and immediately sought Roc. He stood at ease by the fireplace, leaning a velvet-clad elbow on the mantelpiece. Gwen's knees went strangely weak, and the air seemed to thicken between them as their eyes met.

"Ah, yes, our neighbors," the dowager began. She raked a disapproving eye over Gwen's green and yellow striped gown, shiny with worn patches.

Why did I agree to come here and have insulting glances sent my way? Gwen wondered, but she already knew the answer. Roc. Her longing for him followed her everywhere, like a chronic disease. How was it going to end? He appeared to be just as drawn to her as she was to him, but perhaps it was only in her imagination. As she met his topaz gaze, she knew the unspoken passion between them could not exist much longer without expression. She pressed her fingernails into the palms of her hands, reminding herself that her responsibility was to her smuggling friends. As long as she continued to be Dandelion, Roc remained her enemy. The word reverberated in her head as she lowered her gaze. What if she abandoned her secret identity . . . what then? And who would take up the leadership if she resigned?

"Lady Landregan, how very kind of you to invite us," she said, managing a weak smile. She glanced at Louise, who giggled. The marchioness of Camelford looked forbidding and bored.

"Hmm, not going to bark at me today, eh?" the dowager commented in a gruff voice. "Well? Don't stand there like a gawk, come and sit down. And you may call me Philomela." She patted an overstuffed wing chair next to hers, and Gwen fought a sudden urge to laugh. *Philomela?*

"Squire Tremayne, I daresay I haven't exchanged one word with you since I arrived in this godforsaken hole," the dowager continued.

"Ah, well—no loss," the squire replied absentmindedly, earning one of the dowager's icy stares. "Is Morgan at home? I have a theory I'd like to discuss with him." He glanced hopefully toward the door.

The dowager turned to Roc. "Call your brother."

He complied without protest, and Gwen's eyes followed his beloved form to the door as he issued the order to Enedoc. Longing tore at her heart.

As Morgan stepped into the salon, Gwen was aware of a subtle change in Louise. The girl's green eyes flew wide, full of warm speculation. Good Lord, was she hatching plans for the bookworm? Gwen had not noticed their attraction before. She eyed Morgan with new interest. With his bright eyes and engaging smile Morgan was not unattractive. If he took some interest in his appearance, he might actually become quite the ladies' man. But at this moment his hair was disheveled, and his spectacles pinched his prominent nose. His coat looked as if it had been pulled from under a hedge, his jabot was askew, and his waistcoat was too large and buttoned unevenly.

"Ah, see what the cat dragged in." The dowager snorted, but Morgan did not appear to hear the barb. His eyes were fastened on the glorious Louise, shy admiration shining in his gaze. A red flush appeared on his cheeks as he nervously fingered the book in his hand. Gwen regarded him with surprise since she had never before seen Morgan interested in any woman.

So that's the way of it, she thought, amused. She looked up and happened to glance into Roc's warmly gleaming eyes. Had he noticed what was happening to his brother? With difficulty, she tore her gaze away. Every day she kept dreaming of him, of his hands on her hot skin, caressing, wooing; of his lips on hers, conquering, melting; of his body pressed to hers, fitting perfectly into that place between her thighs which throbbed with longing. She jumped with shame when the dowager barked her name.

"Gwendolyn! Are we boring you to such an extent that you are falling asleep?" Rapier-sharp eyes speared Gwen, and she colored with confusion.

"You're quite mistaken, Philomela. I was merely woolgathering." Looking through her lowered lashes, she noticed a knowing smile playing over Roc's lips.

Enedoc wheeled in the tea trolley, and the dowager did the honors. Gwen helped her pass around the cups, and her fingertips brushed Roc's as she handed him his cup. He managed to give her hand a quick caress.

His eyes caught hers once more, and a fire glowed in those topaz depths, smoldering with what could only be passion. Her heart leaped to her throat, and she could barely make it back to her chair. The delicious cake served to her on a gold-edged plate tasted of nothing. All she could think of was Roc's touch and her own raging longing.

The tea party went fairly well, as long as no one argued with the dowager. She kept up a monologue, and the guests said yes and no in the right places. Every time Gwen looked up, Roc was gazing at her. As soon as she set down her teacup, he spoke.

"Miss Tremayne, would you like to take a stroll in the rose garden? 'Tis so very hot in here."

She glanced sharply at him to see if he was mocking her. Since his expression was wholly serious, she accepted gratefully.

"A splendid idea! I'm sure Louise would love a stroll, too," the marchioness of Camelford hastened to insert, pushing her daughter forward to attach herself to the earl's arm.

"Morgan!" Roc imperiously called his brother back from

ancient Greece, where he had spent the last fifteen minutes with the squire.

"Huh?" Morgan's spectacles had slid down the length of his nose, and he pushed them back up with an awkward movement.

"You'll accompany us into the gardens, won't you, old shoe?" Roc strode to the French doors and opened them wide to invite inside the sounds and smells of the ripe summer. " 'Tis pilchard time," he commented to all in the room, with Louise hanging like a limpet from his sleeve.

"Ah, yes, that reminds me," said the dowager. "The night the pilchards are brought in from the sea, we're going to have a feast in the gardens to celebrate. After the spectacle on the beach, you'll come directly to the grounds for ale and meat. When we're rusticating like this, we might as well follow the local traditions."

Roc and Louise led the way down the shallow stone steps of the terrace. Gwen, following, gratefully left behind the stifling atmosphere of the salon. She threw a furtive glance at the library window, noticing that the broken windowpane had been replaced. Stepping onto the garden path, she held Morgan's arm loosely, wishing it were Roc's. All of a sudden, Morgan began limping, and Gwen glanced down to his feet. She noticed the heel of his boot was wedged between two flagstones some distance away.

"Why, you've lost your heel, Morgan."

"Eh?" He looked at her as if he had difficulty remembering what he was doing in the garden.

"Your boot heel."

He looked down at his feet. "By Jove, you're right. For a moment I found it somewhat difficult to walk. I thought the path was that uneven."

Roc and Louise paused, waiting for them to catch up. Morgan looked around, a dazed expression on his face. "Where is it?"

"What's happening?" Roc called out, and he and Louise retraced their steps.

Seeing Morgan's predicament, Louise squealed, "You poor man, let me help you find your heel."

Morgan colored, a delighted smile spreading over his lips. "You would be that kind? Splendid!" He turned to Gwen.

"I'm sorry, but I won't be able to escort you now. I'm sure you can find your way around here on your own."

Gwen laughed. "I'm sure I can."

"You don't have to if you let me escort you," Roc suggested, his voice soft with insinuation. She sent him a probing glance. His eyes danced with mischief.

"I don't know if I should leave your side, Roc," Louise whined. "If Mama sees me with Mr. Tyrrell, she won't speak to me for weeks."

Roc patted her tiny hand on his sleeve. "Just stay away from the windows," he suggested. "I don't think Morgan can refuse you anything you want to do." He jabbed his brother in the ribs. "Try to stay in the present, old shoe. And mind your manners."

In a flash, Louise had gripped Morgan's hand and was pulling him down a path bordered by a tall hedge which shrouded them from any inquisitive eye in the salon. Morgan was limping badly.

"Shall we?" Roc offered the crook of his arm to Gwen and bore her down a path in the opposite direction. "I feel an apology is in order since I rushed away from the rose arbor the other day with barely a good-day." He sighed. "You see, I don't know what I might have done to you had not Marva appeared to protect you."

"Oh." Gwen laughed. "You don't think I can protect myself?"

He chuckled. "I think you're wholly capable of protecting your virtue. However, I'm not so sure you want to protect it. Am I right?"

"You're very sure of your attraction," she murmured. She tried hard to look unperturbed, but embarrassment burned in her cheeks.

"Be honest with me, Gwen. Tell me what you feel."

She glanced at him, and she was sure he could read the longing in her eyes. "Yes, I find you very—very attractive." As she confessed, her heart began to thunder in her chest, and she knew they had reached another threshold in their relationship. Gwen yearned for him so much that she ached all over. In sheer desperation, she took refuge in the first topic that came to mind.

"By the way, did you find the missing brandy?" She gazed at the distant rocky horizon.

"No. All the people around the square swore they saw and heard nothing, as did everyone else. There's a wild rumor flying around that three women stole the brandy. Have you ever heard anything so preposterous?"

Gwen laughed, vastly relieved. "Who told you?"

A smile curled his lips. "Why, you will not believe it. The squire."

"Oh, well, he gave us the same story," Gwen said in dismissing tones. "Said he'd seen it with his own eyes."

Roc turned pensive for a few moments, and Gwen shook his sleeve. "You don't believe him, do you?" When he didn't respond immediately, she added, "Don't start acting like Morgan—as if you are in another world." Suddenly she was afraid he would find out the identity of the "women" and link them to her. "I'm sure Papa was dreaming. You know how he is."

Roc sent her a shrewd glance. "Don't want to see him ridiculed, eh? That's understandable. Men like him and Morgan are like bumbling fools or children; they seldom lie, not consciously that is."

"And you do?" Now she wanted at all costs to turn his thoughts from the brandy and the smuggling.

He chuckled. "No, not if I can help it. Talking about children, I remember a dirty little girl who used to follow me around like a puppy when I came down from Oxford during the holidays." His voice had deepened to a tender caress. "I wonder if she still harbors that blind devotion for her handsome prince."

A droning bumblebee hovered in the still air as if waiting for her answer. The leaves on the trees and the clouds in the sky seemed to stand still. Time ceased to exist, a cocoon of intimate warmth wrapping around them. A monarch butterfly landed on Roc's shoulder, as if to listen to her reply. Gwen dared not look into his eyes for fear of what she would read there. She concentrated on the shining buttons of his handsome blue waistcoat.

"Blind I might have been then, but I am no longer," she said. "I think that prince has grown puff-headed over the years," she teased, not daring to admit the depth of her feelings. Not yet.

Roc chuckled, and the world began moving in its customary course once more. He stepped along the graveled path, evidently unperturbed. "Your adoration never bothered me, you know, except that one time when I brought a certain young lady home to meet my parents—a long time ago," he added, laughter crinkling his eyes. "Enedoc saw you shoveling earth onto the floor of her traveling chaise just before she and her chaperone were to return home. What an upheaval that act caused."

Gwen blushed at the memory. What an idiot she had been!

"You were about ten years old, or perhaps eleven, and I was a greenhorn of eighteen." He halted. One long finger lifted her chin, and she was forced to look into his golden eyes. "I think you did me a favor then, a great favor, since I never saw that young lady again. I've heard she is married to someone else and has six cross-eyed children." He studied Gwen intently, turning her face this way and that.

Gwen squirmed uncomfortably. "Do I have dirty smudges on my nose?"

He laughed. "No, I just hadn't quite realized your many beautiful points, such translucent skin, such expressive eyes, such a kissable neck." He proceeded to trail a line of hot kisses down her long neck.

She shoved him away. "Roc! You're forgetting yourself again." Her voice trembled with hope mixed with melancholy.

"Ah! That seems to be my fate every time I'm around you—forgetting myself. Why do you think that is?" He pointed to a wrought-iron bench under the shade of a huge oak tree. "Let's sit down and ponder that question."

"You're chaffing me, milord."

His eyes twinkled. "Next you'll be calling me a rakehell."

"And well you deserve it, milord."

She did not put up a struggle when he pulled her to him, murmuring, "I can't seem to help myself."

Transfixed, she watched his lips descend toward hers. His lips tasted of strawberry tart and clotted cream, of spice, of wildness, of virile eagerness. They sparked her own flaring desire until her defenses broke, and she became a flame of passion in his arms.

Her fingers dug into his hair. Her body arched against his, hungry to mold its rounded curves to his hard muscles.

"Gwennie . . . delicious, maddening siren," he muttered. "Lovable . . . eccentric . . . ragamuffin."

Words that might have stung her seemed like a caress coming from his tongue, and she sensed how deeply he had accepted her just the way she was. He saw beyond her tattered appearance; he saw her as a part of what he loved most in the world. She recalled the love he had expressed for Cornwall and Landregan on their impromptu fishing trip. She realized he had come back to Landregan because he could stay away no longer. He was as bound to this magic bit of earth as she was. He always had been. They shared a passion that need not be spoken of.

His hand glided over the soft skin above the lacy edge of her bodice, and she shivered with delight. He untied the front lacing and freed one of her full breasts. She could not stop him when she saw the reverence and pleasure on his face as he admired her in the golden sunlight.

She sighed, drugged by his intoxicating closeness and by the stillness of this garden paradise. His tawny gaze laughed into hers, his lips once again dreamily sought hers, and at the hot contact, Roc and Gwen floated into an intimate oblivion where nothing existed but their shared wonder. Steadying her against his hard arm, he moved his mouth down her neck in a slow trance. His lips encircled the rosy crest of her breast, and she melted inside. As if of their own volition, her legs parted beneath her wide skirts, and she longed for him to touch her.

Responding to her every mood, he let his hand travel up the length of her leg under the skirts. As he arrived at her knee, he lifted her leg across his lap and caressed the soft inside of her thigh. She moaned helplessly. Seeking to quench the fire between her legs, she pressed up against his hand.

A trilling sound pierced the air, and she stiffened.

"Did you giggle?" Roc withdrew his hand dreamily and lifted his head, his voice thick with desire. Tense, he peered into the gold-flecked greenery around them. "Someone is spying on us."

"Huh?" Gwen languorously opened her eyes. A giggle came like a waterfall from behind the hedge. Roc's smile was at least ten inches wide, his face flushed from their shared passion. "Seems somebody found the bench on the other side of this venerable oak," he whispered. He smoothed down Gwen's skirts. "However much I long to go on, this won't do, y'know. We'll be discovered, and then I'll have to answer to the squire."

"The thought never seemed to bother you before." Gwen felt almost sick with disappointment. She pushed away from him, laced up her bodice, and straightened her hair.

"Come," he murmured, mischief bubbling in his voice. "Let's do some spying of our own, shall we?" He lifted Gwen to her feet and pulled her by the hand. Another sound of delight pierced the air.

"Louise and Morgan! I don't believe it! This must be the first time Morgan has ever fondled a woman."

Roc pointed at Morgan's hand roving under Louise's skirt, and Gwen had to stifle her laughter. She smacked Roc's arm. " 'Tis not fair. Let's tell them we're here."

Roc placed a finger on his lips and inched around the curving hedge. Motioning with his hands, he urged Gwen to crouch. When Roc started caterwauling like a cat in heat, she pressed her hands convulsively to her mouth to suppress her mirth.

The giggle stopped abruptly, and Morgan shot out of the green alcove as if his coattails were on fire. Louise followed, blushing furiously and patting her curls back into place. Their guilty faces spoke volumes.

"Ah, we were just looking for you," Roc lied, and winked at Gwen. "Did you see the yellow tomcat that lives in the stables? I heard him clearly."

The embarrassed couple glanced furtively among the bushes. "No, I don't believe we did. What do you want him for?" Morgan asked with his usual lopsided logic. Some of the vagueness so customary on his face had been replaced with the wonder of finding love, but the experience was evidently still too new to keep him from reverting back to his old ways. "Must speak to the squire about something before he leaves," he muttered, running a hand gingerly through his disheveled hair.

Louise had by then regained her usual aplomb. On tiptoe, she smoothed his brown curls into place and bound them with the ribbon that had fallen to his shoulder. "I suppose I should enter the house on the earl's arm, or Mama will make mincemeat of me," she said, studying her handiwork.

Gwen reluctantly relinquished her hold on Roc's arm, feeling his hot, piercing gaze on her as she hastened to grip Morgan's arm before he limped into the Hall. Her newly discovered sensuality battled with a need to control her rioting feelings. She was eager to hide behind the normalcy of Aunt Clo and her father. This wondrous new development in her body seemed so unreal that she feared it would evaporate like a puff of smoke. She knew she would mentally relive the wonder during the night, but for now she needed to put her armor back in place. She also needed Roc. She needed him if she was ever to dare emerge from the shell of prim spinsterhood she had erected around herself.

"Well, well, *there* you are!" exclaimed the dowager countess. "We almost sent Enedoc out to search for you."

Three pairs of eyes assessed them as they entered the salon. Gwen was sure they would notice her face bore the imprints of Roc's lips. She hastened to don a proud mask, hiding her vulnerability. Louise clearly did not have equal strength. When the marchioness inquired if she had spent an edifying walk in the gardens, she dimpled prettily at Morgan. Lady Camelford shot a meaningful glance at the earl, who took up his former position by the fireplace. She evidently wanted to know if the earl had proposed to her daughter.

"Lud! What is wrong with your gait, Morgan?" the dowager inquired, goggling at his broken boot. "Good God!" she exclaimed, her napkin falling from her pudgy, nerveless fingers. "He belongs in the stables," she muttered to no one in particular.

Morgan had stopped in the middle of the floor, his stare fixed upon his mother, who returned it with frigid hauteur. "Corkbrain! Find yourself another pair of shoes," she ordered.

Morgan, unworldly innocent that he was, turned instead to the marchioness of Camelford. He seemed to be struggling with himself, but the burning question on his lips evidently drove him to speak. "Ahem, I— My dear Lady Camelford—

Eulalie—I would like to, er, if you allow, to—m-m-marry your daughter.''

Tension exploded in the room as all eyes turned with varying degrees of incredulity on the wretched man, who colored uncomfortably under the onslaught. He scraped the carpet with the toe of his boot and scratched his head. His spectacles hung lopsided over his beaky nose.

The marchioness gulped for air like a beached fish and proceeded to swoon into the arms of her startled daughter. Judging from her expression, Gwen concluded that Louise, too, had obviously not expected such immediate action from her admirer.

"A vinaigrette, instantly," Louise wailed, distraught under the heavy burden of her shocked mamá. She fanned the woman's sagging face with desperate vigor and tried to slide away before she suffocated under the load.

Enedoc entered waving a vinaigrette. Morgan wandered dejectedly to a corner of the room, but Roc took pity on him and led him into the hallway.

The dowager had bristled at Morgan's clumsy proposal, but she also eyed her old friend with distaste. "Calm yourself, Eulalie. *I* am never one to buckle under when the world goes awry. And Morgan is my own son; the bluest blood runs in his veins, you must know. And he's no pauper since Roc, upon returning from India, kindly settled a large sum on him." She puffed out her chest. "One cannot hold it against the poor boy that he's a younger son. That his offer should be such a nightmare to you, Eulalie, is sheer exaggeration," the dowager maintained archly.

Like a hawk she followed the progress of her guest's revival, from feigned swoon to hurt pride. When Gwen and her family finally took a subdued farewell, the marchioness only nodded regally. It was with a sigh of relief that Gwen exited the Hall. The visit had ended in chaos, but on the whole it had turned out to be—edifying, to use the marchioness's own word.

Chapter 17

Gwen opened one bleary eye and stared unseeing at Marva who, bending over the bed, was shaking her shoulder.

"Th' pilchards are bein' spotted," the fat cook kept repeating like a nursery rhyme. " 'Urry then!"

Automatically Gwen threw off the covers and placed her feet on the floor. Standing, her arms aloft, she quivered in a catlike stretch and blinked several times, awake at last. Hiding a huge yawn behind her hand, she glowered at Marva. " 'Tis still the middle of the night."

"Dawn'll be 'ere any minute now, so 'urry up. Ye don't want to miss them, do ye—them nice pilchards?"

Gwen gave another yawn. "No, but why do they always have to come at such an ungodly hour, eh? Explain that if you can."

Marva left, mumbling to herself and shaking her head. Gwen sleepily pulled on an old gown. This would be a busy day, indeed, what with the salting down of the pilchards in barrels for the winter—thousands, no millions, of the small, silvery fish. Afterward everyone would attend a feast at the Hall.

After winding her hair into a simple chignon, Gwen stuffed it into the crown of an old straw hat and tied the faded blue ribbons under her chin, then hurried to catch up with the rest of her family, who were already heading down to the village.

Wild excitement spread through town as every citizen, old and young alike, stood on the rocks around the harbor, scanning the sea for the dark shadow that would herald the first shoal of pilchards.

Gwen mingled with the spectators, enjoying the sight of

163

the dawn light caressing the sea with a golden tint. Then the sky turned a striking palette of colors, a transparent eggshell-green slashed with streaks of iridescent pink and red.

"There they are!" cried a lad from the lookout above the harbor.

An intense flurry of activity ensued as the boats that would take out the nets were launched. They darted over the mercurial surface of the bay to encircle the shoal with the seine. The tucking nets were attached to the seines, hemming in the leaping and writhing mass of fish. The bay came alive, the water churning with the frantic movement of silver bodies trying to escape the nets. The boats turned back, and the fishermen on shore helped pull the nets onto the beach, where the pilchards jumped and convulsed in a last desperate struggle.

Gwen followed the others rushing down to the waterline. Hundreds of hands worked to load the pilchards into baskets, barrows, and carts. The fish were brought into the stone salting house where Gwen joined the other women packing salt and pilchards, layers upon layers. Any fish that was not eaten fresh or preserved for the villagers was packed in hogsheads to be exported.

Gwen, her skirt hitched well above her knees and her feet bare, emptied basket after basket of fish onto the wide wooden tables. This addition to the food supply would help tide the Tremaynes over the winter.

Seeing Roc among the working men came as no surprise to Gwen. Like herself, he wore no shoes or stockings. As he hoisted up a keg, his knee breeches molded his powerful thighs, and he looked dangerously attractive in a white shirt open at the neck. A warm sensation spread like wildfire through her veins as she studied the open neckline of his shirt, which revealed a dusting of black hair and a patch of well-muscled chest. His shirt sleeves were folded up past his elbows, and he was hatless. His long hair gleamed, bound at the back with a leather thong, a loose curl falling over his forehead.

Unbeknownst to Roc, Gwen watched him, drinking in her fill of him. He was so strong, his muscles bulging as he loaded two more kegs onto the cart. Her breath caught in her throat when his face lit up in a bright smile at somebody's joke. He mingled easily with the fishermen, all constraint about the smuggling obviously gone for the time being. The yearly arrival of the pilchards was an adventure for everyone. Feuds and class differences disappeared in the excitement of the moment.

Gwen bent to unload one of the barrows. Glancing sideways, she met Roc's laughing eyes. They turned velvety, suggestive, and she remembered her last delicious encounter with him. A small voice in her head kept warning her to stay away from him since any deeper involvement would inevitably spell disaster, but she was helpless against the clamors of her own body.

Resting now, Roc leaned against a trestle table and drank a tankard of ale, two barrels of which he'd made available to the villagers. The fishermen had rapidly developed perpetually parched throats.

Roc's gaze pointedly caressed Gwen's bare legs and, blushing, she instantly lowered the soggy hem of her skirt. His eyes wandered up the length of her body, following every curve with avid interest until he reached her scarlet cheeks. Then his face split into a wide, appreciative grin. She took a step toward him, threatening him with her fist.

"The fair damsel has lost her composure for once," he called across the room, his voice husky with suggestion. The other women laughed and nudged Gwen.

She tried to make her voice light, hating to show her embarrassment. "There was never any composure to be found this morning. It got lost in the hubbub." She swept a damp tendril of hair from her face and noticed how his eyes irresistibly wandered to the fabric straining across her full breasts. Hastily she lowered her arm and turned her back on him. Her skin felt hot and tingling, as if not only his gaze but his hands as well had caressed her curves. How she wanted to be in his arms!

Although it had become clear that Louise did not want to marry Roc, it didn't mean Gwen would have the chance. What would he do with a squire's daughter when he could have his pick of ladies from the finest families in the kingdom? How could she even dream about him? She was considered a spinster by everyone in Landregan, and she would remain so for the rest of her days. A spinster—*and* a smuggling lady, to those who knew. Sometimes she wished she could tell Roc the truth, if only to see the surprise on his face, but that would be the day he would turn away from her forever. A sharp pain of anguish jabbed her heart.

Above the loud chatter of the women she did not hear him come forward. He held out his tankard to her, and she gripped it gratefully, her fingers awkward and stiff with tension. Their eyes locked over the rim, and Gwen almost choked at the sight of the naked desire glittering in his hooded gaze. When he reached for her hand, she placed it in his warm grip.

"Let us take a breath of fresh air," he suggested and stepped out of the salting house. Gwen nodded, too intoxicated by his closeness to speak. Hand in hand they ran down to the pebbly beach where the sea gurgled against the docks. Seagulls wheeled above their heads, calling in ecstasy over the free meal of pilchards lying on the shale. The sun was moving slowly across the blue sky, reflected on the shifting water.

Gwen heard the rumble of wheels on the dock, and Louise's high-pitched voice mingled with the seagulls' cries. *"There* you are!"

Gwen and Roc turned simultaneously to behold Louise in a dainty white gown covered with embroidered rosebuds and stretched over enormous paniers. Sitting in the Landregan landau, the girl pressed a scrap of lacy fabric to her delicate nose. She was guarded on both sides by the two tabbies from the Hall. Roc's mother waved an orange pierced with cloves under her hawk nose to ward off the fish smell.

"How *exotic* you two look." Louise squealed in delight. "I wish I could bathe my feet in the water, too." She looked wistfully at their bare toes. " 'Tis positively romantic."

"Why don't you come down and take off your shoes," Gwen suggested, never once remembering how improper her suggestion was. "There is nothing to it, you know."

Lady Camelford clutched her vinaigrette to her nose and spoke in defeated tones. "Had I known it would come to this, I would never have consented to take this drive, or come to Landregan Hall in the first place. My poor lamb will be ruined in this coarse company." She clung to Louise's arm to prevent her from descending.

"Poppycock!" the dowager countess barked, the bobbing

ostrich feathers in her wide-brimmed straw hat emphasizing her words. "It is the tradition. You can't salt pilchards dressed in a hooped skirt and satin slippers."

Lady Camelford wailed in horror. " 'Tis all *her* fault," she declared, pointing an accusing finger at Gwen. "She has led my little girl astray, destroying her chances for a good match." She gave the earl an acid stare.

The dowager countess puffed up like an angry parrot. "Piffle! If you keep on like this, I vow I will drive you back to the Hall this instant."

"Only imagine, I was forced out of bed at dawn and scalded my lips on the tea," Lady Camelford complained to no one in particular. "Then the impudent butler literally shoved me into the carriage. How *crude!*"

"Mama, since this outing is so unpleasant for you, I believe you should return to the Hall," said her daughter. "I, however, wish to stay here with my friends. I have never seen a pilchard before." Escaping the claws of her offended mama, Louise resolutely stepped from the landau and joined Gwen and Roc on the beach.

Before the marchioness could initiate one of her spells, the dowager ordered the driver to return to the Hall. As she turned a haughty eye on the threesome, a streak of amusement flashed across her face.

Roc turned to Louise and explained, "You're late; all the fish have already been caught and are being salted just now."

"Oh, no! I had the most difficult time convincing Mother to venture out of bed to attend this event."

Roc's mouth quirked. "That much was obvious."

"She finally agreed—after making me promise to try to fix your interest on me." She dimpled prettily. "I'm only warning you."

Roc bowed, a sardonic smile on his lips. "Thank you. I will strive to remember that."

A shout reached them, and they turned to see Morgan, atop his horse Blacky, descending the steep cliff path, a covered basket hanging from the saddle. He waved, and Louise began jumping up and down with excitement in a highly unladylike fashion.

"I had the devil's own time staying out of the path of the old bats," he explained. He was dressed haphazardly in a rumpled shirt and old breeches, and he wore his own hair, the brown curls spilling to his shoulders. He seemed a different man, younger, happier.

"What's in the basket, old shoe?" Roc asked.

"Huh? Ah, yes, Enedoc passed this on to me. Breakfast, I believe. I forgot to look."

"Splendid! Let's partake of it in some sunny spot," Roc said. "I'm sure there is enough for everyone."

Louise clapped her hands. "Yes, let's go to where the smugglers hide the brandy. I'm yearning to see one of those places."

Gwen felt a rivulet of unease curl through her, Roc frowned. "They don't exactly hide it at any scenic spots, Louise," he said.

Louise's face fell.

"I believe Wrecker's Ruin is as good a place as any," Roc said. "They used to store brandy there, but haven't for a long time now. 'Tis too obvious a hiding place."

Leading Louise up the slope, Gwen trailing behind, Roc related what he knew about the smugglers. "They use many hiding places, some that I don't know about or I would have unearthed the stolen brandy kegs by now." He snorted. "If it suited them, they would even stoop so low as to hide the cargo clandestinely in the church, or in *my* cellars."

Gwen smiled secretly. Little did he know.

Roc went on, "They used Brandy Cove and Lucky Hole to land the brandy the last times, but since I've posted guards there, I don't know where they'll land next."

We don't know either, Gwen thought. 'Tis a dashed problem.

"I will not rest until I find out," Roc continued. "One day soon Dandelion will make a mistake and I'll capture him. Until that day I'll make it more and more difficult for him to continue his lawless pursuits."

Gwen's eyes stabbed daggers into his back, her lips set in a stubborn line. "I predict Roc will have any number of difficulties," she said sweetly, "since he's not used to dealing with such rough characters as the smugglers."

He waited for her to draw level with him on the path. "You've forgotten that I spent hard years in the Orient."

"With servants waiting on you hand and foot, most likely," she retorted.

"*I* don't see why you have to capture the smugglers at all. They are *so* romantic," Louise insisted in a swooning voice, covering her heart with her hand for dramatic effect. Gwen loved her for her encouraging—if naïve—opinion on the subject.

"Yes, Roc has such a dull view of the issue," Gwen maintained.

He sent her a dark look which warned her not to turn the conversation into an argument. But his implied order only raised her hackles.

"Gwen is the smugglers' staunchest supporter," Roc explained, evidently noticing the mulish set of her chin.

"I don't blame her. After all, what else does she have to dream about during her lonely nights—oh!" Louise clapped her hand to her mouth in embarrassment. "How very rude of me." She laid her fingertips on Gwen's arm. "I'm sorry, I didn't mean—"

"Don't be distressed. You're quite right, you know," Gwen said with wry amusement. "Life in a small village can become tedious at times, so I do dream a lot."

They had finally reached the grassy plateau in front of the ruin. Waves slapped and froth fizzled against the rocks far below, and a light breeze wafted through the greenery behind the ruin.

"Here we are." Roc led Louise to a sunny spot, obviously relieved to have left the subject of Gwen's lonely dreams. Below the rocky outcroppings lay Brandy Cove, the beach shielded from view by the steep cliffs.

Morgan dismounted and unfastened the basket from the pommel. "Deuced uncomfortable to ride with this thing." Roc and Morgan busied themselves with spreading the tablecloth that Enedoc had been thoughtful enough to pack.

"Where's your cousin Vincent?" asked Louise, looking back toward the harbor. "Is he still busy with the pilchards?"

Gwen frowned. "No, he would never consider soiling his hands with dead fish. Besides, he never leaves his bedroom before noon." Probably because he creeps about the lanes at night with drawn knives and no limp, she added to herself. Her cousin had been conspicuous in his absence ever since the night she had hit him over the head at Landregan Hall. Thinking about him put a pall on Gwen's bright morning.

A flash of red in the trees behind the ruin caught Gwen's attention. With a frown she stared into the gold- and green-dappled shadows. There it was again, a piece of red cloth waving furiously.

Clem! Her mind working frantically, she tried to figure out what the warning meant. The last load had not yet been shipped since a pony train had to take the kegs to Exeter. Gwen had decided it would be wise to wait until Roc's zealous search for the kegs had ceased. She had forgotten to ask Clem the whereabouts of the kegs they had taken from the square. Trusting him implicitly, she knew he had hidden the cargo in a safe place. But was he indicating that he'd stowed it at Wrecker's Ruin? It couldn't be! Everyone in the village knew about Wrecker's Ruin. She gave Roc a long, calculating stare. In a way the ruin might be as safe as any other spot since Roc would never expect them to hide the booty in a place he knew. But what if he got a whiff of the smell . . .

"Eeek, *ants*, the ground is crawling with ants!" Gwen cried, scuttling across the grass on her bare feet, away from the ruin.

Louise was not late in following her, her hooped skirts billowing around her like sails in a storm. "I cannot abide ants," she squealed.

"Females!" exclaimed their exasperated escorts.

But in the next instant Gwen was more successful in diverting their attention than she had hoped. Although she hadn't wished harm to anyone, her ruse went awry as Louise stepped into a hole and fell headlong to the ground, screaming with genuine pain.

Horrified, Gwen rushed to her side and pulled her into her arms. Roc and Morgan fell to their knees in their eagerness to assist the distressed girl, who resembled a bright butterfly with broken wings.

"My ankle," wailed the wounded butterfly.

Morgan instantly relieved her feet of the tiny satin slippers, and when he touched her right ankle, a new wail erupted from her rosy lips.

" 'Tis swelling badly," he commented, distraught, riffling

through his hair in agitation. Turning to Roc for support, he asked, "What shall we do?"

"You'll take Louise to the Hall on Blacky, and I will fetch Dr. Penfield." Roc glared at Gwen. "I don't believe your gall, Gwennie! That was the most harebrained, the most thoughtless, act I've ever seen. Ants, bah! I'm appalled. You, of all people, ought to know better than to tease innocent guests." He lifted Louise easily in his arms and carried her to the old horse, while Morgan trailed irresolutely behind him. "This is all your fault, Gwen, and I expect Louise will never forgive you," came Roc's parting shot.

A hot wave of anger and distress surging through her, Gwen watched them leave. "No!" she whispered, but she was burning with shame. Roc knew there had been no ants.

Morgan, his face filled with wonder, held his precious burden in his arms as Blacky ambled placidly toward the Hall. Roc strode away without a backward glance, leaving Gwen to fend for herself.

Tears streamed down her face, but she cried silently. Roc was angry with her. A large hand touched her arm. "Miss Gwen?"

She knew without looking that the hand belonged to Clem, but she was too upset and embarrassed to meet his concerned gaze. " 'Twasn't yer fault, miss. Ye only did what ye 'ad to do. I guess I shouldn't 'ave 'idden th' kegs in th' ruin." He scratched his head thoughtfully. "Lady Louise is th' prettiest lady I've ever seen," he added in wide-eyed awe. His eyes shifted to the basket, still on the ground.

"Aw, miss, all th' good food goin' to waste . . ." His stomach growled.

Gwen sniffed and dried her eyes with the back of her hand. "Well, why should we let it spoil?" She pounded Clem hard on the back. "We free traders don't let anything go to waste, do we?"

Clem chuckled. "Not if we can 'elp it, miss."

With renewed defiance, Gwen sat down cross-legged on the grass. She was not going to let Roc's harsh words ruin her day, and since they didn't want her assistance at the Hall, she might as well . . . A new wave of tears flooded her eyes.

Clem seated himself next to the basket, which he eagerly emptied after removing the bottle of wine. They feasted on

crusty white bread, paté—which Clem assured Gwen he had
never tasted before—and cold chicken breasts, plumcake, and
strawberry tarts, all washed down with fine claret.

"Aw, what a treat, miss," Clem said with his mouth full
of food. He wiped his sleeve across his mouth, grunting with
satisfaction. "I feel like a lord."

Gwen grimaced. "I'm glad the food wasn't lost to the
ants." To her it tasted like dry wood.

Clem chewed hurriedly, as if he feared such delicacies
would magically vanish from his sight. After eating all he
could, he burped boisterously. " 'Twas a good trick, miss.
Ye did what ye 'ad to do, to protect th' cargo.'Twas unfortunate th' young lady was 'urt." He rose, wiping his mouth
once more. "I'll take th' basket back to th' 'All."

Gwen lay back on the grass, the wind stirring gently over
her bare arms. She pulled off her straw hat and placed it over
her face, but first she peered at him. "Yes, do that. I'm grateful that you warned me about the brandy. 'Twould not do to
have the earl come back in search of the picnic basket and
find the casks."

"Aye, that's 'ow I see it.'E's right enough, but 'e shouldn't
put 'is nose into our business, as we don't put ours into
'is.'Ow would it be if we started findin' faults with th' way
'e takes care o' th' 'All?''

Gwen giggled at the thought. "Go off with you before I
laugh so hard I get a bellyache."

"Yer a right 'un, Miss Gwen, that's what I've always said."
Clem eyed her fondly and donned his grimy cap. Whistling,
he strode through the tall grass, the basket dangling from his
arm.

Chapter 18

"Look at you!" Aunt Clo cried in horror as Gwen entered the parlor of Tremayne House. "Your face is sunburned—like that of a common wench—and your nose looks like a beet."

Gwen glanced at her reflection in the mirror. Her aunt was right. Her delicate skin shone an angry red, especially her nose. "Oh, well." Shrugging, she sat down and picked up her hated embroidery. "I dozed off in the sun, and my straw hat must have blown off my face." She bent over the crumpled canvas.

"How can you attend the party tonight with a face like that?" Aunt Clo exclaimed.

"I'm not going," Gwen said flatly. She stabbed the needle into the flower garland motif.

Aunt Clo's hands dropped to her lap. "Not going?" she echoed. "Why?"

"As you said, I can't show myself like this. Furthermore, I don't want to be the butt of their jokes."

"Whose jokes? Roc's mother's? You don't have to sit next to the dowager countess. The party is being held in the gardens. Just imagine all that good food. 'Twould be a waste not to attend."

"Nothing will stop *you* from attending."

Aunt Clo glowered. "Why are you so stubborn? What happened to change your mind?"

"You might as well know. Sooner or later you will, anyway." Gwen heaved a shuddering sigh. "I caused Louise to wrench her ankle—or even break it—this morning." She could speak freely about the picnic, but she had to bear the burden of her lie about the ants alone.

"Oh, dear." All the breath seemed to go out of Aunt Clo at once. "Well, how could you divine she was going to fall into a hole? It could have happened to anyone. Is it really that bad?"

"I don't know." Gwen did not add that Roc's condemning words had hurt the most. He was the sole reason she didn't want to attend the party. How could she face his disgust? Besides, she hated herself for lying yet again to protect Dandelion. The more she cared about Roc, the more she resented hiding the truth from him. Lies were not a base on which to build a strong relationship.

"I will brook no nonsense from you, Gwennie." Aunt Clo's thin body bristled with indignation. "I will not have you ruin what could be a delightful evening. I'm fed up with your quirks, and you will accompany me tonight. You'll not stop us from partaking of any free entertainment offered in this depressingly remote place."

Gwen could not help but smile at her aunt's sudden vehemence.

"Anyway, you don't know what young man you might meet at the Hall," Aunt Clo continued, her voice softer now.

"You win, of course, but I'm in no mood for idle conversation with the guests," Gwen warned. She sighed. She could not deny her aunt the simple pleasure of a sumptuous meal.

Aunt Clo muttered with disapproval. "Come, we have to try to do something to cover that color on your face. You look like a fishmonger's wife."

With a heavy heart Gwen entered the lighted gardens at the Hall. Darkness had fallen. Colored lanterns swung from tree limbs and brilliant, heavily scented flowers filled every marble urn along the terrace. Long trestle tables laden with food lined the graveled paths, and over an open fire a whole pig roasted on a spit. It looked as if all the inhabitants of Landregan were present, making merry at the barrels where ale and wine flowed freely, or dancing around the fire to the wailing tones of violins, music provided by the villagers.

Like a queen, the dowager countess held court at the head of the longest table, which was covered with a damask tablecloth. Her stern but benevolent gaze followed the merriment of the villagers, who seemed not in the least daunted by such august company.

Next to the countess sat Lady Camelford, and propped against the pillows of a chaise longue reclined Louise, her face pale but composed. Her foot, heavily bandaged, lay like a trophy atop a plump pillow. Morgan hovered around her like an indecisive moth, Lady Camelford's disapproving gaze following his every movement.

Gwen automatically scanned the crowd for a glimpse of Roc and located him in the midst of the merrymakers, dancing with one of the village beauties.

Jealousy gnawed at Gwen's suffering heart, and she wanted to turn on her heel and leave. It pained her to see him so carefree, so handsome, so excruciatingly attractive. Why did love have to hurt so much? she pondered angrily.

"Ah, the Tremaynes at last," the dowager said to indicate she had noticed Aunt Clo and Gwen. Her tone of voice implied it did not make the least difference if they attended or not.

"Kind of you to invite us," Aunt Clo said with a titter.

Ignoring Miss Pettigrew, the dowager turned to Lady Camelford and pointed at the earl with a trembling finger. "I declare Roc learned those outlandish ways in India. I have *never* before seen him behave in such a . . . wild and shocking manner. Like a veritable gypsy. No shoes, and no coat. Wholly indecent! I blush at the sight."

Louise waved energetically, and Gwen hurried past the dowager to join her friend. "Hello, Louise. How serious are your injuries?" she asked worriedly, glancing at the bandage.

"Oh, I will be right as rain in a few weeks," Louise explained quite happily.

"One of the bones is cracked," Lady Camelford uttered in sepulchral tones. "She'll have a limp for the rest of her life, and no gentleman will ever look at her again." She glared at Gwen. "I hear it was all your fault. You should know I was quite set on leaving tomorrow, and now we are forced to stay until my daughter's foot mends."

Louise did not share her lament. Beckoning Gwen closer, she impulsively clutched her arm and whispered, "I'm grateful that this happened, although I'm in pain right now. But the doctor said the pain won't last. Thanks to you, I'll have a chance to get to know Morgan better. It's a blessing in disguise, so don't berate yourself."

Gwen smiled, her melancholy lifting. Although the earl held her accountable for the accident, the victim did not.

Louise squeezed her hand. "You shouldn't heed Roc's hard words this morning. I don't blame you at all. At the time I was well aware of your feelings of guilt. However, I must confess, lying pressed to Morgan's chest, I had difficulty thinking clearly so I never spoke up. How delicious is his embrace!" she whispered conspiratorially.

Gwen sent a furtive glance at Lady Camelford's forbidding face, but no sign indicated she had heard Louise's highly unladylike description. "I'm curious to know why you're interested in Morgan," Gwen said. "He's not exactly a ladies' man."

Louise leaned closer. "He has the most beautiful eyes, and he's so kind."

"Oh."

"He isn't romantic and shrouded in mystery like the smugglers, but who could marry a smuggler?" Louise asked, turning shining eyes on Gwen.

"I see your point," she said faintly. "But are you sure you wouldn't rather marry some man of standing back in London?"

Louise blushed prettily. "I could, but no one has touched my heart like Morgan. I've never known love before."

"Oh." Gwen had difficulty seeing how anyone could fall in love with her bumbling playmate of old. Not that there was anything wrong with Morgan, but he wasn't . . . well, he wasn't Roc.

Gwen's eyes were drawn to the earl with the force of iron dust to a magnet. She watched him swing around the fire, laughing. Holding the village miss by the waist, he lifted her high in the air until she squealed with terror and delight. A dance with the earl would be fodder for endless gossip later in the village. The golden light from the leaping flames undulated over his face, transforming him into someone exotic and dangerous.

Gwen went hot and cold all over, yearning to be with him. Then she turned scarlet with shame. In his simple shirt and breeches he could be mistaken for any one of the village men, his vitality as strong as any young farmer's. It was that male vitality, earthy and sensual, that so attracted her. His strength and determination pulled her to him but also frightened her,

He laughed, his head thrown back, teeth gleaming white against his dark skin. What had the village girl said to amuse him? Gwen wondered as the green-eyed monster of jealousy pushed his fangs deeper into her miserable heart.

"Naturally Mama won't let me have Morgan," Louise continued. Gwen started, torn from her absorption in the earl. "He isn't lofty enough for me, she says." Louise thrust out her chin. "But I don't care what she says."

"You're in a difficult dilemma, of course." Gwen smiled knowingly. "But I'm sure you'll find a solution to your problem, if you set your mind to it."

Louise laughed. "You're so droll, Gwen. I declare, I've never met a more sensible woman in my life. *You* always do exactly as you wish."

"Yes, I have quite a reputation as a headstrong and acid-tongued lady in these parts. You see, when one gains a few years, it becomes easier to do what one wants." In a flash, Gwen realized how little she knew about life, especially about the feelings Roc evoked so strongly in her.

Louise peered at her, curious. "Are you feeling well?" Her soft hand touched Gwen's arm lightly. "You look a trifle peaked, and your face is so *red*."

"It has been a full day." Gwen sighed, tearing her eyes from Roc's twirling body. "And I stayed too long in the sun."

Louise motioned toward Roc with her head. "He behaved rudely this morning, and I let him know it when we arrived at the Hall." Her eyes probed into Gwen's guarded heart. "I thought he was taken with you."

"You have a fertile imagination." Gwen rose awkwardly. "I'll go and refresh myself," she said, needing an excuse to leave. Standing in the shadow of a tree, she watched the dancers. From the tray of a passing footman, she took a glass of wine and sipped gingerly.

Engrossed in the delicacies heaped on a plate before her, Aunt Clo was sitting close to the dowager countess. Standing behind Louise's chair, Morgan, without his ever-present books

and his spectacles, had the look of a lost puppy. He would
have to learn what to do with his hands when not holding on
to a book, Gwen mused, some of her usual aplomb returning.

On the illuminated terrace Gwen caught a glimpse of Vincent sneaking inside the hall. What was her devious cousin
up to now? With a shiver of uneasiness, she decided to follow
him inside. After setting down her wineglass, she kept to the
shadows of the trees until she had reached the terrace. Taking
a deep breath, she darted across the foyer and listened at the
study door. She had a feeling that was where Vincent was
hiding. There was a sound of movement in the room. The
entrance hall was silent, the candles in the wall sconces sending out flickering lights. The house was quiet, the servants
having evidently joined the crowd in the garden.

Although fear rippled through Gwen, she had to find out
what Vincent was doing. Should she first inform Roc that
Vincent was skulking in his study? She hesitated for a moment, then cautiously opened the door. Through the crack,
she spied Vincent pulling out one desk drawer after another.
Only a single candle illuminated the room, and the corners
were swathed in deep shadows. He was so intent on his
stealthy search that he didn't notice her eye in the door opening. Swearing under his breath, he finally closed the last
drawer with a slam and sank down in Roc's chair. With an
insolent smile, he leaned back and lifted his legs to the desk-
top, heedless of the grime his boots left on the papers strewn
there.

Anger burst within Gwen when she saw his smile. She tore
the door open and stepped inside, her body stiff with outrage.
"What are you doing here?" she demanded. "Take your
boots down this instant!"

He laughed. "What are *you* doing, dear coz? Spying on
me or looking for something?"

Refusing to reply, she crossed the room and shoved his
boots off the mahogany surface. "You have no right to put
your feet on Roc's desk. Have you no manners?"

He rose, looming over her, his shoulders stiff with pad-
ding, his eyes glittering with malice. "I take no orders from
you," he said, slowly inserting his hands into his pockets.

As she watched his slow movement, Gwen felt afraid. What
did his pockets conceal? She had been foolish to confront

him alone. "You make me ashamed of you, Vinnie," she said. "Your manners seem to have gone abegging since you left the army."

His smile made her take a step back. "When did you begin noticing my behavior so closely? I'm flattered."

"It wasn't a compliment." Gwen felt the warmth seep from her cheeks at the suggestion she read in his eyes. He was purposely misinterpreting everything she said. She recoiled as he reached out to touch her arm.

The door banged back against the wall. "What's going on? A secret tête-à-tête?" said Roc's cold voice.

Gwen whirled around and ran to his side. "I'm so glad to see you," she said, her voice choking.

He glanced at her through narrowed eyes, then gave Vincent a thorough scrutiny. "I might be wrong, but I sense a tension here," he said slowly, as if testing the words.

Gwen pulled his arm, noticing the hostility between the two men. "Please, let's go back to the garden."

"Were you forcing yourself on Gwendolyn?" Roc challenged, taking a step toward Vincent.

Gwen looked with fear at her cousin, wondering how he would twist his words to blame her. To her surprise, he said cheerfully, "Forcing myself? Come now, what a preposterous suggestion."

"But what were you doing with her alone in my study?"

Vincent shrugged. "Gwen's a dead bore, always nagging me about my manners, my clothes, my whereabouts." He threw up his arms. "Yes, my very *existence!*" He sighed and took on the mien of a naughty schoolboy. "I merely came in here in search of a book of poetry. Wanted to impress one of the village ladies with a bit of dulcet verse, y'know. There's no crime in that, surely?"

Liar! Gwen wanted to scream, but she pressed her lips tightly together. Once again, Vincent had taken the upper hand. He had been going through Roc's private desk drawers. But before she told Roc, she had to find out what Vincent was after. He was part of her family, and any smirch on his name would be a smirch on the Tremayne family. She was almost sure he'd been looking for money, since he'd no doubt spent every penny Squire Tremayne had given him so far, as well as what he'd stolen from her.

Roc gave her a last penetrating glance, and she managed a stiff smile. Seemingly satisfied, he walked over to one of the bookcases and extracted a slim, leather-bound volume. Handing it to Vincent, he said, "Take this, Tremayne, but please return it later."

Vincent bowed subserviently and hurried through the open French doors onto the terrace. Smiling, Roc took Gwen's elbow and led her outside. Vincent had disappeared, and Gwen felt safe again. Glancing into Roc's warm eyes, she soon forgot her odious cousin.

"Dreaming?" Roc asked, his deep voice as soft as velvet. "You seem so far away tonight." He touched her hair, sending waves of longing through her. He stood so close she could smell his warm skin, his musky virility. Inexplicably nervous, she licked her dry lips and shifted from one foot to the other. Barely daring to meet his searing gaze, his sensual smile, she said, "After what happened this morning, I'm surprised you're talking to me." She could not control the injured tone in her voice.

"I realize I was unforgivably rude this morning, and I offer you my humblest apologies. It just seemed so silly to play a prank on Lady Louise, so unlike the Gwen I know."

Still hurting from his wounding words of that morning, she said, "You don't know me very well, milord. And you didn't complain of Louise's fear of ants."

He chuckled, a deep throaty sound. "You're so different from her, so strong and decisive, wholly capable of taking care of yourself."

Gwen's eyes blazed with anger. "She's more womanly and pretty, is that it? I'm just good old Gwen, one of the chaps, eh?"

He grasped her arm, his burning touch sending flames of desire through her. "You said that, Gwen, I never did." He leaned closer, his breath fanning her face. "I never want to touch her like I want to touch you." His whisper rasped along her nerves, making her raw with need.

"Come, let's join the country dance." He pulled her with him, his enthusiasm rubbing off on her. When his hands encircled her waist, she wanted to press herself against him in wanton desire. Laughing, he swung her around and around, caressing her with his topaz gaze which darkened to dusky velvet in the firelight. She had eyes for no one but him.

"Am I forgiven?" he asked during a pause in the music.

How could she keep a grudge when he was begging her under the mellow stars, under the eyes of all the villagers. His gaze smoldered, and his smile pleaded. Her heart lodged in her throat.

"If you don't forgive me, I'll kiss you right here, with everyone looking."

Her heart racing, she managed to form the necessary words. "I forgive you, you scalawag!"

Grinning from ear to ear, he murmured, "I think I will kiss you, but not here. I want to do it where no one but the stars and the sky, and perhaps a bird or two, can see us."

She could not answer. Her heart made a somersault and she could feel her whole face shine with the love she had borne him all her life. It was flowering at last, after long, lonely years. Emotion overwhelmed her, and she felt a strong urge to cry for the deep and wondrous pain of her love.

When Roc lifted her high in the air, she laughed with happiness and a sense of freedom. All eyes were on her, but she did not care if people thought she was making a spectacle of herself.

Roc bore her away from the dowager's disapproving gaze and they mingled with the villagers, who did not take exception to their buoyant spirits.

Panting and smiling, Roc set her down, her body sliding along his. Breathless, Gwen looked at him. A hot urge to kiss his stubborn chin and hard lips overcame her. Only shyness, and a last thread of propriety, stopped her from doing so in public.

"Tired?" When she nodded, he added, "I'll fetch you a plate of food." He placed a finger under her chin. "And don't you dare escape," he murmured, his voice spinning a web of promises around her.

Gwen stood perfectly still, filled with luminous wonder as she watched him move toward the tables with earthy grace. Then her gaze traveled over the happy faces of the villagers. Gone were the habitual taciturn expressions, replaced by smiles and open chatter. Clem waved at her and winked, tossing the earl's broad back a meaning glance. She blushed. What did her fellow smugglers think of her now? Perhaps they had sampled enough ale not to think anything. They might grumble in the morning that Dandelion was consorting with the enemy, but tonight there was peace on all fronts.

Roc didn't seem to notice her pensive mood when he returned, balancing two glasses of wine and a plate with slices of roast pork and warm bread. He led her along a secluded path past a stand of lilacs to a wooden bench. He set down the glasses and pulled her next to him.

His every movement like a caress, he offered her a glass. The wine tasted like nectar on her dry tongue. They ate in silence, the moment too precious to waste on small talk, the air fraught with unspoken longings.

Although their shared closeness invited Gwen to pour forth the love she had stored for so long, to empty her heart of the guilt of her deception, she could not bear to see his face change in horror. What would he do if he knew he was sharing refreshments with Dandelion? She shuddered with unease.

Yet there was that reckless part of her that liked the subterfuge, the suspense. It was that part which had urged her to become Dandelion in the first place. She liked to see how close she could go to the edge without falling. "Shall we take a walk by the sea?" the devilish part of her made her say. "Who knows, we might meet Dandelion."

He laughed mirthlessly. "No chance of that. I'm sure I've met him many times this evening; he's probably at this very moment eating his fill at *my* table."

To her ears, Gwen's laughter rang false.

"Come along before the dowager gets it into her head to call me," Roc demanded.

Gwen's fingers trembled slightly as she placed them in his strong grip. "I'm ready." She followed him, her hand still cradled in his.

The moon bathed the sea with silver. The breakers churned against the rocks and reefs, spraying the air with a fine mist. A warm wind from the south wafted gently against their heated faces and whispered in furze and reed. The sand crunched softly under their feet.

"This is the kind of night when nymphs come out of the

sea to entice sailors, and when sprites dance on the misty moors,'' Roc mused aloud.

"If we walk quietly, we might be able to see them."

"They'll see us first." He stopped and turned to her, placing his hands on her shoulders. "I'm glad you believe in mythical creatures."

She waited expectantly for his kiss, but he stood motionless, his face cast in light and darkness, his eyes wells of thought.

"Kiss me," she urged recklessly. "You said you would."

Silence grew full and heavy between them.

"If I do, I might not be able to stop," he said, his voice harsh with emotion.

As if propelled by an inner force, Gwen leaned slowly toward him, and when he did not enfold her immediately into his arms, she reached up, curled her arms around his neck, and pressed herself against him. "Kiss me," she whispered.

With a groan, he molded his mouth hotly to hers, all resistance melting between them. As he pushed his hand through her hair, the pins scattered across the sand, lost forever. "Oh, Gwennie, what are you doing to me?" he whispered, sliding his lips frenziedly down her slender neck.

"Something I've always wanted . . . with you."

He pulled his head up a fraction. "Then I was right when I thought you might harbor a soft spot for me."

"Oh, Roc," she said, "how can you joke at a time like this?"

She gasped with pleasure as his lips found the soft swell of her breasts above the edge of her low-cut bodice. His fingers worked on the laces of her robings, until he managed to loosen the tight bodice and slide his hand under the padded stomacher. As he pushed it aside, her moonlit breasts were revealed to his eyes in their soft and intimate glory. The moon lent silver to her smile and to her bare arms as she twined them around his chest under his open shirt. His breath flowed over the soft skin of her shoulders, down to the taut peaks of her breasts, and when his lips encircled one nipple greedily, Gwen laughed softly, a chuckle that changed to a moan of pleasure. Her fingers explored the rippling muscles of his back and shoulders, the strong column of his neck, and the long, curling hair at the nape.

He lifted his face, and in the moonlight, Gwen saw pain battling with desire.

"We can't go on like this, Gwennie, even though I'm wild with desire to bed you," he said, his voice thick with need. "I cannot compromise you. Even to take you on this nightly walk was a mistake."

"No one will know . . . Please, don't stop now," she urged, and pulled his mouth to her lips, raining light kisses.

"Oh . . . Gwen, you . . . will be my ruin!" He tried to release her clinging arms, but she forced him down in the sand with her. When he lay on top of her, his bare chest pressed to her breasts, his legs in the valley between her thighs, he could hold back no longer. With a moan of defeat, he buried his face in the sweetly scented cleft between her breasts.

Gwen knew she must have him, must find out what making love truly meant. She would be an untouched spinster no longer. She would know a man intimately.

She eagerly helped him undo her cumbersome paniers and layers of petticoats and overskirt, leaving only the sheerest shift next to her skin. He flung off his shirt in one fluid movement. Shivering with delicious anticipation, Gwen undid the lacing of his breeches.

For the first time she saw the splendid body of a naked man, the perfect symmetry of muscles rippling over chest, arms, thighs, and the hard, flat abdomen tapering down to a shadowed nest of curls from which sprang the evidence of his ardor. His fingers gently peeled off her shift to reveal her slender nakedness. Moonlight highlighted the curves and valleys, caught the softness of the hair at the joining of her thighs, and played over her long slender legs, spread in anticipation of revelations to come.

"Sweet, lovely nymph," he breathed, his hands sliding trancelike over her tantalizing curves.

The very center of Gwen's being opened to his touch. A love so strong that she could only sigh flooded through her. She moaned softly as the heel of his hand dipped between her thighs, pressing, teasing, loving.

Instinctively, her hands strayed over his skin, sought and found his velvety length, begging for her attention. Fitting it eagerly into her hand, she discovered she had the power to create goosebumps on his skin and make him writhe against her.

A molten ecstasy began to build slowly within her as she felt herself swell and throb under his gentle but insistent touch. The pleasure centered in the hidden place between her opened thighs, and she urged him on, eager to learn more about the depths of love. A short moment of pain, then sheer wonder surged through her as he filled her. His movements increased the delicious torment slowly, relentlessly. He filled and emptied her of himself, until her world swirled into hot, rapturous waves, until she ceased to exist. She became one with him as he melted into her over and over again.

Her languorous moans filled her ears. His velvety skin was a constant caress sliding over hers. Her whole body was covered with him—Roc . . . her dream, her love, hotly on her, within her. His breath came in harsh gasps as he wound his arms around her, half lifting her out of the sand as he pounded his release into her.

"Gwen, my . . . love," he breathed as he carefully lowered her back onto the sand. "Glorious love." He gasped for breath, joy radiating from him. She sensed his smile in the darkness. "Utterly glorious." He kissed every inch of her face and licked her earlobes until she giggled. "Vixen . . . sea witch." He accentuated his words with tiny kisses on her eyelids, cheeks, the tip of her nose, her swollen lips. "Dear enchantress."

Gazing reverently at her moonlit face, he asked, "Did I hurt you?" Gently he stroked the wild tangle of her hair.

"Only a little at first." She trailed a shy finger along his chest. "Now I've truly lost my last treasure to you."

He laughed, a full, rich sound. "I'm a lucky man. Such madness, such enchantment," he enthused. "Such rapture!"

"A night of secrecy, of stolen pleasures," Gwen whispered. "A memory to cherish forever."

Roc glanced at her, puzzlement clouding his face. Then he rose with a forceful movement. Pulling her with him, he caressed her face and lifted her easily into his arms. As if carrying a priceless treasure, he waded into the chilly waves and lowered her into the water. A freezing tremor ran through her but was soon replaced by a refreshed feeling as the salty water lapped over her naked body. It stung between her legs for a short time, a healing sting. Roc held her lovingly, his hands wandering over every curve and hollow of her body, creating a new languor, easing every ounce of tension from her muscles. She stood, doing the same to him, and like two happy children they wallowed in the water until the chill got under their skin.

Shouting and laughing, they returned to the beach, where they found new secrets to share and create with each other as the summer wind caressed them dry.

And as once again they slowly descended from the dulcet pinnacles of bliss, Roc asked, ''Will you marry me, Gwen?''

Chapter 19

"Marry you?" Gwen sat up, her eyes like dark pools in her face.

"Of course! You can't think I would compromise you like this and not offer for your hand?" Roc sounded incredulous. He regarded her warily.

"I . . . I can't marry you." With a jerky movement she pushed the wild tangle of hair from her face.

"Nonsense. There's no need to be shy with me, Gwen. Tomorrow morning I'll speak to the squire and formally ask for your hand." He stroked her reassuringly across her tense shoulders. "Why are you looking at me like that?"

Gwen shook herself out of her trance. "I just can't marry you."

Suspicion slowly clouded his happy face. "Why?" Growing angrier when she did not answer, he said, "Is there another man? Are you promised to another? Vincent?"

"No!" Gwen impatiently dismissed his preposterous suggestion. How could she explain to him about Dandelion? She twisted her hands. "You know there is no other man." She grasped at the first idea she could think of. "I need to look after the squire in his old age; he'd be lost without me."

"That's a lame excuse, and well you know it, Gwen." He rested his hand on her warm shoulder. "Don't you see? We have to get married. What if there are consequences from this night of love? You'd be shunned by everybody, including the squire." His voice caressed her softly, and she shuddered. Why had she not thought of this possibility before throwing herself into his arms? Naïvely she had believed everything would continue as before.

187

She rose hesitantly. "I want to go home now." Distraught, she gathered her rumpled garments, shaking the sand from the folds. One after the other, she pulled them on.

Roc stood, his face pale with bewilderment. "I thought you'd raise no objection to our marriage. You would never have to worry about Tremayne House again. Together we'd have it repaired from top to bottom. And at the Hall, you'd be close enough to look after the squire."

"I'll take no charity," she retorted. If only she could admit she wanted to marry him more than anything else in the world. But if he ever found out about Dandelion, he would never forgive her for deceiving him. She needed to be alone and think. "Roc, you mustn't feel that you *have* to marry me. *I* seduced you, remember?"

He chuckled. "I was a willing victim. No, I have to do the right thing by you, Gwen."

"You sound as if you're concluding a business transaction. I told you—I don't want your charity."

That obviously touched a sore nerve. His whole body stiff with disapproval, he proceeded to dress, and Gwen released a sigh of relief. She desperately needed a reprieve.

"And how many people do you think saw us disappear together tonight and not return?" he snapped. "The party must be long over by now, and your aunt—"

"She knows I can take care of myself," Gwen shot back.

She heard him mutter something like, "Useless old chaperone," and smiled into the darkness. What an honorable man Roc was, all that a woman could wish for and more. He assaulted her with more questions, but Gwen deflected them, promising she would consider his proposal.

Before leaving her in the spinney behind Tremayne House, he said, "I thought you loved me. Was that a silly assumption?"

Gwen blushed, worrying that he would wear down her resistance if he knew just how deeply she felt. "I do love you, Roc, but please don't press me."

He looked crestfallen, but a stubborn set to his chin told her he wasn't ready to give up. He bent to kiss her lightly on the lips. "Sweet dreams, my darling. We'll discuss this matter later."

Gwen nodded and disappeared into the shadows, glad to

shield her guilt from his probing gaze. She had no difficulty creeping into the house without being seen.

His parting kiss still burned hotly on her lips, and thrills of pleasure coursed through her when she remembered how his hands and lips had roamed over her body. She was now wholly his, and nothing could change that.

She slept late, and when she came downstairs the following morning breakfast was being removed from the table in the dining room. "Please leave me some, Marva," Gwen said brightly, to hide that anything untoward had happened. "I'm fairly starved."

Aunt Clo greeted her with a withering stare, and the squire murmured an absentminded greeting. Vincent had not yet come downstairs.

"Where did you go last night? I waited up for you," Aunt Clo said.

Gwen decided it was best to tell the truth. With an uneasy glance at the squire, she said, "I took a walk on the beach with the earl."

A falling feather could have been heard in the silence that ensued. Aunt Clo bore an expression of utter horror.

"A walk with a *man* in the middle of the night? Gwennie, how could you! And the earl! *I* always knew he had no honor. It will be your ruin if it comes out." She studied Gwen's face speculatively, but dared not pose the unspoken question: had he taken advantage of her?

"Nothing untoward happened," Gwen said, squarely meeting her aunt's probing gaze. Yet she shivered with delight at the memory of Roc's embrace. No irate relative could take that from her.

Aunt Clo shook her head. "I'm sure a score of guests saw you disappear with him," she uttered in funereal tones. "You are ruined. What shall we do now?"

Gwen turned to the squire, expecting to hear a roar of outrage, but he had not listened to their conversation. She drew a sigh of relief, her eyes warning her aunt to keep silent.

Gwen consumed a big breakfast of fried kidneys and pilchards, eggs, and toast. She washed it all down with tea. Amazingly refreshed, she knew her body was still savoring the aftermath of her magic night with Roc. When she heard the sound of a galloping horse, she wanted to rush to the window to see if the visitor was Roc. But keeping her impulse at bay, she calmly continued to eat.

A heavy knock sounded on the door, and Gwen's heart somersaulted. She heard Roc's deep voice as he spoke with Arthur in the hallway. The feebleminded footman, who took his duties very seriously entered the parlor and announced in a grave voice, "His lordship the earl of Landregan."

As Roc swept into the room, his gaze instantly sought Gwen. For a moment fleeting desire filled the topaz depths as his eyes raked over her languid body. Gwen shivered with pleasure, as if he had caressed her intimately. Her heart wanted to burst, but she could think of nothing to say.

He looked splendid in a close-fitting blue silk frock coat with a matching waistcoat, embellished with gold buttons and embroidered with gold thread in a leaf pattern. Gwen's eyes wandered up the defined muscles of his thighs, and she blushed with embarrassment, then bent to retrieve her napkin, which had slid to the floor.

When she glanced at him again, a knowing smile hovered on his lips. "Good morning to all. What a lovely day!" He bowed.

Aunt Clo acknowledged his greeting with a suspicious nod and the squire muttered a dazed good morning. Gwen said nothing.

"I wish to speak with you, Squire Tremayne, if you can tear yourself away from your studies for a few minutes. I assure you, the matter is very important, or I would not claim your time."

Lionel Tremayne glanced at Roc over his spectacles and murmured, "What for? I'd rather speak with Morgan if you don't mind." When the earl insisted, he snapped, "Dashed nuisance. I'm in the middle of a very important theory." With a sigh he finally rose, his napkin falling into the teacup. "I will see you in the study, Roc. This had better be important," he added peevishly, wagging a fat finger under Roc's nose.

Gwen dreaded the coming half hour, knowing that Roc was going to ask for her hand. How could she explain to her father why she could not marry Roc? She wanted to marry him, so much so that her heart ached. *Dear God, what shall I do?*

The answer stared her blatantly in the face—bury Dandelion and marry the love of her heart.

She must talk to Clem, to ask him to take over the responsibility of the free trading, to handle the large sums of money that paid for the contraband, and distribute the shares to the others. Clem would be a strong, loyal leader, although he had rash ideas at times and a bad head for mathematics.

As Gwen contemplated these plans, Marva entered and told her Gus Lane was at the door selling strawberries.

"Oh, good! I will purchase a basket." Gwen rose and followed the waddling cook to the kitchen where sunlight bathed the room with inviting warmth. Gus sat on the steps outside the door, munching on a wedge of mutton pie. He wiped his dirty hat from his head as Gwen appeared in the doorway.

"Miss Gwen!" His voice urgent, he told her Clem had sent him. "Early this mornin' th' earl began to build a gallows in th' middle o' th' square. 'E says 'tis for Dandelion, and 'e was doin' it as a warnin' to th' whole village. 'E laughed and said 'e would 'ave th' bloke soon. Dandelion would swing in th' wind before th' end o' August."

A jumble of thoughts rushed madly through Gwen's head.

If she agreed to become the countess of Landregan, Roc could not capture her, since Dandelion would be no more. Then anger flared within her. After such a wonderful night with her, how could he go out and build a gallows to hang a man! Such callousness, such insufferable arrogance!

Gwen seethed, her hands clenching into fists at her sides and her chin jutting upward with determination. She marveled that even for a moment she had dreamed she could marry him. In a state of weakness she had forgotten his insolent vow to capture and punish Dandelion. Well, not as long as she had breath in her body. Gallows, bah!

"Tell Clem to make an effigy of the earl and hang it from the gallows tonight," she ordered frostily.

"Effi— What?" Gus stared in awe.

"Oh, a doll of hay, dressed in the earl's clothes. If Clem cannot persuade Enedoc to give him some clothes, just paint the earl's name on a piece of wood and hang it around the neck of the doll. And make sure the earl's there to see the burning."

A devastating coldness came over her. She did not want to do this! But if it took the rest of her life, she would force Roc to take down the gallows with his bare hands.

"Ye're a sharp 'un, miss. Nuffin' can ruffle ye up." Gus's eyes were as large as saucers as he trotted down the lane, pushing his wheelbarrow in front of him. Too late Gwen remembered the strawberries. Well, who could eat after receiving this news? Gallows, indeed. The bloodthirsty sod!

Aunt Clo had moved to the front parlor, leaving the door open, her eyes peeled on the hallway so as not to miss any unusual goings-on. Gwen joined her, still seething inside. How easily things could change from moment to moment. Ten minutes ago she had been ready to marry Roc, and now all such hopes were gone.

Roc's voice trailed into the hallway as he left the study. The squire's voice held an oddly excited note, and Gwen well knew the reason. When Roc entered the parlor, she kept her blazing eyes lowered to the embroidery frame in her hands so that he could not see her wrath. All the stitches she angrily poked into the canvas would have to be taken out at a later date, but she'd rather sew than pretend to be happy at the prospect of becoming the countess of Landregan.

She sensed Roc's eyes on her but stubbornly refused to look up.

"Miss Pettigrew, would you please leave us for a few minutes? I have something very important to ask Gwen."

"Of course." Gwen heard the excitement in Aunt Clo's voice as the older woman fluttered out of the room. Gwen jabbed her needle into the garland pattern, wishing it was Roc's black heart. The threadbare sofa sagged under his weight as he sat down next to her.

"Gwen, is something wrong?" He took a deep breath. "Look at me, please."

Reluctantly she raised her gaze to his face, her anger hidden behind a cold mask. "Yes? What is it you want to tell me that Aunt Clo mustn't hear?"

He laughed, a puzzled sound. "You're pulling my leg, Gwen. You know my business well enough, or have you already forgotten. I'm here to ask you to become my wife."

When no ecstatic response was forthcoming, he took her hand, stopping the nervous stabbing of the canvas. "Gwen, please say yes. We'll deal very well together, and I eagerly admit that you've, ahem, stolen my heart."

Gwen realized how hard it was for him to utter those words, to leave himself vulnerable to her. She had to give him credit for honesty and heartfelt feeling. She ached with unshed tears, love, and disappointment. Why did she not live her life like other females, filling her days with embroidery and painting watercolors instead of leading a ring of smugglers?

"No, Roc. I told you before I will not marry you, so you might as well forget the idea." She dared to shoot him a glance and suffered when she saw the pain and disbelief in his eyes. "I'm surprised you'd insist on talking to Father after I told you in no uncertain terms—"

"But why? There is no reason to reject me." He paused. "If what happened last night is any indication, I'd say you wouldn't be adverse to spending your life with me. You liked me well enough then."

"Pure moonlight madness." Her tears were close. "Please leave, Roc. I don't want to talk with you any longer."

As tense as a bowstring, he stood, misery pouring from him. He bowed stiffly. "I shall do as you wish, but I shall be back. I feel you're hiding the real reason from me, and I won't rest until you tell me the truth."

Gwen refused to answer, her head bent, her eyes brimming. He hesitated for a few moments, then strode from the room, anger accentuating his every footstep.

As soon as the front door closed behind him, Aunt Clo entered, her curiosity overflowing. "Well? Did he offer for you?"

Before Gwen could answer, the squire burst into the parlor in high fettle. "I daresay our Gwennie has nabbed herself a husband at last, and none too early at that. The earl's quite a catch, and I don't know how you managed to entice him, but you did, and that's what's important. He promised a huge settlement, which will put us back into our former comforts." The squire rubbed his hands together with pleasure.

"I will not marry the earl, Papa."

Her relatives seemed to lose their breath in bafflement. A few tense moments passed before the squire found his voice.

"But—but you *cannot* turn him down. You'll never get another chance at matrimony," he said. His voice trailed off as if he already believed the whole morning had been nothing but a dream.

"Ungrateful minx, that's what you are!" Aunt Clo, made of sterner stuff than the squire, would not as easily give up the battle. Here was the perfect solution to all their problems. "Think of our struggle here. 'Twould be extremely foolish to turn him down."

"I already did, so don't waste your efforts on me." A tear fell from Gwen's eye onto the limp embroidery lying useless in her lap.

Her aunt bristled with indignation. "How could you? What's wrong with you? Do you want to live the rest of your life in poverty and be an old maid like me? Pressing forth a few tears, she added, "Roc is a personable young man, and I know you like him well enough." Aunt Clo dabbed at her eyes with her handkerchief as she paced the room.

"Don't wear a hole in the carpet, Auntie, I won't change my mind, however much you try to sway me," Gwen said in her most stubborn voice. "That's my last word."

With a wail Aunt Clo threw herself onto the sofa, while the squire's face bore the expression of one who wished himself elsewhere. "How can you be so heartless?" Aunt Clo cried with disgust. "Only thinking of yourself."

"I beg you to spare us your histrionics, Aunt Clo. They will get you nowhere." Gwen rose, her features set in a stern mask. Wails followed her out of the room, and she hated herself for disappointing her family. In her wildest imaginings she had never dreamed that her identity as Dandelion would complicate her life to such an extent.

In the beginning it had been easy; she had enjoyed herself every time a load was brought in. Now she wondered if the time had come to put Dandelion to rest. She clenched her fists at her sides as she paced the floor of her bedchamber. She could not do it, not until Roc had given up his dastardly pursuit. Gallows! She would show him. Principles were at stake, and she knew she could never live with herself if she abandoned the villagers at this crucial stage in their struggle for a decent existence.

Chapter 20

Roc did not return to Tremayne House for several days, and Gwen was grateful to be spared the pain of arguing with him. In her heart she longed for him every moment, and the days dragged on forever. Guilt stabbed her every time she looked at her family's glum faces. The squire recovered from his disappointment at Gwen's refusal to marry Roc, but every morning at breakfast Gwen saw that her aunt's eyes were red from crying.

The effigy had been hung in the square, just as she had ordered. According to Gus, many gleeful comments were flying about the village. The earl had been in a thunderous rage upon finding a hay scarecrow dressed in one of his old suits—supplied by Enedoc—swinging from the sinister gallows on the square. His eyes as big as saucers, Gus told her that the earl had cut down the doll with one slash of his sword and called the spectators cowards for not daring to step forward and tell him Dandelion's real name.

A glimmer of a smile crept across Gwen's lips at that. "I take it they all gave him the view of their backs."

"Aye, miss, they 'urried away from there. Ye know nobody in th' village wants th' free tradin' to stop, and people don't take kindly to 'is lordship's threat to catch Dandelion. That earl, 'e is workin' too 'ard if ye arsk me."

"Yes, he is quite diligent in his role as magistrate. But I think he's working in vain this time."

Later that afternoon, as Gwen was riding home after visiting Mrs. Padstow's shop, she saw a woman step out of The Pilchard. It wasn't just any woman; she was a so-called bird of paradise, if her brightly painted face, henna-dyed hair, and scarlet gown were any indication. But what gave her away was her penetrating voice hurling invectives at the poor ostler who was struggling with a nervous horse.

"Bring th' critter right over 'ere, ye great looby," the woman demanded. "I arsked for 'im 'alf an 'our ago, didn't I?"

"But ye cannot ride a 'orse," said the ostler, evidently resenting her demands.

"That's neither 'ere nor there. I 'ave to get around this godforsaken 'ole, don't I?" She pulled her skirts up past her knee and wiggled her dainty foot at the ostler. "Can't walk in these slippers, now can I?"

The ostler ogled the trim ankle and the inviting smile, then offered to drive her anywhere she wanted. While the prostitute laughed at the suggestion, Gwen followed the exchange with interest.

When the woman's demands grew louder, the ostler finally gave in and fetched the oldest nag in the stables, the horse most likely not to throw an inept rider.

"Who is she?" Gwen asked the ostler as the woman, holding unsteadily to the pommel of the saddle, disappeared around the corner of the stables.

The ostler shrugged. "She's from Lunnon, that's all I know. Mr. Trelawny wouldn't put 'er up, but she 'as a 'eavy purse, and ye know me employer niver is adverse to th' glimmer o' gold."

Gwen alighted from Buttercup and stepped into the taproom, which was almost empty at this time of the day. The host, leaning against the ale barrel in a corner, looked as if he was sleeping standing up. He started as Gwen called out, "Who was that woman, Mr. Trelawny?"

"Eh?" He cleared his throat and scratched his neck under a grimy cravat. "Woman? Ah, she's Miss Mabel Noble, from Lunnon, Miss Tremayne."

The name Mabel stirred Gwen's memory. It was the name on the note she had taken from Vincent's room. "What's she doing here?"

The proprietor looked put out. "I don't pry into my customers' business," he said, pursing his lips.

"I see. Well, thank you."

"A pint, miss?" Mr. Trelawny gestured toward the ale barrel.

Gwen glanced around the room once again. The men there were all smugglers who were pretending not to see her. No one who might object would find out if she indulged in a tankard of ale at the inn. "Yes, please," she said, imagining the marchioness of Camelford's outrage if she ever knew what Gwen was about to do. Gwen smiled and hoisted the tankard in the air. "Cheers to Landregan and all its inhabitants!"

Mr. Trelawny chuckled. "Ye always was an odd bird, Miss Tremayne, if ye don't mind me sayin' so. But there's no lady in these parts who could 'old a candle to yer charm."

"Well, thank you," Gwen said, grinning. "There's no better remedy for a parched throat." She drank deeply of the cold, bitter ale, then almost choked as she recognized her cousin standing in the doorway.

"Well, coz, if this isn't an unexpected sight, I don't know what is. Does the squire know?" Vincent sauntered forward, a faint smile stretching his lips.

"He will as soon as you tattle." Gwen took another swallow and studied her cousin. He was dressed and painted as elaborately as if ready to saunter the length of Bond Street in London. His almost-white hair was brushed and tied back with a velvet bow, and his pale eyelashes had been darkened. This was only Landregan, but she suspected why he was dressed up—for Mabel.

Vincent ordered a pint and sat down at one of the tables. Gwen joined him. "You're too late, dear coz."

He quirked a darkened eyebrow. "Late? For what?"

"You're here to meet Miss Mabel Noble, aren't you, Vinnie?"

He straightened, suddenly alert. "What are you talking about?"

Gwen lowered her voice. "I don't know if you've noticed that it's gone, but I took your letter from Mabel."

His pale features paled even more. "*You* searched my room, snooped through my things?"

Gwen shrugged, savoring his outrage. "I remember a certain incident when I found you in my room. After that, my money was gone. I know you took it." She paused, studying his narrow face closely.

Something cold and calculating had crept into his features. "I went into your room," she continued, "to retrieve my money pouch—a foolish idea since no doubt you couldn't wait to spend the gold. So I took your letter from Mabel. Now, why don't you tell me about your little secret, eh?"

A spiral of fear curled along her spine as his eyes grew hard and ruthless. "I have business to take care of, that's all. You have no right to pry into my private affairs."

"If it includes hurting people I care about, I certainly have a right. I hoped you'd leave Landregan long before this, but I see that something is keeping you here." She rose. "I intend to find out what it is."

"You may be sorry for those words one day," he snarled, clamping his bony hand around her wrist. "Don't you dare threaten me."

Pain shot through her as he wrenched harder. Furious, she didn't care who heard her outburst. "Let me go!" she shouted, and clouted him over the head. Her smuggler friends rose from their seats and advanced toward her. At the sight of the belligerent men Vincent released his grip. Gwen clouted him once more and hurried outside.

She was queasy with fear, but she could not stand by and let Vincent think he had the right to do anything he pleased without retaliation. Nevertheless, he was a dangerous enemy, and from now on she would sleep with her bedroom door locked.

The dark of the moon in August came with a restless, humid wind that chased tattered clouds across the sky. It was a perfect night to execute Gwen's plan of fetching the contraband directly from the *Alouette* with Morgan's sailboat. She had decided to haul the cargo to Dead Man's Cove.

The sinister name of the cove had been coined long ago because many a drowned body had washed up on the beach. The ruthless wreckers had plied their business on dark, stormy nights, luring unsuspecting ships onto the deadly reefs with signals from the house that now bore the name of Wrecker's Ruin. Hundreds of innocent people had lost their lives because of the greedy wreckers, who worked to seize the rich cargo from the capsized vessels. Gwen was grateful that the evil trade was at an end in Landregan, although it continued in other parts of Cornwall.

According to their plan, Clem and the best sailor in Landregan, Troy Polson, would set out in the *Seahawk* in the dead of night. The smugglers had two reasons for using Morgan's sailboat. One, it was large enough to hold the kegs, and two, it was sturdy enough to avoid being tossed onto the reefs if sailed properly.

Gwen had a personal reason for using the boat—it represented another way to thwart Roc. She had not seen him since that fateful morning two weeks ago when she had turned down his proposal. Anger and sorrow ached like a bruise on her chest. She could find no way to stop the racing tide of events that was taking her farther away from Roc.

Since no gossip, true or false, had leaked out about this expedition, the representatives of the law were fumbling in the dark for any clue that would lead them to the smugglers. Officer Biggles, who had not given up hope of being the one to capture the infamous Dandelion, trailed behind Roc, who was scouting the area around Wrecker's Ruin on horseback.

The smugglers headed for Dead Man's Cove on the cliff path—all except Alfie and Thomas Strutt, who had set off to lay a false trail for the soldiers. Alfie hoped to round up the dragoons posted at Brandy Cove by delivering a deafening shot in the air, thus alerting every waking soul within a five-mile radius, and a few sleeping ones as well. With the dragoons blundering like a herd of sheep behind him in the darkness, Alfie led them east to the path off Lucky Hole. There he met up with his brother Thomas, who was being followed by the rest of the soldiers pursuing him from Lucky Hole.

By preordained plan, they swung effortlessly up into a huge oak tree that bordered the path through a copse. From a high tree limb they watched, with soundless mirth, the eruption of confusion below as the two groups converged together on the dark path.

"Dammit, where did those scoundrels go?" somebody shouted angrily.

"What are *you* doing here? We thought there was some strange to-do at Brandy Cove. Were you not posted there?"

"You blockheads! We're chasing the smugglers, and they were heading toward Lucky Hole."

"Ain't seen no one 'round 'ere. Quiet as a graveyard at Lucky Hole, except for one lanky fella shoutin' and gesticulatin' on th' top o' th' ridge."

"You idiots, he must have been one of them!"

"Saw only one fella."

Hoofbeats echoed on the path, announcing Roc's arrival. His deep voice cut through the confusion. " 'Tis yet another trick. Have you no idea where they are landing the load? The French cutter is certainly hovering out there."

"Naw, not th' faintest idea. Dandelion's plans are mighty odd tonight."

Alfie clutched Thomas's arm, almost falling out of the tree with suppressed mirth. It would spell disaster to fall into the middle of the wolfpack below. In their irate state, the soldiers might take it into their heads to do something horrible to them. If Roc knew that Thomas Strutt, one of his own footmen, was at this very moment sitting in a tree above him, contorted with glee, he would be livid.

Fortunately for the two smugglers, the soldiers marched off in a huff when the earl ordered them back to their previous posts. Roc himself rode off at a spanking pace heading toward the village. But by now the *Seahawk* would be safely out in the bay meeting the Frenchies, Alfie assured his brother.

While Thomas and Alfie had diverted the soldiers, Clem and Captain Polson had boarded the sailboat. At midnight the *Seahawk* glided from its moorings in the harbor. It would rendezvous with the French vessel and then meet the other smugglers and Gwen at Dead Man's Cove.

Dressed like one of her men, in breeches and a dark shirt, a tricorne pressed low over her eyes, Gwen left Tremayne House and sneaked down to the harbor. After making sure that the *Seahawk* was well on its way, she headed toward Dead Man's Cove.

The wind tore at her hat and she pressed it down over her ears as she darted along the dock. She didn't get far before a booming voice halted her.

"Ho! Who goes there?"

Gwen jumped with surprise, slid into the shadow of a beached boat, and waited breathlessly. The sound of hooves cut through the night.

"Step forward if you have nothing to hide," came the decisive command.

Roc. She should have known. Within seconds he might realize that the *Seahawk* was missing. Unless she could divert his attention . . .

Acting instinctively, she darted out in front of Tristan, who neighed and reared, almost unseating his master. Fortunately, Gwen knew every nook and cranny of the docks, and she had a good start while Roc struggled to regain control of his mount.

She slunk down a narrow alley behind the first row of cottages on the waterfront. Running rapidly, she reached the end of the lane as Roc galloped around the corner of the first house. Though she sprinted as fast as she possibly could, he was relentlessly closing the distance between them.

Gwen knew of a narrow stony path that would bring her to the top of the hill bordering the harbor. Jumping over a stone fence, she pushed through tall bracken and bounded over small rocks, hoping that the obstacles she knew so well would slow the horse. Losing her breath, she struggled up the overgrown path. Roc swore behind her as Tristan stumbled. As she reached the top of the hill, she leaned forward to regain her breath.

When she heard the horse's unsteady ascent, she continued into the darkness, slower now as exhaustion began to overwhelm her. Realizing she had nowhere to hide on the open hill, she doubled back down the other side, choosing the roughest path she could find. Tristan would have trouble descending in the loose shale—he might even hurt himself—but she had no choice. She could not risk being recognized.

Lithely she slid along the dark walls of the village. If Roc had noticed which lane she had chosen, he would be upon her faster than she could bat an eyelash.

The Pilchard. Raucous laughter echoed from the taproom, and a few drunk customers staggered around the yard. Patches of yellow light reflected through the grimy windows. The stables. She would have to hide in the stables. Darting from tree to tree, she managed to stay hidden from the blurred eyesight of the drunkards. The horses in the dark stalls did not object to her intrusion. A lantern hanging on a peg by the door shone weakly on six shiny flanks, and six pairs of eyes stared at her.

"Did you see a man pass here a short moment ago?" Gwen heard Roc shout across the yard to the men outside the inn. She waited inside the doorway as her heart slowly returned to its normal pace. Trembling, she leaned against the stone wall and prayed he would leave so that she could sneak back outside. But Roc evidently believed he would find what he was looking for within the buildings attached to The Pilchard because Gwen heard him call out to the ostler, enlisting his help.

If he entered the stables, where would he look first? In the corners and empty boxes and in the loft. Only one other hiding place existed—the opening leading to the dung heap. The inn had a very large heap behind the stables due to the many horses that came and went from this, the only respectable inn in the neighborhood.

Gwen did not think twice. When she heard the ostler's peevish voice outside the door, assuring Roc that no one was hiding in the stables, she opened the heavy wooden hatch and swung both legs over the ledge, then jumped, landing knee-deep in the muck below.

A shudder of revulsion shook her. She closed her eyes and pressed against the wall, pinching two fingers around her nostrils. At least she had not fallen in the middle of the heap, a slender comfort. Slightly above her to her left a head appeared in the hatchway.

"This door should be closed, and I think I did close it, but then I might be wrong," the ostler mused aloud to Roc, standing inside the stables. "Ain't no one there. Who would want to sit in a dung 'eap?" he concluded logically. "Naw, milord, ain't no one 'ere, like I told ye."

Gwen drew a sigh of relief. They had not seen her. However noisome the dung heap was, she would stay where she was until Roc left. Only then would she join the men at Dead Man's Cove. How close she had come to being captured! Her heart still hammered painfully against her ribs, and she breathed deeply to recover her calm.

When she finally thought she was safe, she heard them.

"I told yer lordship, nobody would 'ide in th' dung 'eap, no matter 'ow desperate th' situation."

"He could easily have jumped out and run off. I'm convinced he has slipped through my fingers again." Roc's string of curses drew a chuckle from the ostler.

"I can understand yer ire, but to tell ye th' truth, I don't know what th' bloke 'as done, milord. Who is 'e?"

"I'm not sure . . . but I would swear the chap is a smuggler, perhaps even Dandelion himself," the earl said, his voice thoughtful.

The ostler whistled, then followed with a derisive snort. "Naw, that chap's busy elsewhere tonight. 'Tis th' dark o' th' moon."

"What do you know about him?" Roc barked.

"Nuffin', yer lordship. Only guessin' 'e's at 'is business tonight." The ostler fidgeted, obviously desiring to leave Roc's uncomfortable company.

Gwen pressed flat up against the wall.

" 'Tis possible the smugglers already took in their haul and he was on his way home." Roc sighed. "Well, perhaps you're right; I'm clutching at straws."

The ostler must have tried Roc's patience severely by adding, "Mark me words, guv, ye'll never catch th' bloke. The only way's if 'e stops free tradin' all by 'imself."

Gwen's lips parted in a wide smile. Thank you! Her reputation was as solid as a rock among the villagers.

Roc's voice snapped with anger. "We'll see." He stalked off into the darkness, and Gwen sagged against the wall in relief and weariness. She waited until the slow clip-clop of Tristan's hooves had disappeared into the night, then she waited longer. This incident had been uncomfortably close, and she was shaken enough not to take another risk until she was quite sure the danger had passed.

Like a wraith, she finally crept away from The Pilchard. When she reached the hills, she ran to Dead Man's Cove and met the men on their way home. They assured her the load was safely stowed in the cove below and the *Seahawk* was returning to the docks.

"They had no problem with the reefs, then?"

"With Troy Polson at th' 'elm? 'Ave no fear, 'e cut between th' reefs as easily as a knife cuts through butter," one burly fisherman confirmed, smoothing his bushy mustache. Gwen knew he was exaggerating to impress the others. Sailing among the reefs was a dangerous pursuit even in the most clement weather.

"There are thirty plump kegs o' French brandy in th' cove," said Clem, "some ten 'ogs'eads of th' finest 'Olland gin, and two bales of silk."

"Splendid! We'll have to wait to move them out until the search has been abandoned."

After washing her legs and feet in the cove, Gwen was pleased to return home. She had lived through enough adventure for one night, and the smugglers had teased her abominably for her smelly boots and clothes.

As she neared Tremayne House, she saw the shadow of a man creeping stealthily toward the house. She stiffened in fear, wondering if Roc had invented a new tactic of persecution. But why would he be spying on her home? He didn't suspect her, did he? Unease spilled through her veins. What was he after?

In the shadow of a hedge, she hurried closer, trying not to make a sound. The man halted and turned slightly, as if listening. To her relief, she recognized her cousin Vincent. What was he doing out in the middle of the night? Something strange was definitely afoot, and she was sure his actions were unlawful. But how could she prove it? He looked furtively left then right before heading once more toward the door.

She waited until he had entered the house. When candlelight flickered in his bedchamber, she sneaked inside. Next time he decided to make a nightly excursion, she would be close behind him.

The next morning the villagers buzzed with the news that another load had been safely landed and one of the smugglers almost caught. No one believed the rumor that Dandelion himself had been that man.

Rising late, Gwen ate her breakfast, feeling unaccountably depressed. Not even thoughts of the successful mission of the load could cheer her. The memory of being chased in the dark by the man she loved subdued her. If Roc found out the truth, would he hate her for the rest of his life? She knew no answer to that question. And what was Vincent up to? His presence grew more ominous every day. He never made an

effort to find work to support himself and never showed any
inclination to leave.

Gus came to the kitchen door, as usual full of news. Neat
as a pin, the boat had been safely returned to its moorings in
the harbor, he informed her. All in all the run had been very
good for the smugglers. And the poor soldiers heard no end
of it as the villagers took every opportunity to tease them
about their latest failure.

That morning Officer Biggles was the first caller at Tremayne House. Bursting with news about the night, and how
he had almost been shot by the smugglers—a gross exaggeration—he strode into the parlor.

"The new magistrate has sworn he will capture Dandelion
and let him hang, if 'tis the last thing he ever does! Those
were his precise words, Miss Tremayne."

Aunt Clo's eyes widened. Evidently she thought Biggles a
brave fellow, indeed, Gwen noted. She failed, however, to
understand what charm her aunt could possibly see in the
tedious little man. She was surprised Roc had not yet gotten
rid of him.

She waited anxiously for Roc to pay her a visit, but at the
same time she knew she could not bear to see him. The
memory of their shared ecstasy was like an open wound, and
one glance from his penetrating eyes would surely cause her
to burst with despair.

At last he did come, filling the parlor with his disturbing
presence, until an unforeseen thing happened to distract Gwen
from the awkward situation.

Just as the tension in the parlor grew unbearable, Marva
hurried into the room. Bobbing a curtsy, she informed them
all that Gus was at the door again, crying because his mum
had taken ill.

Gwen rushed to the kitchen to speak to the distraught child.
Roc's decisive steps rang on the floor behind her, the sound
oddly comforting to Gwen in her distress.

"Mum i-is d-dyin'," Gus sobbed, wiping his swollen eyes
on a dirty sleeve.

Gwen kneeled and pulled the boy to her. "Piffle! Don't
cry, Gus, I'll go to her."

"Take th' basket o' 'erbs, Miss Gwen. Ye never know
what ye'll need," Marva reminded her.

Gwen resolutely pulled her old straw hat over her chestnut curls, tied the ribbon under her chin, and hooked her arm around the handle of the basket which contained labeled cloth bags of medicinal herbs.

"I'll drive you," Roc offered, his eyes burning into her. "I'm taking the Landregan coach to the wagon makers for repairs."

Gwen could not possibly refuse when a woman's life might hang in the balance. She nodded curtly and turned to Gus.

"Run and fetch Dr. Penfield while we go to assist your mother."

Gus hesitated on the threshold. "We can't pay for any doctor." His face flushed red with embarrassment.

"Don't you worry about that, Gus. I will take care of any bill the doctor sees fit to send," Gwen comforted him, urging his tense body gently out the door. She watched him dash off, a small, frightened figure, and her heart constricted with compassion.

To Gwen, the drive to the dilapidated cottage on the outskirts of the village was an ordeal. Roc's thighs pressed persistently against hers on the box. Her eyes were fixed rigidly on Roc's strong hands holding the reins. A powerful urge to lean against his shoulder and cry, to empty herself of all her misery, came over her.

He gazed at her, a deep and knowing scrutiny, and said simply, "How long are you going to deny yourself happiness?"

She tried to pull her leg away from his. "I don't know why you go on about it. I've given you my answer." She immediately hated herself for saying the words.

"I cannot for the world fathom what objection you have to me. We would be happy together, I know it."

How could she stop him once and for all? "If you believe you're so irresistible that no woman would turn you down, then you're more conceited than I thought possible." She cringed as his face paled and his eyes narrowed with shock and anger. How could she be so cruel? She fixed her thoughts on the starving villagers, forcing herself to justify her cruelty.

Roc drove on in smoldering silence, and when they arrived at the cottage, he assisted her down from the box and carried the basket for her. He was always the perfect gentleman, she mused.

The door creaked on its hinges as Roc opened it. The wood had rotted away at the bottom, and a scrawny cat slipped fearfully through the gaping hole.

The small room was dim, filled with an odor of cabbage. The plank walls were covered with soot, and where the wood had rotted away, layers of sod kept out the roughest wind. The mortar in the stone fireplace was crumbling, and one of the walls sagged inward, threatening to fall at any minute. On a wooden cot piled with straw lay Meg Lane, Gus's mother. Perspiration covered her forehead, plastering the damp curls, and her emaciated body shivered with recurring spasms.

"Mrs. Lane!" Gwen knelt on the dirt floor next to the cot.

The woman turned pain-filled eyes on her. "Gus? Where's Gus?"

"He went to fetch the doctor, Mrs. Lane. What's wrong with you? Are you in pain?" Gwen told Roc, standing rigid in the middle of the room, to fetch some water.

"Miss Tremayne . . ." A tired smile lit the gaunt face. "My Gus is mighty fond o' ye. 'E says ye buy strawberries every day." Her face contorted as another spasm racked her body. "Don't worry 'bout me. I need no doctor. See . . . I'm in th' family way an' th' babe's comin' too early."

Gwen stared at the suffering woman, clasping her bony hand. "Who's the father? He should be here with you now," she whispered, and accepted the cracked cup brimming with water that Roc offered. She gently placed the cup to the woman's lips. " 'E ain't 'round . . . One o' them peddlers 'e is. Won't come back 'ere no more."

Gwen knew there was nothing she could do to alleviate Mrs. Lane's suffering. The fact that Gus's mother did not possess very strict morals was well known in the village, and no one knew the identity of Gus's father. Yet Mrs. Lane was widely liked for her garrulous friendliness. The woman and her little boy played their small parts in the village and in the smuggling business. Gus was, indeed, an important link.

All Gwen could do to soothe the sick woman was to keep cold compresses on her forehead until Dr. Penfield arrived, which he did an hour later. He proceeded to order first Roc and then Gwen out of the house. When Gwen exited, she saw Roc crouching by the small boy, trying to cheer him up. From his pocket, Roc fished out a penny and pressed it into Gus's hand. "This is for a sweet at Mrs. Padstow's shop," he explained, smiling. "You're a brave boy, someone I could employ at Landregan Hall when you grow older."

Gwen's heart contracted at the tender sight. Roc's expression turned serious as she joined them. "I had no knowledge of the poverty they live in," he murmured.

She answered in a hushed voice. "Now you know why the smuggling is important. They barely survive as it is, get by on one meal a day. In Landregan people help each other, although they have little to share." Gwen's eyes burned with unshed tears. For Gus's sake she controlled herself.

"Listen, mite," said Roc to Gus, "your mum is going to be right as rain in a few days. You have to make sure she eats well. I'll get you a basket of food from Landregan Hall."

Roc set the boy down and Gwen placed her arm protectively around his thin shoulders. "Come, show me your strawberry patch," she said.

She pushed his sagging form toward the back of the cottage. Before she turned the corner, she noticed Roc's gaze gliding thoughtfully over the thin, leaking thatch on the roof, the crumbling whitewashed walls full of damp patches, the unkempt garden, the cracked windowpanes. Was he finally understanding the extent of the villagers' needs? Would that make him change his views on the free trading?

Half an hour later, the doctor came out and announced cheerfully that Mrs. Lane would survive. Letting out a squeal of happiness, Gus darted into the cottage.

"A miscarriage, I'm afraid," the doctor said. "Was almost over by the time I arrived. She's weak, should not become in the, hmm, family way again."

"Thank you for coming so rapidly," said Gwen. "Gus was beside himself with worry. I'll help him look after her until she gets her strength back. I'll see to it that she eats enough."

The doctor peered at her from under bushy eyebrows. "Mighty generous of you, Miss Tremayne." He dried his newly washed hands on a worn towel. "I will send the midwife over to sit with her tonight."

When the doctor had disappeared in his trap, Gwen went

inside to make sure Gus and his mother had everything they needed for the time being.

"Thank ye for yer 'elp, dear Miss Tremayne," Mrs. Lane whispered, holding out a weak hand.

Gwen squeezed it reassuringly. "I'll be back tomorrow and I'll bring some of Marva's good food."

A nod and a smile was the only response the weakened woman managed before her chin fell toward her flat chest in exhaustion.

As Gwen left, she slipped a few coins into Gus's grimy hand and gave him a stern order to go and buy milk and eggs from Farmer Polpenny. His dirty face shone with gratitude. "Ye're a right 'un, miss. I've always said so."

Gwen burst out laughing. "That you have; in fact, you tell me that every time we meet."

Roc took her hand in a firm grip to assist her into the carriage, his expression thoughtful. She detected a new softness on his face that made her want to cry. Her heart ached with longing and despair.

Chapter 21

On the way back to Tremayne House, Gwen, no longer worrying about Mrs. Lane, was doubly aware of Roc's muscled thigh pressing against hers on the narrow seat. Waves of sweet yearning rippled through her, reminding her of the night when they had been one, nothing between them except a few grains of sand. A raindrop spattered on her cheek.

Roc glanced toward the sky, which was rapidly changing from gray to leaden. "Looks like we're going to have a heavy storm." He urged the horse on. "I'll get you home before we get drenched."

Just as he spoke a gust of wind swirled around them, whipping Gwen's hat from her head to her back, the faded blue ribbons fluttering under her chin.

"The first taste of autumn," Roc commented. "Won't be long now."

Gwen suddenly remembered their bet—that he would catch Dandelion before the dark of the moon in August, which had already come and gone. She had won. But she decided against pointing that out to Roc. He must have forgotten all about it.

The rain fell faster. "I'm afraid we'll have to seek shelter under a tree 'til this blows over," Roc said, a frown between his brows.

Gwen held on to the side of the seat as he turned the equipage sharply and pulled under the wide, dense branches of an ancient elm.

After making fast the reins to the brake shaft, he shifted on the seat to face her. "There. What do we do now?" A suggestive smile danced in the back of his eyes. Gwen studied his face, unable to tear her gaze away. He was so dangerously attractive.

"Watch the rain," she said meekly, feeling a surge of color spreading across her cheeks. "There's nothing else to do."

A damp mist rose under the tree, and the strident patter on the foliage isolated them in a private world. The rain pounded onto the ground with thousands of glittering spears. The horses whinnied with fear as a sudden gust of wind bore a sheet of water swirling under their shelter.

Was Roc going to propose to her again? Gwen wondered. She was trapped. She clutched her fists in the folds of her skirt, fighting an urge to escape. She could not go on lying, not if she wanted to be true to herself.

His voice dry, Roc said, "You look distressed, m'dear. Are you afraid I've turned into the big bad wolf, ready to pounce on you?" Playfully twisting his face into an evil mask, he lifted his hands, curling his fingers like talons and leaning over her.

A nervous laugh escaped her lips. "Humbug! I'm not afraid of you . . . you big, bumbling . . . wretch!"

"Wretch, is it?" he growled with mock ferocity. "Well, I'll show you—" A swift change stole over his features, a blur of desire clouding his tawny eyes. His long fingers buried themselves deeply into her curls, and his breath came warm and inviting over her face, tantalizing her senses, caressing, promising. She wanted him madly when his lips descended softly, like butterfly wings to hers, to court, to steal her acquiescence, before he devoured her. The dormant fire inside her flamed to life, and Gwen sighed with a long-denied pleasure. How she loved him!

Roc was awed by the love glowing in the hazel eyes so close to his face. The warm golden knowledge coursed along his nerves. So, nothing was wrong with her feelings. He burned to find out why she had refused his offer of marriage. He let his fingers glide slowly along the slender column of her neck to delve under the lacy shawl crossed over her bosom. Beneath his fingertips he felt her rapid pulse at the base of her throat. She was not the only one with a racing heartbeat. To show her just what her sweet lips did to him, he took her hand and placed it inside his coat just over his heart, then crushed her to him, wanting to peel off all the layers that separated them.

He murmured into her hair. "Why do you reject the pleasure wedlock could bring us? How can you deny the attraction flowing between us? The first moment I laid eyes on you, the world quaked from the impact." He chuckled. "I admit I was somewhat taken aback at your sharp repartee, but I have since learned to admire you—not only your delectable curves, but your care for others who are less fortunate than yourself. And I admire you for daring to say straight out what's on your mind."

"Stop it," she whispered, pushing against his chest. His kind words made her feel worse than ever. "I'm not the paragon you make me. I'm as full of flaws as anyone else."

"That's what makes you the delightful woman you are."

She managed to wrench away from him and jumped down from the box. "I'll remind you of those words when your opinion changes, Roc. You're blind to my weaknesses." To get away from the rain, she opened the carriage door and climbed inside. She desperately wanted to cry, and she pressed a handkerchief to her eyes to suppress the threatening tears. When she heard him scramble down from the box, she shoved the handkerchief into her pocket and swallowed hard. Dear God, don't let me cry.

"I'm aware of your character flaws, Gwennie, but I also see your kindness and your strength," he said as soon as he had opened the door. He climbed inside and closed the door behind him. He sat beside her and gripped her trembling hands. "Please look at me." He sighed when she refused to comply. "Stubborn wench! At first I thought I would have a nice pastime flirting and teasing my 'shadow' of old, but I did not count on falling in love with you." He lifted her chin so he could gaze into her eyes. "I dared not speak of it before, for fear you would turn me away with one of your scathing remarks, but I have come to love you, Gwen. That's why I want to marry you, don't you see? Don't disappoint me by saying no again."

He watched her eyes fill with tears, her face with dismay, as she struggled with her emotions. So many feelings crossed her face, but the most prevalent was fear and—despair?

"Please marry me, Gwen; I don't want to waste any more

time." He placed his warm hands over hers and pulled them to his lips. "Come, let me kiss you." He dragged her hands back under his coat and pulled her close.

She wanted to scream in frustration, but could not stop him. His heart raced under her hand, and her arms of their own volition went around his chest. He felt warm and comfortable. Murmuring endearments in her ear, he eagerly explored her muslin-covered back, his fingers lighting fires of need. The world swirled around her with dizzying delight as his mouth claimed hers once more. His hands wandered to her waist, then across one rounded hip, down to squeeze a thigh. She had to stop him! Giving in to him now would be more than unfair; it would be a mockery of herself and his feelings.

When he finally relinquished her lips, the world once more righted itself, and Gwen gained some semblance of control. She gazed reverently into those beloved tawny eyes. How could she refuse his offer without completely alienating him? And yet she must, because between them stood a gallows, waiting for the neck of a hapless "gentleman." She could almost feel the hard twine of the noose closing around her throat.

"Roc, I've already given you my answer, and let me tell you yet again, I've no desire to marry you or anyone else," she lied, her heart protesting painfully. "And I would appreciate it if you didn't mention it again." She pushed away from him and bit down on her bottom lip in agitation. She dared not look into his eyes, fearing what she would see there. She was well aware of his rising anger.

He jerked his hands through his hair. "I see that I have made a complete fool of myself once more. 'Twill not happen again, I promise," he said ominously.

Gwen saw her future stretch in front of her, barren, lonely. Was the price worth paying? But she could not forget the gallows, and she could not tell him the truth. She could not bear to see his love turn to hate.

"I had no time to tell you the reason I came to Tremayne House this morning," he said. "Louise begged me to invite you for a visit. Unable to walk, she's fretting with boredom." Roc's voice had turned chilly, impersonal.

"Oh, I meant to visit her, but so many things—"

"If 'tis convenient, I'll be happy to convey you to the Hall right now." He peered out the window. "The rain has stopped, and the horses are becoming restive."

"That will be fine." Gwen glanced at the clearing sky. "The storm passed quickly."

How flat and meaningless the words sounded, as if they were two strangers talking at a road crossing. Back on the box, she clenched her fists in her lap, her eyes fixed on a spot between the horse's ears.

Roc flipped the reins and muttered something unintelligible. His bearing was hostile, and Gwen regretted having accepted his offer of conveying her to the Hall. Suffering his punishment of wooden silence, she counted the horse's every step. When Roc reined in at the front of the Hall, she slid from the box and fled inside before he had time to assist her.

"Goodbye," she called over her shoulder.

He followed her without responding.

It so happened that Louise was not wallowing in her sick-bed but hobbling around the Green Salon on crutches under Morgan's adoring supervision and Lady Camelford's sour gaze. The dowager countess's bored countenance viewed the proceedings, her hand traveling back and forth between her mouth and an open box of bonbons on a mother-of-pearl inlaid table. When Louise noticed Gwen's presence, her face lit up. "Gwen! How wonderful of you to come. Just the person I hoped to see."

With a hesitant glance at the dowager countess, Gwen stepped forward to press Louise's small hand. "I'm sorry I didn't come earlier, but we had an emergency this morning. How is your ankle?"

Louise sent an adoring glance at Morgan. "I've never felt better. Morgan is attentive and delightful company."

Those words provoked an angry snort from Lady Camelford. "Louise! You silly girl, have you lost all your sense?" Turning to the dowager, the marchioness said, "I don't know what the world is coming to when a girl dares to compliment a gentleman in public. We'll have to leave before her manners are completely ruined in this crude place."

The dowager did not deign to answer, her cheeks bulging

with bonbons. She fixed first Gwen with her ferocious stare, then Roc, who had entered behind her.

"Ha! Mischief brewing, isn't it, son? She has turned you down," she greeted him. "Again." She chuckled gleefully at the dark scowl on his face. "Told you she would."

Roc sauntered forward and stood before his mother. "Whatever else you might think, you've no right to put your long nose in my private business," he informed her in his most authoritative voice.

"Stings that male pride of yours, eh?" The dowager took not the slightest heed of his humiliation. Unperturbed, she popped another bonbon into her mouth as an angry dark flush crept into his cheeks. She cackled with mirth. "Stubborn young man. Always was and always will be. Just like your father."

Hushed embarrassment filled the room as everyone shot furtive glances at the seething victim of the dowager's spite. Gwen burned with shame, hating the old woman. In a flash of anger she said, "You're unfair to Roc, milady. Instead of supporting him, you're acting like his enemy."

Louise squealed with delight at the daring words. Hands clapped to her mouth, she watched the two older women's jaws fall in surprise.

"One should expect that from the *squire's* daughter," Lady Camelford breathed with outrage. "I say, we should leave this house *immediately*. Louise! Go supervise the packing of your trunks."

"Don't be ridiculous, Eulalie," the dowager snapped. "Louise can't leave in her poor condition." She turned to Roc. "So Miss Tremayne has accepted you after all? She's defending you like a lioness with a cub." She leveled a hard stare at Gwen.

"If you must know, no she hasn't," he said drily. "And now, if you'll excuse me." He turned on his heel and stalked out of the room, leaving an uncomfortable silence behind him.

"I should ask you to apologize to me, young gel, but I see that you're acting in Roc's best interests, so you're forgiven." The dowager gave Gwen a shrewd glance filled with grudging respect. "What I don't see is how you have the *gall* to turn down such an advantageous proposal."

Color surged into Gwen's cheeks, and she had a heated reply ready on her lips when Louise gripped her hand convulsively. "Come, let's sit on the window seat, away from these two vultures," she whispered, and hopped across the floor before Gwen could protest. Miserable and angry, Gwen followed.

"Has Roc really offered for you?" Louise whispered. "But that's splendid!" Her gaze probed into Gwen as if trying to read her innermost secrets. "Why did you turn him down? The dowager is right, he's a marvelous catch."

"We would not suit," came Gwen's tight-lipped response. "Had I but known that my business would be aired in public, I would have—"

"Don't take on so. I'm sure 'twill all come out right at the end." Louise leaned toward Gwen. "One has to *make it* come out right when it doesn't by itself, you know."

"What do you mean?" Gwen gazed narrowly at the spirited young girl, whose countenance glowed with excitement.

"What are you two whispering about?" Lady Camelford demanded imperiously. "Louise, I told you to see to your packing."

"Yes, Mother, presently," Louise answered automatically. To Gwen, she said, "I have great plans."

Unease caught Gwen instantly. "Plans?"

"Since Mother won't consent to a marriage between me and Morgan, we're planning to elope." The information was conveyed in a theatrical whisper.

Taken by surprise, Gwen had an urge to laugh, but she managed at the last second to contain herself. It was a mad day. What would happen next? "Elope? Your mother will have one of her turns, you know, from which she might never recover."

"She has them when she pleases, and they won't change my plans," Louise explained, her chin thrust forward. "Of course we can't do anything until my ankle is better, so we won't be able to leave just yet."

Gwen marveled at Louise's audacity. "Why would you elope? The marchioness will come around eventually, if you try your persuasive powers."

"And endure her spasms and dying fits? There will be no

end to it, you know, and to elope is so romantic." Louise sighed.

"Yes, you would always choose the romantic course if you had a choice," Gwen said with a wry smile. "And Morgan? What's his opinion?"

The young woman fidgeted guiltily. Looking at Gwen from under her long eyelashes, she confessed, "Well . . . he doesn't know about it, yet."

Silence fell. Gwen regarded the innocent victim sitting in a wing chair, his gaunt body bent over a book in his lap. "Oh. And how do you intend to bring him around, if I may ask?"

"I don't foresee any difficulties, especially when he realizes we have no other choice."

"Hmm, we'll see. Morgan might appear to be easy to rule, but he's still a gentleman; he would wish to marry you in the proper way."

Louise sighed dreamily. "You have to admit the idea's terribly romantic." She laid an urgent hand on Gwen's arm. "I'm quite forgetting myself. You must be very sad after this trying afternoon. The earl can be so very difficult." She leaned closer, whispering, "Is it really true that you turned him down?"

Gwen smiled and glanced at the floor. "Yes, I did turn him down." She placed a restraining hand on Louise's arm. "And I don't want to talk about it."

Louise's face fell. "Oh, I had hoped I could help you in some way. The earl has behaved like a bear with a sore head these last few days."

"Yes, I'm sure it hurts his great self-esteem to be refused by an old maid from a country village."

Louise's eyes bored into her. "*I* wonder what your reason is. After all, he's quite a catch, and a handsome man to boot."

"As I told you, I don't want to talk about it."

Louise shrugged. "Very well. Anyhow *I* don't plan on letting my opportunity for love slip through my fingers."

Gwen could not help but smile. "The longer I know you, the more I see that you take the opportunities as they come, however rash." She squeezed Louise's hand. "Promise me you won't do anything you might regret later. Don't ruin your life on some romantic whim. I will leave now, and I don't know if I can return, at least not while the dowager countess looks at me as if she wishes me dead. You can understand what a blow it must have been for her to face the possibility that I would become the new countess of Landregan.''

Louise responded with words that hit Gwen in the center of her heart. "If you want to waste your life, 'tis your own choice, and no one else's. The dowager has no say in the matter. You should listen to your heart.'' She patted Gwen's hand. "I'm sure Roc wouldn't have offered for you unless he really loved you.''

Gwen pondered those words as she was conveyed home in style, in the dowager's ancient barouche emblazoned with the Landregan crest. Was she wasting her life by choosing free trading instead of Roc? If only he wasn't so intent on bringing justice to Dandelion. It rankled too much, and she seethed every time she thought about it. If he knew she was Dandelion, would he hang her? He would have to, so as not to lose face after all his threats.

What a muddle her life was! How he would resent knowing he had proposed to the infamous Dandelion! It would almost be worth revealing herself to him if only to see the expression on his face.

Yet the thought wasn't amusing.

Chaos reigned at Tremayne House. Gwen found her aunt, Marva, Arthur, and even her father up in the attic in the servants' quarters. A part of the roof had finally caved in—not unexpected, but a nuisance all the same.

"Th' rain did it, Miss Gwen. It came down right 'ard, and ye know 'ow it's been leakin' this last year or more.''

What Marva said was true. No matter how many times the village carpenter had mended it temporarily, it had continued leaking at some other spot.

Gwen studied the gaping hole and the rotten planks under the slates. "There's nothing else to do but to put on a new roof,'' she concluded.

Aunt Clo gasped. "We cannot afford it.''

"We'll manage somehow. I'll speak with Mr. Tregony immediately,'' Gwen informed them wearily.

Aunt Clo stared at her narrowly. *"Where* are you going to

get the funds?'' Arms akimbo, she thrust her thin face close to Gwen's. Gwen felt all eyes in the room directed at her.

"I'm sure I can make a favorable deal with Mr. Tregony." She did not mention that the village carpenter was part of the smuggling ring, and that he knew very well she could pay for his services.

The squire regarded her over the rim of his spectacles. "I'm sure you know best, Gwennie. I will leave it in your capable hands. And now I believe I must return to pressing business downstairs." Like a sleepwalker, he skirted Marva's narrow bed and tripped on a wooden bucket placed in the middle of the room to catch the dripping water. Astonishment written all over his face, he toppled to the floor like a felled tree in a storm.

"Oh, dear, oh dear!"Aunt Clo squealed. "Did you hurt yourself, Lionel?" She fluttered around the squire, uttering noises of worry.

He grunted. "Odd place to keep a bucket."

Arthur helped the shaken squire to his feet, and Gwen's lips quivered. "The roof *is* leaking, you know."

"Hrmph . . . leaking? Yes, of course." Aligning his wig and spectacles, he tottered to the door. "Deuced nuisance all the same!"

By midmorning the next day, work on the new roof was already in progress. Gwen held her breath with worry as she stood in the sunny garden watching Mr. Tregony and his two sons braving the steep slate roof. Secured with ropes attached to the chimneys, they began tearing off the old cracked slates, sending them crashing to the ground. Her contentment grew at the thought of having a new roof, the first major step in restoring Tremayne House to its former elegance. She stubbornly shoved away her misgivings about the questions such repairs would raise in the neighborhood. In her mind she could already see Roc staring speculatively at the work, probing her conscience with his daunting topaz gaze.

But she was tired of holding back, of living like a pauper when funds existed to improve her life. She owed no explanations, and only her imagination painted the horror pictures in her guilty mind. If necessary, she would invent some convincing lies. Lies and more lies. She dashed away a tear.

As it happened, she did not have to worry about explaining to Roc because he avoided Tremayne House assiduously. She saw him sometimes at a distance in the village, and her heart ached with longing. She'd made the mistake of her life by turning down his offer, and now it was too late to reverse the damage.

Chapter 22

At the next dark of the moon, the new slate roof shone on Tremayne House. Every time Gwen came up the carriage sweep, she admired the dignity the new roof gave to the old house. The only one who pestered her with questions about where she had obtained the wherewithal for the major repair was Aunt Clo, and Gwen managed to evade her probing inquiries, to Aunt Clo's increasing ire. And now, more importantly, the *Alouette* was hovering in the bay with another load.

Gwen had decided to haul it in on the night before the actual dark, to confuse the lawmen. The trick had worked before, and once again they would make use of Morgan's sailboat, the *Seahawk*. How angry Roc would be if he ever learned they used the boat for smuggling!

Roc sat brooding in his study. The clock in the hallway had already chimed midnight, but he felt no urge to retire. His mind traveled from detail to detail of what he had learned about the free trading over the months since his return. He knew all the common hiding places, whose cellars stored the contraband, and whose ponies sometimes carried the kegs to Exeter. After seeing the poverty in Mrs. Lane's cottage, he'd concluded that he had no interest in capturing and punishing those men. To catch the leader Dandelion was his goal, since the smuggling business would undoubtedly fall apart once the leader was gone. Yet Roc held a grudging admiration for the daring "weed."

And then there were the jewels. Three times he had tried to leave for France, but the dowager had thwarted his efforts in every case. All he could do now was to wait for an answer to his letter to Alistair Borrodale's friends in France. Perhaps one of them could come fetch the gems; it was the only way out since he hadn't heard from the person who had ordered him to place the stones in the wood bin outside The Pilchard.

He laughed out loud at the preposterous demand. Who had scrawled that sloppy, almost illegible letter?

Enedoc shuffled over the gleaming parquet floor, carrying a tray with a full brandy decanter and a glass. Old and trembling, he placed it on the round table next to the earl.

"Oh? Enedoc, you still up? You might as well retire for the night. I won't need anything else this evening."

"Since I knew your lordship was here, I assumed you might like a nip of brandy."

"Very perceptive of you. I see you've already filled a tumbler." Roc took the glass from the tray and sipped the potent liquid. He eyed Enedoc thoughtfully. "Is there something wrong? You look . . . nervous."

"Oh, no, milord. It has been a trying day, that's all."

"I gather the dowager countess has been hard to please?"

"I don't wish to complain, milord." Enedoc stood straight and stiff, his face white.

"By the look on your face, you need a good night's rest." He touched the old man's arm. "It might give you pleasure to know that the dowager will be returning to Tunbridge Wells shortly."

Enedoc bowed. "Whatever you say, milord." He left the room. Before he closed the door, he glanced furtively at the brandy tumbler in the earl's grip. He drew a deep, shuddering breath as he entered the hallway, and wiped his sweaty palms on his blue satin knee breeches. "I've followed the orders," he whispered to Thomas Strutt, the footman standing against the wall, waiting.

"Good! Well then, I'll be off to report to Clem. 'E be waitin' in th' spinney."

Enedoc did not like to pull the wool over the earl's eyes. He thought it underhanded of the free traders to resort to such a cheap trick as to drug the earl with laudanum to keep him out of the way. Enedoc hadn't liked being the one chosen to lace the earl's brandy with the sleeping draught.

Thomas slipped into the darkness outside, and Enedoc hovered anxiously in the hallway to make sure the earl went to his bedchamber. Half an hour passed and Thomas failed to return, which convinced Enedoc he had joined the smugglers on their rendezvous with the Frenchmen.

Wearily he waited up, propped on a hard chair in the hallway. His chin had begun to tilt toward his chest when the door to the study slammed. Enedoc started, heaved himself upright, and hid behind the draperies next to the front door just as Roc entered the hallway. The old retainer was shocked to see his employer bounding up the stairs two steps at a time.

When the earl had disappeared in the corridor above, Enedoc sneaked into the study. One look told him that the earl had imbibed only half of the amber liquid in the tumbler, not enough to knock him out for the night.

From behind the open study door, he heard the heels of the earl's riding boots click resolutely against the white and black marble floor of the hallway. The entrance door banged shut behind him.

Enedoc paced the room. Where was Thomas? How could he send a warning to the smugglers now? He would have to light a candle in the pantry and hope one of the smugglers noticed it.

Roc knew in his bones that the "gentlemen" would be bringing in the load tonight. It was as if an invisible cord linked him with the infamous smuggler. He could almost sense the villain; he understood Dandelion's devious mind more than ever before, and all he now needed was a face and a name. He would not rest until he had patrolled the usual landing spots.

It galled him no end that they had brought in the previous load right under his nose, without leaving a single clue to point to the cargo's whereabouts. But he was convinced he had chased one of the smugglers that night. Had he only managed to catch the man, he'd have made him talk. But the catch had eluded him. Swearing under his breath, he recalled every moment of that night when he'd been so close to finding out the truth.

The wind whirled around him as he galloped down the oak-lined drive, heading toward the harbor. The air smelled pungently of moist earth and autumn leaves. Soon a heavy, raw mist would envelope the sea and the shoreline. Soon summer would be just a memory, a dream of hot flagstones, cool lemonade, bees buzzing, flowers spicing the air with their sweetness, birds wheeling and chattering, swooping into the glittering fountains.

He would especially cherish the memory of his night with Gwen on the moonlit beach. She had melted into his arms like a siren, and he into hers. How could she have been so hopelessly stubborn as to reject him? He ached with longing for her, his heart heavy with sorrow. He hated her for her refusal to accept his proposal, and he hated being in love. What a fool he'd been to let his heart rule his head. But he would never grovel, not after being rejected twice.

At the rocky outcrop above Brandy Cove, Roc yanked on the reins and Tristan protested with a snort. Roc alighted and listened for any sound indicating that the cove hid the smugglers. But the only noises he heard were the churr of a night-jar and the surge of the tide. The ageless pounding of the waves echoed in his head, making him feel strangely restless and preoccupied. He climbed down to the cove, but the strip of beach was deserted. The wind whistled eerily in the caves and crevices, and he felt as lonely as the bird swooping past his head.

Wrecker's Ruin was empty, as were the numerous caves at Lucky Hole. The cottage at Yellow Rock had not been used for months. Where did they land the brandy? Had he been an idiot to suspect they would bring it in tonight? Rumor said the cargo would be delivered on the following night, but he had learned to ignore the rumors. Still, no men stirred abroad this night.

He passed The Pilchard. A few candles still burned in the taproom, and he saw a blur of red uniforms inside. The soldiers were wasting their time drinking ale and gossiping. Officer Biggles probably lay snoring in his bed—his favorite pastime.

Defeated, Roc alighted and stepped into the taproom. If a few of the men he knew to be smugglers were inside, it might mean the load really was arriving on the following night. He looked around the smoke-laden room. Some of the villagers sat around the rough tables, but none he suspected of smuggling. He decided not to waste any more time by downing a tankard of ale. This had to be the night, just as the nagging feeling inside had told him. Abruptly he pivoted and left the aproom before some gossip-hungry soul involved him in peech. Curious glances were thrown his way as he strode outside.

One person who had no wish whatsoever to be seen by the earl was Thomas, the footman. Roc's powerful frame was caught in relief against the light from the taproom as he stood in the doorway. That was enough to alarm Thomas on his way up the path toward the inn. "Lawks, th' earl's not sleepin' in 'is bed as expected!" the young footman said to himself and scratched his chin.

From the shadow of a tree, Thomas watched the earl mount his stallion and trot off down the lane leading to the harbor. If the earl reached the harbor, he would immediately notice that the *Seahawk* was gone. What to do now? Thomas knew a way to divert the earl's attention before he reached the harbor, but he had no wish to engage in fisticuffs. The only one in the village who could match the earl in strength was Clem, who at this very minute was meeting the *Alouette* in the bay with the *Seahawk*. Thomas decided to do the next best thing, to run all the way to Dead Man's Cove and warn Dandelion. She would know what to do.

Setting off along the cliff path, Thomas ignored the mud spattering and thorns ripping his immaculate white silk stockings and satin livery. Enedoc would give him a fearful scold, but he had no time for such worries. His only thought was to save the smugglers from being caught red-handed.

On the lookout for danger, Gwen marched back and forth at the top of the path leading down to Dead Man's Cove. She tensed as she heard the sound of running steps behind her. Turning, her rock-in-the-stocking weapon ready, she waited for the sudden intruder. Expelling her breath with relief, she recognized Thomas. He stopped in front of her, panting. "You're back," she said. "Did something happen?"

"Trouble brewin'. Meant to take 'im on meself, but 'e's too 'andy with 'is fives, th' earl is."

"What are you talking about?" Gwen knit her brows in worry, trying to decipher Thomas's garbled speech.

"Th' earl. 'E bain't asleep in 'is bed at all, though I saw Enedoc serve 'im th' brandy with th' sleepin' draught. 'E's snoopin' around, sniffin' th' air like some cur, down at th' 'arbor. 'E knows th' load is bein' brought in tonight."

Thomas stared round-eyed at the breeches-clad woman in front of him.

"You've been very quick, Thomas, and you'll be rewarded handsomely." Gwen placed a reassuring hand on his arm. "Go back to the Hall and alert Enedoc. I will take care of the earl."

Thomas burst out with relief, "I knew ye would. That earl, 'e never gives up."

Gwen stared grimly over the black bay. "No, he doesn't. We'll need a lot of luck tonight. Now, go! And be sure to clean your livery. It won't do to have the earl suspect you're one of the 'gentlemen.' "

Thomas liked the sound of those last words, and he left, his chest puffed out with pride. He could give his life for that Dandelion. A plucky cove, she was.

Gwen knew what she had to do. She climbed down to the rock-strewn beach below. Finding Alfie, she grasped his shirt sleeve. "Is the *Seahawk* coming back in?"

"Aye, miss, we've one more load."

"Good!" Without explaining her abrupt behavior, she went to the water's edge and stared into the darkness. Soaring skyward between two jagged rocks was the sailboat, trim as a mallard on top of the waves. Gwen could not see the French cutter hovering farther out in the Channel.

As soon as the boat reached the shallows, Polson threw in the anchor. Gwen ran into the water and hauled in the line to secure the boat, and the smugglers waded out to unload the kegs. Clem slogged through the backwash and reached the beach.

"Miss Gwen? What are ye doin' 'ere? Trouble atop th' ridge?"

"The earl is on the prowl. He got wind of the haul." She related Thomas's warning, and Clem scratched his ear in consternation.

" 'E doesn't know we're usin' this 'ere cove."

"I know, but 'tis only a matter of time before he figures it out, especially if he notices that the *Seahawk*'s missing." She leaned closer to his dark face. "You'll have to keep the boat out of sight until the next tide."

"That'll mean bringin' 'er to th' docks at midmorn. Everyone will see us. Or we could dump th' boat elsewhere, in Fowey per'aps.''

"Yes, that might be for the best. If Roc's waiting for you at the harbor, the noose on the square will be your next stop."

"Niver liked th' idea o' a rope 'round me neck. Bound to be deuced uncomfortable."

Gwen thought for a few moments. "I will scout the area first. In half an hour I'll signal you from either Wrecker's Ruin or from the lookout point; two flashes if everything is clear, one if he's still lurking about."

"I could plant 'im a facer for dippin' 'is long nose into our business," Clem said heatedly. " 'E's gone too far!"

Gwen chuckled. "I agree he's a pest. But if we manage to sneak the *Seahawk* to the harbor right under his nose, we'll leave him a memento." Her brow pleated thoughtfully, she viewed the smugglers working efficiently with the kegs. "If I signal you to return tonight, furl the sails at the mouth of the harbor and pole her in along the shore. The trees and cliffs will give you cover."

"Aye, that thcy'll do."

"I'll leave immediately. Tell the men to hide the kegs well under the seaweed. This is still the safest place to leave them for now. Good luck!"

Gwen ran lithely up the path, a shielded lantern in hand. Her stomach had turned into a tight knot of anxiety as she faced another harrowing ordeal. She prayed the earl was nowhere near the sea.

She skirted the village in a wide circle and sneaked up the hills to the Hall. As she had feared, a candle shone in the window of the butler's pantry, the signal used by Enedoc if the earl was abroad. Enedoc must be worrying himself sick, but she had no time to stop and reassure him. Where was Roc at this moment? She had to be careful not to suddenly run into him. The harbor. She prayed he wasn't there, waiting and armed with a musket.

Gwen ran swift-footed through the spinney behind the Hall, along well-known paths to the sea. She cautiously passed Wrecker's Ruin and Brandy Cove, straining her ears for sounds. She heard nothing but the wind and the crashing of the waves. Keeping to the shadows, she descended the hill and turned toward the village. She passed The Pilchard and

saw lights still burning within. Tonight no sounds of song
and laughter floated on the air. She waited tensely for a clue,
but the night was quiet, everyone asleep. Hesitating for a
moment, she decided at last to creep down to the harbor. She
hoped she would hear or see Tristan before Roc noticed her.

Reaching the paved docks, she skirted the walls of the
fishermen's cottages. The black windows suggested people
were sleeping peacefully in their beds. She could see no sign
of Tristan or any soldiers anywhere. Gradually she neared the
Seahawk's usual mooring spot. Still there was no sign of man
or beast. Where could Roc be?

On a hunch, she drew closer to the steep lookout right next
to the harbor. If someone wanted to spy across the bay, that
would be a good spot.

She reached a stand of trees at the bottom of the hill. A
low snort startled her. Tristan. He was bound to a tree, the
greenery effectively concealing him but his chomping jaws
giving him away. Gwen sensed him listening to her steps, his
long face turned in her direction, but he did not move or
neigh. Gwen feared she'd stumble headlong into Roc's arms.
She crept slowly forward, not knowing where to look for
him. Halting, she listened. Was he at this moment looking
straight at her?

Gwen shuddered and then a tiny smile began to play about
her lips. An unmistakable snore had reached her ears, and it
didn't come from Tristan.

She inched at a snail's pace toward the sound, and soon
she saw Roc's dark form leaning against a tree, fast asleep.
Frowning, Gwen calculated the possibility of letting the *Seahawk* move into the harbor while the winds were still favorable. She had no idea how hard the earl slept. Perhaps the
smallest sound would alert him, but that was a chance she
would have to take.

From the top of the lookout, only a short distance from
Roc, she signaled twice out to sea, knowing that Clem would
keep his sharp eyes peeled on the shore.

They were there. An answering flash came from the bay.
Staying well away from Roc's sleeping form, she kept her
gaze on the harbor. She could barely discern the outline of
the sailboat, sails furled and hugging the shoreline as she had
instructed them. Even if Roc had been on the lookout with

his telescope, he'd still have had difficulty noticing the *Seahawk*. But one thing was certain: he knew they were using the sailboat. They could not do so again. Gwen clenched her fists in vexation.

How ironic! Here she was in the small hours of the morning, sitting fifty yards from the man she loved, the man who had sworn to capture and hang her. She longed to awaken him with a kiss, to lie down beside him and ask him to embrace her. Life was a bizarre affair at best, she thought wryly, and sneaked past him without making a sound. Once she was well out of earshot of the earl, she ran as fast as she could down to the docks to meet the *Seahawk*. The sooner the men left the harbor, the better.

Clem and Captain Polson didn't speak as they moored the sailboat; they knew speed was of the essence. Gwen clasped Polson's hand warmly before he hurried away, melting into the shadows. Clem pointed to the bottom of the sailboat. "I left one o' th' kegs as payment for th' use o' th' boat," he whispered.

Gwen pulled him with her up the slope toward Wrecker's Ruin, as far away from Roc as possible. "That's a stroke of genius, Clem," she said at last, laughing. "He will be angry as a bee when he finds out."

"Aye, that 'e'll be. I'll spread th' rumor that I saw a brandy keg in th' *Seahawk,* and that th' earl is Dandelion."

"Do that, but be careful. You don't want to be the only one who has seen the keg or people will wonder." She rubbed her hands together. "Perhaps this will force him to take down the gallows in the square."

"Naw, stubborn as a mule 'e is, 'e won't do that." Clem continued, "We got a 'undred kegs this time, and th' Frogs say we can 'ave two loads a month if we care to."

She sighed wistfully. "I wish we could, but you know how difficult 'tis bringing in even one load, what with the earl breathing down our necks. I fear it would be too dangerous to attempt more."

"That earl's a loose fish if I ever saw 'un; needs a good millin', as much is clear," Clem blurted out hotly.

Gwen chuckled. "Might be, but we have to be wily, to make him understand that he has no right to take our livelihood from us."

"I fairly long to plant me fist 'ard on 'is lordship's jaw," Clem insisted. "That popinjay!"

"And you're a hothead. One of these days it will cost you dearly. You'd better go and cool off. See you tomorrow, you great muttonhead," she teased.

On her way home, Gwen knew she would give a kingdom to be able to see the look on Roc's face when he found that the sailboat was back, containing one plump cask of brandy and a small surprise from Dandelion.

Chapter 23

Roc awakened, his neck stiff and both legs cramped. Sharp needles of pain prickled through him as the circulation returned to his limbs. All he could remember was that he had planned on fetching Sergeant Adams, and then an irresistible urge to sleep had come over him. The first rays of dawn filtered through the blackness as he stretched, wondering what he was doing outside, sleeping against a tree. Memory flowed back, and he stiffened with suspicion mixed with dismay. If the smugglers had returned with Morgan's sailboat, he had lost the best opportunity he would ever get to catch them red-handed!

"Damnation!" he swore. He had never before fallen asleep while on guard. The overpowering urge to sleep had sneaked upon him without warning. Had there been something in his food or drink? What was the last thing he had drunk? The brandy! He rubbed the stubble on his chin. Enedoc had served it himself and he would never put anything in his brandy, Roc decided. But the nagging suspicion would not leave him. Walking to the top of the lookout, he was not surprised to see the *Seahawk* bobbing in the harbor.

"Devil take it!" Roc hurled a handful of pebbles. "He made a fool of me again!"

As dawn got a firmer hold on the world, Roc ran down to the docks and jumped into the *Seahawk*. He came eye to eye with the brandy keg. Frozen with explosive outrage, he stared at the offending keg at the bottom of his boat. On top of it lay a bouquet of wilting dandelions.

"A pox on the plaguey scoundrel!" he shouted. He had

been right to assume that the load would be hauled in during the wee hours of the morning.

How would he ever live down this latest failure? He wouldn't be able to show himself in the village. Oh, how he yearned to wring Dandelion's miserable neck! "You make a mockery of me," he snarled at the keg and gave it a vicious kick. Pain shot up his leg, and he hopped about on one leg, groaning. "You might be laughing at me, Dandelion, but I'll have the last laugh." Fortified by that vow, he emptied the brandy into the harbor and rolled the keg onto the dock. Then he carried it to the square and placed it on the platform holding the gallows. This would show the villagers that he hadn't given up. He would never admit defeat.

After sleeping until midmorning and eating a late breakfast, Gwen entered the morning room. Her cheerful gaze alighted on Officer Biggles ensconced in an old wing chair by the fireplace. Aunt Clo sat pink-cheeked on the opposite side, her gaze riveted on the pompous revenue man.

"Good morning," Gwen greeted them, picking up her embroidery frame from a wicker basket on the floor.

The older people murmured a response, and Officer Biggles rose, presenting her a spindly leg.

"Oh, come now, Officer Biggles, you don't have to be so formal with me," she declared. "Here we don't stand on ceremony, as you might have noticed by now."

"I enjoy doing the polite thing by a pretty lady," the officer replied gallantly and gave her a smile full of yellow teeth.

Gwen eyed him shrewdly from under her lashes. "What brings you here this lovely morning?"

"The most baffling incident occurred last night," he began, barely containing his excitement. He proceeded to tell them about the brandy keg in the *Seahawk,* adding that Dandelion surely was a most remarkable fellow. "He's getting as wily as John Carter at Prussia Cove." Officer Biggles leaned closer as if to impart a stunning secret. " 'Tis widely whispered in the village that 'tis *him,* the earl himself, who is that bloke Dandelion."

Gwen laughed heartily. "Nonsense! We all know Dandelion existed long before the earl returned to these parts."

Deep in thought, Officer Biggles worried the wart on his chin. "You're right, of course, but one has to admit that Dandelion is too cunning by far to be one of the simple villagers. The earl might have had a substitute until he could come here himself."

"Too farfetched. How could Dandelion be a free trader and a magistrate at the same time?"

"Let me tell you, it has been done before," Officer Biggles imparted in sepulchral tones. "And it would be a perfect cover. No one would suspect the *magistrate* of such dastardly deeds, and think!—to erect a gallows would throw everybody off the scent."

Gwen stifled another laugh. The villagers were becoming stirred up, thanks to Clem's rumor. She watched the revenue man, her eyes twinkling. "Well? Do *you* believe these rumors?"

The officer hemmed and hawed. "Can't say I'm especially partial to the earl. He has been inconsiderate toward me, taking over this whole business without so much as a by-your-leave. And *I* have been here much longer than he. *I* showed him all the landing spots and introduced him to Sergeant Adams, who's another ne'er-do-well, if you want to know."

"Oh, 'tis a thankless position, I'm sure. By the way, how long are the soldiers going to be posted in the area?"

Officer Biggles chortled. "Aha, got yourself a young admirer among the officers, eh?"

Gwen marveled at the workings of his mind. She would be the last one in the village he would suspect of smuggling, except for the vicar, of course. "Not exactly," she demurred, assuming an expression that suggested the opposite.

He patted her hand in a fatherly way. "Don't you worry, they'll be stationed here until that weed Dandelion is uprooted." He chuckled at his own wit and failed to notice the fleeting dismay in Gwen's eyes.

Wheels crunched along the carriage drive and, craning her neck, Gwen recognized the Landregan carriage with Louise's angelic face in the window. Gwen ran to the front door to welcome her friend. She expected Morgan to alight from the coach to assist Louise, but instead Roc stepped down, his tawny gaze bearing down on her in anger.

Roc! How will I live through this next half hour? Gwen's heart almost stopped with the shock of seeing him.

Behind Roc, Morgan alighted and lifted Louise out of the carriage. Gwen's gaze skirted Roc's scowling face and she attached her arm to Louise's as a drowning man grabs hold of a piece of flotsam.

"How excessively kind of you to come for a visit," she blurted out, smiling in an affected manner which earned her another withering stare from the earl. Gwen felt as if he could see straight through her black heart, but he made no indication that he had discerned her secret.

" 'Tis our pleasure," Louise said with a pretty dimple. "I could not stand to spend another *second* with the dragons at the Hall. 'Tis so very tedious." Louise slipped her arm happily through Morgan's and leaned heavily against him. He flushed to the roots of his hair. Bracketed on both sides by Morgan and Gwen, Louise limped into the house. Roc followed, and Gwen imagined his angry gaze boring into her back.

"Mother sent Roc to chaperone us. She flatly refused to come herself, and my maid has been packing my things ever since the accident. Naturally, I order her to unpack each evening, as I have no wish to leave." Louise prattled on for anyone who wanted to listen. Arthur held open the door to the morning room and hurried to pull forward chairs and a footstool for Louise. In response to Aunt Clo's inquiry as to the state of her foot, Louise responded happily that it had almost healed and that she couldn't wait to walk normally once more.

Louise evidently knew how to play for time, Gwen mused. A broken leg, let alone a crack in the bone, didn't take two months to heal . . .

"Bring in cakes and wine," Gwen ordered Arthur. Seeing Roc's continued frown, a small devil of mischief flew into her mind. "Officer Biggles told us the most shocking news, something we cannot believe for one second, but rumor evidently holds the entire village enthralled."

Morgan's and Louise's expectant eyes instantly turned to her, but Roc's tawny pair stared stonily out the window.

" 'Tis whispered in the village that Lord Landregan is Dandelion." She let the words fall into the silence like a spell of doom. Glancing quickly at Roc, she noticed that all color had drained from his face.

Louise's giggle broke the tension. "How utterly ridiculous!"

Morgan stared uncomfortably from Roc to Gwen, obviously noting the silent battle going on between them. "Of all the idiotic rumors flying about in the village, this surely takes the prize," he said, looking uncertainly at his elder brother for support. None appeared, and Roc looked as if he was about to explode at any moment.

"That is my sincere opinion exactly. Total lunacy," Officer Biggles echoed, obviously being careful not to earn the earl's displeasure.

Roc turned to Gwen, his eyes frosty. "I'm sure you know better than to believe such nonsense, Miss Tremayne. If you're trying to upset me, you'll not succeed. I'll deal with the villagers in due time."

"By the looks of you, Roc, I'd say she has already succeeded in upsetting you," Louise piped up, her face wreathed in friendly sincerity.

Gwen knew that if Roc had been standing by Louise's chair, he would gladly have strangled her. Pressing his lips together in a thin line, and clasping his hands behind his back, he strode to the window.

"What's bothering him? Can't he take a little joke?" Louise continued, unperturbed.

Morgan patted her nervously on the shoulder. "Perhaps we could talk about something else. We all know how hard Roc works and how frustrating is his task."

To everyone's relief, Arthur entered bearing a tray of refreshments.

"Ah, there are the wine and cakes," Gwen said in a brittle voice, worrying that she had offended Roc beyond repair. After seeing that everyone had received a glass, she rose and joined Roc at the window, her knees shaking. "I want to apologize for suggesting such a rotten thing."

His eyes blazed. "I will try to forget," he allowed icily. " 'Twas not my idea to visit you, you know."

"Come, have a glass of wine." Gwen placed her hand on his sleeve. "I know you had no desire to visit me."

His searing gaze mocked her, resting momentarily on her

bosom swelling gently over the square-cut neckline. His anger could not disguise the smoldering desire in the golden depths of his eyes, and he held her fingers a trifle longer than necessary as he lifted them from his arm. "As Louise said, I came as a chaperone, but also to admire the new roof on Tremayne House," he explained as they strolled across to the company seated around the refreshment table.

A wispy smile covered Gwen's dismay. "Oh, yes, we're happy with it. You know, the old roof literally fell down over our heads during the last heavy storm."

His glance probed into her soul. Nervously she smoothed the material of her gown. "Well, here we are." She offered him a glass of wine.

"Don't you have something stronger?" he chided. "I've heard one can obtain the finest French cognac in the lowliest of cottages here in Landregan."

"Of course . . . we—we have some," Gwen stammered, and she sent Arthur to fetch the decanter from the study.

Biggles's voice boomed above the others. "I say, Lord Landregan, when do you think we'll have the scoundrel smuggling chief hanging from that gallows on the square? I warned you he's as difficult as a weasel."

"We'll catch him. Now he has no other method to bring in the cargo except by way of the coves we already know. We'll post guards everywhere. To use Morgan's sailboat was the most devilish impudence I've ever had the misfortune to encounter. And presenting me with a keg of brandy with a bunch of dandelions on top goes beyond gall."

"What a stroke of luck for you!" Officer Biggles mused. "A whole keg. Brandy being so expensive these days."

"I didn't keep it," Roc snapped, and the revenue officer jumped at the outrage in his voice.

Officer Biggles fidgeted in his seat and smiled blandly. "Of course not! I wouldn't either." He barked a hollow laugh. "The rogue must have been inspired to name himself after the many dandelions on your lawn, Miss Tremayne."

Gwen flinched and paled but kept a calm face. She spread out her hands disarmingly. "My weeds are innocent as far as I know," she said with a charming smile. "But I'm sure many of the villagers laugh behind my back and say I cultivate them on a large scale."

Officer Biggles laughed. Roc sat very still, regarding her speculatively.

Gwen's spirits plummeted to the soles of her slippers. *He knows!* she thought in desperation. He slowly pulled his gaze from her face.

"Why, Lord Landregan, you look as if you just saw a ghost," she blurted with false gaiety.

"Oh," he muttered, "I was lost in thought. I must beg your forgiveness for letting my mind wander so rudely." There was an edge of derision in his voice. He sipped his brandy gingerly. "Excellent stuff." His anger had miraculously dissipated.

Gwen trembled with nervousness. Cold sweat broke out along her spine. He must have seen through her charade. What was going to happen now?

Roc sat quietly eating cakes and sipping brandy. Gwen could barely follow the conversation going on around her, and Louise's high voice grated on her nerves.

Louise broke the tension by placing a calming hand on her clenched fist. "Isn't it famous that I'll be here to attend the county fair?" she asked.

"The fair?" Gwen echoed. "Oh . . . yes, of course, the event of the year. Yes, that will be splendid. I promise you'll have a wonderful time. All sorts of entertainment for every taste."

"Mama has forbidden me to go, says I will attract all sorts of diseases."

"But that won't stop you."

"Of course not!" Louise fixed her friend with an indignant glare. "*You* must have been to many fairs, and you're still alive and well."

"And you pointed out that fact to Lady Camelford."

"Naturally."

"I wager she commented that I have all manner of dread diseases and should be avoided at all cost?"

Louise colored and shifted in her chair as much as her wide hoops allowed. "Well, perhaps not in such brash words."

Gwen laughed, and the others cleared their throats in embarrassment. Only Roc remained silent.

"I assure you the fair's quite harmless . . . as long as you don't touch anything," Gwen teased.

Louise dimpled, her smile hesitant. "Oh, you're teasing me, aren't you?"

"I've heard that the entertainment includes a cockfight and a mill. Famous good sport!" Officer Biggles exclaimed.

The ladies shivered and looked askance.

" 'Tis beyond me how gentlemen can be interested in such savage pastimes," Aunt Clo observed. "No more than wild animals, that's what they are."

"Don't take on so, Miss Clorinda," Officer Biggles wheedled. "A man must have his sport."

So 'tis Clorinda now, Gwen thought, staring with new interest at her aunt, who blanched, guilt written across her face.

"Well, I cannot wait until Saturday," Louise chimed in, clapping her hands in excitement.

Roc added with some asperity, "I'm sure the finest French brandy will flow freely the entire week of the county fair." His warm fingers brushed Gwen's forearm, and she jumped at his touch.

He spoke solely to her. "May we take a walk in the garden? I would like to have a word with you." Evidently sensing her tension, he assured her, "No, Miss Gwen, you don't have to worry that I'll propose again. I promise to behave myself." He rose. "You haven't shown me your new roof."

"I don't understand how a new roof can be of any interest to you," Gwen said.

"I'd like to inspect Mr. Tregony's work since I'm planning to have a new roof put on the Hall." He bent over to whisper in her ear. "Perhaps you could ask him to give me a discount if I don't lock him in the dungeons for smuggling." His words sent dread through her veins. He knew Mr. Tregony was part of the gang. What else did he know?

"I'm sure my word doesn't carry any weight with the village carpenter," she said breathlessly.

"Now, shall we?" Roc offered his arm. To the others he said, "I will steal the hostess for a few moments."

"Don't stay outside above five minutes," Aunt Clo warned, "or tongues will start to wag."

"Just so. I will deliver Miss Gwen back to you in exactly five minutes, Miss Pettigrew."

Filled with a mixture of trepidation and excitement, Gwen

placed her fingertips on his sleeve and accompanied him outside.

"Lovely day, isn't it?" Roc commented blandly, gazing at the bright blue sky. "The end of a beautiful summer." He turned to her. "It has been the best and the worst summer of my life. Best because I'm back home, and worst because of Dandelion. He's been a veritable thorn in my flesh—"

Gwen dared not answer or look at him. Was he fishing for a confession, or was he still floundering in the dark? Oh, dear. She wished she could have read his thoughts when he looked at the dandelions on the lawn earlier.

He dutifully eyed the black slate roof. "Excellent craftsmanship. I will remember to hire Tregony to do the work at the Hall."

"Why, how kind of you. He needs all the extra work he can get."

Roc shot her a shrewd glance. "Since you're such a staunch supporter of the villagers, tell me, how is Mrs. Lane faring?"

" 'Tis kind of you to ask. Can it be that you now have a better understanding of the plight of the poor?" Her eyes blazed a challenge.

"Perhaps, but you didn't answer my question." He did not give an inch. Was he playing a game with her?

"She has quite regained her strength. I've seen her a few times, and she treats me like a goddess descended from heaven."

"Perhaps you are." His voice flowed softly over her. "You have a singular capacity for compassion, and I admire that." His hand traveled over her back to rest on her shoulder as they strolled along the dilapidated terrace. A bee buzzed around the huge blossom of a late yellow tea rose.

"Oh, you're exaggerating," she said. "They all help me, and I like the villagers. They are my friends."

"Not mine," Roc mocked. "They have nothing but black glares and snickers for me every time I enter the village. Especially after what happened last night."

"They do like you, but they're vexed by your interference in their affairs." Gwen held her breath, waiting nervously for his response. Why had she brought up that subject?

"Their *affairs?* Their crimes, more likely," he said, eyeing her angrily.

"We should perhaps drop the subject before we scratch each other's eyes out." Gwen fought back a hysterical laugh. Now or never would he mention the identity of Dandelion. If he knew. Or maybe he was playing with her, waiting for the perfect moment to pounce.

His voice became a soft, menacing growl. "Tell me, where did you get the funds for a new roof? I thought your family was—"

"What are you trying to say?" Gwen tore free and faced him, praying nothing but anger showed in her eyes, though guilt and fear made every muscle in her body tense.

He shrugged. "I just wondered where you found the means to repair the roof."

" 'Tis a subject you should raise with my father, not with me. But if you must know, we sold off a piece of land to Farmer Polpenny." She had already made sure the farmer would support her claim if Roc asked him. The lie felt uncomfortable on her tongue, and she almost took it back. This would perhaps be the only opportunity she would have to make a clean breast of her deceit. There was still perhaps a chance he would forgive her if she confessed now. But the words wouldn't come. The deception had gone on for too long.

He was silent for a long time, scanning her face as if seeing it for the first time. How much could he read in her expression?

"Selling off land is a tragic event," he observed. "Tell me, Gwen, would you do me one favor? I despair of ever finding the identity of Dandelion." He sighed deeply, and defeat trembled in his voice. "I need help."

Was he merely playing with her, or did he trust her to feel compassion for his plight and help him? She wished she knew, but nothing but despair stood written on his face.

"How in the world can you suggest that I'd know where to contact Dandelion—or even how to give him a message?"

Holding her shoulders in a firm grip, he allowed his hard glare to drill into her. "In all likelihood, you know his identity, and if you won't help me, at least stop your pretense of innocence." He dropped his hands to his sides in a weary gesture. "I don't like to be harsh with you, but I'm fed up with the plaguey character."

Gwen saw a flash of purple in the rose arbor. Vincent was lurking about in the garden. Was he spying on them?

Roc had seen him, too. "Perhaps Dandelion lives in this house. 'Twouldn't surprise me."

Her breath clogged in her throat. "Here? That's ridiculous." She grabbed at straws. "You mean Vincent?"

He didn't respond at first, but his eyes were narrowed in calculation. "Mayhap. Not impossible."

"Nonsense! Vincent just returned to Landregan this summer. The smuggling has been going on much longer than that."

Abruptly Roc made a valiant effort to lighten the mood. "Where did my manners go? I didn't mean to berate you. All I wanted was to ask for your help." He cleared his throat. "Do you have an escort for the fair on Saturday?" He gazed down at her, seeing only the top of her simply coiffed chestnut curls. The sunlight picked out strands of red, and tiny blond wisps curled at the nape of her neck. She was lovely. There was a deep sadness in his heart, so powerful he thought it'd be the end of him unless he could find a way to dissolve it. Tenderly he lifted her chin and looked into the sorrow-filled hazel eyes so close to his own.

"No, Roc, 'tis no use. Why torture yourself and me? I can't give you anything but more pain." She pulled away from him, turning her back on him.

"Oh well, I'm sure I'll survive alone at the fair," he said, unable to hide the additional pain of her refusal.

A seagull wheeled high above their heads, screeching.

"Perhaps some other time." Gwen turned sharply on the terrace. "I believe those five minutes expired a long time ago. I'll hear no end of Aunt Clo's complaints."

"Very well, so be it."

With nothing resolved, and misery their companion, they walked back into the house.

Chapter 24

Somehow Gwen had managed to convince Roc of her innocence. Or had she? She could not be sure he wasn't toying with her. She wasn't sure about anything anymore. Had he accepted her lie about selling off a piece of land to pay for the new roof? She wished she could read his mind, but there was a barrier of pain between them, and it was growing more impenetrable every day.

Once Roc left with Louise and Morgan, the very air seemed gray and lackluster. Gwen stepped onto the terrace and breathed deeply of the crisp air, but it didn't soothe her.

Vincent was strolling toward the stables, still dressed in his hideous purple coat. Set into a tight mask of anger, his face was almost as pale as his hair. What was he angry about? Gwen wondered.

She went up to her bedchamber, but could find no peace within its walls. They appeared to be crowding in on her, making breathing difficult. To clear her head, she decided to take a ride. After donning her old brown riding habit and a cloak to shield her from the wind, she ran downstairs and out to the stables. As the stable lad saddled Buttercup, Gwen noticed that the squire's old hunter was missing. Vincent must have taken it out for a ride. She thought no more about it until she rode up the hill toward the ridge path bordering the sea.

The sharp wind slapped her face and tossed her hair. She reveled in its force and jabbed her heels into Buttercup's flanks, galloping all the way to Fisherman's Creek, then cantering back toward the village.

Gwen stopped at her favorite spot above Dead Man's Cove,

remembering the day she and Roc had found the drowned man there. It was a long time ago. Were there still Jacobites fleeing for their lives? News filtered slowly into Landregan. Most likely they would never find out who had killed poor James Murray. The thought made her sad and uneasy. Such a waste of life. She glanced across the harbor to the steep lookout point. To her surprise, she recognized Vincent's purple coat and the squire's chestnut hunter at the top. Vincent was staring down at Roc's yacht, bobbing at anchor in the bay. The crew was scrubbing the deck and inspecting the sails.

Gwen scanned the village. A line of fishermen sat on benches in the harbor, having already returned from their daily fishing trip. Women and children stood in the doorways, chatting. The village looked deceptively peaceful. Everyone must be talking about the upcoming fair.

The sun disappeared behind a bank of clouds, and the air lost its warmth. Gwen turned her attention back to the lookout point, but Vincent had left. There was no sign of him in the harbor, so he must have chosen the path toward Brandy Cove and Wrecker's Ruin.

Gwen's eyes were drawn repeatedly to the *Blackbird,* and she swallowed a surge of sadness. Was Roc going away? Perhaps he was so sick of the villagers' mockery—and hers— that he meant to turn his back on Landregan. She couldn't blame him if he did, yet he wasn't the type of person who admitted defeat.

Sighing, she rode down to the harbor. There was no sign of Roc, so she chatted with the fishermen, who always had wide smiles for her. Before returning to Tremayne House, she rode up the path toward Brandy Cove for a last slap of salty wind on her face. It almost knocked her out of the saddle, and she laughed, gathering together the corners of her flapping cloak.

Buttercup whinnied and shied toward the trees. Without heeding Gwen's protests, the mare ambled into the shelter of the greenery. A corner of Wrecker's Ruin was visible between the swaying boughs. At the ruin's base was a square patch of red. Frowning, Gwen wondered if Clem had dropped his red handkerchief in the grass. She slid from the saddle and waded through the tall grass.

The red patch grew as she drew closer. Though the bracken against the crumbling wall shielded most of it, Gwen recognized the sweep of a red skirt. Gripped by sudden fear, she clasped a hand to her mouth. "Who's there?" she called, but no one answered.

Her gaze darted among the trees, but she saw no one. Fearing what she would find, she took a cautious step forward. A moan reached her ears.

Forgetting her fear, she rushed ahead and parted the bracken. She recognized Mabel Noble, the woman she had seen arguing with the ostler at The Pilchard. She sank down on her knees beside the woman. Mabel's face was bloody and bruised.

"What happened?" Gwen asked, filled with dread. She inserted her arm under the disheveled red curly head and lifted it into her lap. Mabel moaned, and her eyes fluttered open.

"Who're ye?" she asked. Blood flowed from her nose and a purpling contusion was swelling on one frail cheekbone. Her skin was deathly pale, and cold sweat sheened her forehead. Gwen gently wiped her face with a handkerchief. The nosebleed wouldn't stop, so she gently lowered Mabel's head to the ground and ran down to Brandy Cove to dip the handkerchief in cold water.

Returning, she pressed the cloth against Mabel's nose and forced her head back. "What happened to you? Can you tell me?" Fear rippled through Gwen. She knew Vincent must be involved.

The woman moaned and tossed her head back and forth.

"Lie still, or the nosebleed won't stop," Gwen warned. "Did Vincent Tremayne do this to you?"

Mabel's eyes flew open, and Gwen noticed they were a pale shade of gray, a washed-out color. " 'Ow did ye know?" Mabel asked, evidently having difficulty forming the words with her swollen lips.

"I know you're friends, and I saw him ride this way not too long ago."

"A bloomin' snake in th' grass, 'e is!" Mabel spat. "To think I loved 'im once. 'Ow silly can a girl get? 'E used me, and now 'e kicks me in th' arse—'is way o' showin' 'is gratitude."

Gwen didn't press for more information. The nosebleed finally stopped, and Mabel tried to sit up. She leaned heavily against the ruin wall and threaded her trembling fingers through her riotous curls.

"Did you have an argument?" Gwen asked and wrapped her cloak around Mabel's shaking body. The shiny red dress with the swooping decolletage provided inadequate protection against the cold wind.

"Not exactly. We 'ad a business deal, and now 'e wants bloody all o' it. When I argued, 'e beat me. A snake, I told ye!" She dashed a grimy hand across her eyes. "We were to sell some gems and share th' profit."

"Do you want to tell me about it? Perhaps I can help." Gwen glanced hopefully at the woman. She might be the clue to Vincent's strange behavior since he had returned to Landregan.

"Who're ye?" Mabel's tone was suspicious.

"I'm Vincent's cousin, Gwen Tremayne."

Mabel's eyes grew wide with fear, and she tried to scramble away. Gwen placed a hand on her arm. "Please don't be afraid, Miss Noble. I'm as set against Vincent as you are."

Mabel assessed her honesty. "I see." She sighed. "I suppose that snake 'as nothin' but enemies. I was stupid to see 'im as gallant and refined."

"He can be charming when he chooses to be. It's not your fault for trusting him." Gwen sat down beside Mabel and leaned against the disintegrating stone wall. "I'm very good at listening."

Mabel pressed her eyes shut and knotted her fists in frustration. "It all began in Lunnon. I had a lover, a Scotsman in th' Eighty-seventh Dragoons, a 'andsome young man who 'eaped presents over me 'ead." Mabel's voice trembled. " 'Twas a wonderful time, but 'e tired o' me company and stopped sendin' gifts. I was broken'earted."

"I understand," Gwen said. "But how did you come in contact with Vincent?"

"They were in th' same division. I met Vincent in a coffee'ouse at Covent Garden. James introduced us, y'see. Vinnie offered me 'is protection." She patted her wild curls. "I still 'ave me looks if nothin' else, don't I? There are always willin' men as long as I 'ave me looks."

"Yes, you're very pretty."

"I was sad after me breakup with me 'andsome Scot. 'E tore me 'eart out and trampled it in th' mud." Her voice broke momentarily before she continued, "But in my profession nothin' ever lasts, y'see. And a girl's better off without a 'eart, y'see."

"I agree," Gwen said with much feeling. She could understand Mabel's pain as if it were her own.

"Vinnie gave me ever'thin' a girl would want, when 'e 'ad th' funds. 'E gambled 'eavily. More often than not, 'e 'ad nothin'. But I stuck with 'im, 'elpin' 'im without complaint when 'e needed me." Her voice petered out while she struggled against her tears.

"I 'ad a secret which I shared with Vinnie. Me Scot, James, 'ad contacts in France, y'see. They were friends o' that bloke Charles Stuart what led a rebellion in Scotland."

"Yes, I know about it. Was the Scot's name James Murray?"

Mabel's mouth dropped. " 'Ow did ye know that?"

Gwen braced herself against the grief that would come when Mabel learned the truth. "A man by that name was found dead in one of the coves around here. In May. No one knows what he was doing in these parts."

"Dead?" Mabel's voice was barely audible. "That's why 'e disappeared, then. I waited to 'ear somethin' from 'im, but 'e was off th' face o' th' earth. 'E was a traitor to England, y'see." Mabel's lips trembled, but she didn't cry. " 'E was involved in th' business what would 'elp Charles Stuart. They were to smuggle jewels from France, y'see."

"And you told Vinnie about it?" Gwen asked, now understanding why her cousin had been lurking about at night. He'd evidently been searching for something worth a lot of money—the jewels.

"Yes, and in a fit o' rage when James left me, I decided to join Vinnie in 'is plan to lay 'is 'ands on th' gems." She looked thoughtful. "I niver understood why Vinnie returned 'ere, but if this was th' last place James was seen alive . . ."

"He was dead when he was washed ashore, but it looked like he was . . . murdered."

"Murdered?" Mabel paled. "D'ye think Vinnie—?"

"I don't know, but he could have. He's very unpleasant

these days. 'Tis an ordeal to have him living in the house, and I haven't found a way to throw him out since Father approves of everything he does and says.'' Gwen kicked a loose rock. She had gleaned only parts of the puzzle.

"You think James was going to fetch the jewels here in Landregan?" she asked.

"Yes. I didn't know at th' time, but Vinnie must 'ave followed 'im 'ere.'E must 'ave figured out this was th' place James was goin' to collect th' gems."

They pondered the thought in silence. Gwen rose finally and held out a hand to Mabel, whose nose had stopped bleeding. The bruises ranged from black to purple, and Gwen's heart constricted with pity.

"You'd better stay away from Vincent from now on, Miss Noble. He wouldn't hesitate to hurt you again."

Mabel swore at length and straightened her bodice with an angry twist of her hands. "I'll pay 'im back for maulin' me, don't ye worry 'bout that, Miss Tremayne." She smiled suddenly. "Ye've been very kind to me. I thank ye."

"Don't mention it. You may have helped me solve a problem." Gwen hoisted Mabel into Buttercup's saddle and led the horse down the hill to The Pilchard.

If she could prove that Vinnie had killed James Murray, Gwen thought, it would be the perfect way to get rid of him.

They rode into the yard at The Pilchard, and Gwen helped Mabel down. She decided to see Mabel settled in her room, and followed her across the yard. One of her smuggler friends, Troy Polson, approached her. "Miss Tremayne," he greeted, dragging off his stocking cap. His face bore an air of importance.

"Yes?"

"I found an old sack washed up at Fisherman's Creek. Thought it might belong to the dead man you found. I left it here at the Pilchard."

"How intriguing. I'll take a look at it."

Inside, Mabel thanked her once again and, seated like a queen at the best table in the taproom, she ordered a dram of brandy and a tankard of stout. That the patrons were staring at her battered face didn't seem to bother her.

"Mr. Trelawny, I'd like to take a look at the drowned

man's belongings,'' Gwen said to the proprietor as soon as
he had served Mabel.

''What wrong with 'er?'' he whispered, tossing his head
in Mabel's direction.

''A bit of an altercation, I'm afraid,'' Gwen replied. ''Mr.
Murray's things, please.''

Mr. Trelawny grumbled and led her through the steaming
kitchen, which smelled of boiled chicken. In the scullery, he
pulled a sack from a shelf and placed it on the lead sink.
'' 'Ere ye are, Miss Tremayne. Not that I understand why ye
would like to go through a dead man's thin's. 'Tis morbid.''

''I'm investigating his death,'' Gwen replied. ''Don't you
mind me.''

When she was left alone, she opened the sack. A shiver
traveled through her as she touched the dead man's clothes.
They were rolled up and nested in the middle was a lead
pencil, a handkerchief, a comb, a stout iron key, and a
leather-bound notebook wrapped in oilcloth. She flipped
through the pages, realizing it was an address book. The sea
had blurred the ink on most of the pages, but a few names
in the middle pages were legible. She glanced at the last
entry. It was a column of names, with a few words in Gaelic.
At the very bottom she read: *Watch out for the Stork. He's
planning to kill me if I don't give him the gems.*

Gwen frowned. The Stork? That was the name she had
given Vincent when they were children because he'd looked
like a stork, with his narrow shoulders and puffed-out chest.

Murray must have known Vincent was following him. As
far as she could see, Vincent had not found the jewels, or
he'd be long gone by now. She would have to find them before he hurt someone else. But what did they look like, and
where should she start looking? Another problem faced her:
if James Murray had been a Jacobite, what was Roc, his good
friend? Roc, too, could very well be involved in the disastrous Jacobite Cause!

Chapter 25

Gwen tucked the notebook into her pocket and returned to Tremayne House. Until she knew the extent of Roc's involvement, she would keep the notebook a secret. How much did Vinnie know about Roc's friendship with James Murray?

And what about the jewels that Vinnie was looking for? Did Roc know of their existence? Was he even now hiding them at the Hall? After all, Vinnie had been searching Roc's desk at the pilchard festivities.

As Gwen led Buttercup to the stables, she yearned to go to Landregan Hall and look for the gems. But that was impossible.

At least she could confront Vinnie about beating Mabel. As she entered the house and hurried upstairs, Gwen glanced at Arthur, who was sitting on a chair in the hallway, snoring. The whole house was somnolent.

She knocked on Vincent's door and waited. Tension further stiffened her shoulders with every passing moment. No sound came from within. Finally she tried the door handle and looked inside.

Vincent was not there. She looked on top of the armoire where he kept his portmanteau. It was gone.

The rat! He had sneaked away.

Gwen ran downstairs and knocked on her father's door. No answer was forthcoming, but she found the squire snoring with his nose in a thick tome spread open on his desk.

"Father!" she called.

"Huh?" The squire's head jerked up and he peered at Gwen through his spectacles, which were tilted haphazardly on the bridge of his nose. "Gwen?" he asked sleepily.

"Where's Vinnie?" she demanded and sank down in a chair. Reaching for the brandy decanter at a side table, she poured herself a measure. The strong liquid fortified her.

"Eh? . . . Ah, Vincent. He went off to London for a spell. Said he had some urgent business to take care of there and might have to stay awhile."

Gwen's eyes narrowed with suspicion. "Where did he find the funds to travel to London?"

The squire's eyebrows rose in surprise. "Why, I gave him some money to tide him over. No more than right. After all, he's my nephew."

"Father! Haven't you realized by now that he's a parasite? He doesn't do anything to alleviate his financial problems."

The squire tut-tutted and pushed up his spectacles. "I won't hear another word of complaint from you, Gwennie. You show a distressing tendency toward envy."

Gwen burned to show him James Murray's notebook and tell him about her suspicion that Vincent had murdered the Scot. She rose slowly, her hands clenched into fists. Her father would not believe her. He was totally blind when it came to Vincent's character.

"Very well, Father, I will not speak against him again. Forgive me for disturbing your rest." Fuming inside but with head held high, Gwen left the study. At the door she turned to look at him. He was already snoring in his book.

Later that day, as Gwen was calculating the best strategy for searching Landregan Hall for the gems, Louise arrived, claiming her whole attention. The younger lady insisted they embark together on a shopping trip to Plymouth, which lasted three interminable days. And when they returned, it was the eve of the county fair.

The morning of the first day of the fair, a Saturday, dawned nippy. Damp mist curled under the trees and over the sea with stubborn persistence, and every yellowing leaf tip balanced a water diamond. Gwen sensed melancholy in the air, the sadness of a dying summer, each day a little more defeated by the conquering autumn with its brisk cool air and cold rains. Yet summer was not quite ready to give up. To everyone's delight the sun bravely chased away the mist, and shone with mellow benevolence on the cluster of tents and stalls erected on the village common.

Accompanied by the chime of the church bells, the villagers set out toward the fair. Gwen traveled in the Landregan carriage with Louise and Morgan. For the occasion, Louise walked without a stick, quite recovered. Like Gwen, she had chosen a simple muslin gown with moderate hoops for the country entertainment. Fringed shawls modestly covered their shoulders, and clogs protected their feet. They wore wide straw hats to protect their complexions from the sun, Louise's sporting a bunch of violets tucked into the pink ribbon around the crown.

Although it was still early in the morning, people were already milling among the stalls.

The driver stopped at the edge of the large field, and Morgan gallantly assisted the ladies out of the carriage. Farm wagons, carts, and coaches thronged the roads and the outskirts of the common. Horses and cows had been crowded into a fenced area for the upcoming auction. Loud voices and laughter echoed.

The scent of freshly baked pastries, cakes, and tarts filled the air, mingling with the smells of flowers, fish, and roasted meat.

"Oh, Gwennie, look at that lovely silk handkerchief," exclaimed Louise. "I must buy one, the one with the red stripes. And look at that pale blue one, so perfect for you." Louise dragged Gwen to a stall groaning under the considerable load of colorful cottons, cambrics, damasks, flowered silks, satins, and crepes. In a wooden box, red and white whisper-thin silk stockings beckoned.

"What's yer 'eart's desire?" asked the merry-faced man at the stall. "Here, feel th' quality o' these lovely fabrics. A bargain for a beautiful lady." He held a bunch of iridescent squares of cloth between his fat fingers, waving them in front of Louise's enraptured face.

She promptly bargained with him on the price of the blue handkerchief and presented it to Gwen.

"Surely I can't take it," Gwen demurred.

"Don't be silly. Here, 'tis but a tiny gift from me, to a dear friend." She resolutely bound it around Gwen's wrist.

"There." Her gaze traveled immediately to the next stall where cream-filled pastries tempted customers.

"Now, 'tis my turn to treat you," Gwen insisted as she saw her friend's avid eyes on the baked goods. She bought them each a confection. Morgan had no interest in sweets, but the stall filled with old books and journals from the capital instantly drew him like a bumblebee to nectar.

The villagers had donned their Sunday finery for the fair. Hair had been brushed and parted, ringlets freshly curled, aprons starched, and dazzling white neckerchiefs and shirts laundered and pressed.

At a corner of the common a cockpit had been set up. Raucous laughter and curses burst from the excited crowd around the pit, and Gwen shuddered with revulsion. How could men find it intriguing to watch two cockerels fight each other to death?

"Oh, Gwen, look! Isn't it absolutely *divine!*" Louise said with starlight in her eyes. She rushed to a stall displaying ribbons of all colors, and Gwen followed her at a more sedate pace. Her eyes traveled over the crowd; she had the uncomfortable feeling that someone was staring at her. Her hazel gaze locked with Roc's. He was sitting on top of the fence next to the horses, his booted legs dangling carelessly.

Through the opened neck of his shirt, she glimpsed his torso, smooth skin stretching over bunching muscles. His hair was mussed and his skin gleamed with perspiration as if he had been working very hard. His dark face split into a grin, and he waved. She blushed and a shiver coursed through her, making her hot with desire. How she longed to be at his side! But she stubbornly turned her back on him without so much as a greeting. What was he doing there looking so disheveled?

Gwen followed Louise to another stall. Had her friend later asked her what was sold at the stall, she would not have been able to answer. Her thoughts revolved completely around the man she loved.

"Look, a monkey." Louise pointed to the scrawny animal attached to the wrist of an organ-grinder by a thin chain. The monkey begged the passersby for coins, his tiny hand outstretched. "Isn't he the most adorable creature you've ever seen, Gwennie?" The monkey proceeded to scuttle up

Louise's gown and settle on her shoulder, oblivious to her squeals.

"Your mother would have one of her turns if she saw you with that creature," Roc's deep voice came from behind them.

Gwen whirled as Louise cried, "Take him away, Roc, he . . . he smells!"

Roc laughingly relieved her of the clinging, chattering animal and set it gently to the ground, pressing a small coin into its hairy hand. It promptly bit into the metal with sharp teeth.

Roc's cautious gaze brushed past Gwen, as if not quite seeing her. She was mortified by the obvious snub.

"This may be a stupid question, but where is that scholarly brother of mine?" Roc asked lightly, addressing Louise.

"At the bookstall, where else?" Louise's eyes grew wide as she took in Roc's unkempt appearance. "I say, what have you done to yourself?"

Just then Morgan joined them. "Ah, there you are. Roc, old chap, you look as if you've been tossed about in a gale," he said. "A fight?"

"Yes, I'm challenging the burly fellows of Cornwall to a fair mill. I miss the sparring matches at the Amphitheater in London." He pointed to a patch of grass surrounded by a horde of men packed together like pilchards in a hogshead. They were standing almost on top of each other to get a glimpse of the fighters. "I've seen Jack Broughton fight in London, y'know."

"The great champion?" Morgan's eyes widened in awe. "Must have been a sight." He pressed Roc's hefty biceps playfully. "You topple these men like straws, don't you?" Morgan then addressed Louise and Gwen. "My brother is also a champion with his fives, just like Broughton," he explained proudly.

"I can't see any pleasure in punching each other's faces. All the nosebleeds and the bruises," Louise said with a shudder. Gwen added her own comment of disgust.

Louise grasped Gwen's arm. "Come, let's leave them to their barbaric customs. I'd like to buy some lemons and oranges before they're sold out."

Gwen darted a glance at Roc, but he was staring beyond her. Crushed, she hurried after Louise. He hated her!

After buying fruit, Louise set her heart on visiting every single stall and tent, especially the tent with the gypsy fortune-teller. "This is great fun, don't you agree? I'm so glad I'm here. I wager we'll be friends forever, and if you marry Roc, you'll be my sister-in-law, y'know. How splendid."

"That won't happen," Gwen said glumly. "And you're not married to Morgan yet."

Louise waved dismissingly. " 'Tis only a matter of time. If he doesn't propose, I'll ask him to marry me."

Gwen believed her. Morgan hadn't a chance of escape if Louise had truly set her heart on wedding him.

"And I predict you'll be married to Roc before the year is out," Louise added matter-of-factly. "I would wager all the oranges in my basket on that fact." She tossed one high in the air.

Gwen shook her head. "You're wrong this time."

"No. You mark my words! Haven't you noticed the way he looks at you, as if he wants to . . . eat you whole." Her eyes grew misty. "He's madly in love with you. Why, at night he sits in the study until the early morning hours, brooding . . . over you, I'm sure. Morgan told me."

Her words did strange things to Gwen's heart, melting her with longing for the man who was her enemy. She laughed shakily. "You're dreaming, Louise. He's only brooding over a way to catch Dandelion, that's all."

"I hope he never catches the daring smuggler. Life wouldn't seem so exciting if he did." Louise's voice held an edge of urgency. "If you know who Dandelion is, you ought to warn him. Roc can be positively *dangerous* when he's angry, and he's so mulish."

"You're right there," Gwen said in her driest voice. Over Louise's shoulder she spied Clem's massive shoulders and dark mop of hair in the crowd. "Listen, why don't you look through the wares at this stall while I go and speak with the village blacksmith. I have some trouble with the wheel on the squire's rig."

Louise happily agreed, and Gwen did not have to worry about the girl's safety in the rough crowd, because Morgan arrived at her side at that very moment. She left the happy couple and went off to speak with Clem, a move she instantly regretted for he was clearly more than a little merry with drink.

"You big oaf! You'll be bragging of Dandelion before the day is over," she scolded.

"Fiddle-de-dee, what's eatin' ye, Miss Gwen?" he asked with a huge smile.

"I think the earl's getting closer to the truth. He voiced a suspicion that someone at Tremayne House is involved in the smuggling. I suspect he's mingling with the villagers for the sole purpose of gathering information from loosened tongues." She waggled a finger under his nose. "And it might be yours, you old braggart! He cannot voice his suspicions openly, because everyone would laugh at him after his latest failure. But now he only needs some proof, a sentence spoken by one of my men, a thoughtless mention of my name, and he'll happily hang me by my reckless neck."

"Naw, 'e won't 'ang ye, Miss Gwen. 'Yere too beautiful to string up by th' neck.'E would 'ave to answer to me for that." He looked lovingly at his old playmate. "I would mightily like to kiss yer red mouth, miss." He lurched closer. Brave with ale, he grasped her by the waist and lifted her high in the air, then planted a resounding kiss on her lips and was greatly applauded for his endeavor by his cronies. Gwen blushed furiously as he set her down.

"You hothead!" The men who heard her scalding words roared with laughter, unduly attracting attention to the group. Gwen had never felt so mortified in her life.

And that was not the end of it. When she tried to melt away from the scene, a dozen hands held her back, pushing her against Clem's broad chest. She glowered at the men. How could they do this to her?

"Get me out of this, Clem!" she ordered over the uproar. He held her loosely in the circle of his arms, peering tenderly down at her. Like a lightning bolt from a clear sky she understood. How could she have been so blind? Clem was head over heels in love with her. Had probably always been, although he'd never expressed his feelings. But he had never married, either, and he was past the age when most of the villagers did so. They married very young, and he was going on twenty-one. How could she have been so corkbrained as not to see it? He had never touched her like this before, only today when he was three sheets to the wind.

She tore herself free. "Good God, Clem! What has gotten into you?"

The coarse voices, punctuated by wild laughter, still flew around her. Gwen watched, horrified, as the dense ranks opened up like the Red Sea parted for Moses, and Roc strode into the circle. "What's going on here?" he snapped, his voice ringing with chilly authority. His eyes swept coldly over her crimson face.

"We're just cheerin' on ol' Clem 'ere. 'E's found 'imself a li'l sweet'eart."

Roc's eyes ravaged her, and his brow darkened in a ferocious scowl. "Get out of here!" he ordered her harshly.

Gwen had no other choice but to leave, and she shamefacedly joined Louise and Morgan, standing only a few feet away from the group.

"As you can see, I didn't get very far with my errand," Gwen explained to Louise with burning cheeks.

Louise regarded her speculatively. "Isn't he the blacksmith's son?"

"Yes, but I only wanted to leave a message for his father," Gwen explained lamely. "Clem's bosky and I couldn't get him to listen to me."

Louise clapped her hands together. "How romantic! Clem's your secret beau!" She had evidently forgotten her prediction that Gwen would marry Roc.

Morgan gave Gwen unexpected help. "No . . . he isn't her beau. We've all known each other since we were in short coats. I suspect Clem was only teasing her."

Thank you, Gwen mouthed silently.

"Oh." With an air of disappointment, Louise turned away, her interest rapidly caught by a display of brass wares.

Still shaken, Gwen could not take her eyes from the scene being enacted between Roc and Clem. The two men eyed each other like angry bulls, murder flaring in their narrowed gazes.

" 'Ere comes th' 'igh an' mighty lord 'imself from th' palace on th' 'ill," Clem taunted, his speech followed by a hiccup.

"You're foxed, Clem Toboggan! Why did you act so freely with Miss Tremayne?" Roc demanded in a deadly soft voice.

Gwen flinched with embarrassment. She ached for both of them and could not stand to see them angry at each other. She knew now why Clem always had such a low opinion of the earl. Jealousy, pure and simple. Clem had always remembered how she used to follow Roc around with stars in her eyes. She sighed. How it must have rankled Clem when Roc had returned to Landregan. And Clem had never dared to speak to her of his love, as he had no more than a blacksmith's cottage to offer her. All these years he'd kept his feelings to himself. And now, with Roc's provocation, the situation was finally coming to a head.

"Miss Gwen is th' sweetest creature alive," Clem slurred. Suddenly he lifted his huge arm and took a swing at Roc. "Defend yerself, lord 'igh and mighty." He almost lost his balance when his swing did not hit the mark.

A deafening cheer went up. " 'Ave at 'im, yer lordship! Don't just stand there, give 'im a blow," the rough voices urged.

The earl straightened defiantly, his angry gaze scanning the crowd. "How about a real mill in the ring, so that you men can wager, fair and square?"

"I 'ave long wanted to plant a shiner on that bleary eye o' yers. 'Tis too dim, and I'd like to polish it up for ye," Clem threatened. "No matter if 'tis in th' ring or without."

Good God! Gwen thought. Clem could blurt out anything in the heat of the moment. Transfixed, she followed the men to the improvised ring, where the betting started with a frenzy. Morgan tried to pull her away, but she brushed off his detaining hand.

Clem discarded his blue wool vest and opened his shirt, just as Roc had done earlier. He flung his new silk neckerchief to the winds and it landed outside the ring to be trampled by rough boots and clogs. A few women had gathered on Clem's side of the ring, cheering him on, and quite a few more on the other side, casting sheep's eyes at Roc's gleaming chest.

The combatants faced each other in the middle of the ring, animosity flowing thick between them. Gwen held her breath. This mess was all because of her. To her surprise, she felt a steadying arm around her shoulders. Morgan remained, lending his support. She buried her face in his waistcoat, tears swimming in her eyes.

When the first punch crunched bone, she flinched and could not stop her tears from flowing. Every time the sound of a fist grinding against flesh reached her ears, she jumped with pain, as if she had been hit.

" 'Ave at 'im, yer lordship! 'Ave at 'im!'' Catcalls and whistles followed. "Flatten 'im!''

"Clem Toboggan, show 'im yer brawn! Part 'is nose from 'is face, will ye.'' Cheers flew in all directions, some more ribald than others.

"Don't worry, Gwennie, Roc has a terrific right cross,'' Morgan said. "He can knock the daylights out of Clem with one swing if he can get to his jaw. That Clem's strong as an ox. I bet you a guinea 'tis going to be a draw.'' Morgan had completely forgotten Gwen's despair as he was caught up in the loud exultation around the ring. "By Jove, this is worth watching!''

Suddenly Gwen found herself standing alone at the edge of the crowd, which had swelled enormously.

"Never saw such a turn-up!'' someone commented behind Gwen. "Those coves 'avin' a wallopin' go at each other is a mighty rare sight. That lordship got an upper cut that could shatter th' jaw o' a giant.''

"An' all for a wench. Ohhh, did ye see that! 'E got 'im in th' bone box. 'E'll be spitting teeth now.''

The air was instantly filled with a thunderous uproar. " 'Ave at 'im! D'ye 'ear!''

Gwen closed her eyes and pressed her palms to her ears to shut out the sound. All in vain.

"Th' best mill I've seen so far this year,'' a toothless hag piped. "Give 'im a go! Punch 'im one, yer lordship!'' she screeched. "A jab and a right cross, that's right!''

"Devil the lot, 'e drew 'is cork! Did ye see that?'' someone bellowed into Gwen's ear. Bewildered, she stood on tiptoe to see who had suffered the nosebleed. Roc's face was unrecognizable, his nose swollen and covered with blood.

" 'E's goin' to 'ave not one but *two* shiners tomorrow. Blister me, 'e went down! Lawks!''

Gwen frantically elbowed her way closer to the ring, craning her neck to see what was happening. "Who?" she demanded. "Who went down?"

"Th' dark 'un, 'e got 'imself punched with a deadly cross cut."

Gwen glared at the man next to her in a nankeen coat and a cocked hat. "They're both dark, you clod!" she snarled, tears of frustration and anger streaming down her cheeks.

"Don't cry, pretty wench, they ain't worth it." He peered at her. "Why are ye cryin', anyway? Ye should be cheerin' 'em on." His voice rose. "Thunder and turf, I betted on th' wrong 'un!"

The crowd clamored deafeningly. " 'E's down, the cove's down!"

A temporary shift in the throng made space for Gwen. She reached the ring and watched in horror as Clem struggled to get up. His eyes were swollen shut, and he grunted with pain as he wove across the grass, clasping his head. The hatred had disappeared from the two men's faces, replaced by pain and exhaustion. Gwen heard Roc throw Clem a question over the din, and the latter shook his head.

"One more round! One more round!" the audience urged.

With her stomach in a tight coil of fear, Gwen watched them start over, raw fists up, muscles bunched on shiny torsos and arms, shirts torn to shreds.

Clem jabbed his meaty fist under Roc's defense, giving him a crashing uppercut, and Roc fell like a tree in a storm.

"No!" Gwen screamed. She tried to rush forward, but the crowd was too dense. Arms flailed, hats flew in the air, and flowers rained over Clem's head.

To her surprise she saw Roc struggle up, sluggish with weariness. His face swollen beyond recognition, he threw himself at Clem for a last flurry of blows. Gwen bit her knuckles until she tasted blood, whimpering every time a jab hit home. Then, in a split second, Roc's right arm shot straight out with enormous force, colliding with Clem's jaw. Clem fell without so much as a sound and lay perfectly still on the ground. The fight was over, at last.

"Oh, no! He has killed him." Gwen moaned, pushing forward to get to Clem's inert body.

"Naw, 'e bain't dead. Takes more to fell that ox," a rough neighbor commented.

Somebody emptied a bucket of water over Clem's head, and he sputtered. He sat up with difficulty, swearing and wearily clutching his jaw.

The whoops of the crowd grew to impossible heights as Roc was lifted onto the shoulders of two burly spectators to receive the ovations. He smiled, white teeth flashing between swollen lips, and waved, his torn shirt hanging in tatters about him.

Men! Gwen thought in disgust. She managed to reach Clem's side. A flash of recognition lit his eyes before he turned away in embarrassment. Gwen heard him slur, "I'm sorry, Miss Gwen, I truly am, but I didn't let slip a word, did I?"

She fumbled for something to say. "How could you do this to yourself?" she scolded. "Look at you, your face is cut to strips." Pulling off the new silk handkerchief from her wrist, she dipped it in a bucket of water and dabbed at his wounds.

"Ouch, it 'urts, miss." Clem pushed her away and grabbed the pail. As she watched in awe, he upended the second bucket over his head and drenched himself. "Ah, much better," he growled and shook his head, whipping water drops in every direction. Then he peered at her through his swollen eyes. "Go away, Miss Gwen. Ye shouldn't be 'ere. Bad for yer reputation."

She hesitated, glancing at the milling crowd. The men had set Roc down. What would he do now? She flinched as he fixed her with hard, predatory eyes and steered his steps inexorably toward her. Gwen's only urge was to flee from the scene, but she was hemmed in on all sides by the cheering mob.

In a flash Roc stood over her, his hot, virile presence enveloping her. She stared transfixed into his swollen face, shrinking at the cold glitter in his eyes. She had no time to protest as he placed his strong hands around her waist, lifted her in the air, and carried her triumphantly around the ring. She had never felt more mortified. The din rose to a crescendo.

"Let me down!" she shouted, pummeling his broad chest with her fists.

"Never," he declared, tipping her unceremoniously over his shoulder. Holding on to her legs, he stepped out of the ring, the audience parting miraculously. Gwen saw cheerful faces peer up at her, catcalls echoed in her ears, and she burned with embarrassment and utter defeat.

"You . . . *hateful* . . . scoundrel!" she shouted in his ear, tears of anger clouding her eyes. "Set me down this instant!"

A derisive chuckle answered her. Accompanied by the intolerable hoots of the crowd, he deposited her on Tristan's saddle. Before she had a chance to slide off, he jumped up behind her. His thighs pressing hard into hers, he took the reins and pulled onto the road at a spanking clip.

"Where are we going?" Gwen snapped furiously.

"I'm going to show you once and for all that you're mine, not Clem's or anybody else's," came the arrogant answer. "I'm tired of this capricious game of yours."

Chapter 26

"I'm going to compromise you beyond repair so that you'll have to marry me," Roc said, his face contorted with fury and swelling contusions.

"You just did," Gwen replied in her driest tone of voice.

He laughed. "Yes, by God! At least a hundred people saw me carry you off, and no one doubts what's on my mind, you can be sure of that."

Calming down, Gwen began to see the desperation behind his action. "You don't need to prove anything to anybody. We know where we stand in amorous matters," she said, her voice softening.

"Yes, but I won't watch while the woman I love is being mauled by some drunken ape of a man," he blurted out.

"Clem did not maul me. He's one of my oldest friends and has never done anything to hurt me. He was merry with drink, that's all. You saw that he kissed me only once, and only a brotherly peck."

"A brotherly peck? Humbug! He's mad for you, don't you see? He's burning to toss you into the hay and lift up those skirts of yours and explore what's underneath."

Gwen laughed at his outburst. "The pot calling the kettle black?" she chided. "Really, Roc." But deep inside she knew he was right. How could she have been so blind? she asked herself again. Her cheeks blossomed red as she felt his scorching glance rake over her.

"Was it really necessary to rearrange his face?" she dared ask.

"Of course! Only a fool would let him get away with

touching you." Grudgingly he added, "But I had a devilish time showing him his lesson. He's a bruiser with his fists."

"And you're a big silly infant," Gwen countered. "I can see no pleasure in fisticuffs."

"Fisticuffs? Boxing is pure science, m'dear, and great sport." He smiled through cracked lips.

"Barbaric, that's the word for it. You're no better than the fighting cockerels." Anger made her want to heap as many insults on his head as possible, but no others came to mind. She stared ahead. Tristan had passed through the village and was climbing up the cliff path. She realized Roc was taking her to Fisherman's Creek, the favorite haunt of his childhood. When Tristan could go no further, Roc alighted and pulled the horse to a tree where he fastened the reins loosely around a branch.

Too tired to argue, Gwen only watched him. He lifted her down and, holding her close to his chest, pinned her with a glittering glare. "Are you going to try to escape if I set you free?"

She could not hold back a smile. "You're ridiculous," she taunted. "Where would I go? You'd be at my heels before I could take the first step."

He did not deign to answer as he carried her down the narrow path to the secluded strip of white beach by the creek. He set her down under the trailing fronds of the weeping willow. "Don't move!" Scowling down at her, he began to peel off the shreds of his shirt, revealing his golden-brown chest to her eyes. A spiral of butterflies tickled her insides at the tempting sight. His gaze still riveted to her face, he untied the opening of his breeches and let them slide down to his ankles. Gwen stared motionless before him. Soon he stood naked, gorgeous, vital, and wholly irresistible.

Expecting he would invite her into his embrace, she was surprised when he turned and rushed into the water. "Eeaaahh!" he bellowed as the cold water enfolded him. Laughing wildly, he swam and cavorted in the still water of the creek.

"Won't you join me, or are you too lily-livered?" he challenged.

"You've gone completely mad," she replied, her arms akimbo as she watched him from the water's edge.

"No, just trying to glue myself back into one piece. It has been a most upsetting day, and my wounds sting like the devil." He disappeared momentarily under the water and emerged, his hair plastered to his head. He snorted and gulped for air.

"Come, you fainthearted wench!"

"I'm not going to discard my garments in broad daylight and have it said in the village that I was swimming in the creek with a naked man."

"There is no one else here, and you know it. The only way down is by the path we just used, and we didn't meet anyone, did we?" He sprayed some water toward her, but the shining drops fell short.

"I can easily escape you now," she taunted, her tension slowly seeping away as he became more like his usual good-natured self.

It amazed her how fast he moved through the hampering water. He stood dripping before her, his fingers digging into her shoulders. "You should not tease me when I'm angry or aroused," he warned, "and now I'm both."

She paled. He pulled her harshly to him, crushing his mouth down on hers. Her nose was flattened against his cheek so that she could barely breathe. He tasted of salt and cool water, and his hot, demanding tongue forced her teeth apart to ravish the velvet insides of her mouth. He pressed her breasts against his slick chest, one hand ripping loose the knot of her laced bodice, and tearing the string from the tabs on the robings. As the bodice fell open, he enclosed one heavy breast in his cool, strong hand. Her heart beat wildly against him as his fingers coaxed her rosy crest to a pebble.

"You've longed for this," he said. "As much as I have."

She meant to protest against his high-handed ways, but her lips were instantly covered in a bruising kiss.

"I know you're dying for this because I am." He easily lifted her from the ground by squeezing her buttocks upward. Then his hands slid slowly to her waist. Her toes barely touched the ground.

"Roc?" she said breathlessly, her mind empty of protest. The only thing she noticed was his hands on her body, his brilliant eyes dappled with gold from the sun. "Your wounds must be painful."

"Damn my bruises," he whispered. Without ado he laid her on the soft sand under the willow, the lacy fronds creating a curtain between them and the rest of the world. His fingers impatiently unlaced her skirts from the bodice, tearing them over her slim hips and long legs. He kissed her neck and the hollow of her throat. For a moment he lifted his face to gaze at her curves as one by one they were revealed to him.

"You have no right," she protested, her voice husky with emotion.

"If seducing you is the only thing that will bring you to the altar, then that's what I'm going to do." His golden gaze blazed into her with smoldering desire. "Like this." His tongue swooped into her mouth, taming her, arousing her to such a point of need that she moaned and arched against him. She could not stop her hands from traveling along the hard contours of his face, his neck, his shoulders. She buried her hands in his long hair and brought his lips down to hers once more. She could not get enough of him. His flesh was hard under soft skin, and she was caught up in the exploration of his form. It was a special pleasure to slide her hands over his taut buttocks and hairy thighs. Just as he hungrily reacquainted himself with her shape, she wanted to touch every square inch of him. And she did, even the hard shaft seeking entrance to her body.

His fingers delved in proprietary fashion between her legs, plundering her sweet secrets, crushing the last of her resistance. The wind caressed her heated body as sensually as Roc's smooth fingertips. Goosebumps of pleasure rose on her skin as they wandered slowly along the soft insides of her thighs. She moaned against his mouth, and he chuckled, victorious at last.

"You like it, don't you?" he breathed. "And 'twill get better yet. You haven't forgotten how good it can be, you and me together." He nuzzled her earlobe. "Fireworks go off, inside and out."

Gwen chuckled happily. "You don't have to convince me." Her eyes flew wide as his thumb rotated over the most sensitive nub between her thighs, and she expelled her breath slowly in delight. A molten feeling flowed from her abdomen down her legs, all the way to her toes which curled with pleasure, an ecstasy she could barely contain. His skin was velvet under her hands, and his movements were as natural and enthralling as the light wind playing in the foliage above them. He was the sun and she was the flower, slowly opening to his life-giving warmth.

As she moaned against his lips, he smiled, bright, triumphant. "I know what you like, don't I?" His eyes clouded over with sweet torment as her fingers played along his hard arousal. "And you know how to pleasure me beyond reason. Why would we deny ourselves a future of shared bliss?"

His words slowly seeped into her mind, and she knew he was right. Beyond caring that she had lost the battle of wills, she promised to listen to her heart. At the moment it was singing in her chest, and almost stopped every time he teased the soft folds of her femininity.

"We belong to each other," he muttered hoarsely. "Why did you force me to steal this moment : . . like a common thief?" But he expected no answer from her passion-swollen lips.

Lovingly he gazed down at her flushed face, so full of desire, and so lovely, her eyes closed in concentration. "And I would do it again and again." He found her moist opening, his haven. To enter her was to be enfolded in unbearable sweetness. To move within her, to feel her response, her breath quickening, her lips curving in a seductive smile, her cheeks reddening, was sheer bliss. He felt himself swell even more with rapture. His hands buried in her hair, his elbows on either side of her head, he moved over her.

Rolling in the sand, pulling her on top, he grasped her derriere and pounded relentlessly into her until she threw back her head and shuddered in his arms, a deep moan of satisfaction pouring from her lips. He turned rigid as the vast wave of dizzying release rushed through him, and he emptied the fruit of his ecstasy within her.

"Ah . . . tell me that you love me." He groaned as he held her close in the soothing aftermath. He planted a trail of butterfly kisses along the hard ridge of her collarbone. "Tell me! Because I need to hear you say it." He nibbled her earlobes and bit her chin.

"I love you—always have," Gwen admitted shyly. "And always will."

His laughing topaz eyes captured her embarrassed hazel

ones. "I have won," he said with great contentment. "We will hold a ball to announce our nuptials—next Saturday." He twined his fingers through her tangled hair. "We will not waste any more time." His narrowed gaze bored into her, forcing her to respond. "Well?"

"Your proposal is most forceful. How can I refuse you? But you must give me more time, and don't ask me why. I just need time to think." She held her breath, worrying that he would not be content with her reply.

He became very still for a few moments. "I don't believe that is your wish."

"Please, let's not rush into marriage."

He tossed his head impatiently. "I don't know what's wrong with you, Gwen. You say you love me—"

She placed her fingertips against his lips. "Shhh, I've told you I love you. Just humor me this once."

He gave her a dark, suspicious glance. "I warn you, I'll never give up. At least promise me an engagement party next Saturday. After today, your reputation will be in shreds, so you must become my wife."

"Very well. I agree to a betrothal party." She hesitated. "There are a score of issues we don't see eye to eye on, and I still say you're acting high-handedly. Today was ample proof of that."

He laughed at her sudden black look. "High-handed, but irresistible."

"Not with those purpling shiners, you braggart. You need to cover them with a slab of veal soon, or you'll be blind for the next few days. And how would it look at our betrothal party—me leading you everywhere and you stumbling over every obstacle?"

"That would be one way to keep you at my side," he said with a growl.

Chapter 27

The Tremayne household was in an uproar when Roc delivered Gwen at the front door, her hair down, her dress rumpled and covered with salt rings caused by the brackish creek water.

Aunt Clo whisked her indoors, and even the squire appeared angry. He insisted on seeing the earl in his study at once, and glanced in dismay at the younger man's torn shirt and bruised face.

Aunt Clo dragged Gwen upstairs. "You're behaving like a wayward child, Gwennie," Aunt Clo complained with icy disapproval.

Gwen sighed, too tired to respond to her aunt's anger. "I know, but Roc literally abducted me." She patted the older woman's shoulder. "This piece of news will calm you; I've promised to marry him."

"Has he been pressing you, er, bodily . . . to consent? If he has, I will give him a piece of my mind!"

"I thought you'd welcome the good news," Gwen said.

"He has his high-handed ways. If he's forced—"

"He never forced me into anything." She smiled, squeezing her aunt's arm. "You know that's impossible. Why are we in your bedroom, Auntie?"

"Oh, Gwen! You're incorrigible." Aunt Clo propelled Gwen toward the middle of the floor where a hip bath was filled with hot water. "I was preparing to take a bath, but you seem more in need of one." She clucked at Gwen's bedraggled appearance and frowned at her obviously happy face. Then she left to fetch a towel.

Gwen sang as she stepped into the bath, her contentment

overflowing. What a glorious afternoon it had been in Roc's arms!

Aunt Clo snorted with disgust when she returned. "The earl just left and, according to Lionel, he has renewed his offer and added a very handsome settlement on your father."

"Well, I told you Roc would do the honorable thing. He's a gentleman. Besides, 'twasn't the first time he asked for my hand." Gwen soaped her arms and neck.

Aunt Clo clucked her disapproval. "If you'd said yes then, yours wouldn't have been the name on everyone's lips today. The whole village is abuzz about the boxing match and what happened afterward. How could you, Gwen! I have never been more embarrassed in my life. *My* niece the object of a brawl. And Clem Toboggan. *He* never had any sense. Mark my words, he'll have to leave the village now."

"Nonsense! He can weather a bit of gossip." Gwen paused. "Fancy, I never knew he had a romantic interest in me, and I've known him all my life."

"He's an idiot, just as I said!" Aunt Clo exclaimed.

"Don't say that of Clem. He's got more sense in that hairy top of his than the whole village put together."

"There will be no end to the brawls before this day is forgotten. He will be teased mercilessly." Aunt Clo pursed her lips with worry. "And as soon as you show your face abroad, you will be met with snickers and whispers. The wags must have talked themselves hoarse this afternoon."

"The more the better, then they won't question me, although I'm sure they're dying to hear every sordid detail of the abduction."

"What humiliation! How can *I* go outside after this?" Aunt Clo wailed. "I can already hear the tattle behind my back."

"When I marry Roc, there will be enough funds to send you back home to Devon, and then you can forget all about this unfortunate day."

Her aunt looked aghast. "You haven't even inquired if I wish to return to Devon. Do you want to get rid of me now that I'm of no use?" Her lower lip quivered with hurt and indignation.

Gwen turned innocent eyes on her, a smile twitching her lips. "But you always go on about it—what a nasty, awkward place Landregan in Cornwall is, and so on." That was before you laid eyes on Officer Biggles, Gwen thought, almost laughing, but she schooled her features into a stern mask.

"I suppose it isn't *that* bad," came Aunt Clo's reluctant response. "*Some* people have treated me with due consideration."

"Splendid! Then I hope I'll hear no more about it, Auntie. You may stay here as long as you wish. Besides, someone must look after Father once I move to the Hall."

"Well, if that's what you want, I can't refuse. Yet the earl might turn out to be a skinflint, and then we'll be in the basket here at Tremayne House." Aunt Clo wiped away an imaginary tear.

Gwen's lips curved into a smile. "Don't make me feel sorry for you. The farm will tide you over quite well, and Roc has promised to have the house repaired from top to bottom. You may rest assured I will hold him to it."

"God bless you for your astute business sense, Gwen. I'm sure you won't forget us when you're installed at the Hall."

That is if I ever am. What if Roc finds out the truth? Gwen wondered.

She dried herself and after winding a frayed wrap around herself, she went to her own bedchamber. She brushed her hair and braided it. Curling up in bed, she noticed a letter on the nightstand. Frowning, she viewed the impersonal envelope and broke the red seal. Her fingers trembled as she glanced at the signature: Major William Eppsworth, Vincent's former commanding officer.

Gwen studied the tight scrawl and began reading. Her eyes flew down the page, her breath coming in short gasps. She had been right to suspect Vincent's motive for returning to Landregan. He had never been wounded in battle. He'd been discharged for suspicion of grand theft! Major Eppsworth ended the letter by saying he wished to hear no further from Mr. Tremayne!

Gwen expelled her breath, relieved she had found something else to add to Vincent's list of sins. Suspicion of theft. She could present the letter to her father, but she had no idea what his reaction would be. This letter provided no proof that Vincent really was guilty of theft. Her father was a man who heartily disliked disruptions, especially unpleasant ones. He would be furious if he found out she had investigated Vincent's past. She sighed bitterly, feeling the full load of her secrets weighing her down. Father had never been supportive. She alone must solve the problem of what to do next.

Perhaps Roc would help her. Could she ask him directly if he was involved in the Jacobite Cause? Fear crawled along her spine at the thought of what his answer might be. She would have to plan her next step carefully.

She folded the letter and placed it in the middle of the Bible, certainly not a book Vincent would care to borrow if he got an urge to read when he returned.

When Roc strode up the shallow front steps of the Hall, he was astonished to see a pile of trunks and portmanteaux stacked in the hallway. He passed the open door of the morning room, wanting to refresh himself and treat his wounds before he presented himself to the household. He could barely see between his swollen eyelids, and his knuckles were stiff and sore, as were his ribs. He could take a scold from the squire, who had been easy enough to placate with the promise of instantly marrying Gwen, but the dowager countess would be another matter. He could already hear her going on and on, her face full of shocked outrage.

He had barely passed the door to the Green Salon when his name was spoken in the dowager's stentorian tones. "Roc, get in here!"

He sighed and swore under his breath. "Since you can't wait to rebuke me until I have made myself presentable, I warn you of my appearance," he called in icy tones.

As soon as he entered the salon, Louise squealed in horror and the dowager put up her hands as if to ward him off. "Good God! 'Tis worse than I imagined. Whatever induced you to behave in such a wild and uncouth manner?" she demanded, a frown of disgust on her pudgy face. "I'm speaking of the knockdown fight with a lowly individual in public, and then abducting poor Miss Tremayne." She tapped her fan on the armrest of her chair. "I'll never forgive you for dragging our name through the mud like this." She began to sob noisily, and Louise looked at her in surprise, as she had never seen the dowager display any feelings but anger and dislike.

Roc handed his mother a none-too-clean handkerchief.

"Here. You do understand that I'll wed Miss Tremayne, and I'll not accept another word of censure from you or anyone else. I've had enough of your criticisms of Miss Tremayne. Whether you like it or not, she'll become the next countess of Landregan."

The dowager shrieked in outrage. "She's shockingly *below* you, a nobody!"

"Don't be such a snob, Mother. I happen to love her, whether she's of humble birth or not. At least she's no light-skirt."

"How dare you utter such a soiled word in our company!" the dowager wailed, her face paling in horror.

"Throwing a temper tantrum will not help, Mother. You well know it," Roc said frostily. "And now, tell me what all those trunks are doing in the hallway."

"They are ours, Roc," said Louise, "When the gossip reached the Hall, Mama insisted on our instant departure. We had just finished packing when she was struck with a fever. The doctor says 'tis the influenza and that she needs to rest in a dark room for a week until her fever is quite gone." She rose. "In fact, I should go to her now. She'll need my care. I'll have the trunks removed from the hallway since it seems we'll be imposing on you for another week at least."

"Splendid! Then you'll be here for the engagement ball." A smile lurked at the corners of his mouth. "Perchance we could make a double announcement?"

Louise looked wistful. "I wish, but that would surely be the end of Mama. *You* were the one she wished to have as a son-in-law."

The earl chuckled. "She did not count on fate. She will have learned her lesson this summer, the poor woman."

Louise peered at Roc's face with something like a shudder. "You look like a . . . buccaneer or a ruffian. Ghastly."

The dowager sniffed and wiped her red-rimmed eyes. "The foreign lands changed him so. The savages made him into a-a gypsy, running about in a ripped shirt and without shoes. Your father would turn over in his grave if he knew." She pinned him with a grim glare.

Roc laughed. "Don't exaggerate. I'm wearing boots."

"But you did leave them off on the pilchard festivities. I could see no difference then between you and the village men." She had the air of a large, ruffled parrot. "You're an *earl* after all and should act like one. Think of your heritage, your duty."

"Madam Mother, if you have finished your lecture, would you please excuse me? I need to clean up."

"You look like a backstreet bully, and . . . and the impossible Miss Tremayne will take my place." A new torrent of wails rent the air, and tears flowed down her cheeks, perhaps in a last effort to persuade Roc to drop the idea of marrying Gwen.

But no sorrow, false or true, could budge him from his intention, and he strode lightly to the door. "I will send in Enedoc with a stack of clean handkerchiefs," was his parting remark.

"Odious man! I'll return to Tunbridge Wells this very day," she threw after him.

He stuck his wounded visage around the door. "You will do no such thing! You're to be the gracious hostess at the ball. Now dry your tears and begin to write out invitations. I want all of our old friends to attend. And don't forget to send one to the Tremaynes."

A fresh wail followed him up the stairs, which he took two at a time. He sighed with relief; at least their talk was over, and now only happiness awaited him in the future. The only thing standing in the way was that tedious Dandelion fellow. He would have to think hard on that situation before he took the next step.

Gwen lay in bed, wide awake although the night had already grown old. Her eyes ached from lack of sleep, and in her thoughts she relived the previous day's events. Roc had done something so impudent it put even Dandelion to shame. How could she show herself in the village without blushing? she wondered, and tossed restlessly in the bed. Not that she regretted a single moment of her glorious tryst with Roc. Without him life would be worthless.

Then there was Clem. What should she do about him? Again she marveled at her stupidity in not noticing that his devotion went deeper than friendship. But then, he had always behaved like a friend.

For the first time she considered him as a man. He was

handsome and virile, some young village girl's dream of a husband, but to her, he was the younger brother she had never had. She had never noticed that the sniveling boy who doggedly followed her around—while she followed Roc—had grown into a handsome man, as devoted as ever. What she felt for Roc, could she feel that for any man? Could perhaps Clem's lips bewitch her as Roc's did? No, it wasn't possible. She felt nothing but friendship for Clem.

She tossed and turned, her conscience sore and her nerves on edge. When she finally decided to nip down the stairs to find something to eat, a rain of gravel hit her window. Startled, she tiptoed across the floor as another fistful smattered on the glass.

"Shhh," she whispered as the sound cut too sharply into the stillness of the night. She pulled the curtains aside and peered outside. In the silvery moonlight she recognized Clem's large outline.

"Miss Gwen? May I 'ave a word with ye?"

"Shhh, I'll be down in a moment."

He's come to apologize, she thought as she hastily pulled on a serviceable dress and folded a wool shawl across her shoulders. She brushed her hair and bound it away from her face with a ribbon. The only light to lead her was the weak gleam of the moon, but she easily found her way in the dark as she had done so many times before.

"Is something wrong?" were her first words when she stood in front of him. She dragged him behind a thick oak, away from prying eyes. Clem wrung his cap between his hands.

"Naw, I just needed to speak with ye. Can we take a walk in th' spinney?"

Gwen had never seen him look so serious. She studied him closely. "You look awful, Clem! Has anyone tended to your wounds?" She gingerly touched a contusion on his cheekbone, and he winced, pushing her hand away.

"Don't touch!" he snapped, unusually bad-tempered.

As they walked along the path through the spinney, she glanced furtively at him. In the pale wash of moonlight, she saw his eyes glitter dangerously, emotions boiling close to the surface. "What is it you want to tell me?"

They had reached their old meeting place, the small glade

in the spinney. He motioned to the stone where he always sat waiting for her. "Like ol' times, but they will niver return," he said gruffly. "This will be th' last time I see this place."

"Why?" Gwen asked breathlessly, not sure she wanted to hear his answer.

"I'm goin' away."

"Oh. Has it to do with what happened yesterday?" A twinge of sorrow jolted through her.

"Yes. I'm sorry I lost me 'ead; ye see, I 'ad a wee bit too much ale in me belly." He shifted, visibly uncomfortable. " 'Is lordship is 'andy with 'is fists, that's for sure."

"He behaved in an unpardonable manner, so you don't have to excuse yourself."

Clem began to trample back and forth. "Are ye goin' to do th' decent thin' and marry 'im now? Th' whole village saw 'im takin' ye away on 'is horse."

"Yes, I'm going to marry him. However, 'twill be difficult because I don't know how to give up the smuggling without failing the villagers. They count on my help." She placed a hand on his arm. "And if you leave, there will be no one to take over."

"Aw, Miss Gwen," he said with a groan. " 'Ow can I stay after what 'appened yesterday? I'm th' laughin'stock o' th' whole village."

"Laugh back! You almost knocked down the earl of Landregan in a fair mill. You ought to be proud of yourself. He has trained at a boxing salon in the capital, and you almost sent him into a dead faint."

Clem chortled. "I did draw 'is cork, didn't I, and 'e'll be sportin' as black a shiner as I do."

"Two, in fact! He looks ghastly, probably worse than you do. And you know, I believe people are laughing more at me than at you, because *I* was the cause of the mill. But am I planning to leave? No, I'll have to live it down," she said, adding in a lower voice, "although 'twill be hard."

He snorted. "No one'll dare laugh at th' future countess of Landregan."

"Perhaps not, but I'll always be the same, you know that. I'm sorry things have changed between us, but we can still be friends, I hope."

He sighed heavily. " 'Ow can it go on like afore? I can't

take back what I did.'' A current of despair surged from him. ''And me feelin's, ahem, for ye, 'ave not changed.'' He placed his meaty hand on her forearm, and Gwen could not pull it away. ''Ye're in love with th' enemy,'' he stated, sadness edging his voice. ''May I kiss ye just once, Miss Gwen? I'd always remember it, and th' earl don't 'ave to know that I stole a kiss from ye.''

She smiled in the darkness. ''Yes, I suppose that would be a perfect way to seal eternal friendship, like when we cut our fingertips and mingled our blood when we were children. Remember?''

''O' course,'' he said. ''A kiss'll be th' grown-up way.''

Gwen lifted her face toward his, and he shyly placed his massive arms around her shoulders and pressed her close. Timidly his lips touched hers. He tasted entirely different from Roc, and at that moment Gwen knew she could not feel the same rapturous intensity with anyone except her beloved.

Clem belonged to her past, while Roc was her future. As sweet as Clem's lips were, they evoked no desire within her, only sisterly affection. He lingered, moving slowly over her face, as if memorizing the special moment. Gwen consented, also tucking away the memory, the milestone of a lifelong friendship. Life would never be the same again.

Silence fell for a long time while they each alone came to terms with the inevitable change. Clem, his voice low with emotion, blurted out, ''What about Dandelion and th' next load?''

''I have thought about it. How shall we bring in the load? Roc knows about the *Seahawk*. And, although he might not know for sure that I'm Dandelion, I believe he harbors a strong suspicion.'' She related how Officer Biggles had flung out the words about the yellow-headed weeds on the lawn of Tremayne House; how Roc had looked as if a boulder had fallen on his head, and how calculatingly he had gazed at the new roof.

Clem growled that they would have to be especially careful. Gwen told him of her decision. '' 'Twill be the last time I'm Dandelion. You'll have to inform the others, and whoever feels compelled to assume the leadership should take another name than Dandelion.'' She had hoped Clem would accept the opportunity, but he was stubbornly quiet.

"You're set on leaving Landregan?" she whispered.

"Aye, ye know there ain't much work for me 'ere. And if th' free tradin' stops, I'll 'ave no choice."

He was right. His livelihood came mostly from the smuggling, and the help he lent the farmers in the neighborhood. He had never had a longing to become a blacksmith or a fisherman. He had always had a taste for adventure, and Gwen was not in the least surprised to hear his next words.

"I'm aimin' to go to th' Colonies. 'Tis a rich and plentiful place." But his voice lacked conviction. Like her, he loved Landregan more than any other place on earth. Nevertheless, unhappy though he was, he would not hesitate to leave.

"You'll know what to do when the time comes," Gwen told him. "There's no hurry. Now, speaking of the next load. We'll have to ask the Frenchies either to dump the kegs on a rope or bring them into one of the usual coves. But coves will be crawling with soldiers, and they'll be out for blood this time. That leaves us with only one choice, to dump it."

In the silver haze of the moon she saw Clem nod. A nightjar flapped up on frightened wings as Clem's clog snapped a twig. "Th' earl's a damned nuisance." He shook his fist, and Gwen smiled in the darkness.

"Yes, he's the most stubborn man I've ever met, but we'll tweak his nose for the last time. If Dandelion disappears from the scene, he'll have to give up and take down the gallows."

"Aye, let 'im lose 'is sleep wonderin' who th' fellow was," Clem said with a chuckle.

Gwen had arrived, tense at times, and that was no wonder. With
excitement. This would be a great occasion until Ariel now that
Gwen was to battle every kind of influence... in hand. As she
panned incessantly..., she figured only to remember their fa...

Chapter 28

Gwen believed it was no coincidence that the engagement
ball would take place on the night before the actual dark of
the moon. She smiled at the memory of the last load they
had brought in, the keg in the *Seahawk* and the bouquet of
dandelions. Roc obviously suspected the smugglers would
repeat the pattern, and he had made sure to keep everyone
under his eye for the entire evening. Or was he trying to set
up a trap? She fervently wished she could read his mind.

The *Alouette* had orders to dump the kegs into the bay on
the following night and leave without any of the law enforcers
being the wiser. The "gentlemen" would go out in rowboats
and punts to collect them, a couple at a time during the next
twenty-four hours—the time limit the kegs could withstand
the salt water. The effort needed to gather them together and
transport them out of Landregan would be tiresome, but any
amount of hard work would be preferable to getting caught.

Gwen regarded her image in the mirror as she put the fin-
ishing touches to her toilette. Roc had sent her a new gown
that he wished her to wear, enclosing a note that said he
looked forward to seeing her dressed for her new position as
the future countess of Landregan. The wide skirts billowed
around her, a gossamer cloud of deep sea-green silk, the low-
cut bodice and robings parted over a matching hooped underdress that changed hues like the sea every time she moved.
The tight bodice was edged with exquisite cream lace, which
also adorned the elbow-length sleeves. She could not remember a time when she had looked more elegant. Perhaps never,
and Aunt Clo agreed with her.

Roc had not forgotten the middle-aged aunt. A mauve satin

gown had arrived for her to wear, and she was crowing with excitement. This would be an exceptional ball! And how lucky Gwen was to have caught such an influential husband. As she prattled incessantly, Aunt Clo refused to remember that Roc had literally abducted her niece.

The only dark cloud on Gwen's perfect sky was Dandelion. But "he" would be buried the day after tomorrow when she handed over her responsibilities to the new leader. Roc would never know she'd been the elusive "gentleman." She had a strong inkling as to what his reaction would be if he found proof that she'd made a fool of him all this time. Please, God, let him never find out.

Pinning up a stray curl and stepping into her slippers, dyed to match the gown, Gwen was ready. She looked out the window, but darkness lay dense around the house. She could only see her own reflection distorted in the uneven glass. It was a perfect night for free trading. She hoped the next night would be as good. Her nerves fluttered, not at the thought of the smuggling, but at the prospect of facing the guests, the crème de la crème of Cornwall society.

Roc had ruined her, and no doubt she would have to live with the reputation of being *fast*. But she believed the members of Cornwall aristocracy were not quite such high sticklers for convention as their peers in the capital, who probably would have snubbed the invitation to the ball.

"You look stunning, dear Gwennie," said the squire as Gwen stepped down the stairs. He sported a new peacock-blue coat with gold embroidery, a boldly patterned pink and blue waistcoat, and shiny new shoes with silver buckles.

"Where did you find the money to spend on a new costume, Father?"

The squire beamed. "The earl has settled a very large sum on me for life. I will live my last days in luxury, and all thanks to you, clever Gwen, who had the wits to snare such a splendid husband."

'Tis all settled then, Gwen thought. No turning back now. By providing for the squire, Roc had made sure she could not change her mind.

Squire Tremayne assisted her into the carriage. "I've heard they are all coming, the Rashleighs, the Godolphins, the Penroses, and the Carews,'' the squire surprised everyone by saying.

''Papa, you've forgotten your books. How else could you have had time to find out about the guests?'' Gwen teased.

''Ahem, 'tis that demmed tattlebox Arthur who informed me. 'Tis of no interest to me.''

'' 'Tis a very important day, Lionel, and well you know it,'' Aunt Clo admonished, flashing the squire a disapproving frown. She turned to Gwen. ''I'm relieved that you came to your senses at last. I don't know how many times I've wanted to tell you that.''

''You have made it quite clear, Aunt Clo.'' Gwen stared out the window of the Landregan carriage as it bore them inexorably toward the Hall. She felt an inexplicable apprehension, her fingers toying restlessly with her fan of pale green silk painted with exotic flowers—another gift from Roc. He had explained that it came from Thailand, a country he had visited on his travels.

Looking handsome in a burgundy velvet coat, his wounds from the fight healing, Roc welcomed them on the front steps. He gripped Gwen's hand and pressed his lips to her trembling fingertips. As everyone's eyes were directed at them, an urge to snatch her hand from his grip overcame her. With a smooth smile, a teasing glitter lurking in his eyes, Roc greeted his future father-in-law and Aunt Clo.

''Most of the guests will be arriving at any minute now, and we should be ready to receive them, side by side,'' he murmured to Gwen. She nodded. Might as well get the ordeal over with, she thought.

Squire Tremayne, with Aunt Clo on his arm, entered the brightly lit ballroom. Gwen watched their awed faces. Through the open doors she saw hundreds of candles glowing in the chandeliers. Armloads of cut flowers in all the colors of the rainbow overflowed every urn and vase, filling the room with the sweet scent of summer. They must have been grown in the hothouse. The parquet floor had been polished until it had the sheen of still water, and the brass sconces dividing the cream damask wall panels shone like newly minted gold. The pale blue velvet draperies were tied back with twined gold cords.

The dowager countess greeted Squire Tremayne sourly at

the white and gilt double doors. She was wearing a dark violet gown and a powdered wig with corkscrew curls spilling over her fat shoulders. A garish ruby and gold necklace choked her flabby neck.

Gwen watched her raise her nose at the countrified couple before her. *How* will I ever live with that woman? she wondered.

"Approving of the arrangements?" came Roc's deep voice against her ear. His breath sent a thrill of desire along her spine.

"Yes, 'tis lovely. I was just watching the dowager countess," Gwen added truthfully. She knew she did not have to hide her dislike of the dowager from Roc.

He chuckled. "I've given her stern instructions to behave herself this evening. When we're married, she'll return to Tunbridge Wells where she can bully her old cronies to her heart's content. Come, I want to show you something before more guests arrive."

He pulled her outside to the terrace. Halting behind the pillar where he'd once kissed her, he dragged her to him. "Sweet Gwen, tonight I'm the happiest man alive," he said and gazed deeply into her eyes. Then he imprisoned her lips with his, savoring her slowly until that familiar melting sensation filled her limbs. No one had that power over her senses, no one except Roc. He made her weak, made her reason flee, made her world fade until the only thing she knew was the hot pressure of his lips and the enthralling caress of his bold tongue.

With a growl deep in his chest he finally let her go. "My precious jewel," he breathed. "I never expected to meet someone so enticing, here in Landregan of all places."

"Before now you were quite the confirmed bachelor?" she quizzed, her voice husky with emotion.

His hands traveled along her spine, cupped her buttocks, and pressed her hard against himself. "I knew other women, but I was waiting for love. I never suspected it would come in your shape. I'd like to throw you upon Tristan and take you away from here and make wild love all night," he murmured.

Her laugh was shaky. "Abduct me *again?* Isn't one scandal enough?" She tapped her fan on his sleeve, although she wanted to muss his shining hair, rumple his lace jabot, and pull his shirt from the waistband of his breeches. She wanted to touch his naked flesh, reacquaint herself with his taut muscles. She longed to feel that dizzying sensation of mounting ecstasy, and its glorious release.

"I hear the rumble of coach wheels on the drive. Let's meet our guests together."

Taking her position next to Roc at the front door, she greeted a long line of people, most of them unknown to her, but all on a first-name basis with Roc. The Cornish aristocracy came from near and far, and Gwen smiled, curtsied, and received their congratulations. Although rumor must have traveled far, no one hinted at what had transpired at the fair. Nevertheless, a few male glances strayed to the swell of Gwen's breasts over the edge of her tight bodice, and she caught some malicious stares from envious females. She lowered her eyes self-consciously. Roc was every inch the jovial host. He led ancient ladies to chairs along the walls where the dowager presided with her acid gossip. Cackles of laughter emanated from that direction at regular intervals.

Lady Camelford sat rigid, her face pale with disapproval at the edge of that line of old tartars. She had just risen from her sickbed and was anxious to leave the Hall, although it would not have been seemly to depart before the ball. Outrage filled her face every time her pale gaze touched Roc and Gwen. She failed to understand how anyone as well-connected as Roc could choose to wed a nobody from the village.

"I believe the earl is letting down his class by marrying that hoyden," Lady Camelford commented to her neighbor, who sat snoring with her chins on her chest. Fear clutched Lady Camelford's heart when she saw her radiant Louise on that horrid Morgan Tyrrell's arm. What the girl saw in him was beyond comprehension. Her nostrils quivered with despair as she realized with a flash of renewed conviction that she must remove the girl from the influence of this strange household immediately. It simply would not do to have Morgan Tyrrell as a son-in-law. Louise could not be gainsaid when she got an idea in her willful head. Why, oh why, had she become bedridden with the influenza when their whole future was at stake? Lady Camelford bristled at fate for treating her so cruelly.

Meanwhile, Gwen smiled until it seemed her lips would be forever fixed in an upturned position. Officer Biggles pirouetted in front with Aunt Clo until she grew flustered and entreated Gwen with a look to come to her rescue. Gwen ignored her, knowing her aunt secretly adored the attention.

The entrance of Sergeant Adams sent a flood of unease through Gwen. He embodied the constant threat to the free traders, although he had accomplished less with his soldiers than Roc had done alone.

The hired musicians began to play the first set and the couples, led by Gwen and Roc, trod the floor to form the quadrille. Her hand trembled in Roc's firm grip as she dipped in the first figure.

" 'Tis not all that awful," he whispered with a teasing smile. "No one has snubbed us yet. They all think you're enchanting."

"The men positively ogle me."

"Who wouldn't? You look ravishing in that gown." His gaze burned the wide swath of porcelain skin revealed by the low neckline.

Unable to shake her uneasiness, Gwen endured the evening, smiling and dancing with almost every male in the room other than her father and Morgan. Resting for a moment by the open French door, she fanned herself vigorously and watched Morgan. A great change had come over him since Louise had arrived at the Hall. He still wore a distracted expression on his face, but a new air of confidence and cheerfulness emanated from him, and his eyes adoringly followed Louise everywhere. Louise beamed with happiness as she skipped across the floor to Gwen's side.

"Have you informed Morgan of your plans to elope to Gretna Green?" Gwen asked with a mischievous smile.

"Well . . . yes. He's all for it, y'know." Louise studied her friend for a moment. "If I tell you when, you won't inform Mother, will you?"

"Of course not." Gwen slanted a glance at the marchioness of Camelford. "If glances could kill, I would be dead," she murmured.

"Who? Where?" Louise followed Gwen's gaze. "Oh, yes,

Mama talks about nothing but leaving, so we'll execute our plan very soon.''

Gwen's eyebrows pulled together with worry. "Are you sure you want to go through with it?''

"Yes, quite sure. And if we don't act now, Mama will snatch me away from here and prevent me from ever seeing Morgan again.'' She placed an eager hand on Gwen's arm. "He's such a darling, you know. Not a fop like the London fribbles who have been following me around. Morgan *knows* so much! Granted he's a bit awkward, but such a good man, so kind and thoughtful.''

"Lud, you're really taken with him, aren't you?'' Gwen asked, filled with amusement.

Louise nodded breathlessly and Gwen smiled, her eyes dancing. "I'm so very happy for you.''

A frown marred Louise's brow. "If only we could have had a double wedding. You'll be married soon, and I don't like to sneak off to Scotland to wed, although 'tis very romantic.'' Her eyes turned dreamy as she evidently considered the prospect of riding into the night with her lover, perhaps chased by someone who would fail to overtake them.

Gwen chuckled. "I believe the only way you can marry Morgan is to elope, but *I* don't think 'tis romantic at all. Think of the discomfort, the cold nights with rain and fog.''

Louise turned to her, startled. "You're so—so pragmatic, so *unromantic,* if you'll excuse my expression. I like a bit of adventure, but I wager you don't,'' Louise retorted with a toss of her head.

Memories flashed through Gwen's mind: black waves, the sound of oars dipping into the water; dark-clad men carrying kegs up steep cliff paths; the smell of tangy seaweed; mist swirling mysteriously over the moors.

Leaning forward conspiratorially, her eyes flashing, Gwen whispered, "You don't know me all that well, then. You don't know my secret life of danger.''

A laugh flowed from Louise's lips. "You're so droll, Gwen. I cannot for my life see you involved in any adventure, even though Roc did abduct you at the fair. Now, that *was* excessively daring and romantic.''

Just then Roc joined them, his eyes shining with pleasure

as they fastened on Gwen. "I hear you're enjoying yourselves," he said. "Will you tell me what the joke is about?"

Louise turned instantly to him. "You're very lucky to get Gwen. She's so entertaining. She insists she has a secret life of danger."

Gwen bit her lip in frustration. Dash it all! Now he'd know for sure that she was Dandelion. How careless of her to have even suggested . . .

Aloud she said with a calculated sigh, "I might as well make a clean breast of it. I was pulling your leg, Louise."

"Really?" Roc's voice, as smooth as velvet, sent a flurry of unease along Gwen's spine. His topaz gaze probed into her, revealing none of his thoughts. "What did she tell you, Louise?" he continued.

Louise fluttered her fan. "Nothing, really. I don't know what she was hinting at. Furthermore, she's too old for adventure. No offense meant, of course. At her age one is quite settled down, I believe."

Gwen rolled her eyes and chuckled. "I'm not yet in my dotage," she assured her drily.

Roc looked pleased. "I'm glad you know how to entertain each other," he declared, and walked off to speak with the dowager, who had been waving at him these last five minutes.

Gwen let out a sigh of relief. How could her tongue have slipped in such a careless fashion? It truly was time to abandon her nightly adventures and settle down. Dandelion must disappear without a trace—now, *that* would be romantic. Before long, the villagers' memories would turn into legend, Dandelion's character glorified beyond recognition and swathed in a rosy mist of mystery.

Officer Biggles interrupted her thoughts by requesting the next dance. "I have not yet had a chance to dance with you or to congratulate you on your engagement," he said with a yellow-toothed smile. Gwen's eyes instantly went to the wart bobbing up and down on his chin.

"You're very kind, Officer Biggles." As they joined the couples already on the dance floor, she asked, "Have you heard any news about Dandelion? Has the earl found any clue as to his identity?"

"I thought he would tell you himself." Officer Biggles pivoted on high heels.

Gwen felt a chill along her spine. Did Roc really know? "We don't speak of such things, Officer Biggles, as our time is filled with plans for the wedding."

"But naturally, how silly of me." His brow darkened. "I'm sad to inform you that the earl holds me in very low esteem and doesn't inform me of his finds. However, he's been civil by inviting me to all the festivities here this summer, so I don't hold a grudge."

"That's gracious of you, Officer Biggles. Truly, you don't know anything?" She held her breath in anticipation.

"Well, Sergeant Adams seems to think that the load is being brought in tonight. The soldiers are down at the coves even as we speak."

Gwen let out a sigh of relief and moved down the line of dancers. She had no other chance to speak with her partner until the end of the set. As she had calculated, they were all hoping to catch the smugglers tonight, all except Officer Biggles, of course. She glanced at the ormulu clock on the mantelpiece at the end of the long ballroom. Midnight. The soldiers would be miserable and cold, and no "gentlemen" would appear all night. The corners of her lips lifted in a satisfied smile.

Officer Biggles was unusually perceptive this evening. "You look pleased tonight, and well you should be."

"Oh." Gwen smiled guiltily. "Yes, I—I'm enjoying myself."

Roc escaped the dowager's clutches and joined Gwen after the dance. "A very busy evening. Let's escape outside for a breath of fresh air," he muttered, his eyes caressing her face.

"We can't just leave Officer Biggles in the middle of the floor, you know," Gwen said smoothly.

That worthy individual hemmed and hawed. "I can't rightly tell you how much I enjoyed being here this evening. May I fetch refreshments for you, Miss Tremayne?"

"No, thank you, but it looks as if Miss Pettigrew would enjoy your company," she said, indicating her aunt sitting alone by the wall.

Officer Biggles bowed and minced off to court Aunt Clo.

"What were you two talking about, Gwen? You seemed so . . . well, earnest."

Gwen cringed and thought rapidly. "Oh, he was going on about your hospitality."

Roc laughed. "He's a strange creature."

"Quite harmless." Gwen waved her fan, averting her eyes.

They strolled toward the open doors. Before they managed to escape, Enedoc intercepted them, looking extremely ill at ease. "Milord, I need to speak with you urgently . . . in private, please." The butler wrung his gnarled hands. " 'Tis about Thomas, the footman."

"Of course." Roc sent Gwen an apologetic glance. "I will join you shortly."

Gwen stood in the cool draft from the doors, waiting patiently for Roc's return. The night sky looked almost blue in the clear, sharp air. An owl hooted in the garden, and Gwen would not have thought anything of it except that the hoot was a warning signal used by the smugglers. She took a step onto the terrace and saw a bush move. As her eyes adjusted to the darkness, she saw a pale face peeping out of the greenery.

Clem! Gwen ran down the steps into the garden. "What are you doing here?" she whispered.

"I've been 'ere for ages waitin' for a chance to speak with ye. Th' *Alouette* didn't get our message some'ow. She's out in th' bay expectin' us to pick up th' brandy *tonight*. What are we goin' to do?"

Chapter 29

Gwen looked dazed, as if she'd just received a blow to her head. "The *Alouette* here tonight?"

"Aye, Miss Gwen. We 'ave to do somethin'."

Recovering from the shock, she said, "Meet me in the spinney at the usual spot in one hour."

Clem nodded, ready to leave. Gwen grasped his arm. "And be careful!" she warned, and watched his disappearing bulk.

She was leaning heavily on the stone balustrade when Roc returned. His face set in a stern frown, his chin jutting with determination, he said, "Ah, there you are, sweeting." He peered closely at her. "Are you well? You're as pale as a sheet." Holding her chin, he forced her to look him in the eyes. She wondered if he could see how hunted she felt.

"I'm tired, Roc. The evening has taken its toll, and I'm bone weary. Perhaps . . ."

She had no time to end the sentence as Roc broke in, " 'Twould be a good idea to make our announcement now, so that the guests who are not staying can return to their homes at their leisure."

Gwen glanced at him uncomfortably. She knew he was hiding something. Suddenly she suspected he knew about the *Alouette*. She placed a restraining hand on his arm as he headed back inside. "What did Enedoc have to say, Roc? Problems?"

He laughed, a hard, clipped sound. "I plan to catch a big fish tonight," he answered cryptically. Had Gwen not known about the *Alouette*, she would have wondered what he meant.

"Is Dandelion on the prowl?"

Glancing toward the brightly lit ballroom, he did not an-

288

swer at first. Without looking at her, he spoke over his shoulder. "Perhaps. Shall we go inside?"

Ice-cold fear filled her as she placed her fingertips in the crook of his elbow. He sounded so sure of himself. Was he setting up a trap for her right now? Thoughts swirled wildly in her head. How could he hold a large ball celebrating their engagement if he meant to bring her to the gallows? She must be imagining things. Perchance he did not know after all. *Oh, God, what did he know?* She would have to find a way to force the *Alouette* to leave.

On jellylike legs, Gwen accompanied Roc into the ballroom. He led her to the dais where the musicians were seated, and before they had time to strike up another tune, Roc spoke.

"My dear friends." His voice echoed loud and clear across the room. "I have some news to share. Friends, this is a wonderful opportunity to make my announcement." Turning to Gwen, he continued, "I'm proud to present to you the future countess of Landregan, Miss Gwendolyn Tremayne, who has graciously consented to be my wife."

A murmur of approval rippled through the room, and several guests surged forward to congratulate the couple. But Roc held up his hand, stilling the crowd once more.

"There is something else. As you all know, I returned home with a commission—to act as magistrate until Landregan could be delivered from the intense free trading which has doubled in this last year. Since I returned, I've learned that the smuggling has helped many suffering people who could not survive without it. I've decided that only the leader, the scoundrel Dandelion, will hang. With him gone, the smuggling will stop of its own accord—or at least it will slow down. Dandelion's reputation has traveled as far as London, and I'm sure you've all heard of him. I believe all of you agree with my decision to be lenient toward the villagers, as these are very hard times for the less fortunate."

"Aye, starvation is a problem among the poor. The free trading has helped them all," someone cried. "A man has to live and feed his family, after all."

"That rogue Dandelion has a good brain on his shoulders!" somebody else shouted.

"Yes," Roc admitted with a frown, "one has to give him that. However, tonight I have a good chance to catch the plaguey fellow, so I must ask your forgiveness for abandoning you. Naturally I beg you to stay as long as you wish and partake of the delicacies set out for you in the dining room. Please enjoy yourselves.''

Gwen's heart pounded as she nervously watched Roc shaking hands with the guests and receive compliments and congratulations. The worm! Playing, are we? I'll show him, yet.

He returned to her side. ''Darling Gwen, I must abandon you now, but I'll be back as soon as possible. I'm sorry to leave you like this, but it is too important a chance to let slip through my fingers.''

Gwen nodded. If he knows, why is he putting on this charade? She had no immediate answer, but she would soon find out, she vowed.

Roc bent his head and kissed her cheek gallantly. ''I'll visit you first thing in the morning and tell you all about this adventure,'' he said with a cryptic smile, and then he left.

Gwen watched his broad back as he strode purposefully across the floor. She hurried to her aunt sitting next to the dowager countess, who pinned Gwen with a belligerent eye. ''What is that rapscallion son of mine up to now?'' she snapped.

''I'm afraid he's left you to take up the duties of hostess, milady,'' Gwen replied. ''Or should I take over and pronounce supper served in the dining room?''

''How *dare* he leave us in the lurch!'' She glowered at Gwen. ''I suppose *I'll* have to do it. You're not going to steal my title and my responsibilities just yet, gel.''

''I was just going to ask Aunt Clo to take me home as I have an agonizing headache, milady. I'm sure nobody will miss me.'' Gwen sent her aunt an entreating glance and was grateful to receive a positive response.

''Just what one would expect of you, the dowager muttered. ''You'll make my son very unhappy. I can feel it in my bones.''

''I'm sure you're quite capable of making the rest of the evening a success, Lady Landregan. As far as I can see, the ball is already a triumph.'' With those words Gwen hastened across the room before she could receive another reprimand.

However unorthodox it was of her to leave her own betrothal party, Gwen considered the future of her smuggler friends more important than the opinions of the guests.

"You do look tired," Aunt Clo commented on the way back to Tremayne House. "And not only you." She motioned to the squire nodding in the corner of the carriage. " 'Twas a lovely evening. I'm not complaining, although I must say Lady Landregan's a trifle trying at times."

"To say the least." Gwen fanned herself vigorously to ease her nervous tension. Her thoughts left the dowager to dwell on the more pressing matter of the *Alouette,* bobbing full of brandy kegs out in the bay.

"Where's Vincent?" Aunt Clo asked. "I haven't seen him all evening."

"He rode off to Fowey for a card game," Gwen explained. "Had no desire to attend the ball." To spite me, she thought. Ever since Vincent had returned from London two days ago, she had kept a close eye on him. His presence was making her increasingly uneasy.

Back in her bedchamber at last, Gwen hastily changed her clothes, pulling on her breeches and Arthur's shirt.

When the house grew quiet, she slid out into the night. The wind caught her hair and lashed it loose from the ribbon at the nape of her neck. "Dash it all!" She reached in vain for the flying strands as she ran along the stone wall toward the spinney.

Clem sat on the usual boulder waiting for her. "Miss Gwen, I thought I 'ad to wait all night for ye," he complained, tension making him snappish. "What took ye so long?"

"I'm sorry, but I couldn't very well dash from the ball. I had to try to act normal. You gave me a nasty shock by showing up at the Hall." They walked steadily along the path, steering their steps toward Wrecker's Ruin. A lantern dangled from Clem's meaty hand as he shuffled beside her like a large bear.

"Aye, but I 'ad no choice." He gazed at her in the bluish darkness. "Er, ye looked lovely in that dress, Miss Gwen. Like a royal princess, I swear."

"Forget about balls and dresses, Clem. We have to lure the *Alouette* away from the bay, not an easy task. I wonder what could have gone wrong with the signals. Who was in charge?''

"Thomas Strutt."

Though the name had no special meaning for Clem, it made an impact on Gwen. "Tom! Why, he's a footman at the Hall. And Roc spoke with him right before he left the ball. The earl must have discovered that he's involved with the smugglers and made him talk."

"Naw, 'e wouldn't talk, miss. 'E's stubborn as a mule."

"If the earl threatened to dismiss him from his post he would be eager to talk, and you know it."

" 'E would niver divulge yer name. 'E might babble 'bout everybody else, but not ye, Miss Gwen. First 'e'd make up a name."

"We'll soon find out," Gwen muttered grimly. "If the earl has been bamboozling me with all this talk about marriage, only to destroy Dandelion, I'll . . . I'll push him into the sea and hold his head under water!"

Clem did not speak, and she suspected he liked the idea of Roc disappearing into the ocean.

When they neared Wrecker's Ruin they slowed down, sneaking stealthily from tree to tree, their eyes alert for soldiers. The only sounds were the whining of the wind between the loose stones of the ruin and the death squeal of a mouse. A shiver of apprehension rippled through Gwen.

The waves hurtled endlessly against the rocks below. Was that the sound of a voice floating on the air? Gwen listened intently and inched toward the edge of the cliffs. "Did you hear that?"

"Psst, Miss Gwen, get down! Someone might see ye." Obeying, she crawled on her belly to the edge. Glancing down at Brandy Cove, she gasped when she saw the flashes of a lantern cutting the darkness. One, two . . . *their* signal! The *Alouette* would be bringing in the cargo!

"Clem, did you see that? The soldiers are pretending to be us. Give me that lantern. We have to try to stop the Frogs." She flashed the warning signal, three rapid flares followed by one long, then curled her fingers hard into her palms and prayed that the captain of the French cutter wasn't too bosky to understand the peril of landing the cargo.

"The men . . . they are all at home, aren't they?" Gwen asked grimly. " 'Tis only you and me here?"

"Aye, that they are. Sleepin' in their beds like innocent children." Clem scratched his head. "What are we goin' to do now? Th' soldiers will take our brandy."

"Better that than us getting caught. We can only wait and see what will happen. I know the earl has placed guards at every landing spot in the area, plus the harbor."

The salty wind bore disembodied voices to their ears, and Gwen stiffened. "They might have seen our signal from below. Come, we'd better run!" She stood, her body rigid with fear.

Then everything seemed to happen at once. Like black wraiths, men appeared out of the grass and began to close in slowly. Gwen took Clem's hand in a frantic grip and rushed headlong toward the copse behind the ruin. If they could only reach the trees, they would be safe.

"Halt!" Gwen instantly recognized Roc's voice, and she was dimly aware of the sound of pounding hooves behind her, of Clem panting beside her. Their one advantage was that they knew the area well, every path and pitfall. Their pursuers would have no chance of catching up with them, except the man on the horse—Roc.

"Stop or I'll shoot!" he barked close behind them.

"Let's go separate ways," Gwen said, out of breath.

"No, this time I won't leave ye." Clem had barely spoken when a shot rang out, whistling past Gwen's head. A group of startled birds flapped up, screeching. Blindly she hurled herself toward the welcoming trees. Another shot exploded, and a white-hot pain pierced her body. As she fell into merciful oblivion, an agonized moan passed her lips.

It hurt to open her eyes, and it hurt to turn her head. Her body was throbbing with pain. The effort to raise her head brought tears to her eyes.

"Clem?" she whispered. She squinted and recognized the water-stained ceiling of her bedroom.

"He's not here. Only carried you upstairs and left." Aunt Clo's sharp voice penetrated the fog in Gwen's head. "Lie still or the wound will reopen."

"What happened?" Gwen asked through dry lips.

With a disapproving snort, Aunt Clo leaned over her. "I have never been more shocked in my life than when Clem informed me that *you* are Dandelion! Of all the infamous things! How could you do this to us, bringing such shame to your family! We'll never live down this scandal." Her voice rose several octaves.

"Stop the noise," Gwen begged, her aunt's voice grating on her nerves.

"Clem wouldn't let me send for Dr. Penfield to tend your wound. He said something about the earl not knowing it was you he shot. He forced me to keep it a secret."

Gwen groaned. "Oh, dear. Am I badly hurt?" She gingerly patted the thick bandage on her shoulder.

"The ball hit your shoulder. Marva says 'tis a clean flesh wound, no bones broken, and that you'll be fine in a few days." Aunt Clo shuddered. "All that blood! I thought I was going to swoon."

"Does Papa know?" Gwen held her breath, waiting for the answer.

"No, he's asleep. Nothing but an earthquake could rouse him." Aunt Clo plumped up the pillows behind Gwen and helped her to sit up. Gwen groaned, and the pain produced beads of perspiration on her forehead. "You must keep it a secret," she said, grasping her aunt's hand convulsively. " 'Twould kill him to know the truth. Please promise not to tell him."

Aunt Clo cast her a speculative look. "He has the right to know what you've done, but I don't want to talk about it. Most likely, he'll blame me." She shuddered delicately. "I'll not tell him the truth, only say that you have influenza. After this, I wish I could forget that you're a member of my family. Such unbearable disgrace!"

Gwen drew a sigh of relief. "No one need know. I'll keep to my bed for a week or two and Papa won't be the wiser."

"Rumors are bound to fly. Oh, Gwen, how could *you* of all people concoct such lawless schemes!"

"Well, as long as there's no proof, I'm innocent. I was clumsy to get caught." Gwen mulled over the events of the previous evening, fighting waves of pain. "Aunt, please don't be angry. I did it for us, for Tremayne House."

"I have never been more mortified as when I saw you in a man's, ahem, breeches." Aunt Clo coughed. "And a man's shirt!" Her cheeks turned red with indignation. "How could you, Gwen!" She began pacing, and Gwen grew tired watching her.

"I will rest now. Thank you, Auntie, for your help and your . . . understanding." She smiled weakly, her face ghostly pale. "Tomorrow is another day."

Aunt Clo stopped at the end of the bed. "Your smuggling days are over."

Gwen did not hear her. Her head tilted to the side, she was already asleep.

The next morning Gwen felt a lot better, although her shoulder throbbed with a dull, persistent ache. She dutifully drank the broth Marva brought to her. The cook clucked with worry as she cleaned the wound.

"Dr. Penfield should 'ave looked at this," she stated darkly.

"I'm sure you know as much about healing as does Dr. Penfield. A white witch you are, Marva, and my good friend."

The rotund cook's face lightened, and she cheerfully dusted basilicum powder on the wound and placed a fresh bandage around the shoulder. "Ye'll be right as a trivet in no time. Ye're no simperin' miss. I would 'ave died on th' spot bein' shot at like that. Ye're brave like a man, Miss Gwen, and the villagers adore you for it."

"I knew the risks when I became involved with the smugglers."

Gwen slept most of the morning until Marva hurried into the room. "Miss Gwen! Miss Gwen! What are we goin' to do? 'E's 'ere."

Gwen's eyes widened. "Who?"

"Th' earl, o' course. 'E's in th' parlor with Miss Pettigrew right now, and 'e is arskin' for ye!" She planted her wide bottom on the bed and fanned her face with fat hands. "Dear me, oh, dear me!"

"I must go downstairs and see him." Gwen moaned as she eased herself out of bed.

"Oh, miss, naw! Ye can't do that. Th' wound will open up again."

"I will have to take the risk. If he knows I'm the one who was shot—" She took a deep breath. "I have to know, have to show myself downstairs." The room swayed and her legs shook like currant jelly. She gripped the edge of the night-stand to keep from falling. Biting down hard on her bottom lip, she managed to evade the threatening faint. Sheer will-power bore her to the dressing table. Breathing deeply, she steadied herself by leaning against the top and digging her fingers into the scarred wooden surface. How would she ever get through the next half hour? "I believe he might suspect me of being Dandelion."

"Naw, 'ow could 'e? 'E know no more now than when 'e came. Th' villagers don't talk 'bout th' smugglin'. Accordin' t' them, smugglin' don't exist in Landregan."

Gwen smiled and slumped down on the chair. "He knows something—but what? Marva, please help me dress, and quickly." Clasping a hand to her wound to still the torture spearing through her, she gave Marva an entreating glance.

Marva fussed around her, brushed her hair and wound it into a neat chignon. Her tresses looked lackluster and her complexion was deathly pale, except for two bright red spots on her cheekbones. Her eyes shone unnaturally bright. "Powder my cheeks, too, to conceal those spots."

"Ye're gettin' a fever. 'Tis no good risin' from th' bed too early. Ye'll be makin' yerself ill." Marva wrinkled her fore-head with worry. "What a stew!"

"There is nothing else I can do, Marva. Help me with my toilette." While she waited for Marva to select a dress, she rubbed rouge on her lips and dusted rice powder over the dark circles around her eyes. Her hands trembled.

Red-hot pain stabbed her as she lifted her arms to let Marva pull on the bodice. She had no idea how she survived the procedure, or the tight lacing of the robings over the under-bodice, but she concentrated all her will on staying upright. Marva bustled around her, attaching the skirts into place and covering the shoulders with a wide woolen shawl. Gwen pulled the ends together gratefully, as there was a nip in the air.

"Now, help me downstairs," Gwen said between clenched teeth.

Marva made small noises of anguish all the way down the

stairs. Gwen halted and clenched the cook's hand. "Did the lawmen confiscate the brandy kegs?" she whispered.

Marva shook her head. "Th' cutter must 'ave left."

"Then I want you to take a message to Clem. Tell him that under no circumstances is he to go near the shore tonight. If the *Alouette* returns, tell him to let her go. They'll get caught if they try to bring in the goods," Gwen said hoarsely. Feeling faint, she straightened in front of the door and took a deep breath. Only iron will made her hold her head high as she opened the door to the parlor, her hands numb.

She walked slowly but steadily into the room and crossed the floor without stumbling. The image of Roc blurred and wavered, and then loomed over her as he rose to kiss her.

"Good morning, Roc," she said with false brightness. "What a pleasant surprise." She felt his fingers take hold of her clammy hand and she struggled to keep it steady. His gaze bored into her, and she fancied he could see the bandage under her shawl, could read the pain in her eyes. "A lovely morning, isn't it? I had the worst headache last night, that's why I slept late this morning. I'm sorry if I've kept you waiting." She shot him a nervous glance and saw how set and white he looked under the tan. Surely he must suspect. He must know!

Why didn't he say something? She saw her own weariness reflected in his eyes, but he did not mention it. He acted as if this was a usual morning call, a swain visiting his bride-to-be, holding her hand, kissing it longingly.

Aunt Clo's gaze darted back and forth between them.

"I was distressed to hear that you, too, left the ball and let our guests fend for themselves," he said with a hint of disapproval. "But I'm sorry to find you so out of sorts," he added smoothly. "Are you sure 'tis only a headache? You look rather—worn." It was the only indication he made of his doubt about the seriousness of her complaint, and he did not speak of her health again.

"I'll be myself in a couple of days. Why are you here?" The question emerged rather abruptly.

Roc's lips quirked. "You don't want me here? I was longing to see you, and during the commotion at the ball I forgot to give you this." He delved into the pocket of his waistcoat and extracted a diamond ring that winked in the sunlight. "Let me." He reached for her hand and slipped the ring on her finger. "A small token of my love."

Gwen gasped. She glanced into his enigmatic eyes. "For me? But this must—"

"No buts, please. You're my betrothed, and I like to give you presents now and then. Besides, this is a betrothal ring to seal our alliance."

Gwen felt awful inside, guilt weighing so heavily on her shoulders that she could barely hold her head up. She forced a smile to her lips. "Thank you. I'll cherish it forever," she whispered, clasping his hand convulsively. Then her vision blurred, and she sensed her consciousness threatening to slip away from her.

Taking a deep breath, she managed to say, "What took you away last night in such haste?"

"We knew the French cutter was waiting in the bay, and we almost nabbed Dandelion. I'm sure 'twas him or one of his cohorts—slender, almost not tall enough to be a man." His eyes narrowed, probing her.

"Oh, but he got away then. I'm glad." Gwen felt a nervous twitch go through Aunt Clo next to her on the sofa. "I suppose you'll arrest him soon, and—hang him?" she added softly.

He moved uncomfortably on the lumpy wing chair. "Unless he slips through my fingers again. He's had the slipperiness of an eel."

Aunt Clo tittered. "Would you like a glass of wine, Roc?" she asked nervously.

"No, but perhaps a glass of brandy, some of that excellent *French* brandy you served last time."

Everything began moving in front of Gwen's eyes, swirling colors beckoning her to surrender to the void. She forced herself to sit very straight. She pressed her nails into the palms of her hands and bit her cheek to keep the weakness at bay. With utmost effort she focused her eyes on Roc. His brooding gaze never left her face.

"You cannot . . . let him go if you catch him, can you? You'd lose face," she said. "You'd have to mete out the promised punishment. Hanging," she breathed.

He sat very still. Aunt Clo's rapid breathing was the only sound in the room.

"I could never hang a . . . woman," he muttered, turning the tables on her.

He *did* know! Her world crashed around her. "A woman? What an outlandish idea!" Her thoughts became sluggish and disjointed. Her will to fight was slowly ebbing, and the pain in her shoulder had become unbearable. "You would have to prove her guilt."

Roc was suddenly full of energy. "That would be easy, because I *shot* her." He leaned forward in conspiracy. "I regret deeply to have to tell you that I actually winged a woman." His gaze glittered. "She did not die, so if I find the wound, I find Dandelion."

Gwen's lips curved in a stiff smile. "Are you going to spend the day searching all the women in the village for a wound? You would like that, of course." She felt rivulets of perspiration course along her spine and bead on her forehead. The tension between them crackled, just like the sky right before a thunderstorm. Ominous silence followed, and Gwen shuddered.

Suddenly Roc roared with laughter, deflating the tension. "That might be interesting," he teased. "I was only joking, Gwen, knowing how defensive you are about the smugglers, but you're not very responsive today. I can't seem to raise your hackles in defense of the village women." He sighed deeply. "Dandelion, I believe, could be no woman, but I suddenly remembered the rumor that women exchanged the kegs on the square."

The world righted itself and Gwen seethed. "How could you! How unfeeling of you to tease me so! How can you speak of shooting a woman and remain so cold? And 'tis not amusing to hear your flippant remarks about Dandelion."

"Ah! A bit of fire finally." He rubbed his chin thoughtfully. "I could not help but goad you when I know how protective you are of the villagers. No, we'll take that weed prisoner soon, mark my words. Last night we saw two of the free traders, one large man and one small. I'm certain one of them is Dandelion. He was trying to cover up a mistake with the French cutter."

Gwen took in shallow, anguished breaths. "Why, you know a great deal, it appears."

He looked pleased with himself. "I know I have Dandelion in a corner. There is no place to bring in the cargo, so I imagine he's desperate."

The world slowly began tilting once more. Gwen knew she could not take much more. He was sitting there, talking coolly about her—about his enemy. The whole situation was preposterous, mad.

"Roc, if you please, I think my migraine is getting worse. 'Tis very unfeeling of you to taunt me like this when I can't defend myself properly."

He looked startled. "By Jove, you look ghastly, my dear. I'm so sorry! How very thoughtless of me to tease you so." He stood immediately. "I didn't realize how much I've been tiring you." He gave her an apologetic smile. "I only wanted to give you the ring and keep you informed of the latest happenings, since I know how much it interests you."

Gwen felt herself slip slowly from reality. She grasped the edge of the sofa cushion. "Yes—yes, thank you."

She was saved from disgrace as the door burst open.

"Milord!" Thomas Strutt shouted. He stood in the doorway, uncertainly taking in the scene before him.

"Yes, Thomas. What's the matter?" Roc questioned.

"Lady Landregan wants you to return to th' 'All at once. Master Morgan and Lady Louise 'ave eloped." Thomas covertly glanced at Gwen, a flash of guilt filling his eyes, and a dark flush staining his cheeks.

Ominous silence filled the room as they waited for Roc's anger to explode.

Chapter 30

Roc turned on his heel, a harassed look on his face. "Of
all the blockheaded ideas!" He sighed in defeat. "I suppose
I'll have to try to stop them." He bent over Gwen and placed
a warm kiss on her cheek. "I say, you do feel hot! Are you
developing an influenza or some such evil?"

"I feel awful," Gwen admitted. "You'd better go after
Morgan and Louise. Lady Camelford will blame you for their
elopement if you don't."

He bowed to Aunt Clo, who was unusually quiet, and departed, the heels of his boots clicking across the floor. Just
as he left, Vincent strolled through the doorway, eating a
slice of toast. His eyes scanned Gwen's face, and she flinched.
He was the last person she wanted to see.

"What was that commotion about?" he queried. "The earl
looked positively furious." He slid into a chair, swinging one
leg nonchalantly over the other, and stared hard at Gwen.
"And you look like you're about to draw your last breath,
coz. Are you ill?"

Gwen fought to keep from sliding into a faint. The sound
of Roc's angry voice seeped through the walls as he spoke to
Thomas, the traitor.

"Morgan and Lady Louise have eloped," Aunt Clo explained.

Vincent whistled between his teeth, a supercilious smile
parting his lips.

When the front door closed behind Roc with a bang, Gwen
slumped into a heap on the sofa, unable to stay upright any
longer. She was clammy all over, and dark specks danced

before her eyes. Nausea churned in her stomach, and every bone in her body ached.

"I say! Gwen, you remind me of a fellow at Flanders whom I saw shot. He struggled just like you do." Vincent licked butter off his fingers. "I heard shots last night. Did you get shot, dear coz?"

Gwen trembled as her cousin's knowing gaze jolted her. He must have figured out the truth. She wanted to protest, but her lips worked in vain to form the words.

Dimly she noticed when Arthur carried her up the stairs and placed her in her bed. Never had it felt better to lay stretched out on a soft feather tick. With all the strength sapped from her body, she drifted into oblivion. The last thing she remembered was Vincent's smirk.

A strange underwater world seemed to enfold her as she awakened. Weak as a kitten, she could barely lift her hand or turn her head. She was swimming in perspiration. Her mind blank, she felt curiously light-headed and detached from her surroundings.

"Thank God, ye're comin' to." Marva's round face hovered above her. "Ye've 'ad a nasty fever, and we've been worried sick 'bout ye."

"Really? How long?" It even hurt to speak. "Water, please."

Marva eagerly held a glass to her dry lips. "Ye've been gone for two days, miss."

Gwen tensed. "Two days!" She tried to sit up, but lacked the strength to do it.

"Aye, two days, and plenty 'as 'appened since ye was laid down with th' fever," Marva said with some importance.

"What?" Gwen had a foreboding of disaster.

"Well, th' earl came to see ye, but we said ye had th' influenza. That fobbed 'im off. 'E's been in a real takin', I tell ye." She sat on the edge of the bed sponging Gwen's face with a cool wet cloth. "And yer cousin 'as been tryin' to see ye all day. But ye'd better rest for now. I should not tire ye with talk, and I won't let anyone else tire ye, either."

Gwen grasped Marva's arm weakly. "You can't stop in the middle of your explanation. What has happened?"

"Well, I suppose ye'll find out sooner or later, and it might as well be sooner. They've caught th' smugglers, Clem one o' them. 'E didn't heed me warnin'.''

Gwen drew a sharp breath, seeing her world crumbling around her. She squeezed Marva's stout forearm. ''Continue.''

''They are all shut in th' dungeons at th' 'All. Th' earl was goin' after Morgan and that young lady guest at th' 'All, but 'e returned. Accordin' to th' blacksmith, 'e didn't bother to follow them. Th' earl said 'e wasn't goin' to get mixed into 'is brother's business. 'E says 'e likes th' match and wishes them 'appiness.'' She sighed with a wistful look on her face.

Gwen clutched Marva's shoulder fretfully, rising a fraction from the bed. ''What will happen to the smugglers now?''

''I don't know. Clem keeps sayin' 'e's Dandelion.''

Gwen fell back onto the pillows with a groan. ''Oh, no! Roc will hang him!''

''Naw, I don't think 'e will. Th' earl bain't no monster. Th' villagers will lynch 'im if 'e as much as bends a 'air on Clem's 'ead,'' Marva said with great conviction, then coaxed Gwen to drink some hot broth. She clucked at Gwen's lack of strength. ''We've been rightly worried 'bout ye. Miss Pettigrew sat with ye all night and all day. She kept sayin' we should fetch th' doctor, but ye know I didn't let 'er do it.''

''How did they get caught?'' Gwen whispered.

''Idiots, that's what they are. Ye told 'em not to go out th' followin' night, but did they listen? Naw, silly as goats they are. Th' earl was there takin' 'em red-handed with th' kegs. A 'eap o' simpletons, all o' them, if ye arsk me.''

''Give me some more of that broth, Marva. I have to get my strength back, fast.'' Gwen's lips were set in a white line of determination. ''Nobody is going to hang because of my idiocy.''

That afternoon, while Gwen fretted in bed, Vincent strolled into her room, his usual smirk on his lips.

''What do you want?'' Gwen asked suspiciously.

''Thought I'd come to cheer you up, dear coz.'' He sank onto the edge of the bed, and Gwen moved farther away.

'' 'Twould cheer me up if you'd stay away from my bedchamber.'' She pulled the bedcovers up to her chin.

He gave a calculating chuckle. "We've something to talk about first . . . Dandelion."

She gasped, feeling all her blood drain toward her feet. He knew. The game was up now. Surely he would spread the news abroad if he hadn't already. "Your tactics of terror don't work here," she said, forcing her voice to remain level.

He chuckled again. "We'll see about that." He bent over her, gripped her aching shoulder, and squeezed. "Does it hurt, Dandelion?"

She stifled a scream, meeting his cold gaze measure for measure. "What do you want?" Was that quavering, breathless voice hers?

"Listen carefully, coz. I've looked everywhere for his lordship's hidden French jewels. I want them." He shook her for emphasis. "I want them more than I've ever wanted anything. And you will find them for me." His grip tightened. "After all, you're close to the earl and should have no difficulty searching his things."

Gwen drew shallow breaths as the pain intensified. Until she could learn the whole truth about Roc's involvement with the Jacobites, she had to obey Vincent's wishes. She nodded and made herself speak. "So that's what you've been skulking around Landregan for, a cache of jewels." She pinched his flaccid upper arm as hard as she could. "If I find them for you, will you promise not to divulge my secret to the earl?"

He suddenly let go of his grip, and she slumped back against the pillows. "Yes, I promise—for now anyway. Once you're wed to Roc, you're safe. He can't hang his own wife," he added with a derisive laugh.

If Roc finds out the truth from anyone but myself he'll never speak to me again, Gwen thought, her insides sinking at the thought. He was honest to a fault. "Tell me, how did Roc come by the gems?" she asked as Vincent reached the door.

Vincent sneered and crossed his arms over his chest. "Your fiancé is a traitor to England. He's a Jacobite."

Gwen's eyes flew wide as she feigned surprise.

Vincent's pale eyes glittered with amusement. "That got your full attention, didn't it? 'Tis true. The jewels are from French Jacobite sympathizers—or British exiles. The loot should have reached Charles Stuart in Scotland, but 'tis too late for that now. Stuart returned to France in September, a beaten man.'' Vincent barked a laugh. ''Roc saw fit to keep the gems for himself. A sneaky fellow, don't you agree?'' His face darkened in anger. ''He doesn't need them, but I do.'' He shook a threatening fist in her direction. ''Find the jewels, or else—''

Her patience snapped. ''Don't threaten me! At last everything is falling into place. I suspect you killed James Murray because he came to Landregan to collect the jewels for Charles Stuart. I even have proof. I know who is called the Stork, because I invented the name myself.''

Vincent paled and flinched and took a threatening step toward her.

''Don't try anything,'' Gwen warned. ''I'll keep your secret if you keep mine, but I've proof that you're a murderer. If you try to harm me, it'll all come out into the open.''

He stood as if frozen. ''If Mabel has been spewing out false rumors about me, I'll squeeze her dirty little neck.'' He made a threatening gesture, as if he was encircling an imaginary neck.

''She has said nothing. I have real proof.'' Gwen's heart pounded with fear. Had she been foolish to confront him?

He seemed to deliberate for a long time. At last he said, ''You're bluffing. Nothing but empty threats, Gwen.'' Then he left, slamming the door so hard that Gwen winced. How would she ever deal with the mounting problems? It could not be true that Roc had kept the gems for his own benefit. He would never do anything so underhanded. Or would he?

Two days passed before she gained enough strength to leave her bed, and then she walked on wobbly legs. Black dots of exhaustion danced in her vision. She patiently bore the solicitous visits of her father and Aunt Clo, who wore a perpetual frown.

Gwen's wound was healing nicely, thanks to a poultice Marva had prepared, and no other complications had set in.

On the third day Gwen said, ''This morning I'll go to the Hall and see Roc.''

Marva threw up her hands in horror. ''Ye're too weak to be jauntin' about th' countryside.''

''No matter. I must speak with Roc and make him release

Clem. No one is going to take the blame for my work.'' Word
had reached her that all the smugglers had been set free except Clem. Roc had issued only a stern warning and a threat
of heavy fines if the free trading continued. The village rippled with gossip. Roc's high-handed ways did not go over
well with the stubborn inhabitants of Landregan.

"Help me get dressed, and call for the trap. I'm going to
the Hall.'' Gwen turned imploring eyes on her faithful friend.
"Please.''

Marva muttered something about "madness'' and "idiot''
before she grudgingly assisted Gwen.

As Gwen sat in the trap, ready to flick the reins over Buttercup's back, Vincent intercepted her. He glanced casually
at her shoulder and made a movement as if to touch her. She
evaded him.

"I take it you're going to find the gems,'' he drawled.

"Not yet. I have to speak with Roc today about another
matter. Tomorrow—''

His face turned red with anger. "No! You have to find the
gems before you speak with your fiancé. I cannot trust you
not to confide in him,'' he hissed, standing so close she
smelled the ale on his breath. He looked disheveled and dirty,
and very nervous.

"I'll say nothing to Roc,'' Gwen promised and flicked the
reins. The trap jolted forward.

"I don't trust you,'' he called after her. "You'll regret
this.'' Gwen shivered, but she had no time to lose if she was
going to save Clem.

To walk from the trap to the front steps of the Hall was an
ordeal, but Gwen clamped her teeth together, and not one
complaint fell from her lips. Still feeling faint and feverish,
she waited patiently on a chair in the hallway while Enedoc
informed Roc of her presence. Enedoc looked as if he had
aged ten years in the last week.

He clucked over her pale, drawn face and helped her into
the study where Roc sat behind his desk, working. His face
lit up when he laid eyes on her. "Gwen, dearest. How delighted I am to see you. I hope you're quite recovered.''

"A trifle weak as yet, but doing much better,'' she murmured, forcing a small smile. She searched for something to
lean on as the butler let go of her arm, but there was only a

vast expanse of carpeted floor. Enedoc left, closing the door silently behind him. The flower vines of the carpet seemed to take on life and grow straight out of the pile to twine around her ankles.

Roc strode across the room and enfolded her in a warm embrace. She winced as her wound touched his chest, but bit her lip to stop the cry that threatened to burst forth. She leaned stiffly against him, her knees shaking. Noticing her standoffish posture, he held her at arm's length.

"By Gad, you look worn to the bone! That influenza obviously took its toll."

Gwen nodded. "Yes, I'm still under the weather. I'm sorry I can't show more enthusiasm." She paused, her face serious. "I want to see Clem."

Roc laughed as his arms loosely encircled her. "I suspected he might be Dandelion. He has that air of recklessness. My assumption that Dandelion might be a smallish man was totally wrong. Why would you want to see Clem?"

"I need to speak with him. He's a very old friend."

A flare of jealousy gleamed momentarily in his eyes, and Gwen winced. "I *will* see him, with or without your permission," she said, her voice hard. Moving, she felt as if she was balancing on a thin wire, with a bottomless abyss yawning under her. Vincent's words swirled in her mind. Roc—a traitor—a Jacobite. But *she* was a traitor, too.

Roc shrugged and without another word, he fetched his jacket from the back of a chair. His movements exuded annoyance, but she did not let his anger soften her resolution.

He motioned to Thomas to follow them. Thomas would not meet her gaze, the turncoat! But she couldn't blame him for wanting to keep his position at the Hall, if that had been his reward for tattling on the smugglers. The Strutt family consisted of ten children and needed Tom's wages desperately.

They walked outside in silence, skirting the walls to the back of the house. They rounded a low boxwood hedge and descended three shallow steps. Roc opened a creaking door in the thick stone foundation.

The dungeons loomed dank and cold. Twilight prevailed inside even as bright sunlight streamed through the open door. Gwen squinted to take note of every detail. She remembered when she had played with Morgan down here and how frightened they had been. Roc used to tell them horror stories about ship wreckers perishing in the dripping darkness. Today he was all business; there was not a trace of the boy he'd once been.

Clem sat on a wooden box in his dark cell.

"Clem!" Gwen wanted to rush forward, but she could barely stay erect as it was. He stood uncertainly, staring from her to Roc. He looked dirty and unshaven.

"Aw, Miss Gwen, ye should not 'ave come down 'ere. 'Tis not th' place for a lady like yerself." His eyes ran automatically to her shoulder covered by a woolly shawl. He swept a hand through his hair.

"Oh, Clem. How could you say you're Dandelion? Don't you know the earl means to hang you?" she exclaimed. She eyed Roc from the corner of her eye. At least he had the decency to look uncomfortable. "And you are *not* Dandelion."

Roc glared from one to the other. "What do you mean, not Dandelion? Who's lying?"

Clem shot her a warning glance. "She's speakin' flummery, milord. I *am* Dandelion, and don't ye listen to 'er. She's only tryin' to 'elp an old friend." Gwen opened her mouth to speak, but Clem gave her a ferocious stare that silenced her. She was too tired to argue. To remain on her feet took all her willpower. A tear of frustration rolled down her cheek, and she turned and left the damp hole. Outside, she leaned against the wall and took deep breaths. What a muddle! She would have to confess to Roc now.

It was all over, as she had feared.

Roc's rapid steps rang on the flagstones, and she straightened her back. She glanced at him, all the color drained from her face. "I must speak with you," she whispered, and began walking toward the front door. Roc held a steadying arm around her waist, a crease of concern between his eyebrows.

As they rounded the hedge, they bumped into Vincent. Gwen flinched upon seeing his pale, determined face. Ferocity glittered in his eye.

"Ah! Enedoc told me I would find you here. Gwen has something important to tell you, Roc, and I thought I ought to be here to hear the news." He beckoned to her and made a mocking bow. "By all means tell him, Gwen, or are you still trying to pull the wool over his eyes?"

Roc stiffened, his grip around her waist tightening. "What are you talking about, Tremayne?" He took a threatening step forward. "If you've come to pour insults over Gwen's head, you'll have to deal with me first."

Vincent cackled, a sound that made Gwen want to slap him. "You're so righteous, aren't you, milord. Well, let me tell you the truth at last. You're at this moment holding your arm around the infamous Dandelion." He crossed his arms over his chest and waited for Roc's reaction. He had such a pleased smile on his face, a smile that made Gwen feel sick. His eyes seemed to say: I warned you.

The world tilted, the flagstone path sliding from under her feet. With a sigh, she fell against Roc. "He's right," she managed to whisper.

The last thing she saw before she fainted was Roc's incredulous tawny eyes.

When Gwen awakened to the potent smell of vinegar, she was stretched out on the leather sofa in the study, Roc's anxious gaze inches from her face. A wave of love surged through her, and a vague feeling of regret. What a chase she had led Roc this entire summer! Would he hang her now?

After glancing around the room and seeing that they were alone, she plunged into her confession, her voice a raspy whisper. "Roc . . . I've always loved you."

He held both her hands in a convulsive grip. "Shhh, don't speak. You're still quite ill. We'll talk later."

"No . . . I'm wounded because I truly am . . . Dandelion. Clem . . . is only trying to cover up for me . . . because he's a good . . . friend. I would have done the same for him."

To her surprise Roc laughed. "I don't believe you—although I sometimes had a feeling you might be involved. But Dandelion? How could you be? Vincent was looking for trouble, and I'll deal with him later." He stroked her hair gently.

Roc obviously didn't want to accept the truth. Thank God they were alone. Weakly Gwen raised her arm and opened the shawl at her throat. He followed her movements with a puzzled frown. With shaking fingers she unlaced the top part of the bodice and pulled it down from her shoulder, her eyes on his face as it filled with understanding.

"The shot! You were the one . . . I—I shot you. My God!" He held his head with both hands in sudden despair and anger.

"Yes, you winged me because I was above Brandy Cove flashing signals to the *Alouette*. Do you believe me now? I truly am Dandelion."

He surged to his feet, staring at her with undiluted fury. "Why didn't you tell me?" he demanded in a strangled voice.

"Why?" With an air of rejection, he turned his back on her, massaging one curled fist with the other hand as if in the throes of deep agony.

"I . . . I just couldn't." Gwen knew how lame it sounded. "You may free Clem now, and . . . put me in his place. I will not allow him to take my punishment."

"Why, Gwen, why? The vile duplicity, this whole summer. Damnation! Why, Gwen?" He strode across the room, kicking furniture and overturning chairs. At his desk he roared in wrath and pounded his fist into the polished mahogany surface. Then he rushed across the carpet to drag her up and shake her.

"I needed the income for repairs," she said simply, and a small, sad smile quivered on her lips. "And the smuggling chased away my boredom. 'Tis not comfortable being on the shelf, you know. I didn't want to grow into a woman like Aunt Clo." Her words became a sob. She pried herself away from his hard grip. Weak and deflated, she knew he would never forgive her. She dared not look at him. He was honor bound to put someone's neck in the noose on the square. It might as well be hers. Then all her struggles, this charade, would be over at last. She was drained, but at the same time relieved that the truth had been spoken at last. "I suppose 'tis no use asking your forgiveness."

He whirled on her. "Forgiveness? How could anything that simple rectify what you've done?" His eyes were flat and opaque with anger. "You have a lot of gall, Gwen, a lot of gall."

She wiped her eyes with a handkerchief. His hard hands came around her shoulders once more, jarring her wound. "I assume you took enormous pleasure in making me the laughingstock of the village?'' He shook her until her teeth rattled. ''How did it feel, Gwen? Did you laugh behind my back, eh? Whispering and tittering with the villagers.''

''No! It wasn't like that at all. I was simply angry with you for threatening the livelihood of the villagers. They suffered more than you'll ever know—or understand. You've always had enough food in your belly, while they didn't know if they would eat each day. More often than not they went to bed hungry.'' She glared at him and shoved him in the chest. ''But I helped them. The smuggling ended starvation in this village, and I don't regret a single secret mission down to the coves.'' She took a deep breath. ''And then you came and ruined everything.''

''Smuggling is illegal,'' he said flatly. He dashed a hand through his hair, and the bow at his nape fell to the carpet. He looked wild. ''What shall I do with you?'' he said with a groan.

''It's simple enough. Mete out the punishment.''

His gaze narrowed. ''Are you mocking me?''

''No! What else can you do after erecting a gallows for everyone to see? Now you must use it.'' She paused before plunging ahead with her own accusations. ''Or you can always use it for your own traitorous neck. I've heard rumors that you might be a Jacobite, Roc.''

He stood very still, suddenly quiet. She studied him narrowly, hoping to read the truth. Her fervent wish that he was innocent ached in her chest. ''Well?'' she whispered, her lips almost unable to form the word.

''That's a ridiculous rumor. You should not listen to gossip.''

She sensed he was hiding something, but before she could probe deeper, he took a rapid step toward her.

His face was hard, set, and he grabbed her around the shoulders and under the knees. Swept off her feet, she stiffened in his arms. ''What are you doing?''

''You'll remain under house arrest at Tremayne House until I've decided what to do. I'll post two soldiers outside your room, and there you'll remain until I say differently.''

''Well, I prefer my room to your rat-infested dungeon,'' Gwen said, hanging limply in his arms, too tired to struggle.

''There are no rats there,'' came the terse reply. He strode through the hallway as if she didn't weigh more than a feather and carried her to the trap outside. The agony of utter desolation flowed through her veins. Her world had fallen apart. She had alienated the only man who really mattered in her life. Would this be the last time she would feel the touch of his strong hands on her body?

On an impulse, and although her shoulder protested sharply, she placed her arms around his neck and curled her fingers into his hair. And when he set her down in the trap, she leaned forward and placed a feverish kiss on his lips, tears streaming down her face. She received no response, but his eyes were filled with sorrow. "I'm sorry," she whispered. "I love you."

He groaned. "Enedoc will drive you home." He strode back into the Hall, slamming the door behind him.

Gwen's wound was throbbing when she reached home. She had only strength enough to drag herself to her room. Sinking down on the bed, she believed she would never sleep after the painful confrontation with Roc, but sleep claimed her as soon as she placed her pounding head on the soft pillows.

She awakened an hour later, only to sob forlornly into her elbow curved across her eyes. Never would another rag tell its message on the stable wall, and never would the false cry of a nightjar or owl come from her lips in the middle of a dark night. She had lost the one person who meant the most to her, Roc, and she had also lost her one source of pride, the role of Dandelion.

Apathy kept her abed for another week. To her surprise Roc never posted any soldiers outside her door, and there were no rumors about her in the village. Every day she asked Marva if Roc had released Clem, but the cook stubbornly shook her head. Gwen wondered what Roc was thinking. Marva had heard that he had gone to bed three sheets to the wind five nights in a row. And one night Vincent had returned home with his nose broken after fighting with the earl.

Then another interesting snippet of gossip reached her ears. Morgan and Louise had returned from Scotland, happily married, and Lady Camelford had left the Hall in a tiff, vowing never to speak with her daughter again.

Gwen longed to see Louise, but how could she explain the

estrangement between Roc and herself without divulging the truth?

At the Hall Roc was brooding in his study. His elbows were propped on the desk, his hands cradling his aching head. Large quantities of brandy never solved any problems; in fact, the liquor made them seem worse. All he could think of was Gwen's pale, anguished face as she had revealed the wound on her shoulder. He had been shocked, but at the same time it was as if a part of him had known the truth all along. It had taken him months to capture the smugglers—as if somewhere deep inside he didn't want to apprehend them. If only he had not accepted the appointment as magistrate. If, if, if . . . Regrets never changed anything.

During the years he'd been gone from Cornwall, he had forgotten what it was like to live in a small village. It had been a mistake to think that the smugglers would be a faceless group of villains. In a short time, he had become reacquainted with every man in the village, and most of them played a part in the smuggling trade.

Ever since he had seen the poverty in Mrs. Lane's cottage, his drive to catch the free traders had weakened. Then, too, his love for Gwen had softened him, undermining his determination to mete out just punishment to the lawbreakers.

Yet he had promised to hang Dandelion. "Damn!"

Mortification surged through him. He must find a way to shield Gwen from any blame, even though she deserved a stiff retribution for deceiving him all this time.

The villagers who did not know Gwen was Dandelion should remain ignorant of the fact. And if Clem Toboggan escaped from the dungeon and left Landregan, he would do Roc a great service. His disappearance would seem to confirm Clem's identity as Dandelion, thus giving Roc an excuse to take down the gallows.

Surely Gwen would make the bold move to save her henchman. By not putting her under house arrest, Roc was counting on her to help him out of his dilemma.

Not that he would ever ask for her help. He had to salvage the last of his pride.

* * *

As the days passed, Gwen began to feel more like her old self again. Her shoulder wound was almost healed and no longer painful. As she regained her strength, if not her spirit, she paced her room for hours, evaluating strategies that would reconcile her with Roc, but she could think of no perfect plan. A plain plea for forgiveness was not enough. And something had to be done about Clem's intolerable situation.

After deliberating for several days, she made a decision. She would free Clem from the dungeon. She balked at the idea of deceiving Roc one more time, but she had to do something to help her old friend. She would ask no one for help, that way shielding the other smugglers from blame for Clem's escape. From there it would be up to Clem to choose his fate.

Following her daring decision, that evening Gwen slunk out the kitchen door and fetched Buttercup from the stables. With some difficulty she managed to get into the saddle and set the mare on the familiar path to the Hall. She could sense rain coming, one of the usual autumn storms that drenched the area at this time of year. She kicked her heels into Buttercup's flanks, but the mare had her own rigid ideas about pace. As the horse climbed the hill, the Hall loomed dark and eerie in front of them. Candlelight glowed in a few windows.

Gwen slid off Buttercup's swayback and fastened the reins to a tree behind the estate. Now, where would the dungeon keys be? Inside the kitchen entrance. She remembered the long oak board filled with keys of all sizes. Most of them fit the locks of the storage facilities outside the main building.

The walled-in herb garden outside the kitchen was empty and quiet. The kitchen door opened with a groan, and she stuck her head inside. The glow of dying embers shone red in the stone hearth, but no human sounds disturbed the silence.

Gwen stepped inside and located the oak board. There were all the keys, neatly labeled, including the one to the dungeon. Clearly no one expected the keys to be stolen.

Her gaze darted into the kitchen itself. A loaf of bread and half a leg of mutton lay under a napkin on a plate set on a sturdy bench next to the fire. Someone's supper, no doubt. Perhaps the coachman was working late. Well, he would have to find something else to eat, Gwen thought grimly as she snatched up the food and took the lantern from the table, then sneaked back outside.

Clutching a bunch of keys in one hand, she crept along the wall to the thick door leading to the black prison below. The door creaked alarmingly, but no one came running or shouting, so she stepped inside. The eerie air of the place made her shiver, but she resolutely set to work with her tinderbox, and soon the feeble candle in the lantern chased away the darkness. She made her way into the labyrinth. Lifting the lantern high, she swallowed hard and cautiously stepped forward. A bat flitted past her out the door.

"Clem?" she called, and her voice echoed.

"Miss Gwen?"

She exhaled with relief. He was still there. Following the sound of his voice, she reached the door that kept him imprisoned. She tried several keys in the lock, and minutes later he was free.

"I thought the earl would have freed you by now."

"Naw." Clem chuckled. " 'E would 'ave 'ad to 'ang me first. I 'aven't been sufferin' 'ere—plenty o' good food and ale, and Enedoc gave me three blankets, candles, and a pillow."

"Dear old Enedoc. Well, you're free now. I'm sorry I didn't come earlier, but the wound gave me a fever, and I've been too weak to leave the house."

"I'm no worse for wear." He took the lantern from her. "Let's get out o' 'ere. I knew ye were goin' to come sooner or later." He pulled her out of the dank corridor and into the fresh air. "Ah, 'ow good to breathe real air again." He peered closely at her. " 'Twasn't 'ard to rescue me, eh?"

"No, not at all. In fact, I'm surprised the keys were left out in the open, on the board right inside the door, as always."

"Aye, I believe th' earl was waitin' for ye to come and free me." He stretched his stiff muscles and grunted with satisfaction.

"The earl? What does he have to do with it?" She stared at him in amazement.

" 'E . . . 'e is 'ot for ye, Miss Gwen. I believe 'e cares more for ye than any other livin' bein'. I was thinkin' a lot in that dark 'ole, since there was nuffin' else to do. Aye, if ye freed me, and I left Landregan, 'e could say Dandelion broke out and ran away. Then 'e could marry ye." He shifted his weight, flushing with embarrassment. "I know what 'tis to love ye, Miss Gwen. A man could never forget ye, but I know—"

Gwen placed an urgent hand on his sleeve. "Come, let's go into the spinney and talk." He followed her like a loyal puppy. As soon as they reached Buttercup, Clem spoke eagerly.

"I'd like to go to Lunnon and see some new sights, ye know—an' per'aps find me a job on a big ship sailin' for th' Colonies, or some such place. I've 'eard 'bout those places, and I'm fairly burnin' to see somethin' o' th' world." He scratched his head. "Me and th' earl mix like oil and water. Landregan bain't big enough for th' two o' us."

Gwen knew he spoke in earnest and in a moment of insight she realized it would be for the best if Clem left. "I'll miss you, Clem. I'll never forget the times we've shared."

He hemmed and hawed, looking bashful. "We'll niver forget. But ye wait and see, I'll be back with me own wife someday, and then we can speak o' ol' memories."

Gwen suddenly remembered the food she was carrying. She held out the plate. "Here, I stole this for you in the kitchen. I had no idea the earl had kept you with such a good table."

"Aw, thank ye kindly, Miss Gwen." He took the white parcel and proceeded to place his cap on his head. "I'll be off to say goodbye to me family, and then—Lunnon."

"Wait, I have something else for you." Gwen searched the deep pockets of her cape, and her hand emerged with a heavy, bulging leather pouch. "You are my best friend, and will always be, dear Clem. I want you to have this, since you've been the best help a smuggler can have, and the brother I never had."

"Naw, Miss Gwen, I cannot take yer money."

" 'Tis part of the free trading funds, and I want you to have it, just to get you started. Get yourself some new clothes . . . a good position, whatever." She forced the pouch into his reluctant hands. "And I won't listen to any excuses."

"Miss Gwen . . ." He sounded oddly hoarse. "Ye're an angel." He wiped his sleeve impatiently across his eyes.

" 'Tis but a small price to pay you for saving my life, Clem. I'll always be grateful to you.'' She stood on her toes and planted a kiss on his stubbly cheek.

"Aw, Miss Gwen.'' Dropping everything, he took hold of her and lifted her onto Buttercup. Then he clumsily kissed her hand. "Farewell, Dandelion—the bravest and most darin' smuggler I've ever known.''

He slapped Buttercup on the rump. With an indignant snort, the mare trotted down the lane.

Gwen's eyes swam with tears. Another dear person was lost to her.

Chapter 31

Thoughtful, Gwen gazed toward the sea through her bedroom window before going down to breakfast. Why had Roc not come to see her?

Two days had passed since Clem had escaped. The villagers were full of gossip about his disappearance and Roc's death-defying rides over the countryside. They shook their heads, mumbling knowingly that the earl would come to his end with a broken neck.

And Clem Toboggan, their own Clem, had been Dandelion. Fancy that! Half of the population gossiped and exclaimed, and the other half smiled secretly and shook their heads at the innocents who did not know the truth. The smugglers' lips were sealed on the subject, except sometimes very late at night at The Pilchard, when some drunken fisherman commented on the brandy. "This is rat poison! Where's all that good Frog brandy goin' to now? To Looe? They bain't worth it, those good-for-nothings at Looe."

The gallows disappeared from the square, and Roc resigned from his post as magistrate.

Gwen was privy to the gossip through Marva, who out of long habit shared it with her every morning at breakfast. Marva informed Gwen that Officer Biggles had become the new magistrate, and that it looked as if he was planning to make Miss Pettigrew his missus. Gwen had noticed his growing interest in her aunt, and she was genuinely pleased for the couple.

So Roc had resigned his post, Gwen thought, frowning. It was only right—if he truly was a Jacobite sympathizer.

In her bed that night she could not sleep for her tormented

thoughts. Would Roc ever forgive her and stop berating himself for being bested by her tricks? She had made a fool of him, yet he had let the people believe Clem was Dandelion, thereby shielding her from embarrassment.

She tossed fretfully, moaning. Roc had been an overbearing, impossible, stubborn *darling* from the first, and she loved him. God, how she loved him! Life was intolerable without him.

There was only one way to win him now. She must swallow her pride and take the first step toward a reunion, even if it meant becoming the target of his icy hate.

Roc spent a sleepless night in his study, staring into the night. The clouds moved with majestic grace across the sky, now and then releasing a shaft of silver moonlight.

Gwen had saved Clem as Roc had suspected and hoped she would. The villagers had teased him for his failure as magistrate, but it had been no more than friendly banter. They were content to forgive him for his relentless pursuit during the summer months now that Clem had escaped hanging. Roc was at last accepted in Landregan, just as he had been before he departed for foreign parts.

If only he could forgive Gwen for her impudence and forgive himself for his silly pride. Ever since he had learned the truth of Dandelion's identity, misery had been his constant companion. Now that the matter of the smugglers had been solved, his anger was fading. The need to reconcile with Gwen obsessed him. His very bones ached at the thought of never holding her close again.

Gwen had good reason to doubt his integrity since the rumors of his Jacobite involvement were at least partly true. Gwen might be guilty of smuggling, but he could be accused of treason!

She deserved to know the truth about the Jacobite jewels. The thought of taking her—his future wife—into his confidence vastly appealed to him. She, if anyone, could help him. Lord knew, she'd been willing to accept great risk to lend a helping hand to the villagers.

He laughed out loud and shook his head in wonder. Why had she not chosen a more orthodox way to dole out charity?

Because smuggling suited her character . . . Life with Gwen would never be dull.

The next morning Gwen carefully put up her hair after brushing it until it shone. She must look her best if she was to soften Roc's heart.

There was a knock on her door. "Come in," she called, expecting Marva with her newly pressed riding habit. But Vincent strolled into the room. She whipped around, clutching the edges of her dressing gown together. "What do you want?"

"I've been away for a few days—"

"And a blessing it was! I'm sorry Roc didn't finish you off when he beat you up," she spat. Her hand touched the crumpled letter from Major Eppsworth in her pocket, and she worried Vincent would find it. She had read it over and forgot to put it back in the Bible. He wouldn't be above investigating her pockets if his suspicions were roused.

"Since you didn't keep your end of the bargain, I've decided to visit the earl this morning and confront him. I have enough proof to have him arrested for treason." He chuckled. "They cut the heads off the Jacobites and spear them on poles in a public place as a warning to others. The earl's head would look good outside Mrs. Padstow's shop, don't you think?"

"Stop it!" Gwen shouted and pressed her fingertips to her ears. "That punishment was used two hundred years ago. I don't want to hear any more about it."

"Then it's about time you help me find the jewels. Then I'll disappear out of your life—for good. You'd like that, wouldn't you?"

Gwen refused to answer. She wished she had had an opportunity to search for the jewels earlier.

"You've seen most of the Hall, and you might have more luck than I did in locating the dashed gems." He strolled closer. "Well? Do you want to see your beloved's head on a pike?"

Gwen rose so fast, the chair overturned behind her. "Very well, I'll find the gems for you." She had suddenly remembered the odd-shaped leather box with its glittering contents which Roc had pushed into a drawer on the yacht at the beginning of the summer. It might still be there.

Vincent caressed her arm, and she swung away from him. "I knew I could talk sense into you, dear coz. I'll wait until eight o'clock tonight. If you're not here by then, I'll make that visit to Landregan Hall, accompanied by Sergeant Adams and his men."

She glared at him, her heart pounding so hard she could barely hear her own voice. She wished she knew if he was bluffing. "If you so much as set your foot in here again, I'll prove you were dismissed from the army for stealing." Her breath heaved in and out of her lungs like a bellows. "I haven't been idle since you arrived—did my own bit of snooping. I might even prove that you killed James Murray."

His silky smile turned hard and cold. "Threatening me again, coz? I could easily break your neck."

Her anger was so great that no fear could stop her from pushing him out the door. "Go, and don't let me see you for the rest of the day, or I'll reveal the truth."

When he had gone, she closed and locked the door. She would have to find the gems. For Roc's safety. But she could not row out to the yacht until darkness fell. How would she make the rest of this interminable day pass?

It did pass somehow, and as the shadows lengthened, she grew as tense as a bowstring. When complete darkness had fallen, she set off, once more dressed in breeches and a dark woolen cape. It was a bittersweet experience to be outside at night, and she stopped on the lookout above the harbor, breathing deeply of the salty air. The *Alouette* had gone elsewhere with her cargo, and the villagers were once again living off fish and coarse bread.

But this was not the time or the place to mope. She glanced at the yacht, anchored in the bay. No lights shone in the cabins, which meant that the crew was either at The Pilchard or up at the Hall.

She ran down to the harbor and found three rowboats dragged up on the shale. Pushing one of them off shore, she jumped aboard and rowed stealthily across the calm water. A few stars blinked, their reflections multiplying in the undulating rings made by the dipping oars. Gwen felt lonely and sad. She swallowed convulsively and made fast the line to the rope ladder at the side of the yacht.

Climbing lithely upward, she soon landed on the deck. Not until she was outside Roc's cabin did she dare to light the candle stump she had hidden in her pocket. The passage smelled of tar, brass polish, and fresh paint.

The door was unlocked. She stepped warily inside. Full of shadows, the cabin looked unused and abandoned. Roc must have removed all his personal belongings for the coming winter season. She tried the drawers on the desk. Locked. But she couldn't let that stop her.

"Dashed nuisance," she swore under her breath and inserted a letter opener into the drawer into which Roc had put the leather box. She tried to pry it open, but it didn't budge. Instead the blade broke. Swearing once more, she looked about for something else to use. She should have thought to bring some tool for the locks.

With the broken end of the letter opener, she managed to manipulate the middle drawer. It crashed open, almost flattening her nose. She pushed around a handful of feather quills, a stack of papers, a ball of string, and a set of keys.

"Aha! Luck has not abandoned me entirely," she said to herself, and tried every key in the lock. The last key fit, and the drawer opened. She was surprised to actually find the leather case still there. If it was full of precious stones, why had Roc left it carelessly locked in a desk drawer?

She rattled the box and, yes, there was something in it. Studying the lock, she saw it wouldn't be hard to break open. How was she going to explain the broken lock to Roc? She peered at the bottom of the drawer, which contained an empty inkwell, a stick of red wax, and a key on a chain. Gwen scooped it up and fitted it into the lock. Holding her breath, she turned it and lifted the lid.

In the light from the candle, multicolored gems sparkled, and gold settings gleamed. She gasped. Never in her life had she seen such priceless beauty. These were worth thousands of pounds.

What Vincent had said must be true. Roc was a Jacobite sympathizer. That's why he kept the gems hidden in the yacht, so that no one would find them. The knowledge sent icy dread down her spine. She put the box on the desk and sat down in Roc's chair. She would have to find a way to help Roc out of his dilemma. Perhaps it would be a way to smooth a path of communication between them. If he'd been involved in something unlawful, he'd have no reason to chide her for her smuggling activities.

A flare of hope ignited in her heart, and she hurriedly closed the lid of the box. She glanced at the clock on the cabin wall. Half past seven! She'd have to find a solution to the problem as she traveled back ashore. At this very moment Vincent might be on his way to Sergeant Adams's quarters to implicate Roc.

She reached the docks and pulled the rowboat up in the shale, then fastened the line. Clasping the leather box under her arm, she ran up to the lookout point above the harbor. She had remembered an old lair hidden deep under the roots of a dead tree.

A sudden wind whistled in her ears, and she noticed that the air had grown heavy with moisture. Rain was imminent, and Gwen wrinkled her brow as large drops spattered her face and whispered in the furze. Before the leather could get drenched, she shoved the box into the dark hole.

She ran all the way home, arriving winded and wet. The house was quiet, and she sneaked up to her room to change her clothes. A splendid idea had just occurred to her, an idea so brilliant it would crush Vincent and free Roc of any suspicion.

"God, don't let me be too late," she whispered as she dried her hair with a towel and pulled on a simple sack gown that didn't need to be laced. She rearranged her hair hastily, then hid it under a mobcap and swept a dark wool cloak over her shoulders.

She took the letter from her dressing gown pocket and stuffed it into her cloak pocket. James Murray's notebook followed. Then she walked across the hallway and knocked on Vincent's door. No response there. She pressed her ear to the door and knocked once more. Nothing. He had already left. Anger mixed with fear spurted through her blood, making her heart race. She rushed down the stairs. Outside, the rain had intensified, gurgling in the gutters and stabbing the flagstones.

Buttercup had no desire to take a ride, but Gwen coaxed

her with a carrot and soft words. Rain pelted her mercilessly, but nothing could stop her. Roc's life—and perhaps her own—hung in the balance.

She slowed Buttercup as she reached the barracks where the soldiers were billeted just outside the village. Scanning the yard for Vincent, she slid off the horse. There was no sign of him, but he might have already come and gone.

She banged on the door, all the while glancing at the shadows for Vincent's skulking form. A few minutes later the door opened, and Sergeant Adams appeared, still wearing his red uniform. "What's going on here?" he barked, holding a lantern high to light Gwen's face. "Miss Tremayne!" he cried. "What are you doing here?"

"I need your help, Sergeant. Have you seen my cousin Vincent Tremayne?" When the sergeant shook his head she drew a sigh of relief. "He's a Jacobite traitor trying to smuggle a cache of French jewels to the Stuart sympathizers in Scotland." Gwen took a deep breath. "I believe he might have killed the man James Murray whom we found drowned in May."

"You don't say! Where's he now?" Sergeant Adams shouted to his soldiers, and they scrambled to button their uniforms and ready their muskets.

"I think he's gone up to the Hall to force the earl to surrender his yacht and crew. I believe he's planning to sail to Scotland." It was as good an explanation as any, she thought.

The sergeant swore under his breath. "Just one moment, and we'll accompany you to the Hall. I'll post a few men down at the harbor to stop any attempt to take the yacht."

"I hope we aren't too late," Gwen said, wringing her hands. "I'll ride ahead and wait for you outside the Hall. If Vincent leaves, I can follow him and perhaps lead you to him."

As she ran to Buttercup, there was still no sign of Vincent, thank God. If he arrived and found the soldiers gone, he would most likely discover that they were heading toward the Hall and would follow them there. She managed to get onto Buttercup without a stepping block and galloped down the lane toward the Hall. She rode ahead since she didn't want Vincent to see her in the company of the soldiers.

Candles burned in the study windows and upstairs in Morgan's rooms. As Dandelion she had learned to be cautious. Instead of barging up the front steps as her first impulse urged her to do, she waited in the shadows for the soldiers. From the bushes she glanced through the window next to the entrance door, and her breath stopped.

Vincent was standing in the hallway, pointing a flintlock pistol at Roc's chest. They were arguing, and Vincent was deathly pale. Roc's eyes blazed with anger.

She had not counted on this development. Vincent had said he would denounce Roc if she didn't find the gems. She was sure her cousin would not hesitate to kill Roc if he felt threatened. She had to get him away from Roc, and the only way to do that was to lure him away with the promise of the jewels.

Vincent might not believe her, but she would have to take the risk.

The door creaked softly as she opened it. Vincent's head snapped around, but his aim at Roc's heart never faltered. "Gwen!"

"What are you doing?" she demanded in a low voice. " 'Tisn't time yet."

"No, you're late, coz. You've lost." His voice was tinny with anger. "You failed."

"What are you whispering about?" Roc asked. "Another one of your nefarious schemes, Gwen?" He took a step closer, his hand closing around an ornate candlestick.

Gwen was too agitated to pay attention to Roc's anger. She had to get rid of Vincent. She wrenched her cousin's arm. "You fool! I've found the gems. If you take them and leave, no one will follow you. I promise."

His eyes widened in disbelief. "You found them? Where?"

"I'll tell you if you put down the pistol." From the corner of her eye, she noticed Roc coming closer. "If you want them, you'll have to go after them immediately. You must leave tonight."

Rainwater splashed onto the flagstones outside, and tension hung heavy in the air. Roc's eyes were hooded, but Gwen read anger and suspicion on his face. He obviously didn't trust her, probably believed she was in league with Vincent.

"Very well, I'll do just that," Vincent said. "But I'll have to truss you up with Roc here. You might be fooling me. If that's the case, I'll be back to kill you both.''

"The jewelry doesn't belong to you, Tremayne, and it never will,'' Roc said, his voice harsh with anger. He had crossed the hallway, his face illumined by flickering light from a candelabra.

"You don't frighten me, Roc. You're powerless.'' Vincent's arm trembled against Gwen's. "Well, where are they, dear coz?''

"They are at the lookout. I hid them in a burrow under the dead oak right on the edge of the cliffs.'' To save time, ticking off the minutes it would take the soldiers to arrive, she added, "I thought you would bring Sergeant Adams to the Hall to arrest Roc for treason.''

"Since you didn't appear, I figured you hadn't found the jewels. I realized I had to make Roc give them straight to me.''

"Well, you'd better get on with it.'' Gwen shot Roc a desperate glance, urging him to trust her, but he only sneered.

As Vincent gripped her arm, he averted the pistol for a second. Roc lunged, the candlestick raised. "You have worn out my patience,'' he snapped, slamming the candlestick into Vincent's shoulder. The pistol fell. Roc landed on top of Vincent, both men sprawled on the marble floor.

Gwen's limbs were frozen into immobility as they scrambled to reach the pistol five feet away. Roc grappled with Vincent's legs and managed to turn him onto his back.

A guttural snarl rose from Vincent's throat and he kicked out with surprising speed, hitting Roc in the stomach. With a groan, Roc rolled, clutching his middle.

Panting, sweat dripping from his brow, Vincent reached the pistol. Aiming it at Roc's head, he turned hate-filled eyes on Gwen. "I won't hesitate to shoot if you don't do as I say.''

Gwen nodded. Vincent was capable of anything.

"Get up,'' he ordered Roc.

Roc's eyes blazed as he struggled to stand. "I'm not finished with you, Tremayne.''

Vincent only laughed and gestured toward the front parlor, a small stuffy room that was hardly ever used. "You tie up Roc first, Gwen. And don't leave any loose knots. I'll check them afterward.'' He pulled a roll of twine from his pocket and tossed it to her, then waved Roc to a chair. He sat down, his face impassive with fury, forced his hands together, the hands she loved, and bound them tightly.

"Tie his legs, too," Vincent ordered.

Since he hadn't said to fasten the legs to the chair, she only bound the ankles together. Roc's eyes were full of disgust.

With a heavy heart, she sank down on the chair next to him and let Vincent immobilize her as well. Her cousin had the advantage; there was nothing she could do. If she tried to fight him, he might shoot Roc or herself.

She winced as Vincent tied the rope tight around her wrists. "Very snug. You can sit here and ponder your sins," he said. "I knew I would get the gems in the end. Goodbye."

With a slam of the door, he was gone.

"Where is everybody?" Gwen asked. "Let's call for help."

"It's servants' night off, and Louise and Morgan are upstairs at the back and can't hear a thing. 'Tis no use shouting. Only you and me, Dandelion," Roc said bitterly.

"Don't start," Gwen threatened. "We'll talk later. Now we have to concentrate on stopping Vincent."

He stared at her for a long moment, then his expression softened. She drew a breath of relief. "How did you find the jewels?" Roc asked.

"I saw them once in your cabin on the yacht. What shall we do?" Gwen worked furiously at the bindings, but they were too tight. "I hoped Vincent was lying about you, but obviously you're a Jacobite, Roc."

"Believe me, I'm not. I promise I'll explain later." He jerked to his feet and jumped awkwardly across the room as Gwen watched in surprise. He lost his balance twice, and several precious minutes passed before he managed to push himself upright.

Since her legs were tied to the chair, she could not follow him, but she craned her neck to see his progress. He stopped at the opposite side of the hallway, next to a bureau with cabriole legs and a writing flap that held a branched candlestick.

She watched in awe as he forced his backbound hands into position above one of the flames. Bracing his feet and stiffening his body against the coming pain, he let the fire burn into his wrists, and with them the rope. The lace cuffs flared up, and fire licked the insides of his shirt sleeves, but he stayed. His face paled and his jaw muscles clenched, but not a sound emerged from his lips.

"Be careful," Gwen urged, trembling with fear and agony. He bit his teeth together and closed his eyes. Gwen whimpered as his face contorted, but he didn't back off. He stretched his hands apart with savage force until finally the smoldering rope parted.

With a howl of pain he hopped around the room, flapping his arms, then beat his smoking shirt against the thick draperies, quenching the flames. His wrists were raw, and he looked as if he was about to faint with pain. Then he slowly straightened and turned toward Gwen, perspiration gleaming on his face.

His eyes deep pools of agony, his face twisted into a grimace, he bent down and untied his legs. Then he strode into the study and returned with a dagger which he slid between Gwen's wrists, cutting the rope.

"I'm going after him," he said, his voice hoarse with suffering. Without waiting for her or putting on a coat, he rushed outside.

"Take Buttercup! I hid her around the corner behind the lilacs."

As soon as she had untied the rope around her own legs, she ran into the streaming rain in time to hear the sound of horses' hooves clattering over the gravel. He had taken her advice.

She ran after him as fast as she could. There was no sign of the soldiers in the lane, so she abandoned the road and dashed through the wet foliage onto a path, a shortcut to the ridge along the shore. There was no time to wait for the soldiers now. Where were they? Vincent was armed, and he wouldn't hesitate to use his pistol.

Winded, she was forced to slow down just as she came abreast of Wrecker's Ruin. She was soaked through, and the wind was cold on her skin, but she paid no heed.

She passed Brandy Cove and hurried up the steep incline to the lookout. When she was almost at the top she heard sounds of a struggle. Grunts and curses rose above the crashing waves and the pouring rain. Bracing herself against the whipping wind, she climbed the last few feet and stared at the silhouettes of Roc and Vincent, dark and grotesque against the lighter sky as they twisted and turned in the struggle.

Gwen heard shouts behind her and looked down toward the harbor. The soldiers were coming. She cupped her hands to her mouth and shouted as loud as she could, flailing her arms. A few of the men were already sprinting up the steep cliff path.

Gwen ran forward, anxiously searching for a way to stop the fight. She moaned as Vincent barreled into Roc, sending him teetering on the brink of the abyss. "Stay away," Roc warned her.

Frightened, she hefted a rock and hurled it at Vincent. He ducked, and it bounced over the edge and into the blackness beyond.

"Gwen, you were right, the jewels were here. I'm much obliged." Vincent began running down the incline, the box tucked under his arm.

"You won't get far." Roc was on his knees, panting hard. He staggered to his feet and hurried after Vincent, but lost his footing in the wet mud.

"Stop him!" Gwen shouted at the approaching soldiers, helping Roc to his feet.

Vincent swore and slid to one side, hiding in the shadows of a cluster of rocks. Gwen could no longer see him, and he had evidently sneaked past the first group of soldiers, who were searching for him among the boulders.

"Go after him!" Gwen called angrily and rushed back down. Then she saw him at the bottom of the hill.

Another group of soldiers was marching from the other direction, accompanied by a gesticulating woman. Gwen recognized Mabel's wild curls. "Vincent is there at the bottom. Catch him!"

The party of soldiers broke up and surrounded the path emerging from the incline. Moments of confusion passed, then Gwen gasped as Vincent suddenly shoved her aside and shot past her, back up the path. She gripped a handful of his coat, but he tore free. Sliding in the wet mud, she fell to her knees. Shouting, she gained her foothold and followed him, reaching the peak before the soldiers.

Roc was once again grappling with Vincent, clearly in

much pain and having difficulty maintaining his balance among the rocks. They swore and grunted, performing a macabre dance, coming closer and closer to the edge of the cliff. Vincent ducked one of Roc's forceful blows, and Gwen saw him snatch up a rock from the ground.

As Roc raised his fist to deliver another blow, Vincent dragged the rock along one of Roc's burned forearms. Roc roared with pain and fell to his knees, holding his injured arms stiffly in front of him. "Scoundrel!" he shouted, fury catapulting him to his feet. Vincent raised the rock once more and landed it on the side of Roc's head. But still he failed to stop Roc's attack.

Fearing for Roc's safety so close to the edge, Gwen rushed forward.

Vincent scooped up the leather case and turned to run, furiously pushing Roc aside. But Roc gripped his arm fiercely, twisting it so abruptly that Vincent crumpled to his knees with a moan of pain. With his other hand, Roc jerked back Vincent's head and delivered a thunderous blow to his chin.

Crying out, Vincent fell flat on his face, scraping his cheek on a rock. The jewel case slid to the ground. Dazed, he lifted his head from the mud and delivered a string of expletives. He crawled to his knees and tried to stand.

"Got him!" Sergeant Adams called out, gripping Vincent's collar.

Gwen panted as she struggled against the wind to the small knot of soldiers surrounding Vincent. Braced against a boulder, Roc was gasping hard from pain and exertion. Gwen laid her arm around his shoulders. She wished she could assuage the torture of his burns.

The rest of the soldiers and Mabel arrived at the top of the incline. As soon as Mabel laid eyes on Vincent, she ran up to him, elbowing the soldiers aside, and slapped him hard across the face.

"Ye traitor!" she cried, and struck his other cheek.

Roc moved as if to say something to the soldiers, but Gwen halted him. "Shhh, don't say anything. Let me handle it. Please trust me. This is part of my plan."

In the darkness she met his probing gaze. He touched her arm gently. "Just as I thought, another one of your wild schemes,'' he whispered. ''Like all your Dandelion schemes, this one is bound to be successful. I trust you.''

A warm glow filled her. Trust was the first step toward reconciliation. Smiling, she strode into the ring of soldiers. Sergeant Adams had twisted Vincent's arms behind his back, and Mabel was hurling epithets at him.

''This man is a traitor and a murderer,'' Gwen said calmly. She pointed at the leather box which one of the soldiers had pried open. The gems glittered in the lantern light. ''The jewels are Jacobite loot.''

''She's lying!'' Vincent cried out. ''The stones belong to the earl. He brought them from France for the Jacobite Cause—I didn't.''

''Then how is it you have them?'' Gwen scoffed and caught Mabel's gaze. The prostitute winked, her eyes gleaming in triumph.

Gwen continued, her voice ringing loud and clear. ''Mr. James Murray, who was a Jacobite, must have fetched the jewels from some smuggling vessel along the coast. Unfortunately we cannot ask him since you killed him, then confiscated the jewels.''

''That's right,'' Mabel called out. ''I knew both men in Lunnon. They both were me clients, and I can testify that Murray truly was a Jacobite. I over'eard 'im plan to travel down to Cornwall to collect 'elp for th' Stuart Cause. 'Elp was supposed to come from France, y'see.''

She pointed with hatred at Vincent. ''This man followed Murray 'ere, murdered 'im, and stole th' gems for 'imself instead of givin' 'em up to th' Stuart Cause. So if 'e weren't a Jacobite, 'ow did 'e know 'bout th' gems, eh?''

''Yes, indeed,'' Sergeant Adams said in his most authoritative voice.

''These women are lunatics!'' Vincent exclaimed. ''They're lying because they want revenge on me for sins I never committed.''

''I'm ready to swear in court that 'e's a Jacobite,'' Mabel told Sergeant Adams. '' 'E and James Murray served in th' same regiment. They was partners in crime. Vinnie should 'ang for murder and treason. When I came 'ere to Landregan, Vinnie told me 'e 'ad 'is 'ands on th' jewels. 'E told me we could share th' loot, but when I wanted th' security o' marriage, 'e beat me up and ordered me back to Lunnon.'' Mabel smiled. "Try and gainsay it, Vinnie. You're goin' to 'ang, and I'll be right under th' scaffold, cheerin'.''

Sergeant Adams scratched his head. "Treason's a serious accusation.''

'' 'E 'ad th' jewels, didn't 'e,'' Mabel snapped. "What else proof d'ye need?''

Gwen stepped closer, meeting Vincent's cold eyes measure for measure. She pulled out the letter from Major Eppsworth. "This is a letter from Vincent's former commanding officer. My cousin was dismissed from the army for suspicion of grand theft.'' She pushed the paper into Sergeant Adams's hand. "I also have James Murray's notebook in which appear a series of names, including Vincent's. He was using the nickname the Stork, a name I gave my cousin when we were children.'' She opened the book to the right page and showed the officer. "Look, it says here: 'Watch out for The Stork. He's planning to kill me if I don't give him the gems.' '' She turned to Vincent. "What did you do to him? Strangle him, then send him out in a boat so that it would appear he had drowned?''

Vincent took a step back.

"Father will testify that everyone called you the Stork, Vinnie. 'Tis all over.''

Mabel sashayed around an angry-eyed Vincent, her chin high in the air. "Yes, everythin' Miss Tremayne says is true.''

With a snarl, Vincent lunged for the leather box. "I'll kill you yet!'' The soldier holding it was taken by surprise and didn't have time to defend himself. Clutching the box, Vincent broke out of the ring, pushing Mabel to the ground. But as she fell, her legs rebounded against a rock, tripping him.

With a howl of outrage he staggered forward, the force propelling him right into Roc's arms. Roc's grip on Vincent's upper arm was relentless. "Take him to the dungeon at the Hall. I'll have a word with Magistrate Biggles first thing tomorrow morning.''

The ring of soldiers tightened around Vincent, and Sergeant Adams tied a rope around his wrists.

"Set guards outside the dungeon door. We won't take the risk that he'll escape.''

"Th' jewels will be th' death o' 'im,'' Mabel said with a

sob as Gwen reached out to gather the shivering woman into her arms. Mabel's bravado had seeped away. " 'E was too greedy by far."

Sergeant Adams exclaimed his horror at the deep burns on the earl's arms. "Tremayne did that to you?"

Gwen claimed the sergeant's attention. "I'd appreciate it if you would help the earl home and spare your questions until tomorrow. He has had a terrible ordeal and desperately needs to rest."

"Of course," said Sergeant Adams. "My pleasure."

Roc sent her a questioning glance, and she smiled reassuringly.

"We have a lot to talk about," she said. "Later."

Chapter 32

Gwen spent the rest of the night pacing the Green Salon at Landregan Hall. She would find no peace until she had spoken with Roc. Dr. Penfield had bandaged Roc's arms, shaking his head. "I gave him two drops of laudanum so he could sleep for a few hours. He'll have scars from this ordeal," he added before drinking a glass of brandy and leaving.

"We will all have scars," she replied. Her cousin was a murderer and a thief. She had lived a life of danger and deceit, and Roc had somehow been involved in the Jacobite Cause. She was anxious to learn the whole truth.

The new magistrate, Horatius Biggles, arrived at eight o'clock the next morning and closeted himself with Roc in the study. Gwen wished she could hear their conversation. Mr. Biggles joined her an hour later in the salon, his face grave as he sank down on a straight-backed settle.

"Your cousin is locked in the dungeon for now, but we will take him to Plymouth, where he will be tried before a bench of magistrates. Alone, I cannot judge his crimes; they are too serious." He patted her arm. "I'm sorry, Miss Tremayne, but I'm sure a punishment will be chosen to fit his crime. Murder is a hanging matter. There is no hope . . ."

Sorrow coursed through Gwen. "I'm well aware of it. Nevertheless, Vincent is my cousin and I'm sad he became such a scoundrel."

"He made his own choices," Mr. Biggles said.

"Papa will be crushed."

The magistrate hemmed and hawed, clearly embarrassed. He turned beet-red and fiddled with the buttons on his waistcoat. "He has you, Miss Tremayne, and your aunt and I, we

. . . well, we'll endeavor to take care of the squire in the future.''

Gwen could not stop from jumping up and throwing her arms around Mr. Biggles's neck. "I'm so happy for you. Aunt Clo will make you a splendid wife." She poured two glasses of brandy. Just as they toasted to a bright future, Louise entered on a cloud of perfume, dressed in a gown of heavenly blue silk.

"Louise! I'm so glad to see you," Gwen exclaimed. They embraced. "You look radiant. Marriage seems to agree with you."

Apparently fearful he would become trapped in a conversation about weddings and female fripperies, Mr. Biggles rose, made an elegant bow, and hurried from the room. "Goodbye," he muttered as he closed the door.

Louise pirouetted around the room. "Oh, yes, marriage is heaven. But enough about me. Why is there a rift between you and Roc?"

"Well, 'tis a bit complicated," Gwen hedged. She had no desire to discuss the smuggling business or her cousin's crimes. "To tell you the truth, last night we took the first steps toward healing that rift. Have you spoken to Roc this morning?"

"Oh, no. He's been taking care of urgent business, though he should be resting. But this is ridiculous! Why are you waiting out here? You should be with him."

Evidently, Louise did not know what had transpired last night. "I didn't want to disturb him."

"Come! No one is with him now. He doesn't know you're here, I wager."

On trembling legs Gwen followed Louise. "Tell me, what was the dowager's opinion of your hasty marriage?"

"Actually she thought I would be good for Morgan. She said as much to me before returning to Tunbridge Wells. And she grumbled about you and Roc, asking me why you hadn't patched up your quarrel. In fact, I think she likes you more than she lets on."

"She can make my life difficult if she chooses to do so."

"She won't. Once grandchildren arrive, she'll become a doting grandmother. Well, here we are," Louise said matter-of-factly. "And don't come out of this room until you've decided on a wedding date. This time we'll plan a huge formal wedding.''

Gwen squeezed Louise's hand, grateful for her friendship. ''Do you regret missing a wedding of your own?''

Louise made a moue, then smiled widely. ''No, I could not be happier.'' Winking, she left Gwen outside the closed door.

Gwen's heart lurched at the thought of seeing Roc again. She cleared her throat and knocked.

''Enter!'' he barked.

She opened the door. ''Good morning,'' she said lamely before her breath caught in her throat. Though lines of weariness etched his face and his hair was uncombed, he looked so handsome. His arms were bandaged from his wrists to his elbows, and his shirt was open at the front, his chest barely covered by the thin fabric. A fire crackled in the grate, but Gwen only had eyes for him.

She walked unsteadily across the floor without taking her gaze from his. Sunlight flooded the room. A trace of a smile lit his eyes, and pleasure quivered through her, to the very tips of her toes.

''It seems as if a lifetime has passed since I last saw you, Gwen,'' he said quietly.

She skirted the desk and stood before him, so close she could feel his thigh against hers. He stood slowly.

''The real reason I'm here is that I . . . came to ask for your . . . forgiveness. I don't know if you can ever forget the game I played all summer, but I was so angry at your attitude toward the smuggling. Don't you see, I *had* to go on, to prove to you and to myself that I could win.'' Her voice faded.

A faint smile lit his face. ''I never realized you could be so humble, Gwennie,'' he said. ''It suits you.''

She blushed, and on an impulse she laid her palm against his bare chest. His skin was warm, and his heart thundered under her hand. ''I love you,'' she whispered. Color surged into her cheeks, and she lowered her gaze.

His next words were not much more than a low growl in his chest. ''Show me.''

Blinded by longing, she threw her arms around his neck and pressed herself so close that she could barely breathe. He chuckled.

"You can do better than that, Gwennie. Don't be shy." He led her around the desk and left her standing before the fireplace. Three long strides took him to the door, where he turned the key in the lock.

He strolled toward her, pulling the shirt from his breeches. A bold grin curved his lips, and Gwen's heart careened with love. As he held out his arms toward her, she melted against him, pressing her face against his skin and curling her arms around his back. In that moment she forgot her unspoken questions and doubts. Lit with an inner fire, she buried her fingers in his wavy hair and dragged his face toward hers.

She moaned softly as their lips met. His tongue invaded her mouth forcefully and she responded with consuming passion. Of their own volition, her hands traveled under his shirt and untied the fastenings on either side of his breeches. Her hands wandered over taut buttocks and hard thighs until they reached the nest of wiry hair. He groaned deep in his throat as she encircled him.

She was dimly aware that he had unfastened her gown and slid off her petticoats. A heap of material puddled around her ankles. He soon coaxed off her last garment, and she stood naked before him. He removed his breeches. She helped him off with his shirt.

Paying no heed to the heap of clothes on the floor, they sank on top of them, Gwen almost swooning with happiness as he kissed her breasts.

The blazing logs in the fireplace warmed their skin, but the fire raging in their blood was hotter. Gwen tickled Roc's ear with the tip of her tongue.

"Oh, Roc . . ." she whispered dreamily. His laugh flowed over her. He found her secret, throbbing place and explored it with knowing fingers. She gasped at his audacity and skill, which brought her to the brink of golden rapture.

At the same time he eased himself between her legs, he caught her mouth in a shattering kiss. As their tongues slid wetly against each other, he penetrated to the core of her femininity. His possession of her body made her soar, and every deep stroke brought her farther into the realm where dreams are made. A wave of pleasure so profound and so soothing that she could only sigh rippled through her. He threw back his head and moaned in ecstasy. She cried, and he laughed with delight, though his lashes were wet.

Stillness fell around them, except for the crackling and sputtering of the fire. Roc was lying beside her. He twirled a strand of her long chestnut hair and played with it over her breasts.

"We have wasted a lot of time, don't you think?" His voice was deep with remembered pleasure.

She could only nod and grabbed the corner of her gown to dab at her eyes.

"We're both fools." He chuckled and traced her cheek with one long finger. "I love you, Gwennie. You know that, don't you?"

"You showed me just how much." She kissed him. "Thank you."

They shared a few minutes of silence, their happiness too full for words. Roc's hands moved slowly over her body, stroking every hollow and curve. Gwen wished she could stay there forever. But as time passed, she was gradually aware of her nudity and the rumpled clothes under her. She was also aware of Roc's bandaged arms.

"Are you in pain?" she asked.

"Every inch of me is content at the moment," he said lightly. But she could tell his arms hurt.

She pulled at her hair, which was trapped under his shoulder. "We've reached the heights of decadence, making love on the floor at midmorning," she said with a giggle.

"A desperate remedy to a desperate situation." He heaved himself to his feet and held out his hands to assist her. Smiling and laughing, they helped each other to dress. The clothes were wrinkled beyond recognition, and Gwen gasped as she glanced at herself in the mirror above the mantelpiece. Was that radiant face with dreamy eyes really hers? She wound her hair into a braid and pinned on the cap she'd worn earlier.

Roc pulled her by the hand back to the desk, where he dragged her down on his lap. Cradling her head against his shoulder, he sighed in contentment.

"Please tell me about the Jacobite business," she whispered.

He sighed. "Yes, the Jacobite business. Will you believe my story, I wonder? And will you trust me afterward?"

"I'd trust you with my life. That's why I pushed the entire blame on Vincent last night. And he is guilty. I just don't understand how you could be involved."

"You deliberately lied to the soldiers, didn't you?"

"The only lie was that Vincent and Murray were partners. Vincent found out about the jewels through Mabel. Then he evidently hatched a plan to steal them from Murray. The only snag was that Murray never had the jewels." She sighed. "My cousin was guilty of murdering James Murray, and he tried to kill you at the end."

Roc looked deeply into her eyes. "Gwennie, I'm not a Jacobite. I had a dear friend, another Scot, whom I knew all my life. His father knew my father, and they were always good friends. Alistair—my friend—was a Jacobite, and he begged me on his deathbed to take a cache of jewels from France to England. A contact from London would arrive and pick up the jewels in Landregan." He sighed. "Well, no one came, and then we found James Murray at Dead Man's Cove. I put two and two together and concluded that he was the contact." He rubbed his chin thoughtfully. "Then I had a strange letter from someone who ordered me to place the jewels in the wood bin outside The Pilchard. Perhaps Vincent sent that letter. He might have suspected I had confiscated the jewels, since I dealt with James Murray's burial. When no one else approached me about the gems, I decided to return them to France."

"But you've been here all summer."

"Yes, that was my mistake. I should have taken the jewels back immediately, but I got involved with Dandelion and put off my mission until it was too late. The jewels now belong to the Crown."

Gwen lowered her gaze, shame blossoming in her cheeks. "I'm sorry I ruined your plans," she murmured.

Roc squeezed her hand. "I had no idea Vincent was trying to locate the jewels, though I found him shifty and unpleasant. But he's always been like that."

"Yes. If it hadn't been for Mabel's contact with James Murray, Vincent would never have known about the gems."

She leaned back against Roc's shoulder and closed her eyes as she felt his feather-light touch on her hair. "I'm relieved you're not a Jacobite," she whispered.

"But an accomplice." He sighed heavily.

She raised her eyes to his. "No one will ever know. Just as you shielded me from the gallows, I shielded you from the traitor's noose. We're on equal terms now." Trembling all over, she waited for his reply.

His voice was hoarse when he spoke. "Yes, we certainly are." He paused, gazing at the fire. "I admit you led me on a wild goose chase. Only once did I suspect you of being Dandelion, but it was too preposterous a thought to consider seriously. How could anyone believe a gently bred woman—?"

"Do you think we can put this summer behind us? My shoulder wound is healed, but I will always remember the shot that stopped Dandelion. It will remind me of a glorious summer when all my dreams were fulfilled."

He glowered at her with mock ferocity. "Impudent weed! How you and Clem must have laughed behind my back."

Gwen squirmed uncomfortably. "At first it was a lark, a challenge, but the more I cared for you, the more I wanted to stop deceiving you."

He cradled her face between his hands. "Why didn't you give up Dandelion sooner?"

"You put up the gallows and threatened all and sundry with hanging, that's why!" she exclaimed. "I continued mostly for the villagers." She clawed through the contents of her pocket for a handkerchief as tears of shame gathered in her eyes. The moment stretched tensely between them.

"You ought to hang for what you did," he threatened, "but I must confess I can't live without you." He hugged her fiercely.

"I cannot live without you, either," she breathed into his ear.

"I love you, impudent Lady Midnight!" came his final judgment.

A glorious smile broke through her tears and she lifted her face to his. With a wealth of tenderness she caressed his stubborn jaw.

"The only way I could save face was to let people believe Clem was Dandelion," he explained. "And when he left Landregan, I was free to take down the gallows. Just imagine the stories we will tell our grandchildren. And the legend we've created, the favor we did Clem; he'll be the hero of the village forever.''

Gwen laughed. "What about me? *I* was Dandelion, after all.''

"You will go through history as the seventh countess of Landregan. Isn't that enough? I won't have my wife called a smuggler!''

"A fair bargain.''

"I have something for you.'' He pulled out a desk drawer and drew forth a black velvet case. Round-eyed, Gwen opened it. On the red silk lining lay her mother's locket, but instead of the velvet ribbon, it hung from a string of gleaming, perfectly matched pearls.

"Your winnings from our bet. I lost, for obvious reasons.''

"Thank you,'' Gwen exclaimed with breathless awe. "This will be an heirloom the family will treasure for ages to come.''

He cupped her face, a devil lurking in his eyes. "Let's first create our descendants to inherit it.''

Just as he was about to kiss her, someone rapped on the tall French door. Roc and Gwen turned guilty eyes to Louise and Morgan, who stood outside waving, their faces lit by teasing grins.

Roc set Gwen on her feet and went to open the door.

"What's going on in here?'' Morgan asked, sauntering inside. He glanced at Gwen's red face and laughed. "The door was locked, so we thought—''

"Never mind what you thought, old shoe,'' Roc admonished.

Morgan seemed happier than Gwen had ever seen him. Here was no longer a lost puppy, but a tall, confident man.

Louise looked lovelier than ever. "When is the wedding going to be?'' she demanded.

Gwen and Roc exchanged guilty glances. "As soon as we can arrange it. We're anxious to add to the Landregan family tree.''

"Splendid!'' Morgan said and pulled Louise close. "Although I think we might have beaten you to it.''

"Don't be too sure about that,'' Roc said with a wink at Gwen.

The room filled with their laughter.

Epilogue

When Roc and Gwen were married, a stubborn strain of dandelion weed took hold in the lawns at the Hall. No matter how hard the gardeners tried to uproot it, they fought a losing battle—as did Magistrate Horatius Biggles against the smugglers, whose new leader's identity was veiled in mystery.

MARIA GREENE

A native of Sweden, MARIA GREENE is a blonde, blue-eyed echo of her long-ago ancestors the Vikings. Like them, she roamed the world looking for adventure until she settled down with her American husband, Ray, in New York State's beautiful Finger Lakes region.

Maria likes to read books by Susan Howatch, Jennifer Wilde, Patricia Veryan, James Herriot, Sidney Sheldon, Barbara Pym, and Charlotte Vale Allen. When she is not writing, she does needlepoint, gardens, plays with her cats, and sometimes goes fishing for lake trout and salmon with Ray, an avid fisherman.

Maria, the author of the Avon Romances *Reckless Splendor* and *Desperate Deception*, loves to hear from her readers!

**Everyone Loves
A Lindsey—**

**Coming in June 1989
from Avon Books**

the next breathtakingly
beautiful novel of love and passion
from the *New York Times* bestselling
author

Lindsey Ann 3/89

Avon Romances—
the best in exceptional authors and unforgettable novels!

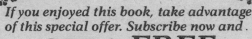